Unbreakable Love

Unbreakable Love

Lance J. Kendrick

Copyright © 2010 by Lance J. Kendrick.

Library of Congress Control Number: 2010917234
ISBN: Hardcover   978-1-4568-1711-4
               Softcover   978-1-4568-1710-7
               Ebook   978-1-4568-1712-1

All rights reserved. No part of this book may be reproduced or transmitted in any form or by any means, electronic or mechanical, including photocopying, recording, or by any information storage and retrieval system, without permission in writing from the copyright owner.

This is a work of fiction. Names, characters, places and incidents either are the product of the author's imagination or are used fictitiously, and any resemblance to any actual persons, living or dead, events, or locales is entirely coincidental.

This book was printed in the United States of America.

To order additional copies of this book, contact:
Xlibris Corporation
1-888-795-4274
www.Xlibris.com
Orders@Xlibris.com
84688

Dedication

This book is dedicated to my Lord and Savior, who has planted this wonderful gift of writing in me. I would like to thank those who have stood by me and believed in me and even supported this project financially: Renee Sandra Barrett, Rosetta Barrow, and others. The truth is that you have made this work a possibility because without your prayers, support, and encouragement, this work would still be a thought. Peace and Love.

Chapter 1

Shawn Cook stood in his huge office, the size of most modern apartments, looking out of his floor to the ceiling window transfixed, lost in thought, trapped in time. He stood there staring at the hustle and bustle of New Yorkers rushing back and forth in the city that never sleeps or takes a nap, for that matter.

It would appear as if Shawn was looking at the intrigue activities of the crazy business of the midtown traffic, tourist reactions, and the attractions of being in the greatest city in the world.

In the past, Shawn would get a kick, looking at the spectacle. It would make his day; he would laugh at how people would practically kill themselves just to put an extra digit in their salary cap. He could never understand that concept. Money didn't make you happy, but what you loved to do did make you happy whether it made you rich or not. If you had a roof over your head, food on the table, clothes, clean underwear, socks, and decent health, then you were on your way to the road of being happy. People worked every day on jobs they hated or worked for supervisors they disliked with such a passion that if that person was in a life and death situation, they would not have any feelings of guilt if they turned and walked away, leaving that person right there to face their demise.

Shawn Cook was voted by magazines as one of the youngest and wealthiest men in the city. He had everything he had ever dreamed of. He was rich, young, thirty-five years old, wealthy, intelligent, and could keep up with those mega business giants. He was in the top ten. Yet one thing Shawn Cook did not master or have and one thing his wealth could not purchase. It was the attention of this mystery woman, not that he was bending over backward to grab her attention. He wasn't jumping through hoops or jumping up and down shouting "look at me, look at me." That wasn't his style or profile, or as they say, it wasn't his MO—modus operandi.

Well, at least, he wasn't jumping through anything at the beginning, but things get crazy before they become sane.

However, speaking of profiles, he fit the profile of a man that should be able to get a woman. Getting women wasn't his problem, getting this one was. He stood tall at six foot three, and his weight shifted from 215 to 220 lbs. So he was tall, dark, well not too dark, but the complexion of soft chocolate, and handsome. To most women he had that yum-yum yummy look, and to top it off, bald not by nature, but by choice. He liked the look, and many women did also. He wished that his face would look good for locks, for if that was the case, he would lock it down, but it wasn't, so he joined the likes of Telly, Jim, Issac, Van Diesel, and even Britney Spears.

He was the chairperson and founder of Shawn Enterprise—a company that designed computer games and worked with film directors and producers, producing animated, full-length movies. He had been referred to as the black Walt Disney of animation. Of course, in his estimation, he was not even close, but that was the direction he was heading in. So he had it going on, and his career continued to blossom and grow, but what remained stagnant was the fact of trying to know this mystery woman, but in vain. That remained at ground zero.

In one sense, she was a mystery or perhaps a paradox. He knew where she worked, or at least the building. He knew what time she went to lunch and where she dined for lunch, well he had an idea. He knew what time she got off from work, including overtime hours, which was no more than thirty minutes to an hour. He even knew what type of car she drove and where she parked it. He had stormed the subject, however, the person had no idea who he was, yet alone exist.

Shawn wasn't the flamboyant type about his career; he wasn't one that had to be in the headlines. If it happened, it happened. If you saw him on the street, you would walk right past him. He didn't stand out like a bright light; he was satisfied with the low profile, and that is why the mystery woman never noticed him. This was the cloak-and-dagger stuff that went on for several months. It was coming to a point that it was starting to interfere with his work; for example, he seemed edgy, irritable at times and apprehensive. He didn't want to hang out with the boys. This thing was really affecting him; this wasn't the Shawn his friends and others had known. The Shawn they knew was easygoing, relaxed, cheerful, unruffled by the small stuff. If there was tension, he would go upstairs to one of the floors he owned which he converted into a gym and self-defense classes, and he would work out and work on some of his Tae Kwon Do moves, which he was a master of. If not there, he would go to the Y and put in some extra volunteer time where he taught Tae Kwon Do, but ever since he had been muddling through this situation, not even these things had given him the solace he once looked for as a sanctuary.

Shawn, despite his wealthy status, was a down-to-earth guy. He had a small circle of friends that hung out together. These weren't the upper crust of smugness or self-important or self-conceited guys, but the cats he grew up with. He had always kept that connection. His ace and homeboy and copilot was Frank Hall, but he and the boys got together every weekend and played basketball either at the Y or on one of the floors of the office building he purchased which he converted into a gym. Despite his wealth and success, he was down-to-earth. He was a natural guy that struck the pot of gold for which he gave honor and recognition to God, but he was a people person, that's why his friends liked him and people gravitated toward him; they liked his style and character.

Shawn always remembered where he came from, raised in the projects in the Northeast Bronx Area. His parents had clawed their way out of the projects little by little, so he wasn't a stranger to poverty, and so he moved from poverty to prosperity with hard work, diligence, and divine intervention. He owned three or four floors in the building where he worked in Mid-Manhattan and in all of that he was still a humble guy. However, one thing he did not have was the mystery woman he saw practically every day, who worked in the Federal building, right next to where Shawn Enterprise came out of.

Shawn and some of the other guys used to say to him, "Yo, Shawn, if you really like her, let her see the real rugged man, the moneymaker, the hunter, you know the Mr. Suit-and-Tie man—the whole nine. Let her get a taste of that. A homegirl is high maintenance. You better come correct if you expect to get with that."

Shawn would respond, "Nah, you see, that is not what I want. I want her to see me whether I'm dressed up or whether I'm coming outside in my workout clothes."

His friends just shook their heads and mumbled some things about that's why things were the way they were.

Shawn, on hearing their protest, said, "Wait, hold up. If clothes and bling-bling is going to turn her head and get her attention, then she is fake like the others, and I am fed up to here with that." Shawn raised his hand up to his chin.

As he stood there by the window, still in a fog, he thought about the time he had gone outside just to see her. He had just got finished working out, so he was in his sweat clothes. He just wanted to see her walk back to her building after her lunch break. It was such a sight to see; he loved the way her hips swayed from side to side, but he also discovered that he wasn't the only one scoping her out.

He was surprised to see most men game, making catcalls, whistling, or hissing like a snake. Some cats were downright out and making bold statements such as, "Hey, baby, what are you doing tonight?" The young dudes would call her "Yo, Shorty." They would also call her other ridiculous names and at the same time wear their clothes down to their butts while talking and holding their crotch, looking for someone to take care of them.

Ms. Good bar, however, did not respond to them. She would keep walking, yet on the other hand, she wasn't responding to Shawn either. He did not know what the problem was, and it frustrated him. Perhaps she was gay, he thought at first, but he came to the conclusion that that wasn't the case. He had been around enough women to know, or perhaps she had a man in her life. There were no indicators: no ring on the finger, no ankle bracelet, nothing. Shawn thought if he had someone like her, he would make sure that other cats would know she was taken. He would have rings on her fingers, ankle bracelets on both ankles, and a tattoo with Shawn and mystery woman engraved forever—something to say she was his.

Chapter 2

Shawn was amazed and mesmerized by her beauty. He wasn't a shy guy. He had had his share of women, but this was a woman to the highest degree. He would see her and say a simple hello to her or speak pleasant words such as "have a nice day," things like that, and she had a class and style about her. She would look at him, smile, and keep going, moving those hypnotic hips and backside. Shawn was hoping soon that she would progress with the communication level and say something like a simple hi, but he had been out there for a while, enjoying New York and waiting for her. However, she just gave him a simple smile.

One day, she smiled and waved. Shawn thought, *Eureka!* He knew it was a matter of time! All that hard work had paid off. The results were right there. She smiled and waved back and said, "Hey, how are you? Where have you been?" Her hands were on her hips playfully as she continued, "It is good to see you."

Shawn thought, *Now she is speaking. What a quantum leap!* "Yes!" he said to her, "I've been right here for the last . . ." Shawn looked up to calculate how long it had been and said, "It doesn't matter. How are you?"

She smiled, shook her head, and said, "I wouldn't have recognized you. What have you done to yourself?"

Shawn was smiling and said with a laugh, "Nothing. I haven't changed, but thanks anyway."

She smiled and said, "I know what it is. It's the lipstick, right?"

Shawn, so happy, not thinking that she wasn't talking to him, smiled and said, "Oh, thank . . ." He then realized that she wasn't speaking to him. How embarrassed he felt! The mystery woman, whose name was Serenity Powers, which he didn't find out too much later, excused herself and squeezed past him to the young lady that she was speaking to. Shawn, from that point, made up his mind that he had to find a different tactic, and like the hunter, he must be patient. OK, perhaps, three months was a little too long, but he was ready to put phase two into effect.

Shawn had thought that phase two had worked, which was to just let her continue to see him and continue to speak to her. *Don't change a thing,* he thought. That day, he went outside just to get some fresh air and also to see the mystery woman walk from the place she dined for lunch back to the Federal building. There go those magical hips swaying from side to side! She was accompanied by her friend Sandra. As those long sexy legs took those long steps, he waved at her, and she smiled, waved back, and kept on swaying. Shawn knew he had to do something. The matter was affecting his work and attitude. He could not concentrate as she was on his mind 24-7, so it seemed.

Now, concerning women, Shawn was a well sought after bachelor having featured in some of the top three magazines a year ago. He dated but was growing weary of what was out there or what he was dating. He met many that were as faked as their weaves. They would put on a façade, a mask that would give an impression of who they want others to think they were. But in time the true colors would come out. He didn't want someone who said or did the right things like some kind of lab rat, but he wanted someone who was genuine. For example, plus-sized women! Why do they try to fit into something they know they would not be comfortable in, or even look good in, for that matter, despite what their friends tell them? Why be something you are not, just to get that dude? Such were some of his issues in general with some women he dated. Or for example, women who wore tight pants! They shouldn't have to go through such extremes to show their figure. Sometimes he wondered how they got into those pants; it had to have been a struggle, and it probably took them forever—pants so tight—if they passed gas, they would bust a hole in the seat, or the whole thing would rip right off. It's either the person likes you or he doesn't. Be true to oneself, which is all he was asking, for one has to face self in the mirror every day.

Chapter 3

Shawn had had his share of both the pretense and the suspense of women. He didn't want drama, especially baby mama drama. Because of his money and wealth, he had dated those who tried to trap him, push him, or seduce him, but because he had a good support network of friends and family, he was able to see through the manipulations. He was tired of such women; he wanted someone like the mystery woman that he saw every day, and when he didn't see her, he thought about her. It wasn't as if he knew her, because he didn't. However, what he did was his homework, and he had inside people that knew her and gave him the inside track. And from their report, the mystery woman was consistent, intelligent, and as far as his spy report, she went out with her best friend more than often. As far as a boyfriend goes, the information was inconclusive.

Shawn, still looking out of his Manhattan office, was still thinking about her, especially when he saw her the day before. She was wearing a modern, white-pleated skirt that came just above the knee; the pleats were centered on the skirt, but the highlights were her firm-looking, shapely long legs—legs that looked like they had strength and endurance. Then she had on a beautiful, rose-colored, semi loose-fitting blouse that highlighted her shoulders and her nicely shaped breasts. He wondered if she had on a wonder bra, because the shape of them was so enchanting like the rest of her. She wore a large belt that went around her waist, highlighting her sexy waist line, and finally, the two other items that stood out in his mind were her designer black shoes with a three-inch heel, which highlighted her nice hips and sexy, firm-looking backside. Every time she walked, her hips and backside did a dance. She had perfect symmetry: 36-24-36. That is a winning hand for any man, or as the commodores say, "she's a brick house." Her walk had rhythm; he could imagine what she looked like in a bathing suit, and then she had on a necklace with a cross. Shawn thought, *Lord have mercy, this woman is finer than fine.*

He continued to stare aimlessly out of the window when his intercom went off. Karen Smith, his secretary, was on the other end. "Uh, Mr. Cook, there is a Mr. Porter on line one." Shawn, lost in thought, heard, yet did not hear his secretary's voice. "Mr. Cook." Karen paused for a response, and then with a little more urgency, she said, "Mr. Cook, Mr. Cook, are you all right?" Karen paused for a few seconds before Shawn realized that he was being brought back to reality, but to be honest, he wasn't in the mood to speak to anyone. He had turned down so many phone calls. He had his good and bad days. This was a freaked up day. He was in a serious funk. He had come to the conclusion that he had no other choice but to respond. He told himself to snap out of it, and then he focused his attention on what Karen was saying.

"Yes, Karen, what is it?" Karen's voice sounded elated to know that her boss was OK. And Karen began to ramble, "Mr. Cook, didn't you hear me calling you? You had me worried. I thought—"

Shawn cut her off as politely as he could, "Karen, please, what is it?" Shawn could hear the hurt in Karen's voice. The last thing he wanted to do was hurt someone the way he had been feeling for the last few months, especially Karen Smith.

Mrs. Smith was Shawn's success story. She had been unemployed—in and out of rehab. She was sent to Shawn because he had gone to the courts here throughout the city letting the judges and lawyers know that he was willing to start a program called "Another Chance," and the main concept was to give those like Karen, who had a revolving door record in and out of court as well as jail, to do their time instead of behind the bars to behind a desk, learning a trade or a skill. The program had been very successful, thus far. Karen had been clean and sober for the past six years, and she had been with Shawn for the past five years. Shawn remembered vividly when Karen had first started. What a mess! No poise, no composure, no home training! Shawn remembered how Karen used to speak to his clients over the phone and in person. We are talking about multi-billion dollar deals, and yet Shawn took a huge risk in putting Karen at the heart of the business. She used to speak to his clients and colleagues, mind you, as if she was about to make a drug deal! Street mentality is an understatement; let's try rude, obnoxious, and just plain nasty, and what a garbage mouth! She made some of your foulmouthed comedians today look like rated PG folks.

She gave new meaning to the term *Ebonics* like, "Yo, what up, he ain't here at the president, holla back, later, aight." Or "Yo, what up, B." This is no joke. She used to put people on hold without telling them to wait. The person would be talking and bam, without warning, she would do some of that Con Ed blackout stuff on them like they did during the summer months of 2003 and then come back on and say, "Who this, yo, B, my bad. Check it, hold tight, and let me see if home boy is chill'n." She would then come back again and say, "Yo, check it, home boy said he will check you out later, peace."

Shawn loved her; people balked, complained, and even threatened to pull their business, but Shawn stuck with her. He invested time, energy, and money, sent her to workshops, brought in folks to teach her proper office etiquette. Shawn even brought outfit after outfit for her, just to break that lack of womanly confidence and make her feel like a woman. He took her to function after function to give her that feeling that she was somebody.

Karen was already an attractive young woman. She had features like Beyonce and a body like Janet Jackson, yet she had such a hard time accepting this on the inside.

Shawn's generosity threw Karen off. You see, in Karen's world, if you got, you gave. Nothing came free, and to have a man like Shawn Cook treat her the way he did, she might as well take up jaw-strengthening exercises. He really taught her how to be a woman. Shawn had always been a gentleman, in every sense of the word, for example, allowing her to walk on the opposite side of the curb when walking with a man, not that she wasn't used to. Her brothers used to take her out and have her walk whatever way, but they did not have the quality that Shawn had. For example, she never had a man pull a chair out for her to sit. Many had raced to get to a chair first and left her behind. She had never experienced a man opening a car door for her. And how about the time they went out to one of Shawn's functions when she got up to be excused to use the women's room? They had just started eating. When Karen got up Shawn did also. She thought it was time to go, but she did not realize that it was a sign of a true gentleman. Those outfits on Karen were stunning, but homegirl took ages to learn how to walk in heels. When she first started, she looked like one of those characters from *The Little Rascals*. It took a lot of work, but in time she learned.

Chapter 4

Shawn's program, "Another Chance," was Shawn's way to give back to the community that had given him so much. Many would assume and even bet their last dollar that he came from a well-off upper middle class family that probably lived in the upper crest of the Bronx or Manhattan among white folks or nifty, uppity black folks. He probably went to the best private schools, which is why he sounded white on the phone and in person. All of these assumptions, and in reality none of it was even close to the real upbringing of Shawn Cook.

Shawn, the youngest of five siblings, three sisters and two brothers, grew up in the projects in the Northeast Bronx. Shawn had a good foundation; he had the privilege of being raised by both parents in the same household together versus some, if not most, of his peers that grew up in households where there was only one parent—mainly the mom. Only on rare occasions do you find a man in the position of a single parent. If this is the case, you can believe it is not because the mom wandered off and shed her responsibility; perhaps, it is due to an unfortunate accident or illness. However, in reality, it is the woman who wears hats as well as the pants and the dress. The father is not around mainly because the reality of the responsibility is too much, and so he leaves and moves away.

Such men want to make babies but do not want the responsibility of taking care of them. Or perhaps they were raised in the way that subtlety taught them to lie back, chill, that ah—what is that Spanish term—yeah, that machismo. Mothers didn't know that they were handicapping their male child by creating a sense of false independence, translated as enabling. Shawn's parents made sure that Shawn did not get caught up in that type of behavior, but they were surrounded by it. It was in the songs they listened to, in the movies they watched, even on the street corners. Shawn's parents did not allow any of their children to rely on anyone but God. His father strongly believed that if you allowed that behavior to exist for even a few years of life, you have just created some serious collateral damage—a generation that is full of excuses, rationalizations, and pity-me stories instead of creating real men.

Shawn's father always said that being a real man takes more than sitting back and chilling, trying to be cool, or it takes more than humping and pumping your seed into a young lady. Unfortunately, like poison, such self-destructive behaviors seem to have seeped into our gene pool, causing a chain reaction of destruction and havoc—the sins of our fathers. Shawn thought and shook his head—a generational curse. For this reason, he gave back to the community to stop or at least slow down the cycle through the "Another Chance" outreach program and other means of building, sustaining, and maintaining the community. Shawn had contributed a whole lot of money to charity, to educational endeavors and had been an inspiration, but now Shawn did not want to be bothered. He was going through his own stuff.

Karen was still on the other end, waiting for Shawn to respond. "Mr. Cook, you stopped in mid-sentence. What do you want me to tell Mr. Porter?" There was another long pause as Shawn tried his best to stay focused.

"Karen," Shawn cleared his throat, "Ah, tell Mike I will call him back."

Karen, with a slight feeling of uneasiness in her voice, said, "Yes, sir, Mr. Cook—"

Karen was about to sign off when the tone of Shawn's voice surprised her, "Karen, from this point, hold all my calls."

Karen responded, "Yes, sir, Mr. Cook, but what if it's an emergency? What should I do?"

Shawn, at this stage, was about to lose all the professionalism and poise that had earned him the title "Mr. Smooth." "Karen, listen to me carefully. I am going to say it one time only."

Karen had never heard Shawn in this manner. Part of her was somewhat intimidated. The other part, the old Karen, the street Karen, was about to be resurrected, and was about to go off and say what needed to be said and let the chips fall where they may, but the polished and trained Karen bit her tongue as Shawn's tirade went on. "When I give a directive, do not question me."

Karen tried to speak, "But Mr.—"

Shawn went on like a steamroller, "Hush . . . Don't interrupt me either."

Karen was about to open up a verbal can of whipping, you know what, but held her restraint.

Shawn continued, "If it's an emergency, Mrs. Smith, I have well-able employees that I pay very well that should be able to handle anything that comes across their path. This is why I spent the dollars to train them, like the way I trained you."

Karen felt the proverbial backhand slap in the face. Shawn realized it, but it was too late. He had gone too far; he had crossed the line. He paused and, in a low voice, said to Karen, "Karen, I am sorry. I haven't been myself lately, uh, if something should come up, ah, pass it to Mr. Johnson. He's good. He'll know what to do."

Karen did not respond quickly but finally said, "Is there anything else, sir?"

Shawn felt Karen's words penetrate right through his heart. Shawn said, "Ah, Karen, take the rest of the day off."

Karen barely said "yes, sir," but Shawn faintly heard it. What he heard when Karen clicked off was the sound of a sniffle. Shawn went to his desk and buried his head in his hands and banged his fist on his desk; the sound of his powerful hit even startled him. He said to himself, "I have to get a grip on this thing. I can't believe I'm letting a woman, who I don't know but want to know, do this to me. I can't even get anything done. Enough is enough, and it's time to do something about this."

Chapter 5

Shawn, his five brothers, and sisters came from what people in the South refer to as good stock. They were taught values, mores, and good manners. Mr. and Mrs. Cook truly believed in a person's character. They felt that a person's character would always reveal the truth about that person. Growing up in the Cook home was an experience in two ways: It was a pleasant experience for one, and it was an experience you will never forget. The Cooks were always strict but fair parents. It was not easy for either one; they both struggled and practically clawed their way to make ends meet.

Both Mr. and Mrs. Cook started out with a limited amount of education—a serious disadvantage. Neither one had completed high school when they got married at the early age of twenty. Despite their educational shortcomings, both possessed the innate wisdom that books or professors cannot teach to their students. Both of them had jobs that barely paid enough to put food on the table and pay the bills, but no one ever went to sleep hungry or went outside with holes in their clothes or shoes. Hand-me-downs maybe, Salvation Army used perhaps, but they did not have to beg, borrow, or steal. They made it from day to day on a wing and a prayer.

Mr. Cook worked for the Port Authority in the center of Manhattan. He was cleaning toilets, while Mrs. Cook did an assortment of things. She was a seamstress, a nurse's aide, and she cleaned apartments. The seamstress and the cleaning of apartments were her own business adventure endeavors. Mrs. Cook, from the start, had an independent eye to be her own boss. Shawn looked back and could not believe how his parents did it, but it planted something deep in his soul. He realized that when you put your mind, heart, and soul into your dreams, with God by your side, you can and will do some amazing things. Shawn's character was built on these principles. God only knows the hectic and busy lifestyle the Cooks had, but they made it work. They pushed their children to the max and did not settle for less. Shawn, and his brothers and sisters had good chemistry. Sibling rivalry was present, but it was not a major factor, and Mr. and Mrs. Cook did not allow sibling rivalry to get out of hand. Mr. Cook always felt that one needs to stand up for what one believes in, but one should not stand up just for the sake of it.

Shawn and his brothers and sisters were poor by certain standards; however, you could not tell them that. Mr. and Mrs. Cook always made sure they had everything they needed. Mr. and Mrs. Cook went back to school, earned their diploma, and kept on going like an express train. They both had enrolled in Lehman College in the Bronx; they struggled, juggled, and tag-teamed their way into the family obligations and responsibilities. Through their busy schedule, they were able to make time for PTA meetings, school nights, special school events, and trips. When they looked back and saw what they had accomplished, they always told their children that God gave them the strength to do what they did.

Mr. and Mrs. Cook received promotion after promotion on their jobs. They both continued school. They both earned their master's degrees. Mr. Cook earned his MBA and Mrs. Cook her Master's in Nursing. Mrs. Cook's business was doing so well that she had to hire some of the high school seniors and college interns to help her out. In a way, the arrangement worked out perfectly. The students received their earnings to help pay for their school supplies and other things as well as learn a trade and the art of business. Mr. Cook moved up in the ranks as well; he was finally promoted to the head administrator at the MTA. Mr. Cook was also working as a part-time professor at Lehman College, while Mrs. Cook was promoted the head administrator RN nurse at Montefiore Hospital in the Bronx.

Shawn sat at his desk, remembering how crazy the house was in those days, but it was fun as well. While his mother and father were doing their thing in school, Shawn, Kelly, and Macon graduated from high school. Malcolm and Alicia were seniors in high school, Jonathan was in his second year in high school, and Joanna was in her first year. Shawn remembered how active he, his brothers, and his sisters were in high school. They all were a part of something political, such as being the president or vice president of their letter class or some other form of activity. Alicia was probably the only one that did not run for president; however, she was the head of the drama department. Shawn remembered the time when Alicia and Malcolm did not like the way their parents were running things, and they decided to go against the grain. They both tried to rebel and go against the beaten path; both were no bigger than toothpicks back then.

Shawn remembered how they had tried to convince him and Kelly, Macon, and Jonathan to stand up for the cause. All four said they would, but something convinced them otherwise. Jonathan didn't want to have anything to do with it, while Shawn wanted to see from a spectator's view how all of this was going to work out; he knew his parents.

Chapter 6

That night, Alicia and Malcolm had it all planned out on paper. They went over it with us. I guess they thought we were excited because of the way we were hyped up, but that was not excitement; that was crazy behind fear. Right then and there, I said to myself that I was going to wait to see how Alicia and Malcolm were going to do.

I will never forget the night. Malcolm and Alicia walked into Mom and Dad's room, knocked, and walked right in, and I kind of peered over Malcolm's shoulder and knew this was a bad idea. Mom and Dad looked at Alicia and Malcolm as if they had lost their mind. Malcolm, to this day, would tell you he thought he caught them off guard, and he had them right where he wanted them.

Malcolm said, "Travis, we need to talk to you,"

Dad said OK, got up, and walked toward his closet. Bad sign number one: he said "give me a minute" or something like that.

Then Malcolm raised his voice and said, "Now Travis and Roberta, front and center."

Bad sign number two: Mom humming a tune. It didn't matter, for once she started humming, and you didn't recognize the tune, trouble was coming like a storm on a hot summer's day. Why and how Malcolm and Alicia missed it as they claimed they were too fired up, but something was about to get fired up soon.

You see, Malcolm and Alicia did not see what I saw; they had turned and pivoted as if they were the parents, but as quick as lightning, Dad grabbed two of the seven belts he had hanging. I think you get the picture why Dad had seven belts—remember he had seven children—well, there you go. The only thing I remember that night is that Malcolm and Alicia never got a chance to say what they wanted to say. Malcolm and Alicia tried to go against the beaten path and were beaten back on the right path. That mutiny was put into check quickly. Mom and Dad looked at Macon, Kelly, Joanna, me, and Jonathan, and the only thing we could say was that we had told them not to do it, but they would not listen. Dad went off on them again for not having listened to us. For the next few meals at the table, Malcolm and Alicia had to stand up and eat. Their choice, as a matter of fact when they sat down, they were reminded the tag team parents would jump on them like flies on doo-doo.

Shawn chuckled every time he thought of that story, but right then his mind was trying to figure out how he was going to make his move with the mystery woman. He had faced challenges before, but she was the toughest challenge he'd ever faced, concerning a woman that is, but he was determined to get her attention, one way or another, but the ordeal was weighing heavily on him.

Chapter 7

Shawn sat there reminiscing about the past—about how growing up seemed so simple—but dealing with love seemed so complex. For about two months or so, Shawn had avoided the usual Friday hangouts with his family and friends; it was now a traditional thing, if you can call it that. On Sundays, after church, everyone would go over to Mom and Dad to have that old southern traditional dinner, and what a time they would have! A good dinner and some Uno or some other card game that black families have known as well as the electric slide! Shawn, for the last couple months or so, had avoided all those things that he used to do with his family. He had even started going to a different church. Some mornings, he would not go to church at all. Shawn sat at his desk, knowing fully well the meetings he had canceled that afternoon and, for that matter, for the rest of the week were meetings that would have and could have put Shawn Enterprise into such a position that they would have dominated the computer software market. Shawn just could not get into his work; he had been trying for the last few months, but thank God for his team. They had been holding things together as best as they could.

Shawn remembered how his family was not always well-to-do, but when they reached that stage and moved out of the projects into a huge mansion-like house in Mount Vernon, the Cooks still sent Shawn and his brothers and sisters to public school.

Funny when the Cooks moved into their new home, some of their white neighbors and black neighbors, whom Mr. Cook called black uppers, because they would get so high, would forget how to come down from off that high horse and help out their own. The Cooks, on the other hand, dealt with those who misjudged them. Many of them spread the rumor that the Cooks got past their bias radar due to affirmative action. *How about that? Unbelievable!* Shawn sat there and thought. The Cooks obtained, many were saying, not brought, mind you, but obtained their home through some form of affirmative action or some other form of government assistance program, or they had helped other black activist groups, such as the NAACP even though the Cooks lived in the right place. They were treated as if they were crooks and thugs, stealing from government programs. Those were the rumors going around until someone did their homework and found out that the Cooks were quite well known in the academic as well as the business world. This shut them up real quick. Then came the welcome band, the smiles, the cigars, and the pats on the backs. However, the Cooks took it with a grain of salt and still lived their humble lifestyle; the children still went to public school and still had friends from the projects whose homes they still went to hang out and have a great time.

Shawn sat there and remembered that some of those homes were jacked up; some were infested with the two Rs: roaches and rodents. Some were overcrowded, while others had beautiful apartments. Many of them had both parents in the home, while others had one. Some even had both parents MIA, and their friends were being taken care of by kinship or relatives. The reality of extended family was a real thing for some of these families. Shawn remembered walking into some of these buildings, and the stench of urine and feces was overwhelming. There was always drama going on in these places. Shawn understood the pressures most of his friends were under, and for this reason, he gave back to the black community. He always gave over and beyond the standard. He could always be seen volunteering his time at the Y, teaching kids the art of self-defense or tutoring some child whose reading or math level was way under the norm or even planting the seeds of positive self-esteem and image.

Shawn had overcome many obstacles and met many challenges, but this thing with Serenity Powers was driving him up the wall. Shawn, in the past, had dated many women; in fact, women flocked to him, but he did not allow the attention to distract him and throw him off his game. He realized that his money would open up many doors, and women would practically give him whatever he wanted without reason. He had been told by some caring friends when he was in grad school while he was on the prowl of hitting big time to watch out for the hoochie mamas, gold diggers, looking for sugar daddies like Flavor Fav looking for a wife.

Chapter 8

Shawn was about six foot three and 220 pounds of firm muscle, a Caesar hairstyle, and wore clothes and footwear that most of us would never be able to afford unless we opt to be homeless. Shawn had dealt with the best of them, and each female that might have come off as one of those "check yourself" sisters as if they bathed in gold could not handle Shawn's suave, cool, and in control behavior. Shawn was Shawn, and many women could not break into that character. If Shawn was a pimp, he could have gotten those women to become his slaves. We are talking about education—PhD, doctors, and lawyers—what have you women! However, he met someone that did not need to be tamed. She was self-confident, strong yet feminine.

Shawn thought about the other night when Jonathan had come over to his house to hang out with his big brother, but mainly to talk with Shawn about this mood he was in. Jonathan was very much concerned. He told his parents that Shawn was not himself since he had been trying to hook up with this woman; he seemed to be losing contact with everything around him. Jonathan could not figure it out. He thought this was only a woman. There were plenty of them, plus with his reputation, he knew his big brother had his share of women. He could pull any of them at anytime, so why this one? What was so special about this one?

Jonathan sat at his parents' table, discussing the issue with them about the brother he loved and had looked up to all his life. Jonathan felt helpless and powerless; he wasn't used to seeing his brother this way. He had always been in control, not controlled. The other thing was that he was used to his big brother helping him out of situations, not the other way around. This is why he felt powerless. What could he do or possibly say to a man who had seen three times as much as him or had had the experience with women more than he would ever know. What spell did this woman have him under? Jonathan had never met her and was already developing a dislike for her. He told his parents that Shawn had been really slacking up at work. "He's not on point, his mind is elsewhere," said Jonathan and asked his parents what he should do.

Mr. Cook told Jonathan that he should go over to the house and confront his brother out of love and concern, nothing more, but he warned Jonathan to go easy. When a man loves a woman he is blind to everything else.

Jonathan laughed and said, "Love, how can you love someone that you don't know? She hasn't said one word to him."

Travis Cook looked at his son and said, "Son, love begins in the heart. A man would do some crazy things to get the attention of a woman." Travis Cook laughed and continued, "Son, I did some crazy things to get the attention of your mother. Good thing she wanted me as bad as I wanted her, but when one is hungry and the other is not . . ." Travis Cook just shook his head and continued, "What your brother is going through is purely from the heart. With some women they see it right away and respond positively, while for others, it takes longer to see. He will have to be patient and choose whether the chase is worth it. Your brother is used to women falling at him. This one is a challenge he's not used to . . . I think Shawn met his match, but knowing him, he'll be OK."

Travis Cook chuckled and hugged Jonathan with his hand on the back of his neck and said, "Be careful in how you approach, remember, you are thinking with your head, while he's thinking with his heart. What you say can be taken the wrong way. It can be a very sensitive time for Shawn."

Travis watched Jonathan go and thought about that song "When a man loves a woman." He just shook his head and chuckled.

Chapter 9

Jonathan took the advice and went over to Shawn's house. Shawn came to the door and was surprised to see his brother. Jonathan walked in; both men exchanged a tribal embrace, but Jonathan could sense and feel that Shawn's embrace was not like his old, strong intense hug. Jonathan made a note of it and stored it in his mind for future ammunition. Shawn and Jonathan played the PlayStation 2—a 2K series basketball game. Jonathan was rocking Shawn in the game; usually, the score was so close it went down to the wire. Shawn looked as if he was new at it—like a complete novice, or as Jonathan thought to himself—*like a complete jerk*. Finally, Jonathan threw down the controls and snatched Shawn's out of his hands. Shawn sat there staring at the television screen as the game was taken over by the computer AI mode.

Shawn was surprised to see Jonathan daring to do such a stupid thing as this. Shawn slowly turned toward Jonathan with bloodshot eyes, which was the result of exhaustion. Jonathan shut off the console, and turned to look at Shawn; both brothers looked at each other as if they were in the center of the ring before a fight.

Jonathan came out with the first swing. "Shawn, get a grip. Look at you. Have you seen yourself lately?"

Shawn countered and struck back with sarcasm, "No, Jonathan, I have not looked in the mirror lately. You know you could be a real idiot sometimes."

Jonathan ducked and dodged Shawn's counter, which did little damage and came back with his own unexpected barrage, "I'm the idiot, Shawn? Think about how you're behaving—like a spoilt brat—can't get that kitty cat."

Shawn cut a warning look at his brother as Jonathan continued, "Look at you, you refuse to take calls, while your punk behind have Karen do your dirty work. Oh, that is a real-time low for you, Shawn."

The blows were breaking down Shawn's defense. "Shut up, Jonathan."

Jonathan continued with the onslaught. "You are having a hard time meeting this so-called mystery woman. She is not giving you the time of day. Is she messing with your head, poor Johnny boy?"

Shawn looked at Jonathan with another warning look. The look even took Jonathan by surprise, but he had to say what he had come to say, and he continued, "Have you ever thought to pause for a minute and move on? That's life! Maybe it's different in the business world, you are the big shot there, but this is the real world, Son. Move on. So why this woman, Shawn? Is she that hot? Maybe too hot to handle! Shawn, this thing is affecting your work, or perhaps you can't see that. You are so preoccupied with her, trying to get with her, while everything else is going to hell . . ."

Shawn looked at him and Jonathan continued, "Yeah, I heard. What! You are surprised! Don't be. I'm sure I am not the only one. I heard how you are slacking."

Shawn thought the only leak that could be was Karen. She was the only one that had close ties with the family, and they treated her like family. *I'll deal with her,* he thought.

Shawn was brought back into focus as Jonathan continued, "Wow, Shawn, this sounds like one flew over the cuckoo nest."

Jonathan was on a roll. He had Shawn against the ropes as he continued, "Move over, Jack. Hereeee's Shawn, the real McCoy idiot!"

The blows had found their target, and not even Shawn, who could bluff and poker face his way through most important deals, begin to show his weak side. He said, "Jonathan, just leave it alone, all right. This is none of your concerns."

Like a shark that smells blood, Jonathan came in for the knockout blow, just the way Shawn had taught him to. Jonathan, wide-eyed at what Shawn had just said, returned fire. "Like hell it is, and like everyone who feels sorry for your butt, it is affecting all of us, you selfish jackass."

Shawn stepped closer to Jonathan. He was now just a breath away. Jonathan stood his ground despite the fact that Shawn outweighed him by twenty-five pounds and blow for blow, if it came down to that, Jonathan had no chance. Shawn looked at Jonathan and pointed a long, hard finger at him and said, "Be so ever careful, little brother, how you tread. I think you need to back off."

As Shawn flexed his muscles, Jonathan looked at Shawn with a look of comical surprise and said, "I need to back off? No, you need to get a backbone, Shawn. Face it, Shawn. You do not want to face the fact that this woman is not interested in you. How long has it been? A few months? Three? Four? Six months? How long? Too damn long and still nothing! Maybe she is not interested in men at all. Maybe she prefers women. I mean I heard she hasn't given you any play. Remember that commercial with Clyde Frazier and Keith Hernandez when they both said in unison, 'Rejected, no play for Mr. Gray?' Likewise, no play for Shawn today, or maybe she is straight and maybe, big brother, you have lost the magic touch. What do you think?"

Shawn knew what he thought. He wanted to give little brother a good butt whipping. Shawn now went to grab Jonathan, but Jonathan still had the grace of a dancer. "You don't want to face the truth, Shawn. You are scared, but you have to face the reality in order to deal with it. Move on, what's up with this bitch?"

Shawn went to grab Jonathan again, "I said, shut up."

Jonathan, still back peddling, said, "Shawn, maybe this woman is either a lesbo or a stuck-up bitch. What do you think, huh?"

Shawn said to himself, "I'll show you what I think." He used a martial-arts move, grabbed Jonathan, and decked him hard in the face. Shawn was in shock. He could not do anything or say anything as he apologetically shook his head and said, "Jonathan, I am sorry, I . . ."

Jonathan was slowly getting up; he touched the side of his face where Shawn had hit him. "You know, big brother, I would have never thought you would be the one hitting me over some bitc . . ." Jonathan corrected himself and continued, "I am sorry." He then got up and walked to the door. "But you better get it together, Shawn. You better get a handle on this. Move on, look at you."

Shawn went to hold his brother's arm as a peace offering gesture, but Jonathan snatched his arm out of Shawn's grip and opened the door to leave. He turned back and looked at Shawn, shook his head, and slammed the door behind him as Shawn tried to apologize to him. But his words fell on deaf ears as he stared at the door his younger brother, who looked up to him, walked out of.

Chapter 10

Shawn, sitting at his desk, was brought back to reality by the intercom. Shawn's patience was wearing thin with Karen. He said to himself, "I told her I do not want to be disturbed. What part did she not understand? And I'm still planning on talking to her about leaking out information to my family. I—" Shawn could not finish his venting to himself before what sounded like the loudest, ear-piercing sound broke his thoughts. *That stupid intercom,* he thought. Shawn quickly pressed the button to silence, ignoring the sound, and to address Karen. "Yes, Karen what is it now?"

Before Karen could respond, Shawn, sounding a bit upset, continued, "Karen, I thought I had made it clear I am not accepting any calls. I don't care who it is, not even the president."

Karen's voice had the sound of sweet-in-your-face victory as she questioned, "Not even if it's your mother?"

Shawn prepared to continue with his tirade stop as if he ran into a brick wall. "Oh, sorry, Karen, please put her through."

Mrs. Cook came on the line, "Hello, Shawn."

Shawn wondered why his mother always asked for him, heard the switchover click, and still said hello, Shawn. Who else would it be?

"Yes, Mother, what can I do for you? I am very busy right now."

Mrs. Cook was a patient woman, but if you press the wrong button, watch her degree fly out the window, and see her transform to GQ—Ghetto Queen. "Shawn, stop right there, let's get something straight. I don't care if your building was on fire. You better talk to me, now. Don't bring that side of me out. You hear me, young man . . ."

Mrs. Cook paused and listened. "Shawn, do you hear me, Shawn?"

One thing Shawn learned was that his mother meant business. If she said she was going to do something, you had better believe it was going to happen. Shawn knew better than to keep up the silent treatment.

"Mother, I am here. What is it?"

"Shawn, what happened between you and your brother the other night?"

Shawn wanted to tell his mother to mind her business, but then again he wanted to live to see a full life, so he opted to give the short version. "Mom, I am going through a little something right now, and I am not trying to be rude, but right now I need space."

Mrs. Cook made the sound of "I see." When Shawn got finished, Mrs. Cook gave him some motherly advice. "Shawn, I know things are a little crazy right now, but by striking and pushing away people who love you is not the answer."

Mr. Cook then came on the line. Shawn thought his mother and father were the most devastating tag team partners around, and even the Legion of Doom would have been envious. "Son, your mother is right. Now, whatever happened between you and Jonathan needs to be cleared up. I don't know what was said, and frankly I don't care, but one of the rules of this family, Son is—"

Shawn, sounding somewhat frustrated, interrupted his father, "Dad, I know, 'let nothing come between family.' Mom, Dad, I am sorry."

Mrs. Cook started to say something but was cut off by Mr. Cook who told Shawn that they will be in touch during the week, and that they hoped to see him the coming Sunday for dinner. The Cooks hung up the phone. Shawn held the phone in his hands longer than expected and then slammed the phone down in its cradle. Shawn pressed the intercom, and Karen came on quickly. "Yes, Mr. Cook."

Shawn was trying to sound calm, but Karen could tell some bottled-up stress was coming through his tone. "Karen, take the rest of the day off."

Karen felt it was not an incentive for working hard, but it had something to do with the phone call from his mother that she had put through to him. Karen tried to defend herself.

Karen, a few minutes later, came into Shawn office. Shawn expected Karen to say "Have a good day" and thank him for the early time off. "Mr. Cook, I had no other choice. It was your mother."

Shawn thought about it for a minute and knew that Karen was correct; he knew his mother could be intimidating at times. "Karen, I know how she is. It is not your fault. Still take the rest of the day off. I know I've been grumpy and not easy to get along with, so take the rest of the day."

Karen's face said that she wasn't convinced. Shawn walked up to her and stood in front of her with his arms on her shoulders, looking down at her. He smiled and said, "Listen, it's OK, this is not your fault. Enjoy your day."

He playfully kissed her on the forehead like a big brother would to his little sister. Shawn tried to sound somewhat cheerful, "Look, tomorrow is Saturday. I am sure this early leave would help you have a jump-start for your day tomorrow. Plus, this gives you a chance to spend more time with your son, TJ."

Karen smiled to herself when she heard her son's name. Her smile turned into a frown. "Mr. Cook, I never saw you like this before. All these years I have worked for you, and you have never been like this. You have always been strong and confident. What's wrong? This is not like you. Are you having girl trouble?" Karen stepped even closer to Shawn. She continued with her flirting, messing with his tie. "I can help you with that."

Shawn smiled; he knew Karen liked him. "One girl in particular," he said with a playful exasperated exhale.

Karen said, "If she can't see who you are, then she is one dizzy chick, Mr. C. You put most men to shame. I wish that one particular girl and I could trade places. You see, I know how to treat and appreciate a man."

Shawn felt that line in the sand being crossed, and in the past they both would get as close to it as possible before pulling away, but this time, Karen saw the opening and now she was going to go for it. Shawn smiled and, in his cool style, backed up. "Karen, I will be all right, it's just a phase, but thank you for your concern, now go."

Shawn playfully pushed her toward the door. Karen was ready to walk out the door when she stopped and thought twice. She quickly turned back to him, made a contemplative face, and said, "Mr. Cook, I am going to say this the way I feel, so if it comes out a certain way . . ." Karen paused, shrugged her shoulders, and continued, "It is meant to sound the way it sounds, no condensing, and no digesting like *Reader's Digest*, OK?"

Shawn just made an unsure sound that said "Oo-kay, sure."

And she continued, "Mr. Cook, you've been there for me. Please give me a chance to be there for you."

Shawn wasn't surprised. He was expecting something like this sooner or later. Karen could feel Shawn's unsure vibe. "Please, Mr. Cook, let me finish, please." She pressed on, "Mr. Cook, I know you have practically saved my life." Karen could hear Shawn getting ready to say something; she assumed it was going to be his denial of such a feat, and she continued, "Yes, Mr. Cook, it's true. You really planted hope in my heart that sprouted up to a confidence I never had before. Let me be there for you. I know you probably think I am just a reform addict and that underneath this veneer is a career-reformed woman who is still an addict. Can't shake the label."

Shawn interrupted and said, "No, that is—"

Karen silenced Shawn with a firm shh. "I just want to show you my appreciation. I understand more than my job, and I think I kind of understand you as well. What I am trying to say is that anytime you need to talk, perhaps we can go out and get something to eat. I'll take care of the tab and the dessert." She winked at him.

Shawn did not know what to say about the play on words, or was it? Was Karen making a pass at him? Of course, she was, and Karen continued, "I just want you to release some steam, that's all." She drew closer to Shawn and touched his arm with such tenderness as she said, "I want to be there for you."

Shawn really did not know what to say. He briefly looked at the hand that held his arm, placed his hand on hers, and slowly caressed her hand with his hands. He looked straight into her eyes with such compassion that Karen thought she was going to melt. "Those words were very kind, Karen." He drew closer to Karen, but he still stood within the boundaries of friendship. One more inch and according to relationship experts, Shawn would have been in that realm of intimacy, but he knew where in the sand of relationships that line was. He continued, "Karen, I've known you for quite some time. I know I've been there for you, and I will continue to be there. You are special to me." He paused and inhaled a deep breath. "Perhaps one day I may take you up on that offer, but thank you."

Karen bent her head and smiled to herself, thinking, "Mr. Cook is so cool and suave that even a rejection from him is like a nice breeze on a summer day."

Shawn slowly lifted up Karen's head, where she was looking up into his eyes. "Karen, enjoy your day off."

Karen, blushing, said, "Yeah, the best exit I ever had, especially after making a fool out of myself."

Shawn let go of Karen's chin and said, "No, I thank you for thinking of me, and you have helped me more than you know."

Karen was all smiles and said like a little girl, "Really?"

Shawn said yes and told Karen to enjoy the rest of the day off and the weekend. Karen went out of Shawn's office with a huge smile. Shawn made his way over to his desk. He thought about Karen's proposition but dismissed it. Shawn knew he had to do something that Karen or no other woman could do for him; he knew in order to move forward, he had to either face this woman head-on or forget about her and move on.

Chapter 11

For the past few months or so Shawn had tried everything in his power to forget about Serenity, and he was doing a good job, so he thought. Shawn became involved in many projects and fund-raisers. He was dating again. He volunteered his time to children events, and he seemed to be doing a good job, blocking out that enticing perfume she wore. He could smell it as she walked past him, heading back to work—that smile that could light up a room—that gesture of her nose she made every time she did not understand what was said. He watched her from every standpoint and that voice, sultry and sexy with a laugh that would cause goose bumps to pop on his skin every time he heard it. Shawn had all of this going for him, so he thought, but as soon as he was done, exhausting himself, the plan was to go straight to bed, but she even met him in his dreams, or, while he was getting ready for work, through a song on the radio.

One day he was rushing to work, looking at his watch when he looked up and saw her walking past him, heading to her job. Once again the usual hi—that was from him, and the smile—that was from her, and she kept going, with those dancing hips and shapely backside. It left Shawn speechless. He sat there and was reminded of her. The little that he knew of her, Serenity Powers was everywhere. Shawn would practice meditation from a Christian standpoint, but that only put a weak dam against those strong-flooded emotions that broke the dam every time. He realized through his own training as a successful businessperson that he would have to deal with this matter head-on. He would have to meet her on her time, which was her lunch hour—no more Mr. Nice Guy—it was time that the hunter went after the game.

As he sat at his desk, he looked at his watch and said to himself, "It's showtime." Shawn got up from the desk, and as he was walking out of the door, he told Karen he was going hunting. Karen gave him a strange look; Shawn looked at her and winked as he headed out the door. Shawn was going to take this from a different approach. If the game didn't go to you, then you go to the game. That was his extremely philosophical way of thinking, and he thought it was time to play the game.

Chapter 12

It was a hot summer day in July, to be exact, and Shawn was feeling good. He knew he had to step up his game. He had no idea about this woman other than the little information he received. This was a busy time at the office; the request for special software and shipment was coming in faster than you could swallow, but Shawn knew he had to meet her. He knew that things were picking up at the office, and he should be there, but that's why he had hired folks, and this was one of those times he had competent folks to oversee the business. To him this was top priority; this was either hit or miss. Shawn was thinking about his agenda. The only thing he had on it that was top priority was making that connection with his mystery lady. Shawn felt a surge of confidence and said out loud, "It's Showtime!"

Shawn, who owned at least four floors to what was referred to as the sky tower in Mid-Manhattan, made sure his team of leaders reached their goals in sales and investments as business was booming. Shawn would have his team meetings in the morning, hang around a bit for any trouble shooting issues, then head over to the Y where he would work out as well as teach his self-defense classes.

Shawn always thought, if he had to give up something, it would be his work as the president and CEO of Shawn Enterprise, and he would spend his time at the Y, helping those underprivileged children. That was more satisfying to him than money or fame.

However, God blessed Shawn to be able to have his cake and eat it too.

He was coming from the Y. He was there, most of the morning, teaching the children self-defense, instead of being at his board meetings. Shawn knew that since the kids were out of school, his time to be at the Y would be very demanding, but Shawn was up for the task.

He decided to go and eat at the "Just As You Like It" diner. He walked in the same time this gorgeous creature of God walked in—the mystery woman. Shawn could not keep his eyes from looking at her. That was the one that he watched day after day go to lunch and come back, so he was right. It was here that she came he thought. Shawn had on a sweat suit he had brought from the local sports store—nothing special. He was still sweating from the workout.

He wanted to kick himself because he knew he was sweating like the proverbial pig, and he had left his towel in his car. The young lady, Shawn was sure, was on her lunch break, but she was dressed in the latest style. Shawn recognized the clothes because he had an investment in the Silverman collection, which was a collection of some of the most beautiful, yet affordable clothing. Shawn was not a designer, but he had invested money into this company, and therefore had the right to check out the items before they hit the stores and give his opinion, since his name would be put on the items. However, Shawn was not the type that had to have his name on everything in order for people to know that an item was his line. He had only his initials SC, and it read like "A SC collection."

Shawn and Serenity had walked in at the same time. Shawn was holding the door for her. As they approached the host, she was in the process of doing three things at once: calling for the next party, directing traffic where to sit for those who had just been called, and taking the names of those waiting their turn to give their names so they could be among the eaters, and not the haters.

Shawn loved coming to this diner. The diner was always busy, but especially around this midmorning lunch-hour time. The quality of service reminded Shawn of the diners and restaurants down south; the workers were very polite and friendly. Shawn looked around at how busy the place was: plates were sliding against each other, the chatter of voices was nonstop, and silverware was clinging and clanging against each other. The busboys were on point with their mini-tubs, throwing plates and saucers and cups, wiping off the tables, and then drying them and zooming off with such grace to put the dirty plates and silverware in the dishwasher so that they could be recycled, cleaned, and used for the next customer. Waiters were handling their business very professionally. Servers wore their outfits with respect, not like some of those establishments where the less you wore, the more you made kind of nonsense—the more cleavage, the shorter the skirt—and the more flirtatious and flimsy the more crowd you drew. Shawn was glad that the owner did not endorse that or believe in that; this place had class. The atmosphere was jumping; it was electric. A nice fuse jazz, mixed with some R&B and classic soul, spread in the air like a blanket lightly spread on a bed. You know how it floats down with such beauty when it is being made up.

Orders were written on an item that looked like a pad, but it was a handheld computer-type iPod. The worker would write down what the customer ordered, and the message would go back to the cooks on a screen, and when the item was ready, the cooks would press a button that corresponded with that order, and the server would go to pick it up. This was the latest in technology. This was better than some Neanderthal yelling out your order or yelling for someone to pick up the order. Chances of someone yelling over your food that way may leave a few wet surprises, courtesy of the filthy animal, the Neanderthal. Therefore, the only talking you have conversationally is from the customers talking with one another, or making an order, or the server having a conversation with the customer. The diner was well kept; on the walls were the halls of black history, paintings of famous black men and women and people of color from all occupations from the past to the present. The lighting was just right, and the seating was mostly booths for privacy, but those without booths had plenty of space and comfort.

Chapter 13

The hostess asked Shawn, "Table or booth for two, sir?"

Shawn smiled and was about to set off a wise remark that he thought would definitely earn him points in this young lady's deposit bank; however, Serenity stepped in front of Shawn ever so ladylike and smiled at the hostess and said, "No, please, table for one, we are not together."

Shawn stood a few feet from Serenity, and he could smell the fragrance of her hair. He noticed the shape of her slender neck; he memorized the sound of that voice: soft and sweet, yet firm and businesslike. It was missing that sultry touch that he had heard many times, but then it was businesslike, and he liked that side of her as well. Shawn dared to get a bit closer as the fragrance of Serenity's hair wafted through him like a starving man smelling a good meal. Shawn recognized the perfume. He closed his eyes and said the French name in his mind perfectly. When he opened his eyes again, Serenity was looking at him as if he had lost his mind.

Shawn apologized for his rudeness, "I am sorry, but that fragrance . . ." He paused for effect and continued, "May I ask you the name of that mesmerizing perfume you are wearing?" He had recognized the fragrance immediately, but he could not tell Serenity that, so he played the role of the out-of-touch person. Serenity brushed it off and looked back at the host as if to say "mind your business, and do your job."

The host blushed a little. She cleared her throat and proceeded as she looked at Serenity. "Ma'am, we don't have a booth at this time, but we have a nice table in the corner. It will give you as much privacy as a booth."

Serenity thought about it for a brief second and agreed to take it. In reality, she didn't care where she sat as long as it was away from that weirdo and as long as she had time to eat and get back to work without feeling rushed. One of the servers led Serenity to her table. Serenity thought about the man in the sweat suit. He looked nice, but he could not handle her, a high-maintenance woman. *Brother, man, please, this perfume probably cost more than what you have on, as well as your underwear,* she thought. She then looked back at Shawn with a smug look on her face.

Shawn said to himself, "I know that hottie did not brush me off with that look." He did not exactly know what to do; well, he knew he had the resources to do and to buy whatever he wanted. He laughed to himself and looked forward to winning this young woman's heart. He thought that the hunt was going to be more interesting than he anticipated. He waited for the host to get to him. While he waited, he could not keep his eyes off Serenity. She was the most beautiful creature on God's earth. Shawn knew women. He dated them quite often, and he had spoken with many on a candid level. Many had tried techniques to trap him but had failed in their attempt.

Shawn looked around the diner and noticed that the servers were bringing out the orders, three and four plates at a time. He was always amazed at this feat. Shawn knew that this woman would be a challenge, but right then and there something within the very core of his being hit him like an eighteen-wheeler. Right there in that diner, Shawn knew he had to have this woman. All of his rationalizations and common sense capabilities right there fell apart, broke down, and collapsed. He was now moving on that primitive and raw thing called emotion and intuition. To watch her was amazing and to stand next to her was breathtaking. Shawn was not the type that would go on feelings or emotions. He was a successful businessman, because he based what he did on hard-core evidence—evidence that would show proof and establish intellectual, analytical, and statistical reasons to pursue or retreat so as not to waste his time with stuff that was bound to fail.

Shawn was the type of person that strongly believed in the Missouri concept—that is, let me see it first, or simply put, put up or shut up.

All that Shawn had been taught seemed to be already there within the spheres of his soul. He could not come up with any rational reason or data that would make him feel the way he was feeling. The thing that bothered him the most was that he did not care. The only thing he knew was that he had to have this woman. Destiny sat only a few feet from where he was standing, and he knew he could not pass up that moment. However, one thing stood in his way—a huge obstacle—and that was the woman herself.

Chapter 14

The host brought Shawn out of his reverie. Shawn cleared his throat and apologized. The host once again, with that professional and friendly tone, said, "Table for one, sir." Shawn knew that the question was rhetorical and out of habit. Shawn jokingly and quickly looked behind him as if to say "are you talking to me or is there a couple behind me?" Shawn turned back around with a warm smile, which caused the host to blush. He said, "Yes, sweetheart, table for one." The host now seemed to have lost the control of her facial muscles and was showing all her teeth with a huge smile—like one of those smiles the joker did on Batman—all the teeth were showing.

Shawn smiled back, but not as wide, but enough to make this host if she had the space to do backflips. One of the female servers came over to escort Shawn to his table. The host whose nametag read Candy said to her, "Beatrice, I'll escort the gentleman to his table. Will you watch the desk for me?"

Beatrice, from the look on her face, did not appreciate Candy messing around with her customer. Beatrice knew from the other servers that Shawn was a regular and tipped very well, plus, he probably did a few other things very well too. Beatrice went with the improvisation and went along with it with a half-smile. Candy knew that she would have to deal with the matter later. She asked Shawn to follow her. Shawn nodded and let Candy lead the way. Candy walked in front of Shawn, shaking everything she had. Her hump was doing some moving that left nothing to imagination. Shawn thought that Candy was really working it. He got her message, which said, "If I move like this walking, can you imagine how I will move riding?"

Shawn had to smile as he followed her. Candy finally got Shawn to the table and said, "Was that good? I mean is this good, sir?"

Shawn looked around as if he was thinking about the question; however, he knew that the seating arrangement wasn't what he wanted. He stalled for a few minutes and said, "Excuse me . . ." He looked at Candy's nametag and looked at her with a smile. "I would like to have that table over there, please." He paused and continued, "If it's not a problem . . . , Candy."

Candy smiled at Shawn with that joker smile again and said, "No problem, sir. I am here to please. Rather, we are here to please our customers." Shawn smiled again at Candy, and to add on the gravy, he said, "That is such a nice name, Candy. How sweet are you?" Candy, leading Shawn to his desired table, had a plastered smile on her face and that walk became more vivid and animated. She just knew she had scored some points.

Serenity was looking at the menu when she looked up at the man in the sweat suit, still waiting at the desk, talking to the host. Serenity looked back at her menu and jerked her head back up toward the front desk and noticed how the man in the sweat suit was flirting with the host—no, the host seemed to be flirting with him—no, they seemed to be flirting with each other. Serenity thought, *What a player! Mr. Sweat Suit is nothing but a player. He gave me a compliment and now he, well she, or perhaps both of them are hitting up on each other.* She concluded that she knew she was right about him—good looking, cool, smooth, oomph, but looking for a sugar mama. She thought he seemed to fit the profile—a dog.

Serenity watched the whole exchange between Mr. Sweat Suit and Ms. Candy. She picked up her menu and shook her head and thought, *Two peas in a pod.* As she went back to reading what she wanted for lunch, she dropped her menu and her jaws as she watched Candy walk Mr. Sweat suit to his table. Serenity thought, *My god, homegirl, you are going to break something if you keep moving like that.* She caught Shawn *smiling* and thought, *Yea, I bet he's enjoying that.* Serenity gave a signal to the waitress to let her know she was ready to order. She had finished ordering when she looked up. Mr. Sweat Suit was sitting at a table, adjacent to hers. She looked down and could tell from the old imprint markings of the table that it had been moved closer to her table. Serenity, very cool, played it off and gave Shawn that smug look, picked up a copy of the *Times*, courtesy of the diner, and began to read.

Shawn tried not to stare at Serenity, but he had to get a look at her. He was trying to think whether he had seen her there at that diner before. It took him only a few seconds to conclude that if he had seen her here before, he would have definitely recognized her face. The five years since this diner had opened, Shawn firmly established that he had not seen the woman before. Serenity caught Shawn looking at her, gave a sort of uncomfortable smile, and continued reading the paper. She thought, *What is this guy's problem? He's been staring at me off and on since he came over here. Maybe he's in deep thought, perhaps thinking about sports like most guys in sweatpants and sport jocks.*

Shawn tried to turn away quickly but knew that the young lady had probably caught him peeking at her two or three times by then. He casually looked away when Serenity for around the third or fourth time caught him sneaking and peaking at her. Shawn wished he had a third leg so that he could kick himself. He could have been a little less obvious, but he was so intrigued with her beauty that he had to somehow meet this Nubian queen.

Shawn had just concluded that he did not know how long she had worked in the area and that her building where she worked was close to his. Why hadn't he discovered this rare jewel before? Whatever the case may be, Shawn was determined to find out more about this goddess. He just had to. He thought to himself.

Chapter 15

Through the third and fourth of Shawn's observations, he was trying to study everything about this rare beauty. As he was looking, he had developed a mental check off list. He first looked for signs that would indicate that this fine sister may or may not have been in a relationship. Shawn checked out her hands to see if any rings were on them. He found rings but not the ones that indicated she belonged to someone. There was no engagement ring and definitely no marriage ring; these are the things he had looked for when he first spotted her. He was glad to see that things had not changed. Next, Shawn's eye scanned down on the woman to see her ankles, but he could not see the woman's ankles due to the angle he was sitting in. But what he saw totally blew him away as he saw the most voluptuous, thick, and well-chiseled legs he had ever seen. He could tell that this woman worked out in the gym, or did something to keep that body looking that fit, attractive and sexy, move over Miss America. Yet he would not be surprised if this beauty queen did not have on an ankle bracelet. He could not see if she had on an ankle bracelet or not, which was a sign of having someone in her life. He knew that a few months ago she did not have an ankle bracelet. He was hoping that was still the case. He sort of laughed at the idea that this woman, as far as he could see, would not allow such customs to invade her liberated womanhood. She did not seem like the type that would allow someone to "own" her. She seemed more independent, but he had to make sure. He could not go by assumptions. He needed solid evidence.

Shawn still could not see that happening with her, yet again one never knows the effect someone has on another person. He pretended he had dropped something and was looking for whatever he may have lost. Serenity was caught up reading the paper when she noticed Shawn had been down there for a few minutes and kind of wondered whatever he may have lost must be very important. While Shawn was down on his knees pretending to have lost something, his server came over to take his order. "Excuse me, sir, is everything OK?" Shawn was somewhat startled by the waitress's voice and quickly lifted his head from under the table, and as he did, his head did not fully clear the edge of the table, and he hit it as he was coming up. The whole thing to Serenity was humorous, and a yelp of laugher escaped out of her mouth. She tried to cover her mouth to restrain herself from further laugher, but the damage was already done.

Shawn, sort of, gave Serenity a rather embarrassed smile, recovered, and gave his order to the waitress. As he was ordering as well as rubbing his baldhead, he noticed Serenity trying to hold back from laughing at his expense, and right there he knew that was going to be his soul mate. Shawn got a good look at Serenity, and her natural beauty mesmerized him. There was no makeup caked all over her face. What he saw was a glow—all natural. Shawn did not realize he was staring at her as well holding the menu that the patient waitress was tugging on. He knew at that moment that it was now or never, and he did something he had not done in such a long time.

Chapter 16

"Excuse me, sir, will there be something else?" The waitress repeated her request before Shawn broke his trance from Serenity and told the waitress "no, thank you." Serenity's food had arrived; she was eating and looking at the paper. Shawn looked at her for a few minutes more and then made his move.

"Excuse me, miss." Serenity Powers, the mystery woman, reluctantly looked up from her reading of the *New York Times*. She inquisitively looked at Shawn, and the look did something to him. Those big brown eyes and long eyelashes put Shawn in a state of disarticulation. No woman had ever made such an impact on him. This was a man who was never for a loss of words, a man who could wheel a deal in a matter of minutes, yet he found himself almost in the most awkward situation.

Serenity, patiently, looked at Shawn, waiting for him to ask his question. She was all of that and then some. She was very attractive as well as sophisticated. Serenity Powers, the mystery woman, worked over in the Federal building, right across Shawn's office. She was the executive secretary for the Law Enforcement Unit—the LFU. All federal cases had to go through her office in order to be processed and sent to Washington. Serenity decided another tactic besides inquisitive looks—perhaps the direct approach. She said to Shawn, "Yes, may I help you?"

Serenity, always the professional, had a very smooth and soft voice, yet very much firm. Shawn, once again, in a matter of minutes, made a brief mental note of Serenity. He was good at that. He could be doing something and quickly give a good detailed description of a person while he was doing what he was doing. Shawn did that with Serenity. Her skin tone, he noticed, was light caramel, and her skin looked soft and smooth. He noticed her hair was hers—no thieving with the weaving—a phrase used when someone had someone else's hair and not their own.

Once again, Shawn was on the other end apologizing for his behavior, "I am sorry for the intrusion, but I find myself lost in your . . ." Shawn stopped himself before he went any further and approached what he had to say from a different angle.

He took a deep breath and started again, "Look, I apologize for staring at you. I usually don't stare at women . . ." He realized how that sounded and raised both arms in a defensive way and then raised one pointer finger as to say "give me a minute."

He realized that the proverbial hole he was digging was getting deeper. Serenity did not know what to think, whether to call for security or find out if Shawn had taken his meds that morning. In a way, Serenity thought it was kind of cute. You know, to have a man get all flustered and nervous because of the effect you may have on him, or maybe, it was not her, maybe, just maybe the elevator did not go up to the top, and it became stuck somewhere. Shawn was surprised of what was happening as never had such a thing happened to him around any woman. Shawn had mastered the gift of vocalization and articulation—the gift of public speaking, or in the street vernacular—the gift of gab, yet he found himself tongue-tied.

Shawn took a deep breath and let it out slowly, and then he said, "Whew, I am so sorry. I don't know what just happened. Wow!" Shawn shook his head. Serenity was still waiting for Shawn to get to his question so she could finish up reading and head back to the office.

Shawn continued, "I see you are reading the *Times*. Do you mind if I check on something?"

Serenity looked at Shawn, then at the paper, and said, "This is only the business section. You probably read sports or the comics." She looked at him as if she was above him, moving her head in a way people who think they are superior do.

She thought, *This guy went through all of that just to ask me for a certain section in the paper! Sports section is not here, and the* New York Times *doesn't do comics, so what else could he possibly want?*

Serenity looked a little closer at Shawn and thought, *He is a good-looking man. And look at his hands: fingers—well-manicured and haircut—just right. The man may have only a sweat suit, but one thing is for sure, he's well groomed.*

Chapter 17

It was Shawn's turn to bring Serenity back into focus. He could not help himself but laugh at the comment about the sports and comics.

Shawn said with a smile, "No, may I look at the business section, particularly, the investment section?"

Serenity wanted to laugh. She thought, *This man is really trying to show me something. I know someone who does not have that quality when I see them, and this man is light years away.*

Serenity looked down at her paper and back up to Shawn with a "you have to be kidding me" look. Shawn, taking advantage of the opportunity, asked Serenity if he may join her at her table. Serenity, still off balance from Shawn's request, absentmindedly nodded yes and under her breath said "sure."

Shawn was sitting across from her before she came to her senses and thought, *Why would I invite a total stranger, who has been looking and staring at me since he walked into this diner to sit at her table?*

As far as she knew, he may be a serial rapist or, even worst, a serial killer. Serenity took a brief look at Shawn and concluded that he seemed harmless; in addition, she thought again about his broad shoulders, his well-manicured large hands, and perfectly shaped fingers. Moreover, that sweat suit fit him like a glove where she could tell this man probably was solid like a rock. However, she was reminded that the guy was probably a smooth player, as Sade says, a smooth operator. She realized she needed to put a stop to this charade even though she enjoyed the attention she was getting.

Serenity looked at Shawn and said, "You want me to stop what I'm doing to find a particular section in the investment section of this giant paper!" Serenity had already put the section back somewhere in the middle of the paper and knew she did not have time to look.

Shawn put on his best G-smile, G stands for game, and in this case major game. "I hope this isn't an inconvenience." Shawn paused and waited to see if Serenity was going to say something, and since she did not, he continued, "I guess I could have waited when I got off work."

Serenity found the section and looked at Shawn with great contempt for making her look through all of the paper for that one section. She thought, *This man had me fight through this paper to get to the section, which he thinks he wants, and then tells me he can wait until after work to check it out.* She looked at Shawn, handed him the investment section, and said, "Here you go, this is the section you wanted, I believe."

Shawn looked at the paper and then looked at the section from arm's length as if he had some type of problem with his eyes, "Yep, this is it, thank you." Serenity looked at him and thought, *This should be good.* And she waited to see what Shawn was going to do with the business section of the *Times*. She wanted to see how far brother-man was going to go with this.

Shawn's food had arrived. He told the waitress to wrap it up as he did not have time to eat. He said to the waitress, "You guys are moving slow today, huh."

The waitress turned and said to Shawn, "I apologize. We have several new people."

Shawn replied, "Yes, I notice, especially ah, Candy, I think that's her name."

Serenity rolled her eyes in a mocking gesture to say, "As if you didn't know her name." She said under her breath, "Now you know her name and her game."

Shawn looked at her and said, "Excuse me?"

Serenity had not realized that she had said it that loud or perhaps she had done it on purpose. The point is Mr. Player got the message as she looked at Shawn and told him she was talking to herself about something. Meanwhile, the waitress, whose name was Beatrice, rolled her eyes after hearing Candy's name and said, "Yes, that is one of them, she's our secret weapon."

Serenity, overhearing Shawn inquire about Candy, made another sound—this time a smug noise—and thought, *That nursery rhyme should be changed, the one about the fingers . . . where is pointer and so forth. It should say: Where is player, where is player and have Shawn stand up and say, here I am, here I am. How are you this morning? He would say, as horny as ever, thank you, you girls better run away.*

Serenity gave one quick burst of laughter out loud and covered her mouth as if she was coughing. Shawn and Beatrice looked at her with concern; she lifted her hand and stated she was OK. She was about finished with her meal. She looked at her watch and noticed she had about twenty minutes before she headed back to work. Shawn was talking with the waitress and caught a glimpse of Serenity looking at her watch, and he realized he better make his move.

Chapter 18

Shawn looked at the investment section as if it was written in a foreign language. He looked up at Serenity with a perplexed look that turned into a smile. "I want to thank you for allowing me to intrude. I am sure you are a busy woman."

Serenity thought, *Yep, just like a player, trying to get information of what I do. The next thing he'll ask is how much do I make, and do I need a roommate.*

Serenity was lost in thought when Shawn got her attention, stuck out his hand, and said, "Hello, I'm Shawn." Serenity, feeling a little better, at least she could put a name to a face, took Shawn's hand with a professional grip and said, "My name is Serenity, Serenity Powers."

Shawn held Serenity's hand a little longer than expected, while Serenity loosened up her grip and let her hand relax in Shawn's big grip. She liked the feeling. She was thinking and hoping that Shawn was not the type of guy you meet, shake hands with, and the next thing you know the guy is moving his pointer finger in your palm, and everyone knew what that message meant. However, Shawn did not do that. Serenity was relieved. She had to admit, he was good and good looking. He had style and class, a player of players, he had done his homework, just like what Sandra called a Mack player, not just a player, but Mack. Player Mack, first name Player, the last name Mack.

Serenity looked at Shawn and said, "Are you interested in the stock market?" Shawn did not know what to say, so he said he dabbed into it every now and then. Serenity figured the next question was obvious, but she felt she had to say something. "Do you know how to read the market?"

Shawn looked at her at first, but deep down, he wanted to show her his track record; instead, he answered her question, "Well, there's always room for improvement." Shawn's laugh was hearty and without restrictions. As a matter of fact, his laughter was so contagious that Serenity had to chuckle out a laugh but quickly caught herself.

Shawn rebounded, smiled, and asked, "Do you understand the market?" He continued, "I mean Wall Street."

Serenity stared at Shawn, longer than she really wanted to, but there was something about this man, she thought, she could not put her finger on to. She answered, "I understand a little bit, like you say, there's always room for improvement."

Shawn looked Serenity in the eyes and asked, "How much?"

Serenity did not like the way Shawn was so-called backing her up against a wall and said, "Enough."

Shawn knew he had come out of his game plan as he thought, *I was too aggressive. I need to back down.*

Serenity seemed a little nervous and began to twirl her *locks*. She was becoming fidgety and flustered. Shawn looked at her and thought that the flustering was cute and so innocent; it made her look so volatile, sexy, and vulnerable. The look, to Shawn, was a turn on in one sense, and in another sense, the look made him want to protect her from anything that would make her feel the way she was feeling. Shawn knew he had better switch gears.

Chapter 19

Shawn cleared his throat and looked at the headline news. "Uh, this should be interesting. The mayor is supposed to be meeting with several entrepreneurs and real estate city leaders this week to discuss building a plaza with stores and a YMCA."

That seemed to perk Serenity up a little bit as she peered over at the story Shawn was reading. She thought, *This guy really seems to know what is going on around him. Probably part of his game to lure women!* Serenity, as she was peering, could smell the mixed aroma of a nice cologne and sweat. The two scents did not create a stench but tweaked her olfactory nerves that created a distinctive smell she could not put a finger on until she thought further while Shawn was talking. The thought hit her like a sudden orgasm. The two odors of yin and yang created a sensation and an image in her mind of Shawn working out naked, chiseled to the core, pumping more than iron. Serenity, at the time of the thought, was finishing up her coffee. She let out a surprised gasp and began to cough. Shawn asked her if she was OK. She raised her hand to gesture she was fine. When she recovered she was still blushing from the thought of the manly smell that was coming from him, invading her space. She said, "Thank you, I am fine. It must have gone down the wrong way."

As Serenity was getting herself together, Beatrice, the waitress, came over. "Is everything OK?" Serenity, still recovering, nodded with a smile that translated to say thank you. Beatrice looked at Shawn and smiled in an overly friendly way. The gesture caught Serenity's eye, and she sort of fumbled at the contents, whatever she was pretending to look for in her bag. Serenity thought, *I could be choking while she is flirting her behind off with that silly grin plastered on her face.*

She noticed Shawn smiling back at Beatrice with that playboy smile and thought, *He is a p-l-a-y-e-r to his heart. That's probably his tip: that* playboy smile with those cute dimples, nice white teeth, and strong-looking hands. Serenity, in her mind, smacked herself for getting pulled in by Mr. Playboy. She thought, *Honey, good looks and a smile will not pay your rent, get with the program, sister.* Serenity smiled at Beatrice but was thinking, *There is a sucker born every minute.*

Beatrice looked at Shawn and said with a smile, of course, "Your food is at the pay counter."

Serenity playfully stomped her foot and thought, *Ah, Beatrice, you forgot to say "your honor." If she keeps that smile up, we would not know the difference between the crap between her teeth and her real teeth.*

Serenity could not believe how those women practically fell for that guy as if he was a magnet. She shook her head and said a little too loud, "I don't get it."

Shawn stood up and responded to her statement, "You don't get what?"

Serenity, still sitting down, looked up at Shawn like a deer caught in the headlights. She began looking for that pretend item in her purse again.

Shawn thought, *As small as this purse is, it must have some secret compartments!*

Serenity, recovered nicely, said, "Oh well, I just don't get where the time goes. I have to get back to work."

Shawn looked at Serenity as if to say "I see right through you." But he said, "I am sure everything will work out. Where do you work? Is it close to here?"

Shawn knew. He watched her every day. He wanted to see what she was going to say. Serenity, looking at her watch, calculating the time she left for lunch, gestured with her hands absently to Shawn's question. "No, it's not far. It's right over there in the Federal building." Serenity stopped, blinked, and thought, *Now why would I give this stranger the exact place where I work?* Serenity had to admit; it was like talking to a friend. Shawn reached into his pocket, took out an old sweaty dollar, and put it on the table. He then wiped his hands on his wet sweatpants. Shawn reached out his hand to Serenity to shake it and said, "Once again, it was a real pleasure spending this time with you. I hope we can do this again."

Serenity, in her mind, was thinking, *Now that was totally gross—nasty wet hands and a nasty wet dollar, and you want to do this again. Yeah, when Bush finds those weapons of mass destruction!* Serenity smiled at Shawn, quickly placed the tip of her hand in Shawn's hand and removed them quickly before Shawn could grasp it. She smiled at Shawn and said, "You have a nice day."

Shawn said thank you, turned, and walked away with a smile so broad on his face that he knew he had given Serenity something to chew on—enough to make the impression he wanted her to see. For some reason, he did not want her to see Shawn Cook—just Shawn.

Chapter 20

As he was making his way to the front door, Serenity was still looking at him. She thought he had a walk of a king—so confident and sure of himself! Shawn took out his cell phone, spoke into it for a few minutes, and placed it back in its case on his waist.

Serenity saw the gesture and thought, *Hey, Casanova! You better save those day minutes.* As she watched Shawn walk toward the door, she shook her head, thinking that Shawn ran a good game, but this was one sister, who refused to play. *Mr. Big Stuff* Serenity thought, *a get over artist, comes in all sweaty, talking all that stuff about stocks and bonds! Oh yeah, he knows how to play the game. All that big talk and leaves such a little tip!*

Serenity continued to shake her head when Beatrice came over and stood next to her. As she joined her, watching Shawn leave, she said, "Oh me, oh my, what a fine man, yum-yum yummy! I know exactly how you feel. I don't blame you for looking."

Serenity realized what Beatrice was saying. "What? Huh, no, it's not like that. There is probably too much women drama with that." She looked at Beatrice. "Believe me, I don't want that. Whoever has him, could keep him."

Beatrice looked at Serenity. "Are you kidding? The man is free, unattached, that's what makes him so desirable, a perfect gentlemen."

Serenity cut her eyes at the dollar tip on the table and thought, *These women are either crazy or stupid.*

Beatrice continued, "Sister, I wish I could have thirty minutes with that man. He'll have me . . ." Beatrice stopped and remembered that she was on duty. Serenity, on the other hand, wanted Beatrice to continue. She was feeling a sensation she had not felt in a long time. Beatrice looked at Serenity and under her breath made a "whew" sound. She tapped her forehead several times as if the thought she had just expressed was too powerful to bottle up. "I'm sorry," she tapped her forehead some more and said, "will that be all? Can I get you something else?"

Serenity looked at Beatrice and told her that everything was splendid. She said, "This is my first time here. I usually go to the place right next door, but this was good. You won another customer. Do I pay you or take it up to the front?" Beatrice smiled and said, "Normally you would give me the money, and I'll bring you back your change." Serenity smiled at Beatrice's cunning hint toward getting a tip.

Serenity said, "Well, all right. I'll just give you the money and . . ." Serenity stopped talking for a brief moment and thought, *Shawn did not pay, so why was he allowed to take his food?* She further thought, *This man could probably charm a snake. He must have charmed that Candy girl with the joker smile and got over like a bandit.* She dismissed the thought and proceeded to take her wallet out.

Beatrice said, "Ma'am, that won't be necessary. It has already been taken care of."

Serenity looked at Beatrice and crinkled her nose, as if to say by whom. Beatrice looked at Serenity for a brief moment and realized that she needed to explain, "Oh, I'm sorry, by the gentlemen that you were sitting next to."

Serenity did not know what to say. She placed her hand on her mouth. "Well, let me at least leave a larger tip." She looked at the measly dollar left on the table and continued, "That is the least I can do."

Beatrice looked at Serenity and said, "Ma'am, that's been taken care of also by the gentleman who was sitting next to you."

Serenity did not know what to say as she hemmed and hawed, trying to find the words to express how she was feeling. Finally, she said to Beatrice, "I will like to pay the gentleman back."

Serenity looked at Beatrice, who looked dumbfounded. She impatiently said, "Can you tell me where he works, if you know?" She paused and asked again, "Do you know?" Beatrice pointed to the building next to the Federal building and told Serenity that that was where Shawn worked.

Serenity felt a sense of relief come on her. At least she knew where he worked. *I need to find him and give him back this money. I do not need any favors from that Casanova.*

Serenity further thought, *His payback might require more than I could give.* In addition, Serenity always felt that borrowing or accepting money from men was a way to open your door, without you saying to come in, and a way for a person to overstay their welcome.

Serenity looked at Beatrice. "That's a big building. Do you know what floor?"

Beatrice said, "Well, you can start on the third floor up to the twenty-fourth floor."

Serenity thought he probably worked in the mail room or something, which meant she needed to reimburse the man as that may have been part of his rent money or some bill. Perhaps, he was trying to look like a big spender. He better put that money on his electric bill to keep those lights on.

Serenity picked up a glass of water to wash down her food and asked Beatrice, "So, how much did the gentleman give for the tip?"

Beatrice looked up, thought, and said, "Uh, forty dollars."

Serenity, upon hearing the amount, ended up having a mouthful of water sprayed all across the table and started coughing again. Beatrice ran over to Serenity and asked her if she was all right. Serenity was about tired of surprises that had caused her to choke on something she was drinking.

Serenity, still flushed from the coughing, pulled away from Beatrice and said,

"No, I am not OK . . . ," which brought concern to Beatrice, and Serenity continued, "A forty dollar tip! How much was the meal?" Beatrice was getting ready to respond when Serenity said, "May I see the bill, please?"

Beatrice, reluctantly, handed the bill over to Serenity. She looked at the cost of her meal and thought, *OK, twelve dollars for my meal and the tip.* She then fell back in her chair. "I can't believe this! My breakfast came out to seventeen dollars!" She thought, *I need to go to the bank to get some money. I will not become a part of this guy's drama. First thing tomorrow morning, this, Mr. Shawn will get not only his money, but also a piece of my mind.*

Chapter 21

Shawn left the diner, feeling like a kid on Christmas morning. He had a smile on his face that was beaming like a bright star. Shawn had been on many dates in the last couple of months, but what happened today had never happened to him before.

He had never, as far as he could remember, been in a relationship that was complete.

But Shawn felt good about this day; he felt like he'd made some progress. Finally, he'd made a positive impression. He started thinking about his next move. He smiled and knew what his next move would be and then he would chill and wait. *The next move will be hers,* he thought. But in the meantime, he was getting ready for round two.

As Shawn was leaving the diner, he made a call to Karen and asked her to call Sandy's floral shop and send three dozen roses to Serenity Powers over at the Federal building. He wasn't sure what floor Serenity worked on, but instructed Karen to inquire with the front desk.

Karen said to Shawn, "How would you like to pay for this?"

Shawn replied, "Sandy will take care of those details. She knows I'll take care of her."

Karen mumbled, "I bet you will."

Shawn said, "I didn't hear you, what was that?"

Karen, feeling a little embarrassed, said, "No, I was just going over what I need to do."

Shawn didn't have time to dispute with Karen about what she really said, but he pretty much had heard it. He was still hyper; he started rambling on about upcoming meetings, appointments, and cancellations. He was back in the driver's seat. He felt it; he was going so fast that Karen had to ask him to slow down. Shawn calmed down for a minute and jumped back into hyper mode.

He said, "Karen, make sure you get back with the people at Disney. Let them know we accept their offer; the same with Paramount. Karen, let Essence know I'll be glad to do the interview with them and make sure my calendar is free for at least one night in the week and on the weekends up to 5:00 p.m. Do you have any questions?"

Karen said, "No, that all was clear." Shawn told Karen he should be there in about another hour or so. He said to Karen, "If you need to get in contact with me, I'll be meeting with Frank and his so-called colleague, Phillip Keys for lunch."

Karen, feeling a bit inquisitive, asked Shawn, "What's up with the attitude toward his colleague? Do you want me to check him out?"

Shawn smiled to himself and thought how proud he was of Karen. She had come a long way, but she still had a few connections with some folks that went around busting kneecaps for a living—people who back in the day she rolled with and now would be glad to bust out a favor for their pretty mama. So when she said "check out," she was not referring to by means of the Internet. It could mean anything, but nothing good, you could believe that. Karen, asking him, brought him out of his reverie. *Was he sure he didn't want her to have her friends do the honors?*

He responded, "Uh, no, you don't have to go through all of that, but thanks." He said to himself, '*But no thanks.*' He continued, "Naw, it's cool. I have my eyes on Keys." Shawn told Karen he would call her later; in the meantime, he was thinking about his next move.

Chapter 22

Serenity took the elevator up to the seventh floor, where she worked as the executive secretary of operations. She was running late. She peeked in and saw her friend and the receptionist Sandra Beck. Sandra was under Serenity, but the two had started the same day. Serenity, however, took advantage of the programs the federal government was offering, which promoted her to her current position.

Sandra never had the desire or the drive to excel. At one time she did, and she could have been up there with Serenity; however, she had some major drama going on, and those things became a distraction and overall a discouragement from pushing forward.

Serenity never looked down at Sandra. She had the utmost respect for someone who had been through the stuff Sandra had been through and still had the drive to survive.

Serenity was never the type whose head became bigger when promoted. Her parents always said to her, "We are only a fine line away from being homeless." Despite her upper middle-class rearing, Serenity knew what her parents were talking about.

Serenity and Sandra, over the years, became very tight; they hung out together after work, even met up on some weekends and had a nice time. As a matter of fact, it was Serenity that helped Sandra get out of her drama with her ex-husband. The man was a certified nutcase, always stalking and threatening to do physical harm to either Sandra or their two children.

Sandra confided in Serenity about what was happening. Serenity said she would take care of it. She made a few phone calls to several big-time lawyers, whom she had connections with. Those powerhouse lawyers had some big-time police officers even on a federal level that could make life very miserable as well as uncomfortable. Well, the rest is history. Put it this way, Sandra's ex-husband had not been seen in the last few years.

Serenity called Sandra on her cell phone; Sandra picked up and asked Serenity, "Where have you been?" Serenity dismissed the question for then and instructed Sandra to meet her in her office in two minutes. She did not want to walk into Mrs. Benita Fry, the senior vice president of operations, or rather the watchdog of operations.

Benita Fry, the senior vice president of operations, was chosen for the position over Serenity due to her seniority and her age. In all reality, Mrs. Fry had two feet out the door for retirement. The heels of her feet were still firmly planted on the inside. Even though Mrs. Fry went to Serenity for advice and to get certain tasks completed, Serenity had always been nice enough to help out Mrs. Fry, while Mrs. Fry had always been consistent in regards to taking all the credit to herself. When Mrs. Fry had no need for Serenity, she displayed such an attitude toward her and wielded her power, but Serenity handled it with ease, because she knew that Mrs. Fry would eventually come to her. Like the old saying goes, "You don't bite the hand that feeds you." And boy, Serenity knew that Mrs. Fry, one of these days, would be starving.

Serenity came inside the double doors, and everyone looked up with greeting smiles. Serenity asked Debra, her intern, as to where Mrs. Fry was. Debra secretly pointed way down the hall. Serenity mouthed a "thank-you" and headed straight to her office where Sandra was waiting. Serenity had a nice-sized office, which she had decorated herself. On the wall behind her, she had her degrees and accolades of accomplishments and letters of promotions. On the other wall, facing the front part of her desk, she had photographs of family, friends, and coworkers. On the huge mahogany desk sat more pictures of family, such as those of her parents and close relatives. She also had little quirky sayings and wisdom sayings, and a Bible verse framed into a beautiful picture frame. Serenity had a huge library of professional as well as nonfictional books, such as love stories and mysteries. She loved her office space, especially the view that looked right at the building where Shawn, the mail guy, worked.

Chapter 23

Serenity opened her office door and closed it softy, facing the door. When she turned around to walk toward her desk, she stopped, frozen right in her tracks and could not move. Serenity stared in awe at her desk. What she saw, totally took her breath away; she felt faint and had to lean against her door for support.

Sandra looked at her with excitement and said, "They just came about an hour ago."

Serenity's eyes were wide open in surprise, not knowing what to say. Who could have done such a thing? Sandra, jumping on the bandwagon, said, "What are you holding out on me, girl?" Sandra continued, "As much as we hook up, you never told me there was someone, whoever it is, you must have given it to him, lovely. Look at all of them."

Serenity looked at Sandra and shook her head in denial with a Girl Scout honor sign. Sandra looked at Serenity and said, "Girl, put those fingers down. You were not a girl scout." Serenity, still shaking her head in denial, said to Sandra, "Come on, you know I would have clued you in on it from day one, so don't even go there."

Sandra gave a "yeah-right face and whatever" look. Serenity waved her hand at Sandra and told her to hush. Both girls laughed like junior high students. Sandra looked at the flowers and said to Serenity, "Well, who do you think may have sent them?"

Sandra paused and continued, "Maybe that guy on the fifth floor, who is always trying to ask you out."

Serenity looked at Sandra and said, "Who, Mr. Payne? He's old enough to be my father."

Sandra continued, "How about that four-eyed brother, you know, the one with the bottle top eye glasses. Those things are so thick you can use the sun to fry an egg. I am scared to look right in his eyes. Those things may make me go blind. When I talk to him, I always look off to side. I know it looks as if I'm talking to someone on the side of us. I don't care. Those things could pop your eyeballs out of their sockets."

Sandra started laughing, and Serenity laughed a little as well but stopped. She picked up the giant vase with the flowers in them and smelled them. She had to close her eyes because the smell was so fresh as if they just were picked from a rose bush. She came to her senses and remembered how Sandra, in her silly joking way, had tried to put a face to the mystery flowers and said, "Sandra, I really don't know who sent these. I have no idea."

Sandra was looking at Serenity like one of those television detectives. Serenity continued, "Come on, Sandra, you know I have not been seeing anyone. Come on, you practically know my social life, and it is the pits."

Sandra agreed and said, "Well, that part is true, or should I say what Isaac Hayes says, 'Damn right.'"

Serenity said, "You don't have to agree with me, you know."

Sandra quickly inhaled her breath in surprise, and Serenity asked, "What is it?"

Sandra smiled in a shy girlish way and said, "You have a secret admirer."

Serenity gave Sandra a look that said "are you kidding." "You have issues. Are you high on something, San?"

Serenity shook her head and said, "A secret admirer? I guess so secretive, I didn't even know about it." Sandra picked up a few flowers that also came in a box, noticed a card, quickly picked it up, looked at Serenity in an accusatory "I got you way," and said, "Oh yea, and then who is Shawn?"

Chapter 24

Shawn took the elevator to his main office on the seventeenth floor. When the elevator door opened, Shawn waved to the people in the elevator and told them to have a nice day.

He stood there for a brief second, thinking about what had taken place at the diner. He opened the main door to the office, danced, and did an awkward waltz right into the waiting area of the office where Karen's desk was. Karen's desk was the first, following which was a slew of large offices and cubicles that had at least three workstations. There were a total of eight working stations that had at least three to seven people per station.

Shawn, very much elated, waved to his employees with a big smile on his lips. They waved back with a little trepidation as they did not know what to make of Shawn's happy mood. For the last few months they didn't know how to deal with his crazy emotions. They said among themselves that maybe his behavior manifested signs of bipolar disorder. Some jokingly said that he had a case of PMS. They tried to figure out what could have sparked the man out of his funk; perhaps a new account from a big-time movie company. They did not know. Shawn's employers, most of the time, caught their founder/CEO in a fairly good mood. This was one of the attributes they loved about him. He was consistent, but this type of manic display was totally out of character.

Shawn stopped at the A-team working station; there were about seven people within that station. He considered this group one of the most important aspect of his enterprise. If this station goes down, it could affect the whole operation.

Shawn leaned on very heavily on this group to troubleshoot issues and problems, such as hackers and viruses, to name only two. The A-team's main mission was to assess the problem and eliminate the problem, and at the final stage, bring the matter up in the next meeting—to teach others about the problem. Shawn got the title "A-team concept" from the television hit that starred Mr. T—a group of former soldiers—always getting into a fix but always finding a way out of it by using whatever they could get their hands on.

Shawn stopped at their workstation and said with that baritone voice and huge smile, "How are you guys doing?"

Everyone in the seven-man group stopped their progress and gave their attention to Shawn. A few brief seconds passed before the supervisor of the group, Sam Hunter, the senior consultant, spoke up, "Good day, sir, we are doing fine, Mr. Cook. That task you assigned to us . . ." Sam paused a minute and continued, "We are about 95 percent sure that we have solved that problem." There was more hesitation, and Shawn felt there was a "but" lingering in the air, so he said, "But?"

Sam continued, being very careful how he was treading. He knew Shawn did not accept excuses. One better have a good reason for having a setback, so Sam said, "We need an extension, sir."

Shawn looked at his A-Team, still with that smile on his face, and said, "How much time you need, Sam?" Sam was caught off guard seeing the "New Shawn" behaving that way. He pondered over how much extended time his team needed, and he looked at his team for assistance. His team looked at him mumbling and brainstorming the question. The team members looked at Sam and shrugged their shoulders. Sam looked at Shawn with a look that suggested the question was one of those jeopardy questions. Shawn imagined the music to *Jeopardy* playing.

Sam was ready to reveal his answer with some apprehension, and he said with hesitation, "Uh, maybe, uh, I think . . ." Sam looked back at the team and back at Shawn as he was giving Shawn bits and pieces of his answer. He continued, "I think three or four, uh." Sam's team did not seem to know the right response either as they were like those bobblehead dolls. Every number Sam threw out his team head with up and down, as they hemmed and hawed and made unsure and sure sounds, "Yeah, uh, that sounds good" thrown back at Sam.

Shawn thought, *Eggheads! You give them the hardest question, and they will solve it for you in no time. Give them a commonsense question, they will start bumping heads.* He cut off the voices of confusion, "Look, I'll give you one more week." He looked at them with a big smile plastered on his face. "Remember, one week." Sam and his team were relieved that the strain on their brains had been relieved with an extension, and Shawn reminded them, "Listen, ladies and gentlemen, Vision Ware is right on our backs. If we fail, you know who these big production companies are going to go to, right?"

Sam and his team looked at each other, some nodded, while others said the affirmative of yeah and yes sir. Shawn paused, he looked around at the empire he was building, looked back at his A-Team, then at Sam, and said, "Listen, fellows, you guys have been at it this whole week, and you guys are doing great. Sam, you and your team, take the rest of the day and tomorrow off."

They all cheered. Shawn continued, "Provided, excuse me . . ." The cheering calmed down as Shawn continued, "Provided, Sam, you and your team use these tickets to the Beacon Theater and enjoy the show."

Sam and his crew looked at each other as if they had won a trip to Malibu or some exotic island, giving each other, which only can be described as, the nerd shake and high fives, which by the way, when they attempted they missed each other's hands. Shawn, standing close to this display, realized what may have started out as a friendly zone had by then turned into a combat zone. He quickly sidestepped away from the combat zone. Sam and his crew were still missing each other with the high fives as hands were flying everywhere but were missing their target. Shawn did not want to become an unattended target. He walked away, heading to his office with pep to his step.

Chapter 25

Shawn waltzed into his area; everyone stopped what they were doing, looked up, smiled, and went back to work. Shawn had people working for him that appreciated him. They saw him as a tough and hard, yet fair and easygoing CEO—one that was easy to talk to and get along with—so this behavior was sort of odd, yet not strange. Shawn had always had a policy on a wall in his office that said: "Work without play is like a man without food and water."

Shawn practiced what he preached. Throughout the year, he would have special marked fun/family days on the calendar. This would include picnics, sports day, family day, and different festive events that Shawn encouraged all his employees and their families to be a part of—all at his expense. Shawn's only requirement was that all employees had to bring one dish each. Shawn did not need the dish, but he strongly believed what you give from the heart will be given back to you in different ways. Shawn called this his idea of a seed blessing: plant it and watch it grow.

Shawn came to Karen's desk, took a mint from Karen's bowl, and said, "Sandy Flowers are going to handle that matter?"

Karen smiled at Shawn and said, "Yes, sir." She paused, looked down and back up at Shawn, and said, "Mr. Cook, are you OK?"

Shawn, in the middle of Karen's question, had waltzed off and was waltzing with some of the employees as he playfully send them off with a spin and looked at Karen and said, "Karen, I never felt better. I have discovered something I hope all of us would find."

Karen looked skeptical and asked, "Mr. C., what is that?"

Shawn looked at Karen, took another mint from her bowl, tossed it high in the air, and caught it with the applause of the employees behind him. Then he turned to them and bowed, turned back to Karen, and said, "Love."

Karen sat there, looking bewildered and confused, and said, "What?"

Shawn came close to Karen, so close that she could smell his mint breath from the candy. He spelled it out, "L-o-v-e, Love, Karen, I found it."

Shawn walked to his office, doing a Tango. "Karen, get Frank on the line. I'll be in my office." Frank was Shawn's closest friend. He called Frank his ace boon koon. They grew up together and went to the same school. Shawn and Frank graduated from the same high school; however, Frank wanted to pursue a career in law enforcement, while Shawn wanted to achieve his career in business. Frank was recruited by the FBI. The two men did not allow their career choices to get in their way of a long-lasting friendship. Both men had been there for each other. Even now they got together with their other friends at least twice a month and went to the state-of-the-art gym, where Shawn chose to work out with the weights or do kickboxing or simply shoot some hoops.

Shawn tangoed his way to his office, excited about talking to his best friend, Frank, about whom he was calling his girlfriend. Shawn basically explained that the funk cloud was gone, and he was in love with the woman he had been looking at for months.

Frank was excited about his best friend's situation especially the fact the funk was gone. Frank questioned whether this woman knew that she was a recipient of Shawn's love. Shawn said, "No, but she will."

Frank told Shawn that he had to go as he had a business luncheon with his supervisor and colleague, Phillip Keys. Shawn made a sound, and Frank said, "What? Come on, Shawn, Keys is cool. He's helping me deal with the situation with my son, Bobby. I know you don't like him, but he's cool."

Shawn refused to allow his cloud nine to be rained on and said, "Look, Frank, I don't care too much for the man. I mean last week when I met up with you guys, I have to admit I didn't like his vibe. I just felt something was wrong. This dude isn't all what you think he is and you are going out again. This is like within the last few months."

Frank appreciated his ace, but sometimes, he let that karate kung fu stuff get in the way, and he could become overprotective like a big brother. Frank stated, "Naw, he's cool, people, it's all good. He's going to try to help me with the medical situation concerning Bobby."

Shawn made a sound that registered as saying that he accepted, but with reservation. He said, "Just be careful. It could have been the funk I was in, but my instincts tells me something different. My advice is that keep your friends close and your enemies closer."

Frank thought, *You see, there goes that kung fu crap again.* The two exchanged pleasant words as if the disagreement had never occurred and hung up. Shawn was concerned, but he brushed it aside and thought about his time with Serenity earlier that afternoon, and as far as he was concerned, nothing was going to get him to come off the cloud he was floating on.

Chapter 26

Sandra was waiting for Serenity to explain who Shawn was. Serenity mouthed the name . . . Shawn, as if she was trying to remember the person and suddenly said, "Oh, Mr. Sweat Suit."

Sandra looked at Serenity and asked her who she was talking about. Serenity didn't want to go into details. She just gave Sandra the basics. "Some guy who was trying to get my attention. I mean he had the women practically falling over backward.

Sandra looked at Serenity and said, "There had to be a reason. Sisters are not going to fall like that unless they know you're packing the green or well packaged." Sandra nudged Serenity with a "bad girl look."

Serenity looked at Sandra, shook her head, and said, "Girl, that is all you think about. You need to get off that one-track mind."

Sandra looked at Serenity and countered, "And you need to just get off, girl. I bet you're so backed up, not even Roto-Rooter can unclog your butt."

Serenity just looked up and said, "Why me, Lord? Why test my patience? Nuts are for squirrels but you, in your humor, gave me . . ." She shook her head and said, "Lord, have mercy."

Sandra laughed and said, "Right there, you need to use that 'Lord, have mercy' prayer to help you get a life."

Serenity looked at Sandra with a smile of humor and said, "Well, anyway, this guy, uh, Shawn, comes in sweat dripping from him, and he's trying to talk to me about business as if he is Mr. Wall Street or something. Then he, get this, has to rush back to work where I think he works in the mail room, or he's a messenger guy, and he was probably coming off one of his runs, because no one goes to work sweating and looking like that unless you work a job where they make you work and sweat like that. And then he pays for my meal and leaves the tip! Guess how much it all came out to?"

Sandra shrugged her shoulders in a gesture to say she did not know. "Fifty-two dollars, girl."

Sandra blew out a whistle of the price tag.

Serenity said, "I thought the same thing, but then I thought the way he was dressed, homeboy probably spent money for one of his bills like his light bill or something." Sandra and Serenity laughed.

Sandra looked at Serenity and said, "Girl, I know you are lying. Homeboy tried to impress you looking like that? And putting down that much cash for lunch, nah, something is wrong somewhere." Sandra continued, "You see, that is what I mean. Brothers these days are trifling. These are the same brothers who will go out with a woman who is all dressed up, and here they come picking you up in a broken-down cab, pulling up to your crib, having the driver blow his horn, trying to get your attention, instead the horn gets everybody else's attention in the hood. You're too embarrassed to come out, so now he's halfway in and halfway out the broken-down cab, yelling your name. If that's not enough punishment, here he comes walking up to your door with a name brand sweat suit, and here you are looking in the mirror with a beautiful dress on. Then when you get to the place, he makes up some story about payroll messed up their check, and if you can take care of the cab and the dinner tab, and then send you home like that boy in that movie, *Home Alone*." Sandra sucked her teeth and waved her hand as if she was really frustrated.

Sandra looked at Serenity and said, "But I don't think this guy fits that MO, Serenity."

Serenity looked at Sandra with curiosity and said, "How did you come to such a conclusion, Sherlock?"

Sandra looked at Serenity and said, "For one, look at his handwriting. If this is his handwriting, but giving him the benefit of the doubt, let's suppose this is his handwriting." Serenity looked at the handwriting and looked backed up at Sandra and agreed to use the handwriting as evidence, "All right, Mrs. Madam bright, get to the point."

Sandra continued, "Well, I read somewhere that the way one writes says a lot about their personality and even their occupation." Serenity looked at Sandra with a look of pessimism and said, "This, I got to hear, go on." Sandra stopped, looked at Serenity, and said, "Forget it. I have to get back to work." Serenity playfully grabbed Sandra by the arm, apologized, and encouraged Sandra to continue.

Sandra, with some hesitation, continued, "Well, as I was saying, from what I see of this person's writing, you are dealing with an intelligent and thought-provoking man—a man that is not afraid to let people see who he is."

Serenity said, trying to hold back her laughter, "Sandra, where do you see all of this?"

Sandra said, "Look at his signature. You see how it's not too big and not too small. It says this guy has a balanced self-esteem. Look, if he was full of himself, the signature would have been exaggerated, but it's not. See here and—"

Serenity cut her off, "OK go on, I want to be entertained some more."

Sandra continued, "The other thing about this man is that he is confident and sure about himself, but he is a man of compassion as well."

Serenity looked at Sandra with a look of skepticism. "Girl, are you telling me you can tell by this man's writing that he is a man of compassion? Now I know you are part of the snap, crackle, and pop crew."

Sandra, once again, pointed out at Shawn's writing. "Serenity, I'm not kidding. I may joke about a lot of things but not this. You see how his writing is very close to each other as if one is holding up the other." Serenity was looking hard but denied seeing what Sandra was seeing even though she did see that Shawn's writing did have that quality. Sandra continued, "Oh my!" Serenity anxiously said, "What, what is it?" Sandra, still looking at the writing, made the same sound, "Oh my, this man is sexy to the core, and he probably knows how to please a woman."

Sandra looked at Serenity's amazed expression and said, "Girl, just inhale and let it out slowly. You are about to hyperventilate."

Serenity looked at Sandra. "No, I'm not. I am fine, and you read into things too much. Now get on with it."

Sandra, teasing Serenity, said, "Oh, at first it's nothing, this is crazy, you went on and on, but now—"

Serenity, sounding frustrated, said, "Sandra, if you don't get on with this, you will be on the unemployment line. Now get to the point."

Sandra acted like she was offended, but Serenity knew better. "OK, you see how his S crosses into his H, and you see how his letters are touching each other. They have an on-top-of-each-other look."

Serenity's mind began to think what Shawn's physique looked like underneath that sweat suit. Her mind started going into areas that were restricted, even prohibited. Serenity looked at Sandra after coming out of her daydreaming fantasy and said, "Sandra, all of this is poppycock."

Sandra said, "Well, it was in the papers for the last few months, and it was in that psychology magazine you order every month." Sandra held up the magazine. This went on back and forth till Sandra said, "Come on, girl, look at you. What happened at lunch? What did Mr. Confident say that got you so flustered? Good thing you're not a shade lighter, or you would be red like a cherry. Oops, sorry, wrong choice of words."

Serenity shook her head. "You are so off target. Stop trying to see something into something where there is nothing there to see, you see." Serenity even looked confused after that one. She shook her head and continued, "Look, you may be right about this theory of his handwriting, but you, as usual, are barking up the wrong tree. This guy, Shawn, is a womanizer, a good con man, a true player to the heart that is pulling a few heartstrings and stringing these ignorant women to him, but not this educated black woman."

Sandra asked, "Was he fine?"

Serenity said, "Oh yes, yes, indeed. But I saw his game." Serenity was beginning to twirl her hair, looking at Sandra.

Sandra smiled at Serenity and said, "I bet you want to be in that game. You can play center, and he can play quarterback, if you know what I mean, 347, 347, 36, 24, 36, hut, hut . . . *hut*, hike."

Serenity could not believe this girl. "You are so nasty with your gutter brain. I'm only going to say this one more time. The only thing this man is looking for is a sugar mama or a buddy or a booty caller, sorry not interested. He may be fine and all, but he's like the number one player. This guy is smooth as silk. I have to admit, but he's a play-er."

Sandra looked at Serenity with uncertainty and said, "Serenity, I'm telling you, this guy is not portraying all who he really is. Secondly, he's got you hot and bothered . . ." Serenity was ready to challenge that statement, but Sandra cut her off, "Don't even deny it. I know what it means when you begin to twirl your hair like the way you were doing it a few minutes ago. I've known you for too long. That gesture means that you are either troubled about something or you, just like in this case, bit off more than you can chew. Pardon the expression again."

Serenity waved a dismissal hand at Sandra. "What else the note said?"

Sandra found where she left off at. "It says, thank you for a wonderful lunch. You stimulated my mind. I enjoy talking to intelligent women like yourself."

Serenity said, "You see, homeboy is a charmer. He has all the right tools. He knows all the right words. I will admit he's one smooth operator."

Sandra laughed at Serenity's statement and said, "Well, you'll have the opportunity again. He would like to meet with you tomorrow at the same place, same time, sounds like me and Mrs. Jones."

Serenity brushed her friend off with a look of aggravation and a dismiss wave of her hand. She did not know what to say. All types of mixed thoughts were busy in her head like cars on a freeway. A part of her wanted to meet this Shawn so she could tell him she was not a charity case and settle that score, then, yes, she would pay back his money when they meet tomorrow. Serenity did not want to admit it, but she wanted to see Shawn again to test Sandra's crazy theory, so she used as an excuse.

Serenity looked at Sandra and said, "You know, I think I'll give Mr. Smooth something to talk about, by the time I am through with him he's going to wish he made a detour to one of his other floundering floozy mamas."

Sandra smiled and said, "All right, lady, start your engines."

Chapter 27

Serenity arrived ten minutes earlier than the last time she was at the restaurant. She thought, *If this guy, Shawn, works in the mail room or as a messenger, there is no telling what time he may get here.*

As Serenity approached the host desk, Candy smiled at her and said, "Welcome back, we are so glad to see you. Are you interested in a table or a booth?"

Serenity's confidence, which she had felt before coming here, was beginning to dwindle or rather deflate. She could not stop thinking what Sandra had said about Shawn's handwriting the previous day. All that morning, she had stood in the mirror practicing her speech she had prepared for Shawn. She had felt strong and confident that morning, but now she was having second thoughts as she was thinking about all the crazy things Sandra was saying about the writing.

Absently, Serenity said, "She is so stupid."

Candy looked up from studying her tables she had left and said, "Excuse me, I'm sorry. What was your preference between a table and a booth?"

Serenity wanted to express a sign of relief with a whistling gesture that suggested a close call that Candy did not hear her. Serenity stared at Candy as if she was caught with her hands in the cookie jar but did not have the sense to take it out. Serenity realized she was staring at Candy, quickly thought about Candy's question, and then played it off, "I'm sorry, I was just thinking which one I wanted."

Serenity paused and continued, "Actually," Serenity looked at Candy's nametag and proceeded, "Actually . . . Candy, I'm waiting for someone to arrive. Do you mind if I sit here?"

Candy smiled at Serenity and said, "Sure, that's fine. Are you looking for the gentleman you had lunch with the other day?"

Serenity wanted to correct Candy and set the record straight. "Actually, we didn't have—"

Candy cut her off. "Yes, he's already arrived, ma'am. He's asked to point you in the direction where he's sitting when you arrive." Serenity wanted to make it clear to Candy that yesterday wasn't what it appeared to have been. However, she felt she was dealing with a more important battle.

She thought that this guy, Shawn, had a lot of nerve to have someone "*point me in the right direction.*" How dare he act as if he and I are here to see each other? As if this was a planned date or something? Serenity continued to let her thoughts build her confidence as she waited for Candy to "*point her in the right direction.*"

Serenity thought, *I am here for one purpose and one purpose only, business, and definitely not pleasure. I'm here because I want to give him back what he spent on me, nothing more, nothing less, and afterward close out this chapter as he is out of his league. He better stay in his place and do some overtime for that money he spent yesterday.*

Candy pointed toward the back booths that had a window view, and what a view! This place was designed by someone who really loved what he or she did as well as someone who was romantic. *This is beautiful,* she thought. The window view had different types of exotic trees and plants. There was a large wishing well with a statue of an exotic man and a woman in the middle of the fountain, drinking and enjoying the water, as the man stood over the woman and the woman was between the man's strong legs. It was an image of strong love. The whole area had footlights, stone benches, and tables set in different areas of the place. Each table had two candlestick holders. The tables were huge. Serenity began to feel goose bumps going up and down her arm like several feathers. She imagined what this place must look like at night as lovers held hands and whispered sweet nothings to each other. She looked at the sign pointing to the outside area. It read "Paradise." Serenity smiled to herself and said, "I bet it is."

She reluctantly told Candy thank you and headed in that direction. She did not see Shawn. The place was enormous, and she hoped that Shawn did not see her coming, because he would probably yell her name across the restaurant.

Serenity saw Shawn before he could notice her as she threaded her way past tables, busboys, and customers coming and going. It was like a speedway: the clinging and clanging of plates and silverware sliding and banging into each other and servers carrying orders like circus performers.

Serenity liked the atmosphere. She could not believe how crowded this place was. No doubt the food and the quality of service were exceptional! She thought whoever was in charge should be commended. Once again, Serenity gave credit to the owner of this well-designed five-star restaurant.

Chapter 28

She was amazed at all the things that were happening around her, but what really caught her attention was that the workers were mainly people of color, and she was astonished how they worked together and the energy they had. She stood there watching, taking it all in with a sense of pride, and arriving to a conclusion that whoever was in charge had her people in mind.

Serenity was just a few feet from Shawn as she observed what he was wearing. He was wearing a Polo matching sweatshirt with a pair of sweat shorts that came just below the knee. Serenity had a perfect view in front of her. She could see Shawn's well-defined calf muscles and tree-truck thighs, no doubt mostly muscles. She noticed Shawn's narrowed waistline even while he was sitting and his wide shoulders. He was no doubt a man who took care of himself. She could not take her eyes off the well-sculptured man in front of her with the almost close-to-perfect symmetry body. Serenity remembered Shawn from their last encounter. She thought how mean and lean Shawn was, and yet he moved with fluidity and grace for someone tall and his size. Serenity shook the thought away from her mind and told herself she was there for one purpose—to settle the score.

As Serenity approached the booth, all what she had practiced last night and this morning in the mirror seemed to have been erased by that revenge emotion called anxiety. Serenity nervously stepped closer to the booth and felt all the signs of anxiety hit her, you know, the sweaty palms, dry throat, the whole bit. Serenity tried to shake it and tell herself to do what you came to do. She was about to turn and go, but Shawn noticed her from the corner of his eye. He got up and greeted her with a huge wide grin. Serenity's heart went out to the man whose smile could win the hearts of millions—so innocent and sincere. Shawn's smile reminded her of a happy child overjoyed to see his long-lost friend.

Serenity, once again, put up the defenses to remind herself that this smile was probably one of the weapons used to break down these women, which mounted in Serenity new vigor, new courage, new inner confidence that was hidden beneath her fears. She told herself that she would not be one of those women.

Shawn looked at Serenity with a smile and said in that baritone voice, "Good day, Mrs. Powers." Shawn paused, and his left eyebrow went up, you know how the wrestler, the Rock, used to do his eyebrow after he said his famous line "If you smell what the Rock is cooking" and then that eyebrow would go up. Shawn continued, "Or is it Miss and gave Serenity that million-dollar smile with that million-dollar white teeth and that million-dollar dimple on each cheek."

Serenity blushed a little and said, "Yes, it's Miss."

Shawn's smile beamed like a two hundred-watt light bulb. He continued as he took Serenity's hand to shake it. "Thank you for accepting my invitation. That was very kind and generous of you."

Serenity was surprised. Shawn grasped her hand, and his touch was so gentle. His hand totally engulfed her hand, almost to the point it disappeared. Serenity started thinking about the words to the song by the Pointer Sisters: "Something like she wanted a man with a slow hand, an easy touch." Serenity was about to think of the words to the whole song when those goose bumps started coming back as she pulled her hand perhaps a little too quickly from Shawn's.

Shawn looked at her with a smile and said, "Pardon me, but may I say you look very nice." His kindness and gentle approach caught Serenity off guard and sort of disarmed her, and the combination of his voice and his kind words melted her plans of what she came to do like butter. Serenity said, "Than . . . Thank you." She pulled together the little composure she had left and said, "Look, I just wanted to settle this mat—"

Shawn cut her off, "Ms. Powers, I hope you enjoyed the flowers. I wasn't sure if flowers were your thing or perhaps an invitation to have dinner with me."

Serenity, once again, smiled and put aside what she wanted to say. She was once again distracted from her game plan. Serenity looked down at her lap, back up at Shawn, and said in a gentle voice, almost a whisper, "Thank you, they were beautiful." Serenity paused and smiled, "All of them . . . thank you."

For a moment, it felt as if time had stood still. It was a very awkward moment for both of them as neither one had anything to say. Serenity broke the ice and said, "I see you are reading the *Times*." She continued, "Do you read a lot?"

Shawn smiled and said, "When I get the chance."

Serenity thought, *When he gets the chance! As a mailroom worker or even a messenger, you get plenty of downtime, or chances, as he put it, but he probably doesn't have the time because he's chasing after all these women.*

Shawn looked at the look on Serenity's face as if she wanted to say something to him, and he said, "Well, I like to read the editorial. I like to read what is on people's minds. It helps me to stay focused."

Serenity chuckled, "Oh, so you're saying that you are a follower."

Shawn looked at her with such intensity she felt as if he could see right through her, and that made her feel both self-conscious as well as if Shawn could tell she was wearing her favorite sexy panties. She shifted in her seat a little, and Shawn noticed her discomfort.

He said, "In that case, I guess we all have had someone we followed. Don't you concur, Ms. Powers?"

Serenity thought, *'Concur', nice, big word! He probably memorized it this morning, or he's probably heard his boss use it.* She thought, *Nice try, player. I'm not impressed.*

Shawn continued bringing Serenity's attention back to him. "Oh, you're not convinced?" Shawn, with that same intensity as if it was only him and her in the room, continued, "Look at businesses in general. The majority are copycats of the other, in many cases, the blind leading the blind, so to speak. One business is hoping to do better than their predecessor had done, but in many cases, they copy the same plan and fail the same way. There you go. We are followers of each other. Now to answer your question, I don't see myself as a follower. I would hope that I am a pacesetter." Shawn smiled and took a sip of his water.

Serenity looked at Shawn with curiosity and said, "Interesting philosophy." She said to herself that enough was enough and it was time to pop the bubble on player. "Shawn, what exactly do you do for a living?"

Chapter 29

Shawn paused for a brief minute and realized he knew he would have to come out and tell who he is, and when he was ready to respond, he opened his mouth to speak, "Hello, folks! May I ask you if you would like something to drink, and may I take your order?" Serenity did not want to be rude and send the young lady away. She looked at the Rosetta nametag. "Yes, I will have your special for the day with a glass of water please."

She noticed Shawn letting out a slow, long breath that seemed like relief, and she made a mental note of it. Rosetta took Serenity's mind from off Shawn because she was very nice, warm, and friendly. And what a talker! Serenity took to Rosetta and got caught up with her energy and her stories that were so funny. Rosetta punched in their order; Shawn requested the special as well. Serenity was still very much impressed with this new way of ordering—no yelling or writing on a pad—but on an instrument that resembled an iPod. She liked that idea, way in advance. The owner was a thinker, and she had to meet him.

Serenity looked at Shawn, trying to figure out his game. She found him to be attractive and handsome, not in a cute way, but in a rugged way. Shawn and Serenity talked about some of the comments in the editorial, some of that day's hot topics. She really liked the way Shawn thought. He was very analytical and had a critical thinker's mind. She was impressed, but what she really liked about Shawn was his passion for what he believed in and how he hung on to every word she spoke as if his life depended on it. However, it was his passion that drew her closer to him. Serenity knew that a mailroom worker or a messenger worker could not work for her. Perhaps in time she could overlook it, but one main thing about this Shawn was that he was a player and that he was holding back the truth about himself. Plus, Serenity thought, *That's not what I am here for.* She laughed and thought, *This guy is trying to swallow me into his player's web, not in this lifetime, player. Serenity, get it over with. Stop stalling for time, yea, you are right.*

"Look, Shawn, I want to . . ." Rosetta came with their food. The aroma was breathtaking. Rosetta set their plates on the table, first Serenity then Shawn. Shawn looked at her get caught up in the wonderful smell of the special which consisted of a nice, medium side bowl of chicken noodle soup with real chicken, none of that can stuff. This was fresh, not just the broth.

Rosetta, after putting their plates down, stood straight up with a smile, looked at both Shawn and Serenity, and said, "You guys really are a nice-looking couple."

Serenity at the time was drinking her soup when she practically spit it out on hearing the comment. Rosetta quickly rubbed her back and said, "Are you all right, honey?" Serenity gave a nod, while she was calming down her cough and regaining her composure. Rosetta said, "The soup is hot. You have to blow it. Why don't you have this last?" Rosetta moved her soup to the side, and put the special entrée in front of her. "Here, enjoy your main meal."

Serenity could not argue with someone like Rosetta. She had that old southern care; she could only thank Rosetta for her concern and her on point service. Rosetta smiled and walked away.

She felt a little embarrassed as she looked down at her meal. Shawn knew she felt somewhat in the spotlight. He wanted to take some of that feeling of embarrassment away and asked, "Are you all right?"

Serenity, still clearing her throat so that she could speak without sounding hoarse, nodded and said, "That Rosetta," More throat clearing sounds as she continued, "is wonderful. She really sparks up the place. You can't find service like that anymore. No wonder this place is always packed, if not for the food, then for the home hospitality, and even with that, some of these people probably aren't treated this way at home. What a place to escape!" Serenity stopped talking, realizing she sounded like a chatterbox and said, "I'm sorry. Sometimes I go on and on. My best friend, Sandra, when I go on like this, says, 'Now where is that turnoff button.'"

Shawn laughed a nice hearty laugh with no restrictions or boundaries on it. Serenity looked around to see if his laugher disturbed anyone. For some reason, which she could not put her finger on, she loved to hear it as well, no restrictions. Shawn looked at her and said, "I don't ever want to find that turnoff button. Personally, I think, it's soothing." There was that awkward moment again. Shawn, once again, broke the ice. "Do you mind if we say grace before we eat?"

Serenity was sitting there, wondering how she was going to squeeze giving thanks for her food, and Shawn, without an ounce of hesitation, asked if that was OK. Serenity looked more than pleased and told that she would not mind. Shawn smiled and gently held her hand. The touch made her heart skip a beat or two. *There go those goose bumps going over time.*

Shawn prayed, "Dear Lord, thank you for this meal and this wonderful person you have placed in my path. May our paths cross again soon! Amen."

Serenity still had her head down as if she was praying, instead she was thinking, *What the heck is going on here?* She raised her head slowly and caught Shawn looking at her. His eyes penetrated right through her, making her feel as if he could read her thoughts. Serenity cleared her throat and looked down at her lunch. "So much food, and it all looks so delicious." She cleared her throat again. She looked at Shawn, who was looking so cool, not even a sign of being nervous, while she was a nervous wreck, and this wasn't even a date. She thought, *He's calm because of his sluttish lifestyle. He's been there, done that and thinks I'm going to be one of his conquest. I don' think so.* And she chuckled a little too loud to herself.

Shawn smiled and said, "Is this a private moment?"

She looked at Shawn and crinkled her nose as if to say "excuse me, can you repeat yourself," but then she caught on to what Shawn meant and fumbled to explain her overt blunder, "Oh no, I was just thinking about something my girlfriend said earlier."

Shawn looked at her, and Serenity looked at Shawn. He said, "Would you like to share it?"

Serenity said a little too quickly, "No, no, uh, girl talk!"

Shawn smiled and said, "I see."

They both ate without saying anything else to each other. Serenity looked at her watch and took out her cell phone. She asked Shawn to excuse her for a moment. Shawn nodded. Serenity at first covered her cell phone with the other hand as if she was telling her cell phone a big secret. Then she sort of turned her body in the profile position and bent her shoulders slightly.

Chapter 30

Shawn watched and saw how cute and animated she looked and how she blushed with whoever she was talking to. He just heard mumbling going back and forth. Apparently, the person wanted to know something, and she kept on saying I'll tell you later, no later. Then she closed the phone on the person who was playfully yelling. He could tell it was a female voice, and he felt good about that. He wondered if she was seeing someone, which he doubted. He just had that feeling that no one was in her life right then.

Serenity turned back toward Shawn and smiled. Shawn smiled back, and she said, "That was my office clerk. I was telling her I would be a little late." Shawn's eyebrow shot up like the Rocks again, as if to say what was all that about.

Shawn said, "Do you always go back and forth with your employees?"

Serenity smiled and said, "No, but she is also my best friend."

Shawn looked at her, and Serenity looked at Shawn, and they both said together, "Girl talk!"

They both chuckled and went back to eating. Shawn looked at Serenity while swallowing his food and asked, "So how long have you been working in the Federal building, and what is your position?"

Serenity was drinking some of her water. She put down her glass. "Whoa, is this an inquisition?"

Shawn laughed and said, "No, I'm sorry. I was just curious, just making conversation. I didn't mean to offend you."

Serenity said, "I know you didn't. I'm only playing." Both Shawn and Serenity laughed lightly about that as Serenity continued, "Uh, I've been there a while, and I'm the executive secretary."

Shawn's eyes opened wide, and he made an impressive sound.

Serenity put down her fork, looked at Shawn, and said, "What's up with the sound effects? What was that for? You know, that can be taken as a sexist remark."

Shawn almost became unglued from the smooth persona he exhibited and said, "Hey, slow down, baby. That so-called sexist remark, as you call it, is my way to say I am impressed."

Serenity was locking and loading another round of verbal assault before she realized what Shawn said, and she could only say, "Oh, sorry." Shawn and Serenity were about finished with their meal when Rosetta came back with coffee and cake. "This is on the house. I hope you drink coffee, and this is our homemade French pound cake, compliments of the owner."

Serenity smiled, thanked Rosetta, and said, "I would like to thank the owner personally. Is he still here?"

Rosetta said, "Yes, ma'am, but he is very busy right now, trying to seal a deal."

Serenity smiled at Rosetta and said, "Well, please tell him thank you."

Rosetta told Serenity that she would make sure the owner got the message and wished her and Shawn the best. Serenity looked at Shawn and said, "Wasn't that sweet of him?" She tasted the French pound cake and made a sound that hit Shawn in his groin, and he squirmed a little in the booth. He had to get his mind off Serenity's sounds and the way she put that cake in her mouth. Right about then was not the time to stand up, one thing was no doubt at attention.

Serenity looked at Shawn, who was not eating his cake, and said, "You don't know what you are missing." She made that sound again, took out her tongue, and slowly licked the cream off her lips.

Shawn had regained his composure; he had to use everything he knew about meditation from his self-defense training in order to overcome that sensation. He asked Serenity, "Republican Senator Thomas runs his office out of the State building, right?"

The question sounded more rhetorical. Serenity said, "Yes, he does, why?"

Shawn just shook his head and made a sound. Serenity thought, *Here we go with the sounds again.* She looked at Shawn and asked why.

Shawn, in short, told Serenity that Senator Thomas was for the rich. He said, "If our senator had his way, he would try to get rid of programs that help the poor, head start, student grants, you name it. The man is the antichrist for people of color."

Serenity just listened and was impressed about how much this guy who worked in the mail room or as a messenger knew.

Shawn continued, "Senator Thomas wanted to cut funding on after school programs. Do you know what problems that would have caused for our young soldiers, excuse me, young men?" Shawn did not give Serenity time to respond. "I tell you what. It's a conspiracy against our boys. Take away the afterschool programs, sport programs, and government-funded jobs, and you have our kids on the street with nothing to do. The next phase is, build more jails for the next generation. This is what our senator, if he had his way, would do."

Shawn had such fire and intensity in his eyes. His fist was clenched. Serenity looked at Shawn and said, "You know it's funny. How is it that you know more about me, and I know nothing about you?"

Shawn smiled and said, "There is not much to tell."

Serenity said to Shawn, "Aren't you going to call your job and let them know you are running late?"

Shawn gave Serenity that smile with all the trimmings, dimples and all, and said, "I have the day off."

She looked at Shawn with suspicion and said, "But you were off yesterday as well."

Shawn just looked at her. He had nothing to say. Shawn's cell phone went off, and he asked Serenity to excuse him. He answered it, said a few brief words, and hung up.

Serenity thought, *That the call was quick. I guess he has to preserve some of those day minutes, probably some baby mama drama. Homegirl said what she had to say and hung up. My kind of girl!*

Shawn looked at her and said, "I'm sorry, I have to cut this short. Something has come up that needs my attention."

Serenity thought, *For sure, right there, that is the code for baby mama drama.*

Shawn stood up and said to her, "I hope we can do this again soon."

She said to Shawn, "Well, at least, let me take care of the bill."

Rosetta came by to thank Shawn and Serenity for coming. It so happened that she overheard Serenity talk about the bill and said to her and Shawn, "Don't worry about the bill. It is on the house, courtesy of the owner."

Serenity was about to fall out, and she had to meet the owner. She was overwhelmed by the generosity of this place. She said, "No, I can't do that. This meal between us both was expensive. I want to give something."

Rosetta looked at Serenity and said, "Please accept this as a gift to both of you. To refuse would be an insult to the owner, so please accept his generosity."

Serenity looked at Shawn in a way that said say something. Shawn shrugged his shoulders and said to her, "You heard Rosetta. There is nothing that can be done."

Serenity looked at Shawn and back at Rosetta and pouted her lips like a spoiled child. Shawn regarded the expression and thought it was cute; it made his heart do a backflip. He didn't want Rosetta to get in trouble by trying to persuade her to disobey the rules, so he just looked down at his sneakers as if something was on them. Serenity thought, *He's no help.*

She looked at Rosetta again in a pleading fashion. Rosetta shrugged her shoulders and said, "I will get in big trouble if I intentionally disobey a direct order."

Shawn looked at his watch again and said, "Sorry, I wish I could stick around and see the outcome, but I can't. Ladies, have a good day, and I hope things work out."

Shawn looked at Rosetta and said, "Rosetta, I don't know what you are doing to keep looking good, but keep it up, baby." He laughed while Rosetta blushed, and Serenity, with a slight turnaway from Shawn and Rosetta, mimicked Shawn's robust laughter and thought to herself, *What a charmer! Just when I thought I was wrong.* She turned back toward Shawn and Rosetta with a smile.

Serenity watched Shawn walk toward the exit. She had to admit that Mr. Shawn had all the right stuff to be somebody—too bad he used his so-called stuff to his advantage over women. She had to admit that he had a walk that got everyone's attention in the place. His six feet three inch stride was so fluid and easy as if he was a king. The walk seemed to tell a story—a story of the seeds of pride and dignity planted a long time ago and now it was bearing fruit. It was a walk that there was no way you could miss. Serenity smiled to herself. She had come there for a purpose, but even she had to admit she had enjoyed his company. She had a wonderful time. She still was reminiscing about the luncheon, and she had a more interesting thought invade her first thought. Perhaps this was the thing that had been nagging her all afternoon, but she pushed it aside, and that was the idea she got pulled in and caught up in his charm just like the rest of them.

She had to admit that his conversation was different and fresh; it was revitalizing to see a man with such passion and conviction. He was stimulating in more ways than one. How he felt, touched her heart, yet again she had to remind herself that he knew how to play the game. Serenity sat there for a few minutes, when Rosetta stood next to her and said, "There goes one busy, fine man." The words pulled Serenity out of her reverie as she responded to Rosetta's comment, "Yep, when a man rushes out like a bat out of hell, there must be some drama in his life."

Rosetta looked at Serenity and said, "Are you kidding? The man has all kinds of drama up the kazoo."

Serenity said to herself, "I knew it. I knew this man had drama."

Rosetta said, "I think he's got too much on his plate."

Serenity made a sarcastic huff sound and said, "No, really."

Rosetta continued, "But I think he's fine. I don't mind being added to that drama, if you know what I mean."

Serenity looked at Rosetta as if she had lost her mind, and she said, "No, I don't know what you mean. Let me get this straight. You want to be a part of that drama—that headache?"

Rosetta had a dreamy look on her face as if she had been seduced.

Serenity said, "What is wrong with you women around here? Here is a man that clearly has a sign on him in neon flashing freaking lights that reads: *Danger* and no one sees it?" She paused and looked at Rosetta as if a light bulb went on in her head and said, "Or do you?"

Rosetta still had that dreamy look on her face as if what Serenity had said did not even penetrate to the slightest degree. Rosetta looked at her and said, "Did you notice that the man is—"

Serenity cut her off and began counting on her fingers. "He's a charmer, a smooth talker, a smooth operator . . ." She was still looking at her fingers, counting, and she continued, "A player, and a . . ." Serenity stopped counting, looked up at Rosetta, and saw that the woman was spellbound by all those descriptions and shook her head and said, "Girl, he may be all of that, but is it worth the drama?"

Rosetta looked at Serenity and said "yes, yes, yes" as if she was about to climax.

Serenity looked around nervously at the other patrons with a smile, hoping that Rosetta did not draw the attention from her expressive moment. Rosetta laughed and said, "Remember that scene in *When Harry Met Sally*?" Rosetta laughed again. Serenity had a look of relief on her face to know that Rosetta's climax was only a reenactment from a movie.

Rosetta looked at Serenity and said, "Girl, in all seriousness, the man is fine, and he handles his business well. You just don't understand, but you will. You're on the list."

Serenity shot Rosetta a look of panic and said, "What list?"

Rosetta laughed at Serenity's expression and said, "Girl, you are so fortunate, you know. Many make the list, but not too many stay on . . ." Rosetta paused and made a gesture that conveyed she talked too much; after that, she smiled at Serenity.

Serenity said, "Rosetta, what list?" Rosetta just shook her head. Serenity continued, "What list . . . Oh, his harem list. I don't think so, girl. He may have some of you girls charmed and seduced, but Shawn's magic will not charm me or seduce me. I don't have time for drama."

Rosetta dismissed Serenity with a polite wave of her hand and gave her a few more mints, complimentary items, and said, "Come back soon, and here is our card. We also do catering parties." Rosetta gave Serenity the card, which she didn't even bother to look at. She was in a rush to get back at the office.

Serenity said, "Oh great! You guys are great. I will be calling on your team." She looked at Rosetta, and for some reason, she gave her a sisterly hug and said, "Thank you, Rosetta, you made me feel at home."

Rosetta, releasing the embrace with a smile, said, "You are welcome, uh . . ." The inflection in Rosetta's voice indicated for Serenity to let Rosetta know her name as well.

Serenity said, "Oh, I'm sorry. It's Serenity, Serenity Powers. My friends call me Sen . . . I want you to do the same." She pointed over in the direction of the Federal building and said, "I work right over at the Federal building."

Rosetta chuckled, and Serenity asked her what was wrong.

Rosetta looked at Serenity and said, "That's pretty close to where Shawn works."

Serenity said, "So I heard . . ." She stopped, looked at Rosetta, smiled, and said, "Don't even go there. This is not a sign or anything . . ." She paused and looked at Rosetta with a look of playful uncertainty and said, "Is it?"

Serenity and Rosetta laughed like old friends and Rosetta said, "Well, if the truth be told, would you admit that the man is fine, handsome, smooth, and has sex appeal?"

Now it was time for Serenity to playfully do the *When Harry Met Sally* scene. Serenity turned off the reenactment like turning off a faucet and said,

"But keep the drama with the mama." She laughed along with Rosetta, gave her a friendly hug, told her bye, and wished her to have a nice day. Rosetta smiled back and wished the same toward Serenity. Rosetta watched Serenity go toward the exit and said under her breath, "Add another one to the list. I just hope this one doesn't get away."

Rosetta smiled as she went to serve a couple at another table with that charm. Serenity could faintly hear that charm of hers, "Welcome to . . ."

Chapter 31

When Serenity got outside from the 'Just as you like' restaurant, she had some mixed feelings about the last two meetings with Mr. Shawn Cook. A part of her was giddy; however, the other part of her was bewildered. She had this strange urge to laugh. Why? She did not know. She just wanted to laugh. She wanted to do something that teenagers in high school would do after their first kiss or their first flirt with the opposite sex. She just wanted to laugh. Serenity was walking toward the building where she worked, and she was getting these moments of giddiness. They would hit her out of the clear blue, and she would smile as if she had no control over her facial muscles. Every now and then, she would put her hand to her mouth to stifle a laugh or a widemouthed smile as she passed people she saw every day. She prayed, even in her giddiness, that no one she knew or worked with would stop her. She knew she would not be able to carry on a conversation without going through a tic of giddiness.

When she finally felt she had some control over the emotional attack, she began to get serious. A thinker by nature and very analytical was her makeup, and she thought, *What had just happened back there?* As she thought about the giddiness she had no control over, she walked, feeling a sense of control when she felt the rumbling start. She didn't know what to make of it at first, then it became stronger and stronger, and the next thing, the giddiness was back. Serenity held her hand to her mouth as people would walk past her, not without cutting an observant eye, which they tried to keep as obtrusive as possible. She cleared her throat and acted as if she was using her earpiece to her walkman, but somehow Serenity thought people knew better, so now she said to herself that she was acting paranoid. She said to herself, "Come on, girl. Pull yourself together. Snap out of it." She thought the pep talk had worked, then out of nowhere, *bam!* She was hit with the giddiness as she covered her mouth trying to get to her building as fast as she could, without drawing attention to herself.

Before going up to her office, she sat on the bench as many of the workers were out, either getting fresh air or taking a smoke break, polluting the air. Some were handling the nice September breeze. The birds were begging for bread, and the squirrels were being fed shell peanuts. It was such a beautiful day! Serenity thought about the dinner and sat there, thinking and going over it in her mind as she said to herself, "This guy, Shawn, is very nice looking and charming. He's smooth, but, he's also a con man, and a player. He may have those other women fooled, but Mr. Player . . ." Serenity did a mock laugh. "He can't play me."

However, the mind strategy Serenity was employing was not working. She knew that Shawn had proven himself to be a gentleman—very kind and intelligent. Serenity thought that Shawn was very friendly as well. Her expression changed as she had a different look in her eyes that went from hot to cold, and she thought, *Yeah, pimps are like that too, until they get their sharp hooks in you, and try to control you and change your name, and now you go from an African name to a slave name, and now the final stage is that you are walking around with a slut's name.* She further thought, *Homeboy is smooth, trying to recruit me.*

Now Serenity was feeling a little more in control as well as justified in her thinking. And what's the deal with all of those calls on his cell phone? He always has to hold the phone away or turn away from whoever is there with him in order to handle his secretive business. Now that is suspicious Serenity said. She jumped when her cell phone went off. She checked the caller ID. It was her office clerk Sandra.

Serenity answered to hear Sandra, "You are so rude. Why did you hang up on me? Homeboy got your head spinning like that and your panties tight?" Serenity put Sandra on speaker phone and turned the volume low enough so that Sandra's loud ghetto voice could not be heard by anyone in a certain radius. Serenity moved the phone further away from her ear as Sandra went on with her babbling. When she was through, Serenity asked her if she was finished, and Sandra in a much more calm and relaxed tone and volume cleared her throat and said that she was finished.

There was a moment of brief silence before Sandra continued, "Well, Serenity, I can't help it. This was a chance for you to meet someone, and Lord knows how long it has been since you had a date. Well, how did it go? And honey, don't be bashful, and don't hold back the details."

Serenity sucked her teeth and let out her breath as if to say "give me a break, girl," and then she began to tell of her experience, "First of all, why are you being so beastly, and why are you sweating me so hard, girl?"

Sandra, feeling a little attitude coming on, replied, "Come on, Serenity, don't go there. You know I am concerned and—"

Serenity laughed and said, "Come on, girl, I am only playing. Chill out now. Second of all, let's call it like it is. This was not a date, never was never will be."

Sandra, becoming serious, said, "Serenity, what happened?"

Serenity explained to Sandra that she was cool and continued with her story, "Homeboy is packing some serious baggage, Sandra."

Sandra, smiling from ear to ear, responded, "Oh yeah! Wow! Oh sugar! Like busting lose. You go girl drop it like it's hot on that brother."

Serenity continued, "Girl, let me tell you . . ." She stopped mid-sentence and realized that she and Sandra were talking about two different things, which did not surprise Serenity one bit, because Sandra had a nasty mind, and she saw sex in everything. Somebody could say that they were going down to the meat market, and Sandra would see that as someone getting their groove on.

Serenity continued, "Not like the way you are thinking. You are so nasty, Sandra."

Sandra said laughing, "Well, what should I think? You meet a man and come back saying 'Oh, my homeboy is packing,' and then you made a slurping sound."

Serenity fired back with a smile in her tone, "That wasn't a slurping sound. That was me shivering out here, having this conversation with you when I could be upstairs having this same conversation."

Sandra quickly responded, "You might forget something from there to here. Now finish."

Serenity smiled to herself and made a "why do I put up with this type of abuse," and she continued, "You need to think outside of the circle, instead of in the hole."

"OK, what do you mean by packing?" Sandra asked.

"Sandra, the man has some serious issues. I'm talking about employment issues and baby mama issues. What else . . ." Serenity was thinking, "Oh yeah, I think . . ." Serenity's voice got low, "I think, this guy is a pimp . . ."

Sandra sucked in her breath and whispered, "What?"

Serenity continued, "You know small-time stuff, and he works in the mail room, pimping at night, mail boy during the day . . . He's pimp man."

Sandra cut her off, "Come on, Serenity, mail room?"

"That's right, Sandra. The way he was dressed, definitely mailroom attire, and get this, he may also be doing some dope dealing on the side."

Sandra had heard enough. "Serenity, come on, not liking the guy is one thing, setting off rumors . . . Serenity, that's not your MO."

"You're right, so why would I lie? This guy is always on his cell phone, whispering or speaking in codes or turning his back and then making excuses he has to make a run . . . definitely dope dealing."

Sandra repeated with a bit of unbelief, "Coded language, huh?"

"That's right, but one thing I will admit. The man is fine and is smooth, and he has game." Serenity proclaimed strongly.

Sandra said, "Wait, but how did it go?"

Serenity smiled. "Dag, Sandra, I'm on my way up now. Stop acting like a thirsty vampire."

Sandra dismissed the comment and made a squeal sound, "Well, get your butt up here, I can't wait. Come on. Give me a little more until you get to the elevator."

"Bye, Sandra, be there in a minute." Sandra tried to get another word in, but Serenity had hung up.

Chapter 32

Sandra warned Serenity about Mrs. Fry, the senior vice president of operations. She told Serenity that Mrs. Fry was on a rampage and that she'd been looking for Serenity, asking everyone questions, but Sandra assured Serenity that everyone covered her back. Serenity smiled to herself regarding the support she always received from her staff. She got off the elevator quickly, pressed redial, and Sandra picked up right away. "Come on, girl."

Serenity told Sandra that she had to wait, but Sandra, feeling the suspense, said, "What, what?"

Serenity wanted to laugh so badly, but she had a more urgent need beckoning her. "Sandra, I need to use the restroom."

She could hear Sandra make sounds of frustration. Serenity wanted to laugh so bad as she rushed down to the ladies' room. She could hear Sandra's voice raise in the background saying, "You hold that water, girl, you hear me. Oh, that's cold, Serenity, but it's all good. I hope you piss on yourself." Serenity heard that and made it just in time in stall to pull down her panties, laughing up a storm.

Serenity walked in the office, smiling at her staff. She knew that her extended lunch hour may have been a bit overkill, but she had been the type of supervisor that was fair and did not take advantage of situations. She had always maintained a decorum that brought out the professional in her, but she was down-to-earth, easy to get along with, yet there was a side you did not cross. She was the type that would stop and speak with her workers, making sure all was well with them. From the cat to the dog to the bird, she was a concerned soul; however, one thing she always maintained was the parameters of professionalism. There had been times on rare occasions when Serenity would even join the girls for a night out, mainly on Fridays after work, but never to the point of losing touch or respect with them.

Serenity realized that as much as she wanted to get out with her staff, more often it would do her good, because at this point, her social life was the pits and at the point of extinction. Sandra was the only "nut" she could be a nut with and someone with whom she could really let her hair down. To this day, she couldn't understand how Sandra and she had become as close as sisters.

Sandra's coworkers knew that Sandra and Serenity had more than a professional relationship. They had an idea that the two were tight, even as tight, according to the office gossip as lovers. Then that gossip was shut down and another rumor circulated, stating that they had grown up together, which was still the prevailing gossip. Serenity did not like either one, but she would choose the latter any day of the week. However, crazy Sandra, also known as the office clown, used to play the role of them being lovers for fun and to see Serenity freak out. Her antics would get her coworkers laughing, while Serenity, each time, would be at the point of embarrassment.

Sandra, for example, during some of their weekly meetings when things were going OK, would break the monotony by saying something or doing something that would have some rolling and others blushing. In one meeting, Sandra started making seductive and flirtatious expressions during Serenity's presentation. That wasn't so bad other than the fact that those expressions were aimed toward Serenity. Expressions such as winking at her, moving her tongue across her lips and teeth, all in fun, and this was the thing that crushed those gossip rumors, because no one would put themselves out there like that.

Most of the workers believed that Sandra and Serenity may be good friends, but they did not envy or complain about the friendship, because Serenity worked Sandra like a slave, and one would think that Serenity did not like Sandra, as hard as she worked her, so the others came to the conclusion if becoming a friend to Serenity meant becoming a slave. Most kept their distance, gave her the utmost respect, and did their work without drawing attention. To Serenity, that was just fine.

Chapter 33

As Serenity walked in the work zone, her staff was busy handling cases as she heard the chatter of workers on the phone and the clicking of the female workers' finger nails, moving at their computers, hitting the keys.

Serenity got their attention as soon as she walked in. Her staff silently pointed in the direction of Mrs. Fry's office, indicating that the soon-to-be-retired worker was back there. Serenity could think of a thousand things her superior was doing back there, and not one of them had anything to do with work. She walked toward her office as if she could care less about returning late from lunch. She looked at Sandra as she has done numerous times—a look that her staff interpreted as it was time to pick on Sandra. However, for Serenity and Sandra, it was their secret code as Serenity would look at her watch while walking to her office, which meant for Sandra to meet her in her office in ten minutes. Or Serenity would adjust her dress or skirt, which meant for Sandra to come in fifteen minutes. Or else, she would simply say to Sandra, "Now, Mrs. Beck, I need to dictate to you a letter." Now that meant, there was some serious gossip she had to tell her, and for Sandra that meant to drop whatever she was doing and get in the office ASAP.

Serenity and Sandra had it down to a science, and every so often they would change the codes so no one would be able to catch on and blow their cover. Serenity got to her door and before she went in, she turned and said to Sandra, "Has anyone contacted us from the mayor's office regarding that matter?"

Sandra, with every bit of professionalism she could muster, which was a good amount because Sandra was a good actor, responded, "No, Ms. Powers, not yet. Do you want me to call them?"

Serenity behaved as if she was upset. She ignored Sandra's question and said, "I need you in my office now." Sandra would say yes, ma'am, and

Serenity loved it. Sometimes Serenity would ask questions so she could hear Sandra say no, ma'am or yes, ma'am. Sandra wanted to barf. Serenity closed her office door, just to fall against it, holding her mouth and laughing up a storm. Sandra knocked and waited for Serenity to tell her to come in. Sometimes, Serenity kept Sandra out there knocking longer than expected. Sometimes Sandra would be right at the door like then, and she could hear Serenity laughing. Sandra said to herself that she was going to get that heifer.

Serenity finally asked Sandra to come into her office. Sandra went in with her pad and pen, looking every way professional, and said as soon as she closed the door, "That was cold Serenity. I heard you laughing." She tossed her pad to the side and said, "Come on with the 411."

Serenity looked at Sandra. "Dag, San, easy, you're like a—"

Sandra cut her off, "Yea, whatever, so I've been told." She sounded exasperated and desperate. "Come on, Serenity, stop playing games. Something had to have gone down. It took you more than an hour to put the man in his place and give him back his money that he spent on you the first time. When you walked out of here today, you had a plan to give him back every penny he spent on you." Sandra smiled at Serenity to rub in that information.

Serenity looked at Sandra, as if she had an attitude, saying, "You see, that's why I hate telling you stuff. You're so mean that you like to throw it right back when the opportunity knocks."

"Well," Sandra continued, "opportunity is not knocking. The baby is banging." Sandra noticed that Serenity wasn't laughing and so became more serious. "Come on, Serenity, I just wanted to know if you stuck to your plan and what was the mail boy's reaction." Sandra looked at Serenity as if to say, eat crow baby. Serenity looked at Sandra as if she could chew her and spit her out. Sandra then gave Serenity one of her overconfident smiles and said, "What's with the look? You know I'm telling the truth, so save the drama for the acting class now that we have cleared the air." She gave Serenity a big ear to ear smile. "Now what happened?"

Serenity said, "San, this restaurant is beyond description. I mean good food, good service, good . . ." Sandra cut in, "That's nice" she sarcastically added, "and I want to hear about your ten-point inspection." Sandra, back to herself, said, "But tell me about Mr. Tall, Dark, and Handsome, what happened?" Serenity, getting serious, walked over to her desk and sat down in her chair. "Well, Mr. Tall, Dark, and Handsome, yes, there is truth to that, but the jury is still deliberating about Mr. Shawn."

Sandra squealed and ran over to Serenity and then leaned on the corner of the desk in excitement. Serenity jumped when she heard Sandra squeal. She looked at Sandra as if she had lost her mind. "You would think I just told you I hit lotto, Sandra."

Sandra, still excited, waved off Serenity's comment. "What happened? What do you mean that the jury is still out?" Serenity got up, walked over, and opened her refrigerator to get a bottle of water, knowing full well that Sandra was about to burst waiting with anticipation for the news. Serenity continued, "Well," she twisted the top off, and Sandra looked like she had ADHD. "Well, what?" Serenity looked at Sandra with inquiring eyes. "I don't know." She took a nice gulp of the water, and Sandra couldn't take it. "You don't know what!" Serenity looked at Sandra, shrugged her shoulders, and lifted the bottle of water to her mouth. Sandra desperately grabbed Serenity's arm and stopped her from putting the bottle to her mouth. "What is it that you don't know?" Serenity looked at Sandra as if she had completely lost it. "OK, relax, take a deep breath." Serenity laughed. Sandra didn't think it was funny.

"OK, in all seriousness, lunch was good. Shawn was sweet, but—"

Sandra interrupted, holding her breath and waiting for Serenity to finish her sentence, "But what?"

Chapter 34

Serenity walked back to her desk and sat down as she took another sip from the bottle of water. Serenity was getting a little tired of this question-and-answer game between her and Sandra. She inhaled a deep breath and said, "But he's not my type . . ." Sandra, looking exasperated, took a deep breath and blew it out, and Serenity, sensing her frustration, said, "Look, Sandra, what. It's a simple matter which you are making complicated. What is there to understand? He's not my type, OK? The man has drama up and down, inside and out, plus he's too secretive, and he has a job that probably pays minimum wage at best. Not to say money is everything, but you better have some aspiration that says you want more than working in a mail room or a messenger boy." Serenity paused and continued, "Do you know what this is about, Sandra?" Sandra did not respond, and Serenity continued, "I didn't think so. Listen, I don't have time to nurse or take care of someone's drama. I have my own." Sandra, after being verbally avalanched upon, could only look at Serenity with a look of disappointment. Her only reaction was "wow." Serenity shook her head at Sandra, not grasping what she had just said and continued to defend herself. "Sandra, I don't need the drama. I enjoy being free, coming and going as I please, yea, it's simple, but it's as stress free as it's going to get. I'm telling you that man has some issues." Sandra softened her look and walked over to stand behind Serenity and massage her shoulders. "I'm sorry, Send. I just want you to be happy. You deserve it. I just thought—"

Serenity cut her off, "You just what? Wanted to make it work? Look, San, playing cupid is one thing, living with drama is another. Perhaps the arrow, which was aimed for the heart, struck me right up my ass."

Serenity was becoming agitated, because she hardly ever used language like that. She got up from her desk abruptly, knocking Sandra's hands off her shoulders. "I don't need that or want that. I don't need to settle for that, San. I asked him a very simple question which was what he did for a living."

Sandra asked, "And what did he say?"

Serenity looked at Sandra, right in her eyes, and said, "Nothing. He said nothing and then had the nerve to play on my intelligence by changing the subject as if I did not notice."

Sandra was speechless as she shrugged her shoulders. Her only reaction was a sincere apology for butting in her best friend's life. Serenity drew near to Sandra and put her arms around her shoulder. "San, you are my best friend, and I know you'll do anything for me." Sandra was nodding her head in agreement as Serenity continued, "And I would not hesitate to do the same for you, and you know that, girl."

Sandra pretended to cough, stifling a laugh, but became serious. "I know, I know."

Serenity looked at her watch and then looked at Sandra in shock. "San, do you know how long you've been in here?" Sandra had a whatever attitude as Serenity continued, "Too long, girl. You better get back out to your desk. We'll pick this one up later." Sandra loved to hang out with Serenity. She enjoyed her down-to-earth attitude, and besides that, she was her best friend whether at work or after working hours.

Sandra didn't want to leave, and it showed in her expression as she got up and half turned to the door when Serenity stopped her. "San, hold up. Give me ten more minutes." Sandra didn't have to be asked twice. She pushed past Serenity and ran to the chair she had just got up from with excitement. Serenity, almost falling from Sandra's craziness, just looked at Sandra as if she had lost her mind. "Relax, girl . . . anyway, this restaurant is incredible. The service is unbelievable and . . . I know I wasn't going to talk about it, but there is this worker there that has worked there for years."

Sandra, feeling the suspense, said, "To the point, Serenity."

Serenity hesitated before continuing, "Anyway, I was talking to her, and well, anyway, she said this guy Shawn always has some type of drama going on in his life."

Sandra gave Serenity a look of exhaustion. "Now this woman you said has been working there for years, correct?" Serenity nodded her head in agreement as Sandra continued, "And this guy Shawn according to this, this . . ." Sandra paused to find the right word that would describe this person and decided to be nice with a smile. "This woman has been going to this eatery, let's call it, for some time, correct?" Serenity smiled as well nodding in agreement. Sandra paused for a brief moment. "Serenity, don't be so gullible." Serenity looked at Sandra with an incredible look that was based on what she had just referred her as . . . gullible. Sandra continued, "Look, I don't mean to insult you." Serenity cut her eyes at Sandra as if to say, yeah right, you could have fooled me. "Think about it. Put the pieces together, girl. Homegirl is marking her territory. She's trying to say keep away from her man."

Serenity sat there trying to follow Sandra's street logic. Sandra continued, "Listen, I know what I am talking about. This is what is happening, trust me." Sandra smiled, "Girl, you better step up your game." Serenity waved in frustration at Sandra's comment. "I have no game. I mean I have game. I mean, I think, I have game. No, wait, I'm not—"

Sandra cut Serenity off, "Let me help you. What you said the first time is true. Does that help?" Sandra smiled.

Serenity gave Sandra a look and said, "Your subtle insult did not go unnoticed, girl. Anyway, how did you come to this conclusion?"

Sandra smiled. "Girl, us women, we are our own worst enemy. When it comes to men, we are vicious. It is like animal kingdom. There is no sisterhood, and it becomes a doggie dog world."

Serenity let out an exasperated breath of frustration. "I don't have time for this nonsense. You see, this is what I'm talking about, drama."

Sandra waved her hand at Serenity dismissively. "Whatever, girl, I bet that heifer wants you out of the picture so she could have him all for herself. You better wake up, girl. You are totally out of the loop. I see it all the time at the clubs and B parties, girl, even in church. Sister would snatch up your man while you are praising the Lord, even while you are in the bathroom, fixing your weave. Some sisters don't have any dignity or respect for themselves."

Serenity had a look of shock on her face. She was speechless, not about what her best friend said about stepping up her game. She had no interest in the man, and even more so now. Her main concern of disappointment was the way sisters treated each other over a man, which bothered her to no end. Serenity could not imagine such a world that Sandra described. Serenity came from a world of corporate business people ever since she was a child, watching her parents head off to the business world. It was in her blood. Things like loyalty and the highest of dignity was the world she had been brought in, but this description that Sandra painted was for people who thought very low of themselves.

Serenity had a look of protest on her face that came out of her mouth a little too overprotective. "San, I think . . . I think . . . you're wrong.

Well . . . I mean you are probably right about some women, but not all women. You can't clump all women in your narrow window of thinking." Serenity, looking confused, said, "I don't know. What do I know? I'm not a street girl, never have been. I am not a party girl, and I don't respond to catcalls or guys calling women like me out of their or my name 'Hey, Shorty.' What is that? Anyway, Rosetta was very sweet."

Sandra, with a look of astonishment on her face, asked, "Rosetta? You even know her name!" Sandra shook her head from side to side, making a sound with her tongue and teeth. Serenity looked at Sandra, fed up with this whole conversation. "What now." Sandra's facial expression changed from calm to battle mode. "Ah, homegirl is very clever." Sandra was thinking her eyes shooting from side to side. "She's probably been well trained in 'operation snatch away.'"

Serenity, at that point, didn't know whether to laugh or cry. She looked at Sandra with her big eyes. "But I don't think she is a fighter." Sandra, looking directly at her friend, made that noise with her tongue and teeth slowly, shaking her head from side to side and said, "Will you stop that? You sound like a broken clock."

Sandra countered, "Honey, I may sound like a broken clock, but you better wake up and see what time it is."

Serenity had reached that point where she was ready to kick her best friend out of her office. "Listen, I don't want to talk about this any longer. The bottom line is, and you can blame Rosetta or whoever, is that the man may be smart and intelligent. He may have the gift of gab. He maybe a player to the tee and now news flash," Serenity sounded like an anchorwoman as she continued, "and for the latest development, this is just in folks. Mr. Shawn, if that's his name, now has women acting like animals, marking their territory, according to field reporter Sandra Beck. We will have more on this developing and disturbing story at the eleven o'clock news. Now back to office gossip."

Sandra pretended to wave the white flag in surrender. "OK, OK, I wasn't there. You had a firsthand account, and so, I throw down my weapons of verbal accusations and judgment."

Chapter 35

Serenity smiled big and wide, but she wondered deep down whether she was more afraid of the drama Shawn has stirred, or was she afraid of the challenge of responding to that drama. She knew, without being told, that Shawn was more advanced in dealing with the opposite sex. She had witnessed firsthand that the man was fast when it came to the opposite sex, and this bothered her. The man had something going on. He had got those women flocking and falling all over him. This, to her was a paradox, because if one had an array of women to chose from, why choose the lonely wallflower?

Serenity considered herself attractively average. She was someone whom a guy wouldn't mind taking home for his mom to see. She was highly educated with a Master's in Business Administration. She was very intelligent, but even if she was interested in the likes of Shawn, she thought and concluded that she did not have those voluptuous bodies those other women had. Serenity had a nice shape; it wasn't like boom, bang, or bang boom, but she told herself that she wasn't interested in the man. Why even be concerned with all of this? Yet she was! But one thing she knew without a doubt. She knew she could run circles around him professionally, in every which way and in any direction, but was it enough.

Serenity, unlike most women, felt that you didn't have to get a man by wearing clothes that would be considered a whore's attire. Keep that for your bedroom fantasies, not for public display. She wasn't one who had flirt appeal. She had sex appeal, but flirting wasn't her thing. She knew she could flirt if she wanted to, but that's not how she had been raised by her parents. She and her brother Eric were raised differently. They both were expected to demonstrate manners, both in and especially out of the house. She remembered how her father used to require Eric to read the *Sunday Times* for that week and write or be prepared to discuss articles their father would bring up, and you better show you knew what you were talking about, and as for her, her mother would have her to read about fashion, and all types of black magazines from *Jet* to *Essence* and anything in between. Then she was required at least once a month to choose an educational field outing that just she and her mother would go to.

Both she and Eric were expected to take up music. For her it was the piano, and for Eric it was the trumpet. Both were still very good at it even till the present time. Serenity's parents pushed them, always drilling in their heads not only to keep up currently, but also to stay a step in front of the mainstream so that they could create their own waves; for example, both she and Eric received their junior driver's license, and both were accepted into colleges of their field when they turned seventeen. Both graduated before turning twenty and went to work on their master's. Serenity went to Harvard, and Eric went to MIT. They completed their studies on time and both had high-paying jobs.

Eric worked on Wall Street, where he was considered the up and coming of new minds of the age, according to the *Business Weekly* magazine. But Serenity, because of her upbringing, had never experienced the drama most girls growing up had experienced in regards to boys. She had been taught to present herself as a young lady at all times. She was taught to use her intelligence, independence, femininity, and polished conversation to weed out the knuckleheads, thugs, and all the other rejects. What was left were the true gentlemen that you could pick and choose from. She thought, *Well, that leaves Shawn out of the picture, because he fits somewhere between knucklehead and player.*

Her parents had always preached to her to set her standards high. By so doing, she wouldn't have to come down or lower her standards to a guy's level, but the guys would have to reach up high to her level. She remembered her mother telling her when she was an adolescent, "If you allow a guy to pull you down to his level because he has a good line or he is good looking, then you will end up with three or four babies before you turn thirty."

Sandra looked at Serenity, who was in a deep daydream. "Girl, you OK?"

Serenity shook off the daydream and smiled at her best friend. "Yea, I'm OK. I was just thinking of my parents. I have to see them this weekend." Serenity felt a shiver and shook it off, "Anyway, Sandra, before you go, listen, we need to go to this place as a group to eat. We've been in this area all this time, and we let these so-called brothers and sisters and our white coworkers take us to eat at places that sold tow food . . . and . . ." Sandra stepped in, which meant the girl was in stand-up comedian mode. The mood was back in full swing, in full affect, and in high definition. The dynamic fool was back in action, cutting up. "Yeah," said Sandra, "Tow food tastes like cardboard seasoned with sawdust. You can tow that crap out of here and bring me the colonel anytime, baby. I mean we went to some crazy places for lunch. Serenity, remember when Bobby and Sandy took us to that . . ." Sandra had a hard time pronouncing the name of the place, and both started laughing.

Serenity said, "Whatever it was, it was Buddha food. I needed some homemade Bubba food."

Sandra jumped in, "That's right. I mean dipped in that southern fried grease with some black-eyed peas and some dirty, no filthy rice."

Serenity jumped in, "Some vegetables mixed with some fat back."

Both started laughing, and Sandra said, "Now, Serenity, you know if we ate that here, these white folks would get a good look of what exactly is . . ." They both said it together, "Nergo-I-tis."

Both fell out laughing, falling against each other. Sandra said, "Tomorrow, I'm going there. Tell them to hook up a sister with some serious soul food smothered in fat back." Both women started laughing.

"You are so ignorant," Serenity said.

Sandra playfully dismissed Serenity and said, "Girl, let me get back to work." Sandra joked, "My supervisor gave me a ton of work to do."

Serenity smiled. "And you better have it ready today for the meeting." Sandra cut her eye at Serenity and started toward the door, but Serenity stopped her. "Oh, Sandra, here is the card to that eatery." Serenity handed Sandra the card. She took the card, glanced at it, and went to put it away but stopped and quickly read it carefully, "Just As You Like It" diner: Soul food/Caribbean cuisine, desserts, and catering available. Owner and founder: Shawn Cook' She stopped and stared at the card. Serenity went back to her desk and was pulling something up from the computer when she noticed that Sandra had stopped reading the business card, and she looked up at her. She noticed Sandra staring at the card as if she had come across a word she could not pronounce, but then she noticed some of the color in her face was gone. Serenity, very much concerned, quickly got up and worked her way around her desk toward Sandra. "Sandra, you OK? What's wrong?"

Sandra, a little startled, quickly shot her eyes up from the card toward Serenity, who was standing just a few feet away from her. She did not verbally respond but quickly nodded her head. Serenity looked at her strangely as if to say, "Are you sure?" Sandra nervously smiled and asked, "Ah, Serenity, what was the name of the guy you met up with yesterday?" Serenity, still concerned about the way Sandra looked, almost dismissed the question to attend to her friend, but Sandra insisted that she answered the question. Serenity thought and concluded if this would help her friend, and she said in all seriousness, "I don't know. He called himself Shawn."

Sandra asked, "That's it, just Shawn?"

Serenity nodded. "That's it. I know I should have gotten his full name, but he was . . . you know, anyway, are you OK?"

Sandra gave her friend the business card. "Here, I got to go to my desk . . ." Sandra nervously picked up a few items so she would walk out, at least give the impression that she and Serenity had been working. She continued, "I'll . . . I'll speak to you in a few minutes. Ah, later, check out the Web site." The next thing, Sandra had dashed out of Serenity's office. Some of the items she was carrying fell from her arms as she nervously picked them up and closed Serenity's door. Serenity looked at her friend's odd behavior as she went from night to day, thought about it, and shook her head, baffled over what had just come over her to make her act like that.

Serenity picked up the card and did a quick reading of it. She read the same thing her friend just read to her, but didn't see anything different so it wasn't the card that caused her friend to go weirdo on her. She looked at the card again and read the small bold print: "For more info, go to the Web site." It gave the Web site address. Serenity thought that she would take the time to find out a little more about this wonderful eatery. She logged on to the Web site and waited for the information. A nice, colorful screen slowly scrolled up with the name of the eatery and pictures of different customers enjoying the food and the soulful atmosphere. The Web site was moving like a snap shot of different parts of the eatery—the special days and jazz nights, weekend parties, and then it stopped, repeating the same thing all over again.

Serenity was impressed; she thought whoever created this Web site knew what they were doing. She looked at the options and read: Download pictures and testimonies; contributions of "Just As You Like It" to Third World countries; the story behind the eatery; how did it come about; and finally, the brains of the operation.

Serenity was really enjoying this. She wanted to first go to "the brains of the operation" to know who had the intelligence to start and run such an establishment, but she decided to first see what others thought. She clicked the mouse onto that option, and the screen rolled up, bright and colorful of pictures of employees mingling with customers, and customers enjoying their meals. The snapshots were in square, little and medium, boxes with testimonies all over the page: people just telling how much they loved the place, how excellent the food and service were, how professional the workers were, how they took time to talk to them, and how quick the service was, et cetera, et cetera. Serenity was more than impressed with this five-star eatery. She noticed that the place had won many awards since opening, and they were listed in the top five best eateries to dine at.

She then thought, *Let's see the brains behind this operation.* But before she did, she had to call Sandra and let her know of her investigation. Sandra picked up the intercom at her desk, and Serenity just went on and on about the place. She told Sandra that she was about to unmask the mastermind behind the operation, and she laughed about her cloak-and-dagger attitude. She hung up and proceeded. As she clicked onto the option to see who was behind this, the screen scrolled up as a little statement was given about Shawn—things like who he, and how he started the eatery and why, and the other accomplishments of the man, but no picture. Serenity was disappointed, but she noticed in fine print, "Click here to continue." She thought why not.

Serenity waited as the screen slowly came up, and as it was coming up, she just remembered not to forget to give Sandra the office supply order form so she could get those items she requested. She found the form and made a mental note to give it to her by the end of the day. Then she called up Sandra, all excited, on the intercom. "Sandra, I'm bringing up this guy's picture. I have to see who the brain behind the business is. Here it comes. It scrolls so slowly. Oh, remind me to give you the office supply form later . . . what! The screen went blank . . . wait, it says to click right here."

Sandra was at her desk, listening to Serenity ramble on while doing a silent countdown, "5, 4, 3, 2, 1." Sandra heard Serenity either dropping something very heavy or probably hitting the floor herself, but before that, she heard Serenity say, "Oh, here goes the . . ." Then she heard her scream, "Oh my god!"

Chapter 36

Serenity called Sandra to come to the office, but Sandra was standing in the office looking at Serenity desperately, trying to get her on the intercom. Sandra said, "What happened?" Serenity startled, yelped, and dropped the phone, pointed to the screen, "Did you see this . . ." Serenity, still pointing, said, "This man Shawn . . ." Sandra could not resist, "Who mister mailroom slash messenger boy, and oh, I forgot my bad, the player . . ." Serenity gave Sandra that look, which said "shut up." Still pointing at the screen, she said, "He's really Mr. Cook, oh, man . . ." Serenity put her face in her hands, then quickly took them off, looked at the screen, and said real shell-shocked slow, "Oh my god!"

Sandra walked over to the desk joking, "So which one, your man or . . ." She looked at the photo on the screen and looked back at Serenity and back at the photo on the screen with a look of seduction. "Wow, yummy, or your god." Sandra, still looking at the screen as if she was going to start salivating, cocked her head to the side. "Well, he sure could pass for . . ." Serenity cut her best friend off, "Don't be stupid."

Sandra dismissed Serenity's comment by waving her hand at her and concentrating on Shawn's photograph. "But damn, he's fine." Serenity rolled her eyes up at the ceiling as Sandra rambled on, "Whatever, girl, Serenity, please don't tell me this is the man you had two lunch meetings with." Serenity made an attempt to respond, but Sandra continued, "You were avoiding this. Ah, girl, put my behind on his waiting-for-drama-to-happen list, because I would give this man some action that he would get rid of his drama and deal with this mama. Serenity, homeboy got it going on. What happened?"

Serenity nervously paced her office, holding her head with both hands, trying to get her thoughts together. "Sandra, you are not helping. I heard you the first five times. Right now my main concern is how I treated the most influential man in the city."

Sandra just shook her head and said, "Girl, the only thing I can say . . ." Sandra paused for affect and then continued, "You blew it. You . . ." Serenity had about enough of her friend. "Sandra, shut up. I mean it." Sandra raised her arms as if to surrender. Both women drew their attention to the knock at the door. Sandra yelled, "Come in." Serenity looked at Sandra as if she had lost her mind. She looked at Sandra and said in a low, firm tone, "Remember, this is my office. If you don't believe me, look at the name on the door. Come in please."

Serenity's community affairs advisor, Marisa, shyly came into the office. "Ms. Powers, this just came in for you—these flowers and this note." Marisa handed the note to Serenity, who thanked Marisa for bringing the flowers and note. Marisa looked at both women shyly, smiled, and left the office.

Sandra ran over to Serenity. "Who is it from?" Serenity ignored Sandra and read the note, "Have dinner with me. I'll pick you up at 5:00 p.m. in front of the Federal Plaza building."

Sandra jumped up and down as if the flowers and note was for her. "Girl, oh my goodness, Shawn Cook, the number one sought-after eligible bachelor has asked you out . . . again." Serenity, didn't know what to say. Sandra's, eyes opened up wide. "That's like being asked out by Denzel! Go ahead and be wined and dined, good food, good music, good sex . . ." Sandra barely got the word sex out before she noticed how quiet Serenity had become. Sandra looked at her with concern. "Serenity, what's wrong? You just got an invitation from the hottest man in the city, even the nation, and you act as if nothing has happened."

Serenity looked at Sandra. "Nothing has happened yet, and I don't know. Why me? Of all the single women in this city, why me? What's going on? Is this take-out-a-plain-Jane date to boost his fan base?" Sandra gently grabbed Serenity by the shoulders. "Why not you? You deserve it. You are more than a good woman, and you are far from being a plain Jane. Look at you. You are beautiful, and you always carry yourself as a lady, and no doubt Shawn saw the same thing. The essence of beauty is all over you."

Serenity was totally speechless. As long as she had known Sandra, this was the first time Sandra had come out like that. Serenity said, "Wow, thank you, Sandra. That was deep, girl."

Sandra smiled. "Girl, you know I love you, plus, you better milk that cow for what it's worth." Serenity, annoyed, rolled her eyes at her friend. "You know that's not me. Now either help me or don't say anything at all."

Sandra nodded her head in all seriousness. "OK, my bad. Listen, I know, let's double date. That way, you won't feel or do anything crazy. I'll be right there to keep you in check."

Serenity looked at her friend, astonished. "A double date? I don't even want to single date. I have to find a way to get around the way I treated this man, plus . . ." Serenity came to an abrupt stop. "A double date? If that was to happen, but don't get too excited, but let's just say, if that should occur, who would you bring?" Serenity could tell just by the endless hours and months and even years she had spent with Sandra, when her mind was in warp drive and clicking and clacking in that thinking mode. Serenity couldn't tell for some time whether Sandra's mind was in warp mold or just plain warped. She could tell just by the way Sandra's eyes shifted from side to side as if she had no control over them. She took the bait and asked Sandra what the problem was. Sandra put her pointer finger to her own mouth to tell Sandra to hush. Then she held her finger up, which she did often when she had to either think or scheme. In this case, Serenity knew it was thinking of a scheme, and if Sandra's past record was correct, she didn't want anything to do with it.

She was getting ready to let Sandra know she didn't want to hear it, but Sandra held up her hands, "Wait, hear me out before you kick me out." Serenity reluctantly agreed and said a slow doubtful OK. Sandra continued, "Now, this guy Shawn whom you have already been to lunch with twice, right?" Serenity blew out a harsh breath and was going to speak, but Sandra cut her off, "Wait, please let me finish." Serenity defended her actions, "Well, you asked me a question, and I was going to respond and speaking of responding, I am about fed up with you bringing up how many times I went out to lunch."

Sandra, absently nodding, dismissed Serenity's statement and continued, "Now, as I was saying, Shawn is a high-profile guy, right. Don't answer, just work with me." Serenity shrugged her shoulders, and Sandra continued, "So, as I was saying, he's a high-profile guy, and we know that high-profile guys hang out with high-profile people, right."

Serenity was nodding, but her eyes narrowed at Sandra, wondering where she was going with this. And she continued, with her pointer finger in the air, telling Serenity to let her finish. "If you could hook up with Shawn, I know without a shadow of a doubt, hear me now . . . the brother could hook up a sister. I mean I'm not picky or anything. I was thinking about someone as fine as Denzel or LL with those thick lips, you know." Serenity was smiling and excited, which made Sandra get excited and happy that her friend agreed with her, and Serenity added on, "Yeah, cool, or maybe we can either hook you up with Bozo, the clown, or Bellevue psychiatric ward to get you admitted. Girl, what is wrong with you? The elevator is not going to the top. You are not wrapped too tight at all. I am trying to do damage control, and you are creating collateral damage."

Sandra looked at Serenity, like a person sinking in quicksand with desperation, and said, "Serenity, don't blow this. Say no to drugs by all means, but say yes to this, because if you don't, then I'll think you are on drugs."

Serenity paced her office with a look of concern. With her back from Sandra, she said, "Listen, this is the second time you were in here for a good amount of time. Do me a favor. Take that stack of files on my desk and bring them to your desk as if you are going to work on them." Sandra looked at the huge pile of folders and files, laughed and turned back at Serenity, and noticed that she wasn't laughing. Sandra stopped in mid-laughter. "Come on, Serenity, you got to be kidding. All those files . . . you are going to make me look like the office slave."

Serenity, placed her hands on her hips, looked Sandra in the eyes, and said, "San, how can I justify you being in here twice already for such long periods of time? And you walk out of here with just a piece of paper, or nothing. So what if they would think I am your slave master. What's the big deal?"

Sandra didn't like the image, but knew that Serenity was right as she further conceded. She pouted like a child. "Well, I guess you're right, but you better not refer to me as Toby's sister." Both women laughed at that, and Serenity helped Sandra pile the files up as Sandra was holding them, watching her best friend hold back her laughter. By the time they were finished, the files went all the way up and were being held in place by Sandra's chin. Sandra looked at her best friend and was barely able to speak due to her holding up the files with the support of her chin, "The things I do for you."

Serenity smiled and ushered Sandra to the door, and before opening the door, she said to Sandra, "Listen, make it look good, and do me one more favor." Sandra was now the impatient one and said, "Now what, Master Powers." Serenity waved her hand at Sandra and told her to stop that. She went to her desk and picked up the business card that was sent with the flowers. She seriously doubted if Shawn had picked out the flowers himself. He probably had sent one of his gofers to get them, and she picked them for him. It had a womanly touch. She shook off the thought, picked up the card, and walked back toward Sandra. Sandra, like a little girl, started to complain about how heavy the files were becoming, and on top of that, she had to go to the bathroom. Serenity admonished Sandra and told her to stop behaving like a baby, and Sandra began to pout. Serenity just shook her head and continued, "OK, look, I want you to call up Mr. Cook."

Sandra then began to smile as she totally forgot how heavy the files she was carrying were becoming. She knew that Serenity would come around and do the logical thing. She had anticipated Serenity's acceptance speech of going out with Mr. Rich and handsome, and she echoed Serenity's instructions with a big smile on her face, "Yes, you want me to take this card. Oo-kay, I got that part. Go ahead and make me proud, girl." Sandra's arms were starting to shake from the constant weight of the files, but Sandra thought the pain was worth it.

Serenity looked at Sandra as if she was stuck on cupid, cocked her head to the side, and asked her, "Are you finished?" Sandra let out a deep breath, smiled widely, and said, "Yes, I am, sorry. My lips are sealed."

Serenity rolled her eyes and continued, but to make sure Sandra did not make any more comments and with her hands already full, Serenity put the card in Sandra's mouth. Sandra had a look of total surprise as her lips clamped down on the card, preventing it from falling out of her mouth. Serenity looking satisfied. She smiled and continued, "Take this card and call Shawn and tell him thanks for inviting me to dinner."

Sandra tried to smile with the card in her mouth as Serenity opened her office door while talking gently. She led Sandra out of her office. Sandra was still facing Serenity, waiting for her to finish, now standing within the doorway of the office and just outside of it as she continued, "Yes, don't forget to call and tell Mr. Cook that I said thank you, but no thank you."

Sandra tried to speak, but the card was in her mouth, and to add fuel to the fire, Serenity said out loud, "Oh, Sandra, please have those items for me by the end of the week. And the ones I gave to you this morning, I need as soon as possible."

Serenity winked at Sandra and did the thumbs-up like a nerd as she closed her office door, leaving Sandra in shock, still facing the door with her arms full of files that went all the way up to her chin that was balancing them and holding Shawn's business card in her mouth. As she turned toward the other workers, they stared at the sight. Some were snickering, and some were whispering. Sandra, as fast as she could, which wasn't very fast, went to her desk with all eyes on her, dropped the files, and took off for the ladies' room, saying a few choice words under her breath as she went.

Chapter 37

Serenity felt bad about what just went down with her best friend. She did not want to put her in a position where she had to act that way in front of the other workers. She could tell that Sandra was caught off guard. Her eyes practically came out of her head when Serenity placed the card in her mouth. If the card wasn't in Sandra's mouth, she could only imagine the new words of profanity Sandra would have invented. Serenity would not be surprised at the verbal eruption that would take place when she and Sandra hooked up later, but she did what she felt was best in regards to Sandra getting that unknown preferential treatment that her other staff workers did not know about. Serenity weighed the cost and did what she had to do. But now Serenity faced a much bigger problem and that was dealing with Shawn Cook. She knew that Shawn Cook was a hunter in every sense of the word. Someone of his caliber did not become who he was or accomplish the things he'd accomplished just by sitting around, watching and waiting for the game to come to him. No, she could tell just by the two times they'd met that Shawn Cook knew what he wanted and how he was going to get it. He went after the game; he went after what he wanted, and did not stop until he got it, but, she smiled and thought, *Mr. Cook will be in for a surprise, and he will find out very quickly. He may put me into his little game, but he'll play by my rules.* Serenity was still pacing her office with a look of anxiety and concern on her face. She bit her bottom lip as she wondered how she was going to deal with him. She was going to need Sandra's ghetto-street support. She knew pound for pound that she was no match for the fine looking, smooth talking, Shawn Cook.

Chapter 38

Shawn received a call from Serenity's office assistant, Sandra Beck, who was behaving very flirtatious. At first Shawn was caught off guard, but then he realized it was probably a test since many women had this stereotyped notion that all men were dogs. Perhaps Ms. Powers was using her assistant to see whether or not Shawn would bite; however, Shawn was not impressed with the little game at all. As a matter of fact, he was delighted that Serenity had struck first; at least he knew that the hunt was on. Shawn spoke to Sandra firmly with an intensity that made her shudder, "Tell your boss, I'm not into playing little schoolhouse games and using you as a distraction to distract me from her won't work. I'm totally focused on what I want, need, and what I will get, and I'll sidestep, crawl, step over, and even run through anyone or anything that gets in my way. She's all the woman I need . . . tell her that, and you have a nice day, Ms. Beck." Shawn added the frosting on the cake by saying in his low and slow baritone voice, "Chow baby." Shawn hung up the phone without giving Sandra a chance to respond, and even if she had a chance to respond, Sandra was totally incapacitated by Shawn. She sat there at her desk frozen. She thought that her idea could bring out the dog in Shawn; instead, it gave him more reason to pursue the hunted. Sandra should have realized that her old street tricks may work on her trifling hood boys because some of them were so desperate that if you put a hole in the wall with a weave around it that was enough for them. However, to pull that mess on someone who had no problem getting women was foolish as he could probably pull them while he was sleeping. Sandra wanted to smack herself. She had not only underestimated the man, but had also totally put him in a category with losers, while Shawn was in a category all by himself. Sandra was trying to do Serenity a favor, but she probably gave Shawn another weapon for his arsenal. She sat there, biting her lower lip, thinking about damage control before things got out of control.

Chapter 39

Shawn sat in his spacious office, thinking about Serenity and the low-cut trick her office assistant had tried to pull on him. He just shook his head thinking. Some women can be so manipulative, but he thought about his ability to attract women. For him, it was very natural. He found talking with women easy, not because he was rich and wealthy—that was another power card that he could play—yet never had it come to that point that he had to use it. Neither was it now, because he knew, according to what essence magazines said about him, that he was voted one of the most attractive men in the city. This vote cut across racial and ethnicity lines, and so forth and so on. In other words, Shawn's looks had practically many women wanting a piece of him, which was mind boggling, yet Shawn took it in stride, never allowing it to control him, nor did he allow himself to use it to control others. He was impressed, but the woman he wanted seemed unaffected by how the majority felt. However, in reality, regarding the surveys, Shawn did not put too much stock in them. As a matter of fact, he seriously wondered how statistically those numbers came about, but anything on a course of action other than what he had to do to that boosted his own self-image was to his advantage. He would gladly accept the handout. But, in reality, he realized there wasn't anything truly special about him; he was a guy who grew up in a home with good parents, and he was surrounded by that village, so to speak, but he knew there were a slew of black men that were much better looking than him. It just so happened that he was famous, and that tended to gravitate toward a capitalistic-free enterprise society. He smiled to himself and thought, *But while the surf is up, why not ride the waves for what it is worth.*

Shawn had just wrapped up a multi-million dollar business meeting with some top-notch business folks that wanted his company to start production with their film company. This company, whose main base was out of New York, made some of the top-notch animated big-screen movies; they wanted Shawn Enterprise to head the job. Shawn was at the top of his game. The competition as well as the media knew it. He was in demand, and the media called him the mystery man behind the helm of the enterprise. The reason for the title was because Shawn did not do interviews whatsoever unless it was for a special cause, such as invites to schools or churches or afterschool programs such as Y-programs. He would do it if he had the time, and for the most part, he would make the time. This was free, pro bono, from his part, but many of these places would give whatever free stuff as possible as a way to show their gratitude. However, for some organizations, he would accept the offer to come, speak, and thank whoever invited him to come and give a few minutes of his time for a reasonable offer. Shawn did not per se hold firm to a retainer fee even though he had one, but most places he went on a heart-to-heart trust of what the place could afford. If he felt he was being duped, then he would play hardball and raise the fee about 10 percent, and if they wanted him, they would pay for his time, but since he did not conduct interviews, rather sent representatives in his place, he went by what these organizations could afford, based on his heart-to-heart policy.

Shawn had it going on—he had the house, the job, his health, family support, materialistic wealth, fame—all of these things he'd worked hard for. Nothing was handed to him on a silver spoon or platter, but one thing he did not have—the woman, Serenity Powers.

Chapter 40

Shawn told Karen that he was leaving early that day to meet up with some of the guys from the gym. He gave her some instructions and some important tasks to complete. He reminded her that if anything should come up, she should reach him on his emergency phone with different codes: 311 meant business; 411 meant important information, and 911 meant family situation. Karen smiled and told him to have fun. Shawn, as he was heading out the door, reminded Karen that he would be working from home the next day. In other words, he would probably go down to the golf range.

While Shawn was out, Karen was in charge of the office and everything that went on. She had several workers under her, and she handled what she had to do very professionally. Many people questioned Shawn when he gave Karen that responsibility, but Shawn just had a burning instinct of confidence that Karen could handle the job. He would say to those who protested in Karen's defense that anyone, particularly, a woman who could handle herself where she came from and survive, could handle this responsibility as well. Shawn was right, and those who thought it was a bad move, now looked back and saw that Shawn had picked the right person for the job.

Karen Smith looked at Shawn as her knight in shining armor, not in a romantic or fantasy sense, even though she wouldn't mind, but in a humanitarian sense. He had rescued her from the muck and mire she was sinking in. If it had not been for him, Karen would probably be a recidivist victim in the New York City shelter system or living with some loser with children from different baby daddies. Karen smiled; her family was so proud of her. She had been the first to do about everything from graduating from college and about to complete her master's degree, to landing a six-figure job. She was so impressed with Shawn that she didn't want to mess up any assignment he gave to her. She was grateful to Shawn for believing in her and for giving her a chance. Deep down, she had some feelings for him. She loved him. She didn't know if it was hero worship or if her feelings for him were genuine. He was on her mind throughout the day, nothing sexual, just feelings and images of how wonderful he was, but she knew nothing would come of it. If anything, those things only happened in fairy tales.

At any rate, Karen had told Shawn to enjoy the gym and to say hello to his friends. She had playfully walked up to him, fixed his tie, smiled, and told him to be a good boy. Shawn had smiled back and said always and headed out. Shawn walked to the elevator, thinking about the open friendship he and Karen had, but they both knew where the line in the sand was drawn, so to speak, and up to this point, neither one had crossed that line. However, he had to admit as he got on the elevator that they both had come pretty close to the edge.

Chapter 41

The next two days Shawn was relentless in his pursuit of Serenity. He had received the message from Serenity, delivered by Sandra, saying thanks but no thanks. However, he wouldn't take no for an answer. He followed the same routine as he had done a couple of days ago. He sent Serenity more flowers and a card asking for a date. The card wasn't one of those expensive ones you purchase in the store. This one was personalized. Serenity thought the idea was very creative, and the card itself was very romantic. The artwork on the face of the card was Shawn and Serenity sitting in the diner, looking and smiling at each other, and their eyes told the story. Serenity stopped to remember how the picture was taken but was mentally stopped cold as she could not recall. Inside the card was a picture of her and Shawn's. They were both laughing. Their hands were so close to each other, and the writing was in big letters—nothing mushy or elaborate—but simple. It said, '*Soul mates.*' And at the bottom, was Shawn's name.

Sandra saw the card and started crying. She thought the man was a rare breed, and she told Serenity that men were not like this anymore and that nowadays a man would send a basic card with a simple poem that matched his creativity with a deep poetic touch that they claimed they made up, such as the "roses are red" stuff. They would send it with a box of candy that they themselves would end up eating. Sandra really tried to persuade her best friend to give the man a shot, but each time something came in from Shawn, Serenity would have Sandra to call Shawn and tell him thank you and decline the offer to go out with him.

This went on for weeks, but Shawn knew, this was the one. She was his soul mate, and he had determined in his mind that he was going to be the only recipient of her love.

Chapter 42

One day Sandra called Shawn and was going to once again thank him for the flowers and the card as requested by Serenity and to decline to go out with him. This had been going on then for several weeks straight. Serenity's office was beginning to look like a floral shop. The more Serenity turned him down, the more Shawn looked at it as a challenge to deal with—a mountain to climb. However, this was the first time anyone had ever held out on his charms, so to speak. Shawn could not come up with the answer. He felt that he was neither making progress, nor was he losing ground. Shawn reasoned to himself that at least Serenity had not sent back both the cards and the flowers. She kept them, so he hoped, and because of that, it was enough for him to think that the scale at that point could tip either way, so Shawn decided to put all the chips on the table and take the direct aggressive approach. Therefore, when Sandra called, Shawn knew it was for the same reason it had been for the past several weeks, but here was the crack in the door, so to speak, he'd been waiting for. Shawn felt that that was the phone call to make his move. The others he had just accepted and given Serenity space, but he had no more space to surrender.

Shawn said to Sandra, "Wait, don't hang up." He knew that it was not the time to put on his sultry, smoky, baritone voice—the one that women practically melted upon listening. It was time for Shawn to be real—baritone and all. He had to find a way to get Sandra to talk. She knew her boss better than he did; he was used to leading, but this time he would have to follow. "I'm sorry, Mr. Cook." Shawn had a smile in his voice. "Please, Sandra, call me Shawn. My business partners call me Mr. Cook. My friends and the ones I want to be my friends call me Shawn."

Sandra heard Shawn laugh, and for a minute, it sounded like Bluto in *Popeye*. She thought, *You have to admit the man is good.* Sandra continued, "Mr. Cook, I mean . . . Shawn, I wish I could help but . . ." Shawn chuckled again, and this time, the deepness of it mesmerized Sandra. She thought, *If this man did that to a woman, he could cause her to have an accident. She better be wearing some of those panty liners.* She was happy that she had hers.

Shawn spoke nice and calm, but there was something else in his voice, and Sandra could not place it. Then it hit her! Desperateness! The man sounded desperate. She thought it was a definite part of any true man, even for Shawn Cook. Whenever a man can sound like that about the woman he cares for, it fulfills the meaning of that song "When a man loves a woman." Sandra could hear it in Shawn's voice. He cared about that silly woman. Sandra thought about the way he sounded, *If Serenity told him to kiss her toes, he'd go beyond the call of duty and probably give them a good licking.*

Then Shawn's voice penetrated through Sandra's thoughts, "Listen, Sandra, you could help. Just tell me where she is and that's it. I could do the rest."

Sandra responded, "Yeah, that's just it. It will be my job. Will you hire me if she fires me? Will you put food on my table or take it out of my children's mouths? Would you buy designer clothes for my three daughters and me?"

Shawn, this time, let out a nice healthy laugh. "I like your style. You are all right, and, yes, without a doubt, if they let you go, you can come and work for me. I'll create a position for you. You'll make enough to buy designer clothes for you, your daughters, and the kids in your block." Shawn laughed again, which made Sandra laugh. Sandra was feeling comfortable with Shawn, she had to admit. Serenity was right about one thing concerning Shawn Cook: the guy was smooth; he was good, very manipulative, and persuasive. Sandra thought, *I thought I was good. This guy is better than good.*

"Listen, Sandra, I have four tickets to see . . ."

Sandra cut him off with excitement in her voice, "Don't you dare tell me Patti Labelle, Gladys Knight, Heather Healy, and special guest appearance by Beyonce in the Divas' Night Out tour. You got tickets? Get out of here. You mean you can get tickets, right?"

Shawn was laughing as Sandra was babbling away. "Come on, are you serious?"

He had a twinkle in his voice, "Yes, indeed." Sandra, still excited, didn't know what to say. "Wow! How in the world did you pull that one . . . forget that. I'm so excited I can't even think question."

Shawn still had a little smile in his voice. "Sandra, I was thinking . . ." Shawn paused; it sounded as if Sandra had hung up the phone. "Sandra, are you still there? Hello?" Sandra, who had dropped the phone, started doing a little shimmy at her desk, not concerned about who was watching. The only thing she had on her mind if she played her cards right, she would have tickets to the Divas' Night Out tour for free. Shawn's voice broke though Sandra's excitement. He had played his last card, and he was right. Sandra fell right for the bait, hook, line, and sinker. Shawn knew he had to move to phase two to overlap the excitement of phase one; otherwise, his generosity would seem endless.

Sandra, calming down, spoke, "Yes, I am here, right with you, Shawn. I dropped the phone, but I am here, baby, you were saying." She was out of breath.

Shawn laughed. "Well, if you know two people that would like to sit with you and whoever you bring in the VIP section, give me a call." When Sandra heard the VIP section, she muffled a scream, and her voice became very excited. Shawn continued, "So listen, Sandra, take care, and if you hear from Serenity, let her know I called, thanks."

Shawn was praying that Sandra would take the bait, and he began to do a countdown from ten with his fingers crossed. Sandra, at this point, did not hang up. He could still hear her breathing. Her breaths were coming out as if she was trying to make a decision. Shawn's countdown was at seven. He didn't want to put Sandra through this, but in the game of love and war, people usually do things that later on, when they look back, totally surprise them. Shawn knew as his count was down to four that Sandra was struggling between loyalty and temptation. Many have gone the route of temptation from the first couple in the garden to a disciple at a dinner table. He could feel Sandra fighting as his count came down to two. He knew that her loyalty to her friend had beat out a night of excitement and pleasure.

As he was about to hang up the phone, he faintly heard Sandra, "Mr. Cook, I mean, Shawn . . ." He quickly put the phone back to his ear and announced that he was still there, and Sandra continued, "Ah, like I was saying, that was some slick, low down stuff you just pulled . . ." Shawn tried to sound innocent of all wrongdoing but was cut off by Sandra, "Don't even play the jackass card. The joker maybe, but the jackass card really doesn't fit you. Anyway, as I was saying, you tried to get over on me, which was low, trying to get me to sell out on my best friend and boss. You have some nerve, but listen to me, mister. I have my pride, integrity, and principle . . ."

Shawn cut her off, "I'll throw in my best friend, Marcus—married material, no children, looking for a strong black woman who can remain loyal to her man, and I think you fit the mold. We could double date. You will really like Marcus, a Wall Street man—no baggage, no nonsense, a pure gentleman."

Sandra, sounding very upset, said, "So, let me get this straight. You will give me tickets to Diva Night, plus a date with a Wall Street brother, and you want to give me that for the loyalty I have for my friend. That is what you are saying, right? Ah, Shawn."

Shawn, feeling defeated, admitted that that was the deal. Sandra made a noise, said something under her breath, and then said to Shawn, "She's at the 'Just As You Like It' diner. She just left ten minutes ago and is not expected back for another hour and an half. If memory serves me right, she likes the booth all the way toward the back on the window side facing the west side. Oh well, if I'm in trouble, at least I'll go down singing and with my Wall Street man holding on to my waist, moving to the music."

Shawn, with a voice of deep relief and satisfaction, thanked Sandra, "Thank you, Sandra. You'll have those tickets by next week, and you'll hear from my man Marcus by the end of the week . . . and Sandra, don't worry. Serenity doesn't have to know how I found her. I so happened to be in the area and decided to stop in and try their special." Sandra sounded as if she was doomed. Shawn told her that it would work out and to leave the rest up to him.

Chapter 43

Shawn walked into "Just As You Like It." He smiled at the irony of the whole situation. The woman whose heart he was trying to win was hiding in his own restaurant. Even though Shawn owned the place, he had made it clear that he didn't want any preferential treatment; he wanted to be treated as if he was a customer and not an owner. Shawn looked around for Serenity and spotted her. At the same time, she spotted him and realized she was caught. There was no place to hide, and she wasn't going to hide under the table, so she sat there waiting for Shawn to get to her table. As she was waiting, her cell phone went off. She opened her *Star Trek* look-alike phone. Serenity didn't even bother to look at the window display to see who it was. She already knew. Serenity, still looking at Shawn as he slowly made his way toward her, without displaying any phone etiquette, said, "You are so dead, traitor." And closed her phone.

She was looking down at her phone when like a phantom he was at the table, smiling with those cute dimples. "May I have a seat?" Serenity was somewhat distracted very briefly by the way Shawn's clothes just cleaved to him—simple wear—a nice, black turtle neck with a pair of black pants that hugged his narrow waist. His shirt brought out his Mr. Universe physique. Shawn, still waiting for Serenity's permission to sit, gave her that billion-dollar smile and said, "Sure, why not? It's your place . . . I am sorry that was not necessary. I do apologize."

Shawn, still smiling, told Serenity that her apology was accepted. He wasted no time with small talk but cut to the chase. "Why are you avoiding me?" Serenity, for a moment, was disarmed by Shawn's passive-aggressive behavior as she sort of fell against the ropes to defend herself, but then she recovered quickly and came out with a sweet-aggressive behavior of her own—just the right amount to knock Shawn off balance, for he wasn't used to women going toe-to-toe with him. He usually won them over with his manly charm, or in business meetings, he transformed into some type of persistent, charming, aggressive business person that usually got what he wanted, but Serenity's boldness caught him off guard as she held back no punches. "Avoiding? I'm not avoiding you," she said with a smile that was as deadly as cyanide, and Shawn could feel it as it traveled through his veins toward his heart.

She continued, "I have no desire to go out with you." Shawn's eyebrows shot up as he was taken aback by her bold admission and aggressiveness, and she continued, "I thought I made that perfectly clear the first time when you sent me the flowers. Thank you, but then I thought I made it crystal clear thereafter, but it's obvious you don't accept rejection gracefully. My only advice and this is free, get over it." Serenity gave him that smile that was laced with something deadly. Shawn practically fell out of the booth where he was sitting. He was no doubt knocked off balance; he wasn't expecting this fine-looking sister to have such a lethal punch, but he smiled, nevertheless.

However, deep within, he knew what he was up against. He quickly studied her and was somewhat handcuffed, but he accepted the challenge. Most guys would have said a few derogatory words and moved on, but Shawn thought he needed to approach this from a different angle or perspective. Shawn, who was good at reading people, despite the aggressive stance she was taking, still felt something tugging him in his heart toward her. He smiled, and Serenity was taken aback. She knew that she had come out stronger than Mike Tyson, but this guy was still standing. She knew most guys would have left her alone, even walked on the other side of the street if they saw her, but this guy just wasn't getting it. *Yeah, he's cute and fine, and perhaps most women would have jumped and acted the fool to get hooked up with him, but I can't be bought with charm, money, and a fine body with a million-dollar smile connected to it.*

Serenity was lost in her present thoughts when Shawn purposely cleared his throat and brought her back to the present. He said, "Look, we got off on the wrong foot. I don't know what happened. Listen, go out with me two times, that's it. If you still feel the same way about me, then I would have to accept defeat gracefully, but I need to know if what I am feeling is real." He paused to look straight into Serenity's eyes as he made his voice smoother and softer—the right touch to cause Serenity to tingle as he continued, "I need to know for my sake whether what I am feeling is right on target or I am totally off base and off the mark. Just give me that chance. I don't want to think I missed the one and only. Like I said that if it doesn't work, then no harm, no foul. I could then walk away with a clear conscious."

Serenity was speechless. Never had a man expressed his feelings for her the way that Shawn had. She could see his sincerity and feel how genuine his emotions were. She was to the point when her insides shook and trembled, but she could not let her guard down. She also realized that Mr. Cook was a master of gab, and he probably had many trophies of women that he'd conquered, but she said to herself, it's going to take more than a few emotional poetic lines to win her over, and she conceded, "Ah, Mr. Cook, you realize you are stalking me." She smiled and Shawn smiled back.

"Ms. Powers . . . I am very much aware, so since we got that roadblock out of the way, let's move on."

They both once again smiled, yet there was a tension between them. They eyed each other as in a standoff—who would draw blood first. Serenity chuckled. It was a chuckle that had a lot of sarcasm, and Serenity drew first. "Mr. Cook, what do you want from me? I am totally out of your league, let alone your social hemisphere. I am out of your loop, so what exactly do you want?" She inhaled a deep breath and came after Shawn again, "So, I ask again, what do you want? And what can I offer you that the rest of my Nubian sisters also can give you? As a matter of fact, you can get that anywhere, and I am sure at anytime, or perhaps you want this." Serenity looked down at her crotch, letting her eyes linger there before she slowly brought them back up, looking at Shawn with a bit of a twinkle in her eye—a trick Sandra taught her. She was shaking inside. She was not used to referring to her body in such a fashion. She shook her head, totally surprised at what she had done. She looked at Shawn and with a plea of desperation, said, "What is it that you want from me?"

Shawn swallowed hard. His throat was getting constricted. A bit of perspiration formed on his forehead. He picked up a napkin, dabbed his forehead, and cleared his throat. He addressed Serenity's question, "I just want to get to know you. It has nothing to do with sex, but everything to do with you." Serenity was the one perspiring now, "OK, two dates, that's it, right?" Shawn nodded with a huge smile. She continued, "Do I get a chance to choose where we are going?"

Shawn, looking at Serenity's twinkling eyes, shook his head and said, "No, unless you're paying. Other than that, I'll make that decision." Serenity did not like the sound of that as her face registered a look of doubt. Shawn could tell that she was contemplating backing out, and he quickly addressed the matter, "Look, I'm not some control freak." Serenity's eyes playfully looked up at the ceiling as if to say "who are you kidding." Shawn laughed at that, and Serenity laughed at the way Shawn laughed. He continued, "As I was saying, I am not a control freak. Whenever you are feeling uncomfortable about anything or anywhere we may go or do, we will stop if it's not your thing."

Serenity's eyebrows suspiciously went up, and Shawn realized he wasn't making things any easier, yet he would give a million dollars if he could capture the look on Serenity's face—the look of innocence as she bit her bottom lip and twirled her locks in a concerned way. Shawn quickly dealt with the damage he had mounted up as he stuttered, hemmed, hawed, and cleared his throat, "Ah, no . . . no, no, nooo. I am not talking about anything crazy or kinky or wild, for that matter."

Serenity, with her arms folded in under her breast, lifted the breasts up a bit, staring right into Shawn's eyes, "So what do you mean?" Shawn tried to ignore Serenity's shapely breasts as her arms continued to press against them. He tried to ignore them as he stated, "OK, let's say we go to a club and . . ." He stopped and looked at her wide and intrigued eyes that were filled with what looked to be a certain naivety. He treasured the look. As the two continued to talk, the tension was starting to break. Serenity, for the first time since Shawn had joined her, was starting to relax. Both sort of put their weapons down metaphorically, so to speak, as Shawn in a backdoor sort of nonthreatening way asked, "So why have you been avoiding my phones calls? My flowers, which by the way, I handpicked myself, just in case you were wondering. You really know how to deflate a man's ego."

Serenity countered, "Ah, poor baby, I am so sorry your ego is so easily bruised. I thought a man of your caliber had tougher skin, a more enduring ego. I guess everything you read can't be taken for face value."

Shawn smiled as he enjoyed the verbal exchange, "You are stalling, and you still haven't answered my question." Shawn lifted up his left eyebrow as to say top that. Serenity smiled at Shawn's impersonation of the former WWE wrestler, the Rock. She said, "Perhaps I don't want to answer your question."

Shawn came back, "Fair enough. I would have thought a woman of your caliber wouldn't be so easily intimidated." Serenity thought, *Touché, Mr. Cook, touché.* Shawn smiled in satisfaction; he knew when an opponent had had enough, and he assumed that Serenity had surrendered. "OK, I am not a sore loser, but I am sure there would be more opportunities where we will clash."

She said it with such dignity like a strong opponent after a defeat. She continued and answered the question, "Well . . . Shawn, to be honest, I don't have time for your drama, and second, I really don't want to become a part of your harem, and . . ." Serenity stopped and looked at his face as he was trying to control his composure, but he could not. His laughter came out very forceful as if it had been bottled up. His laughter came from deep within and just boomed out of his mouth as he leaned back with no inhibitions. Serenity at first enjoyed the display. At that point, she saw him like a child. He laughed as if he was the only one in the room. The sound was so loud that it caused others to stop eating their meals or conversations to stop and look in their direction. Even those who were serving and getting out their orders, rushing in and out of the kitchen stopped to observe. Serenity felt she was on display not her per se, but then she looked at those who had stopped what they were doing and noticed that his laugh had an effect on them. It was actually contagious, and genuine, as others smiled, some chuckled, while some covered their mouths and began to laugh as well, not knowing clearly what they were laughing about.

Serenity put her head down, covered her mouth, and chuckled out of embarrassment as her eyes darted looking to her left and right. Shawn's laughter continued, and to her it seemed as if his laughter echoed throughout the place. Serenity, feeling more and more as if she was under the microscope, looked around nervously with a chuckle and said in a tune barely above a whisper, hoping Shawn could hear her, "What is so funny?" She nervously smiled, touching the items on the table in a nervous fashion, and her eyes darted around the place. "What is so funny?" She repeated, this time with a little more agitation. Shawn, noticing Serenity's agitation and nervousness began to get some control as he wiped the tears of laughter from his eyes.

Under different circumstances, Serenity would have been laughing at the sight of this big, six foot three, 230 plus pounds of solid mass, wiping his eyes. It reminded her of the big bear who got a tact stuck in his foot, so big and mean-looking, crying like a baby, but at this stage, Serenity did not see it that way. She felt a sense of chagrin even confusion. Where was the joke? She was serious and then, out of the blue, this big jerk had started laughing.

Shawn was somewhat under control; he still had that type of smile where he could either start laughing again or he could get more control of it. He said, "I am sorry." And the big bear continued to wipe his eyes. He finally stopped wiping his eyes and continued with that silly grin on his face. "You call me a player, drama, me . . . well, maybe the drama, but it's not what you think, but me a player . . ."

Oh boy! Serenity thought, *Here comes the avalanche of uncontrollable laughter.* Serenity saw it coming and said, "Mr. Cook, if you start that crazy laughter again, as if you lost your senses, I will get up and walk out." Shawn was trying to stifle his laughter as he looked at Serenity with his lips tightly pursed. Serenity looked at him with a stern look, while inside she was smiling, and said to him, "I mean it." Shawn, covered his mouth and slowly dragged his hands down his face as if he was removing a mask, put his head down briefly, and came back up ready to talk, "A player, me, that's funny. Where did you get this or read this . . . who told you this?"

Serenity was now looking as if she had put her foot in her mouth as Shawn continued with all seriousness, "It doesn't bother me. Ignorant people are going to write what they want, and the people who read that crap are as ignorant as the ones who wrote it, but crap like that sells despite how it may affect the lives of people they are writing about. They don't give a damn who they are hurting or chasing or just plain old harassing. They don't care. Why should they? It sells at the expense of those who want one thing: to be treated like a human being, whatever happen to that thing called investigating reporting or seeking out the truth, and not this bull sh . . ." Shawn caught himself before the rest of the word came out, and he continued, "I don't have to, and I usually don't respond to jerks like that or listen to those who think they know Shawn Cook, but no one knows Shawn Cook except Shawn Cook and those who are close to him. Ms. Powers, if you really want to know who the hell I am, speak to my friends. They will tell you. Speak to my family, they will be honest with you, or better yet, speak to the boys and girls I meet three times a week at the Y, teaching them self-respect, conflict resolution, or self-defense. Talk to them instead of believing some idiot who doesn't know me from his butt cheeks."

Serenity was speechless. She just opened up a can of something that was lethal. She was seeing the other side of Shawn. Then she wished the laughing side was back.

Shawn continued, "I have nothing to hide. Wasn't brought up that way. I won't start living that way, Ms. Powers." Serenity didn't know what to say as she looked down at the floor. She had flipped the switch at the wrong time. Now she wasn't sure how to shut it off. Serenity was a little bit intimidated by Shawn's massive built, but she looked him in the eyes just to play it off that she wasn't afraid, but deep within, her bones were slapping against each other as Shawn continued, "And as for you, Ms. Powers, I am totally surprised that someone of your caliber and intelligence would fall for such a stupid rumor without doing your homework." Serenity tried to defend herself, but Shawn put up a big hand as if he was stopping traffic—the traffic being in this case Serenity's words as he continued, "I'm not finished yet, if you don't mind."

Serenity's mouth dropped. Shawn's verbal precise assault was hitting everywhere, leaving no stone unturned, and yet she was impressed at how he expressed himself. In one sense, he could have put her in her place for assuming, but he did something even better than that. He read her the reality check, and there it came, "I ask you for a simple date, and you turn me down with your little cat and mouse games. You don't have the courage to come to the phone, so you send your little me wanna be, whom I like a lot, but she does your dirty work."

Serenity had had enough and had heard enough. Enough was enough. No more tip toeing around the true issue, as the soldiers would say when a bomb was coming their way—one word, *incoming*! Serenity then set off a massive attack. "Let me tell you something, Mr. Cook." Her neck was doing that side to side thing, her hands were going in concert with the neck, and her eyes were opening and closing to what she was putting emphasis on. They were now drawing the attention of the other patrons, as the whispering and finger pointing started, but these two were in a battle of their own, blocking out whatever and whoever was looking or listening.

Serenity intently stared at Shawn and continued, "Let's get something straight, Mr. Cook. I am under no obligation to go out with you, and it is my prerogative whether who I want and when I want to date or not is my choice. You may control a lot of stuff, but you don't control this." Serenity hands scanned her body in one swoop. She continued, "Furthermore, Mr. Cook, let me make this clear. If your dirty laundry is everywhere, then clean up the crap, and if you don't want to clean it up, don't get all bent out of shape when people bring it up. Furthermore . . ." Shawn rubbed his hand on his face as if to say enough already, but Serenity, picking up on the gesture, was more fueled by it and continued, "That's right. I know you don't want to hear it, but hear it. In reality, I do enjoy your company, and that's how far that goes because I am careful who I go out with. Your money, wealth, prestige, and power doesn't do a thing for me. I am not impressed. Those same qualities can buy off, or knock off, or just go off on anyone. So you can put those toys away. They don't do a single thing for me or to me. I hope I am making myself clear, since you wanted to take me there."

Shawn noticed Serenity inhaling for what may be another verbal assault. He quickly mounted up his defenses but did not retaliate. He slowly exhaled and raised the white flag and retreated. He knew he could not make someone like him or go out with him, so he raised his hands in a gesture of surrender. Serenity, seeing the damage she may have caused, felt bad. They both surveyed each other with eyes that told it all—eyes that told the story of going too far. The damage was done, but the question was whether or not it could be fixed.

Shawn then broke the ice as he spoke in his deep, quiet, and gentle voice, "I respect your opinion of me, but don't let it come from a local paper that doesn't even know a thing about me."

Serenity, much calmer, nodded her head and said, "From what I could see the couple of times we met, I think you are a nice guy, but in reality, I don't even know you."

Shawn with eyes of compassion held Serenity's hand so gentle and looking into her eyes, said, "Then get to know me, Serenity. Find out who is the real Shawn Cook, not from a paper that shoots from the hip or builds up a story from those who are my enemies or even women who falsely claim I mistreated them or fathered a baby by them—all nonsense and pure lies. Yes, I have my faults, and I made my mistakes, but I want you to get to know me from your heart. Like my parents always say, you can't judge a book by its cover. You have to open it and take time to read it." Shawn smiled with both dimples full blast.

Serenity smiled at his boyish grin and thought that he was cute and fine put together. She looked down at her hands and looked back up to Shawn. Then twirling her locks and biting her lower lip, she said, "So, where do we go from here?" "Well," Shawn began, "you can let me pick you up next Friday after work. I want to show you who Shawn Cook is. Get it firsthand and not from a tabloid."

Serenity put her head down and looked back up with a twinkle in her eye. "I think I'll like that." She, keeping her enthusiasm under control, continued with a smile, "So, Mr. Tour Guide, after the tour, where to?" Shawn got up from the table and stretched. Serenity got a complete look at his height and even more than that as her eyes briefly slid down his pants and quickly back up to his eyes, hoping Shawn did not notice the look of satisfaction on her face. Shawn, into his stretch, felt the tension leave his body. He felt as if he'd been in a fight, and he'd come out the battered winner. He finally, coming off his stretch, winked at her and gave that million-dollar smile, dimples and all. Serenity just wanted to put her finger in those dimples.

Shawn looked at her and said, "You'll see." Serenity was getting ready to speak when Shawn winked again, turned, and walked off.

Chapter 44

The rest of the week Shawn was on cloud nine. It seemed as if he could not make a bad business decision. He had major companies make serious business agreements with Shawn Enterprise; they brought his plan and wanted his expertise to help advance their business. Shawn, being a serious businessman, knew business had its ups and downs, but right then he was in the zone. However, he also realized as far as black-owned businesses were concerned, he knew the rainbow couldn't last forever, so for however long it lasted, Shawn said he was going to take advantage while the going was good.

Shawn was so excited, he called his parents. They could tell the difference, as slight as it may have been. Shawn's parents always considered him a happy individual. Not too many things got to him, but when he was in one of his slumps, he would do extra workouts at the gym or he would put extra time at the Y to teach the kids defense martial arts. For Shawn these were release stressbusters. But he wasn't talking about his successful business transactions for the last few months. He was telling them about Serenity.

Both Mr. and Mrs. Cook were on the line. Mrs. Cook, being the assertive one of the two, dominated the conversation as usual, and Mr. Cook, as he did most of the time, would listen and make certain confirmation sounds when Mrs. Cook gave him the clue to do so. When Mrs. Cook was off base, Mr. Cook would simply say, "Lord, have mercy" or "Keep us in your prayers, son." Every time Mr. Cook would do that, Shawn would smile to himself, thinking that his father was a wise man, not to tangle with an assertive black woman.

Mrs. Cook spoke, "Wow, son, that's great. It's about time you found someone, so when could we meet her?" Shawn was going to respond when Mr. Cook jumped in, "Son, go slow. I can't wait to meet the young lady." Mrs. Cook chimed in, "Shawn, Shawn." Shawn made a sound that indicated that he wasn't in the mood for all of this. He did not like it when his mother called his name twice like that. He just knew this is where he somehow tuned her off, but he also knew if he didn't respond, he was in for a long night.

Mrs. Cook continued, "Shawn, are you listening to me?" Mr. Cook moaned a "Lord, have mercy," as Shawn responded to his mother, "Yes, Mother, I hear you very much loud and clear, but I am not in the mood to be lectured and . . ." Shawn was cut short by Mrs. Cook, "Stop right there, don't go no further . . ." Mr. Cook let out his second "Lord, have mercy," but this time Mrs. Cook responded and told him to hush his mouth, and Mr. Cook did as he was told. Quite some time ago, Mr. Cook had told Shawn ever since his elementary school days that in life you must choose your battles—a lesson Shawn had applied throughout his life. It had saved him a ton of money on headache medication as well as doctor visits. This was what his father did with his mother, since she was a fighter by nature. Mr. Cook realized some arguments were not worth the time or energy, but Shawn also knew that with Mr. Cook there was a line that Mrs. Cook knew she better not cross, and she didn't. This was one of those battles Mr. Cook didn't have anything to win or lose, plus he knew that Shawn was capable enough to take care of himself. So he sat there smiling and listening to what would turn out to be a good debate. He only wished he had some popcorn as Mrs. Cook continued, "Wait, one minute. I don't care how old and successful you get or how senile I may become. If you forget anything, Shawn Travis Cook, one thing don't you ever forget as long as you are breathing with the genes and all that other stuff that belongs to me inside of you. I'm your mother, and if I choose to lecture you, shut it and zip it and open up those eardrums. Now that's pretty clear, isn't it?"

Mr. Cook blew out a "whew" sound and then came to Shawn's rescue before Shawn put his foot further in his own mouth, "Roberta, the man is grown. He has a right to express himself—"

Mrs. Cook cut off her husband, "Well, show some respect. Don't get beside yourself."

Shawn tried to respond to what his mother had just said, "Mom, I wasn't—"

Mr. Cook cut him off, "Hush, Son. I'm trying to get your foot out of your mouth." Mr. Cook, always the joker, had all three of them chuckling at that as the tension then had a little crack in it. It was enough to release some of that bottled-up energy as Mr. Cook continued to address his lovely wife, "Honey, our apron strings were cut as soon as the boy stuck his head out of your womb."

Mrs. Cook knew what her husband was saying. It seemed like from day one Shawn had an industrious mind, which was independent, and when he left the nest, both Mr. and Mrs. Cook knew that he was more than ready to take on the world and that he would not be looking back, and they were right. Mrs. Cook listened quietly and waited until her husband was finished and said, "Hush, Travis. I'm not out of line, and I know that Shawn is a grown man. Thank you, but—"

Mr. Cook said, "But, now you hold on." When Mrs. Cook heard the "but," she knew that she had crossed the line as Mr. Cook's tone took on a more subtle, yet harder inflection, "Roberta, enough. I usually don't complain when you and Shawn get into it, but I need for you, no, I want you to back off the boy . . . please."

Mrs. Cook cleared her throat, and with a calm voice, she said, "OK, Shawn, your father is right. I do apologize. I said what I had to say. Now, you are still planning to come over for dinner Sunday, correct?"

Shawn made a sound of confirmation. At that point, he did not want to be the one to cause the volcano to erupt. Mrs. Cook continued, "If you like, you can bring your friend, but if you don't want to . . . that's up to you. That's your choice, OK." Shawn once again made a sound that confirmed his response. Mrs. Cook said her good-byes and hung up. Mr. Cook was still on the line, "OK, Son, we will see you Sunday." Shawn confirmed it and hung up. He smiled to himself and knew that this battle with his mother was far from being over by a long shot. He knew it was going to be like the Ali versus Frazier fights, and it just seemed as if they would never end.

Shawn hung up from his parents and called his brothers and sisters since he knew that the gossip train would be running at full speed, driven by no other than the motor mouth . . . his mother. Shawn shared with each of them what had happened and let them know if they heard it differently, then not to believe the hype. Shawn took out a few minutes calling each brother and sister and chatted with them the latest in each other's lives. After that, he focused on the weekend's conference and television interviews he had agreed to do.

Shawn wasn't too big on being in the spotlight. He knew he was fortunate to be blessed by God to have and to do what he did, and he strongly believed that the path he was making, did not point to his success but to the one who made it possible for him to be successful, and that was God. The secret of his success was God. Period. Most of his business peers and competition did not understand that, and they wondered how Shawn ran a billion-dollar business and all the other extracurricular stuff in between. He would tell them when your steps are ordered by God, He doesn't exhaust you. He energizes you to do what you need to do for the kingdom. Shawn looked up to the ceiling and, with both hands raised, pointed up to God and said, "You are the Man."

Shawn was interrupted by Karen's voice on the intercom. He responded, "Yes, Karen?"

Karen spoke, "Yes, sir, ah, there is a call from Mr. Willis who insists I call him Charles. That's gross. Tell him no thank you." Shawn smiled; he was aware that most of his associates called him just to try to get a date with Karen. Shawn, getting some control over his laughter, asked Karen, "Find out what he wants. The man likes you."

Karen said, "Oh gross! Shawn, do I have to find out what he wants? I know what he really wants. The man is so disgusting. He needs to stay within his age limits, and he better be careful. One good sexy look and one good 1-900 number sound bite in his ears and the man's pacemaker is going to skip a few beats, and you're going to lose a client." Karen didn't hear Shawn respond, but she knew the subject was closed. "OK, Mr. C, I'll find out what's going on."

Shawn smiled and said, "That's my girl."

Karen came back to the phone, "Yes, the perv wanted to know you're traveling arrangements and if he can go with you."

Shawn said to Karen, "Tell him no. I already have someone, and I'll call him in about twenty minutes. Ask him to have ready what I am walking into when I get out there. Karen, you know what? Ah, let him know he is free to go, but not with me on this flight. If he wants to go, I'll make the arrangements, but I need to know by yesterday, if you catch what I'm saying."

Karen smiled. She loved to be used in the crunch. It showed Shawn that she was worth her grain and salt.

Shawn continued, "Karen, get in touch with all of those I need to meet. I need times and agendas, best places to eat, ah, workout facilities, let's see what else." Karen was writing it all down even though she knew Shawn like the back of her hand. Shawn continued as he interrupted Karen's thoughts, "Ah, Karen, I need for you to pack a suitcase. I'm taking you with me. That's if you don't have any plans."

Karen couldn't speak at the moment. She was tongue-tied, and her knees felt as if they would collapse any minute. She wanted to scream, but she had second thoughts, since her coworkers would think something was wrong with her. So her scream came out like a long squeal. She had always wanted to go with Shawn, but she didn't know how to express her request, so the only words that came out were "thank you."

Shawn smiled and asked, "Karen, you OK? You have to breathe and let it out, girl." He laughed because he knew to Karen this was like winning lotto. The girl worked hard and did her best to get to know every aspect of the business. Shawn knew that everything Karen earned and received, she was grateful for. Here she was a single mother of two lovely girls—Rebecca, seven years old, and Diamond, five years old—adorable but nevertheless a handful. Shawn knew that Karen could use the trip for the overtime, but he had to make it legit, and this was his way.

"Karen, you OK?" he asked with a smile in his voice. Karen responded with a squeaky yes.

Shawn chuckled and then put on his serious business voice even though he wanted to fall out laughing due to Karen's reaction, "Karen, remember, this is a business trip, not a vacation. But first things first, I need to know if you could go."

Karen was still so excited she could hardly speak. Shawn heard another squeaky yes from her. He smiled but still had that business voice, "OK, good. Now, what about the girls? Can you find someone this short notice of a time?" The squeak came back yes. Shawn continued and gave Karen the basic 411. "Remember, you are going as my secretary, nothing more, nothing less, understood?" Karen's voice was finally returning as she said yes that she understood, and Shawn continued, "I want you to accompany me to all the conferences and take notes, greet those within my circle, and make sure whatever they want to ask, they run it by you first before they shower me with their questions and comments. Then at some point during lunch, or whenever, we would discuss who I should meet with and who we should set up an appointment with. Karen, understand that you are my first and only line of defense. Are you following this?"

Karen confirmed her response as she was writing everything that Shawn was saying in shorthand. Shawn continued, "The lectures that I shall give, I need for you to make sure everything I need is there before I get there. If not, make sure you find whoever is in charge of these things and make sure they have what I need. Be relentless but not a pain, be assertive but not rude. Keep in mind that we are in their house, but we run the show. They asked me to come, and not the other way around, OK? Now, most importantly, Karen," Shawn paused for effect and continued with a smile in his voice, "make sure you have fun in learning and just chill and relax, and please find us . . ." Shawn stopped there. He knew that Karen was very much aware of all of this because she had made the same preparations on all the other trips. The only difference this time was that she was going, and for her she felt as if this was the opportunity she had been praying and waiting for—getting behind the scenes of the movers and shakers, and Shawn Cook was both.

Karen said, "Shawn, I want to thank you for this chance. I promise I won't disappoint you."

Shawn said, "Karen, remember, it's a business trip." Karen made an attempt to cut Shawn off, but he stopped her and continued, "Business, so make sure you bring your bathing suit, tan lotion, comfortable shoes to dance in, and who knows you may find more than you were expecting. You may find Mr. Right."

Karen blushed, laughed, and said, "Mr. C, you are so crazy."

As her laugh trailed off, Shawn responded in a more relaxed voice, "So I've been told." Shawn hung up the phone and smiled nice and wide, but his thoughts weren't on the trip. They were on his luncheon with Serenity, and he knew he had made a great impression. Now he was ready for step three . . . to win her heart.

Chapter 45

Dinner at Mom and Dad's House: Look Who's Coming for Dinner!

Mr. and Mrs. Cook were setting the table for their usual Sunday dinner. This was a tradition that had been going on since they could remember. The Cooks had always been a very busy family, working and going to school as well as keeping up with each child's behavior, school progress, and extracurricular activities. It was at times a miniature New York City in the Cook home. One thing the Cooks enforced, without an excuse, was the Sunday dinner. They didn't care what you were doing or had to do. Come hell or high water, they expected to see everyone at the table on Sunday for dinner.

In addition, this was a beautiful time. The family would come together around the table—the new additions to the family—it was a reunion, so to speak. It would be a very relaxed time. Whatever craziness and nonsense went on during the week, this was a place of restoration. If you couldn't get it out there, everyone knew you will find it right here on Sunday. It was a time of good eating, good bonding, and good fun with each other. Mrs. Cook always felt that one of the most destructive travesties that had subtly worked its way into the family structure was the dismantling of the family gathering around the table with each other. This alone had put a serious obstruction in the family structure.

Mrs. Cook asked her husband to take the bread out of the oven; the two worked together so well you would think each one was in each other's mind.

Mr. Cook responded, "Already done, baby, what else?"

Mrs. Cook, a very attractive, caramel-complexioned woman, who still had a nice figure and took care of herself once a week at the nail salon and beauty salon, and she still had a sex drive that kept Mr. Cook on his Ps and Qs.

Mrs. Cook said, "Well, that's about it for now I guess. The meat should be ready by the time the kids get here." Mrs. Cook hesitated a little too long.

Mr. Cook, knowing his loving wife very well, walked up behind her, hugged her, and interjected, "OK, kitten, what's going on in that pretty head of yours?"

Mrs. Cook smiled at the fact that her husband, who was so in tune with her, tried to downplay her feelings, but she knew with her husband that was a useless task. He was too good to fool. "No, I'm fine. I'm sure it's nothing. I just thought . . . well . . . I wondered if Shawn was going to bring his new friend over, uh, what's her name . . . uh, Jazzman, Jacqueline . . ."

Mr. Cook, still hugging her real tight, took in her natural fragrance, which to him was an instant turn on and interjected, "Her name is Serenity."

He then began to nibble on her ear and neck. Mrs. Cook playfully flinched and laughed at the sensation of Mr. Cook's little pecks, kisses, and nibbles. It was actually turning her on but it wasn't the time and place. It, however, did make her feel more relaxed. She thought to herself that her husband always knew what to do to make her feel better. She really appreciated him so much. She enjoy the fact that the fire had not gone out in their romance; it was burning as bright as ever, and at times, it became a three-alarm blaze, but she was content after all these years that her man still knew what buttons to press, and he was still discovering more buttons as well.

Their lovemaking was different each time. You never knew what the man was going to do next. Most of her friends in the salon talked about how their husbands having got burnt out with not even a flicker of a flame, and most of them were miserable and had accepted to live that way. But Roberta Cook smiled as the only man she ever loved showered kisses in places on her body that were sensitive spots. She thought, *What more can a woman ask for?*

Travis Cook continued the slow assault on his wife's neck as he spoke, causing the vibration of his strong vocals to travel up and down her spine, causing goose bumps to cause a chain reaction, domino effect, throughout her body as he said, "Baby . . . remember, her name is Serenity . . . now I want you to be a good girl tonight and don't hassle Shawn's friend. Let's make a good impression on the young lady, and once she's in after a few visits, then you can tear your claws into her . . ."

Travis Cook laughed as his wife laughed and squirmed from him, "Stop it, Travis. I'm not like that." Roberta paused to think about her behavior.

"Am I? Plus I am more than certain that you will make sure of that." Travis Cook smiled as Roberta continued, "And why are you so frisky? Or to be more politically correct, horny? I just gave you some last night Mr. Cook, didn't I?"

Roberta gave Travis her best turn on flirtatious smile, which went straight to his groin as he moaned the sensation and responded, "You see, that's the thing that got you in trouble last night, and beside that, didn't I do right by you, baby?"

Now it was her turn to blush as she commented in her most sensual voice that she knew will send her husband into orbit, "You always do it right, baby, and last night, you hit areas that I didn't even know existed." And she walked up to him in a slow-stalking motion. "I mean, no kids around, I could express how well big daddy was doing me right. Every time you hit a different spot, I hit a higher note—yum-yum big daddy."

Travis Cook knew that his lovely wife had the art of turning him on down to a science as he became hard and his breathing uneven. Roberta then decided to go for the Oscar performance as she pretended to drop something and slowly bent down to pick it up, rubbing herself slowly with purpose against Travis's crotch area. When she straightened up, he desperately reached for her, but she like a cat was quick and poised and slipped out of his claws. "Not now, big boy. Be good, and I'll have a special treat for you tonight." Roberta laughed at the fact that she could still make her husband go buck wild. Then she looked at him soberly and said, "Travis, to be honest, I don't even know where you get the energy from. I can't even keep up sometimes." She knew how to build her husband's ego.

He laughed with manly pride; as her spell was wearing off, he was back on the original subject, "Kitten, I mean it. No meddling, OK?"

Roberta reluctantly agreed but added, "Baby, I'll be good, but I will not let any woman take advantage of our son."

Travis interjected, "Kitten, Shawn is a smart kid. He has a good head on his shoulders, and he reads people very well."

Roberta thought about it. "Yeah, I guess you are right. He just worries me sometimes. He has such a good heart—"

Travis countered, "He'll be fine. Listen, he takes care of the biggest accounts around, plus don't forget that his business is among the top five in New York. He's probably the youngest president and CEO of his own company. If he could handle all of that, he could handle—"

Roberta cut him off, "Travis, I am surprised you made that statement. Don't think that his business suave and his heart are one and the same.

There is a difference, lover boy." Roberta blew a sexy kiss at Travis as she continued with her flirtations. She continued, "Plus, don't forget, a women's touch is as strong as her scorn. Look what happens when I pour the love on you. I can practically get you to do whatever I want." She smiled playfully with a touch of seduction. That song "when a man loves a woman," need I say more? She concluded with a confident smile.

Travis Cook was speechless. He knew he had no chance when his wife was on a roll, but he was able to interject, "Well, do me a favor. Just keep those claws in and be on your best behavior."

As he kissed her neck, Roberta said, "You mean like you are right now, tiger? Now check on the rice, it's burning."

Travis said, "That's not the rice, baby." Travis's laugh was so contagious it made Roberta laugh as well. The two love birds were in a love embrace when the doorbell rang. Travis made a comment about how time flies when you're having fun. Roberta told Travis that they would pick up where they left off at that night and gave him a quick sensual kiss to hold him until then. Travis went to the door while Roberta went to check on the food.

Travis Cook opened the door. "Wow!" he said in excitement. "Come in, come in, oh my goodness." Travis was all of a sudden swamped by all his grandkids as they hugged his legs with their little cute cartoonlike voices, screaming hi grandpa. Travis Cook was still in good shape and exercised at least four days out of the week and tried to eat as right as possible. He did not feel like a grandfather; nevertheless, he enjoyed his grandkids with all of their energy and innocence. Each of his children had a child, except for Jonathan, with their parents following behind. Travis thought as he tried to walk to the couch without falling on one of the little muffins, who was still attached to his legs like lint to a sweater. As he scuffled his way to the couch, his own children just watched and laughed. Each grandchild tried to gain his/her grandpa's attention. Mr. Cook knew that he had to be fair and even about how his time was spent with each child, and their parents made sure equal time was spent with their child. At times Travis felt like a politician, and at other times, he felt like a union representative, giving everyone equal voice. It was strenuous at times, but one thing was for sure, it kept Travis on his toes. He had to revive every parental skill he had and make sure that he was doing what he was doing fairly, because he was being watched, not only by the grandkids, but also by their parents, specifically the moms. The dads were pretty good at it, but the moms watched with eyes of eagles that their young get proper and equal treatment while at the same time they carrying on with their own conversations. That was one thing Travis could not understand. How did his children talk and play card games or games like chess and checkers and not miss a beat, but make sure that their child was getting equal time with their grandfather. It was another wonder to be added on to the already many wonders of the world. Travis knew that one skip one ounce of particularity given would result in that particular parent blowing a stack and protesting the unfairness and advocating for their child, which in turn could spoil the rest of the evening, so Travis had to tread softly and carefully through this minefield of attention grabbers. As the grandkids were all over him, sounding like little chicks that were hungry, except in this case, the so-called chicks were the grandkids hungry for attention.

They would say, "Grandpa, guess what this and guess what that and, grandpa, look at my boo-boo." And on and on and on it went—a never-ending road until like always his lovely wife came to the rescue by giving him a quick exit and looking at him as if to say you owe me or now we are even, depending on who owns who.

"Oh boy, look what we have here," she would say and the innocent muffins would quickly stop their assault on Travis and turn as if compelled by a magnet toward Roberta, and the results for Travis would be so sweet. "Grandma," the muffins would say and jump off Travis, not caring or paying attention to where they stepped or what they hit when they jumped off, but Travis was of the mind-set that whatever pain that may be experienced from the muffins, the end result was worth it.

Roberta was happy to see the kids and the grandkids. She still referred to her own children as kids and was not afraid to let them know that no matter how old they get, she will refer to them as kids. Roberta looked forward to Sundays; if her week was crazily busy, it was days like Sunday that washed all that craziness away. Her day really began on Saturday night, getting ready for Sunday with church in the morning and rushing home to finish up with what she had started Saturday night. This was something she and Travis decided a long time ago when their schedules were totally insane and the kids were busy in school.

After a passionate night of intense lovemaking, they both lay side by side in a spoon position, with Travis at the back of his lovely shaped wife as they shared their passions and dreams. They both talked in the quietness of the summer night, and one or perhaps both of them talked about how they should make it a practice and eventually a tradition that Sundays would be destined as the family day, no matter how busy or how crazy the week may get. Sundays would be their restoration of rest, thankfulness, and appreciation to God and family. And here they were, years later, with a fulfilled promise.

Chapter 46

The kids were in the playing room, which was bigger than some people's living rooms; the grandkids watched cartoon videos or rather a cartoon video was on, while the kids laughed, screamed, and had a good time just being with each other. Every now and then, someone would cry wolf and their respective mom would kiss the boo-boo or listen to the hyped-up story, make all the necessary faces at the right inflections, and then send them back into the battlefield of muffins. The adults, the men, would be in one room, checking out the game and talking a lot of smack as if they could get on the field or the basketball court and do a better job than the players. That was a men's subculture and women were not allowed. Adult men still acted like young boys, while the women were in another room, talking about everything under the sun from A to Z and anything in between, things like fashions, the latest soap operas, and home improvement projects or nightly shows such as *Grace Anatomy*.

Having to walk into that room was like walking in on a soap opera itself. The atmosphere would be festive as the men in one room would yell and shout at the games, while the women would laugh and shriek at the latest gossip. The two blended together and created such a wonderful symmetry of beauty—a symphony of harmonious unity as the latest in contemporary Gospel Christian music played, filling the air and adding on to the festive moment.

As the two groups came together into the large living room on that particular Sunday, chatting, talking, and laughing with each other, Jonathan asked no one in particular where Shawn was. The group stopped talking to consider the question; some responded with shrugs, while others just said they didn't know and turned and continued where they left off at with their conversations. Jonathan got up and strolled nonchalantly into the kitchen area, easing from the others. Travis and Roberta, knowing their children very well, looked at each other as Travis gave Roberta a quick nod of the head in the direction of the kitchen. She knew immediately that one of the adult kids, as she referred to them, was like a heat-seeking missile heading into the kitchen to do a little taste testing. The funny thing about Jonathan that still held true today, and that was, the boy was never smooth. He would always do something to give away what he was up to. Roberta Cook received the signal from her husband whom she referred to as smoke and he referred to her as fire. She slowly walked up behind Jonathan, just watching her son rub his hands together and saying to himself how good the food smelled and getting happy that he was about to get a pre-taste so he thought. The others, picking up on the hand signals from Travis and Roberta, knew that Jonathan was about to get busted as they all went to get a better view of all of this, without giving anything away. They held their breaths from laughing and just watched.

Jonathan thought about creating a distraction as he lifted the lids of the pots on the stove. "So, has anyone heard from Shawn?" No one responded, so Jonathan thought they were into whatever they were doing and that Mom and Dad were somewhere since they did not answer either. Therefore, Jonathan came to the conclusion that he was home free. With each lid he lifted, he released a sound of satisfaction and put the pot lid back on the pot gently, but it wasn't what his nose was looking for. But when he came to the last pot, Jonathan knew he had hit the pot of gold. He thanked his nose for not deceiving him. Jonathan was excited, but he knew this wasn't the time to get too excited, so he knew he needed another distraction. The inflection of his voice went up a notch, "Has anyone heard from Shawn?" Jonathan waited for a reply, but no one responded. He assumed that they were too busy doing whatever they were doing. He almost did a happy dance when he lifted the lid off the pot, but as the lid hit the pot, making a cling sound, Jonathan froze, listening to the sounds or voices of anyone who may have heard the cling. Thankfully, no one had heard it, so he continued his happy dance. He reached into the pot and pulled out a nice piece of boneless beef rib. Then his mouth opened wide, bringing the rib to his mouth. There was then a *slap* right on the back of his head. Jonathan, in total surprise, dropped the piece back in the pot.

His mother said with satisfaction, "All clear smoke, operation busted completed." Travis Cook responded likewise with satisfaction, "10-4, good job, fire." All the others busted out laughing, pointing at Jonathan while making comments about getting food out of the pots being like breaking out of maxim prison. Jonathan went back to join the rest, feeling a bit embarrassed of getting caught but laughed as well at his greedy self.

"Now, to answer your so-called question of concern," That was Roberta Cook with her hands on her hips, talking to the back of Jonathan's head as he slowly made his way to the group, "yes, he's coming. He's bringing his friend, we hope so, but we're not sure. But one thing we are sure of is that is he's coming." Roberta Cook looked at her youngest son with those eyes that went right through you. Jonathan could do nothing but nod his head, while the others were holding their laughter, which came out in mouth-covering spurts. Roberta Cook's eyes pan all of them. "I hope I answered everyone's question, because I know Jonathan wasn't the only one who wanted to know that answer. Are there any other questions?" They all quickly said in unison a resounding no. Roberta said, "Good." She then looked at her husband. Travis gave her a wink. Roberta smiled and gave Travis a quick wink in return. The group resumed their girl group, and the guys went back to the game in the other room. Alicia, Joanne, and Kelly were talking about the latest gossip from the different magazines to stuff on their jobs; wherever the gossip train went they rode it.

Kelly, the middle one of the sisters, talked about the latest juice on her job, which involved a guy whom all the women seemed to flock over, "I just don't see it. I mean I'm not taking anything away from the brother. He is good looking, but I don't think he's worth all that drama. You know what I mean?"

Alicia, the youngest of the girls, jumped in, "Yeah, I don't understand why sisters trip like that. I mean, how a brother looks is just one aspect of that man. What's up with the rest of the categories? Homeboy better have more ammunition in his arsenal than that."

Joanna responded, "Well, that's why some of those crazy talk shows exist. If it wasn't for these crazy lives, these shows would not be around."

The sisters laughed at that, agreeing. Roberta came in and inquired what was so funny. The sisters clued their mother on the topic. Roberta pulled up a seat and got into the thick of the conversation as well. The women were talking, laughing, and shrieking as the topics became more and more intense about women versus men.

While the women were laughing and giving each other high fives, Jonathan and Malcolm walked in the group, joining the women. "Wait a minute, hold up." That was Jonathan. The laughter came to a streaking halt as the women looked at Jonathan as if he had lost his mind or as if he was from another planet. He continued, "How can you guys sit up here talk or rather trash sisters and brothers as such, especially your own sisters? Has it ever occurred to you how some girls like their rough necks, their thugs, and even their hood boys?"

Alicia told Jonathan and Malcolm jokingly to go back with the guys; the other girls laughed and agreed with her. "Let him finish," came the resounding voice of Alicia, surrounded by Kelly and Joanna's husbands as Jonathan smiled with confidence as the Calvary arrived, and he continued with strong confidence, "Listen, guys will always dog out women and play the game to the hilt."

Roberta Cook chimed in, "All my boys better always remember that you treat a woman with respect because you have a mother that has always been treated with respect, and you learn from that." Jonathan rolled his eyes because of the interruption. His mother noticed the eye-rolling gesture. "You want to keep those things in your head a little while longer, right?"

The group laughed at that, and Jonathan laughed as well as he continued, "Have you ever asked yourself why some girls like guys like that, you know, the ones that will treat them like doo-doo, instead of well-educated and sophisticated guys like myself and Malcolm. We both have good jobs and nice rods and got it together for the most part." Malcolm agreed with his brother.

The women pretended to gag, and someone mentioned that Jonathan loved tooting that horn of his. The men rooted Jonathan on giving him kudos and daps. All three sisters were addressing Jonathan's statement.

Kelly, the oldest of the three, spoke up, "It's a phase some of us girls go through."

Alicia had a look of surprise. "Us girls?"

Alicia said in a way to have her sister to retract the phrase, but Kelly continued, "That's right, Alicia, some of us girls."

Malcolm jumped in, "Hold up a minute. You mean some of us in the sense of representation and not participation, correct? Because I know you're not talking about the 'us' as being a part of the us, right?"

Kelly just made a sound as if to say, you just don't know, and Jonathan pitched in, "You must have done it on another planet or on a sneak tip, because you know Mom and Dad, smoke and fire, would have become your worst nightmare."

Everyone started laughing, even Kelly, as she said, "OK, smarty, not us as in me, but some of the girls I hung out with, and to this day, every single one regrets the decision they've made, but the damage is done, and none of them are with any of those losers today." The other women just shook their heads, feeling sorry for those women who wasted all that time and came up with nothing.

Joanna's husband, Will, spoke, "You see, this is the part that escapes me." Will paused for effect and continued, "Why go that route? Why do these women go that route? Haven't they learned from their fellow sisters? What do they think they are going to do differently?"

David, Kelly's husband, jumped in, "Or perhaps, they are curious about the rumor or the legend of the thug or hood boy, you know, whatever you want to call them. These girls have this fantasy that the sex is different, that living on the edge is exciting, that major break-your-face attitude is the bomb and then reality hits. They are not treated like young ladies but bitches." David looked at Mrs. Cook. "Mom, pardon me." Roberta Cook nodded her head in a gesture of pardon as David continued, "The sad thing is that this behavior affects everyone they come in contact with, even their children. I just don't understand who in their right mind wants to live like that." And David shook his head in disgust.

That's when Alicia jumped in, "Well, if those women could find real men that would act like men—"

Malcolm interrupted his sister, "What do you mean act like men, so I guess the thugs that they had chosen are real men, so you say."

Kelly added, "No, Alicia got a point. I see where she is coming from."

Kelly's husband, David, spoke up, "Well, then explain, because I am confused, and I am a man, so what is the deal, ladies—"

Joanna broke in, "You ladies—"

David continued, this time, with more fervency, "That's what I said. You ladies, for one, you women don't know what you want. And you don't know for the most part how to get it, or maybe you do, but you don't know how to keep it. You just don't know what to do with it."

Alicia added, "Oh really? Is that so? Well, thank you for telling us your sex life, David." Everyone laughed, including his wife, Kelly, as Alicia continued, "So a word to the wise and foolish: don't lump what you hump."

All laughed as David looked around for male support, but Will, Jonathan, and Malcolm were silent as they made a sign that it was getting hot in there. That brought more laugher. David was getting ready to counteract when the doorbell rang. Mrs. Cook, smiling, told them to carry on knowing that the women had the upper hand on the guys.

Mrs. Cook opened the door, expecting to see two people; instead, she saw Shawn standing there by himself as he kissed his mother and said, "Oh, and hi to you too, Mother." He brushed past her into the house. Mrs. Cook ignored the remark as she stuck her head a little further out of the doorway to look around and was slowly closing the door. "I am sorry, Son. I didn't mean to . . . well, I thought that you . . ."

Shawn stopped, turned toward his mother, and said, "You thought what?" Shawn looked at his mother with a bit of confusion, trying to understand what she was talking about even though he had some idea. He continued, "Oh, Mom, I'm sorry. Don't close the door. My guest had to go back to the car to get something." When the others heard that they stopped their conversation. Thank goodness for David, because the women were attacking from all fronts, including his wife as they sat there in suspense, waiting to see Shawn's special guest.

Kelly said, "Oh, she wants to make a grand entrance. I like her already. She knows how to work it."

Jonathan added, "Yep, this is the time to pay attention and take lessons, Kelly." Kelly waved her hand at Jonathan. Roberta quickly reopened the door and could not believe who was walking toward her, smiling.

Chapter 47

The only thing Roberta Cook could do was smile and say hello as Karen walked up to her and gave her a big hug and kiss. Roberta Cook reciprocated the gesture, still in a slight state of shock.

As the two women broke the embrace, Roberta said, "Karen, this is a surprise. What are you doing here? I mean you are welcome anytime. This is such a surprise. I or rather we were expecting—"

Shawn cut her off, "Well, I just wanted to surprise you, and it looks like I did. But what happened? Karen and I are just getting back from my business trip in the Bahamas."

Mrs. Cook, caught off guard, said, "Oh . . . oh . . . well, that's nice, just you and your executive secretary . . . how quaint!" Roberta cleared her throat and continued, "Karen, take off your coat, relax. You are not a stranger here. Someone come and take Karen's coat. Show you've been raised with manners."

Alicia and Jonathan looked at each other. Jonathan, taking the lead, said, "Well, you said she was family. She knows where it goes, right on the bed with the others."

Alicia laughed, and Roberta said, "Oh, a wise guy, Alicia. You could follow your brother all you want, but you know who the first to run when trouble strikes is. Your brother will leave you holding the bag in a heartbeat." They all laughed, and Mrs. Cook continued, "Shawn, your father would like to see you in the kitchen."

Mr. Cook looked up from his paper, with his glasses halfway down the bridge of his nose, and stated, "Huh, no I don't, I'm—" Roberta Cook gave her husband such a stern look he caught the point, "Ah, yeah, that's right, Shawn, I forgot. This will be quick. I just need a little help with something. Karen, excuse us for a minute."

Karen, always feeling at home when she came over, had a nice warm smile and nodded her head.

Shawn followed his father into the kitchen. As they entered the double doors to the kitchen, both of them sat down at the table, mainly used to prepare the meals. Travis Cook smiled and looked at his son, and Shawn returned the warm gesture.

Travis began, "Look, Son, you know, I'm not one who tries to interfere with my children's decisions . . . unless necessary . . ."

Mr. Cook cleared his throat while Shawn looked on in concern, waiting for his father to continue, "OK, Pops, what's going on? What's with the secret meeting?"

Mr. Cook sat down and gestured for Shawn to pull up a chair, which he did and sat across from his father. Shawn smiled, remembering old times when he and his father would sit for hours just talking stuff. Shawn would bring up a subject or problem he'd been going through, and he and his father would discuss it. The bond between them was close, as with his other siblings, but Shawn just felt he had the edge regarding being the closest to his father. Even though his father would not admit it, Shawn felt it.

Travis Cook spoke, "Listen, personally, I am not sure what is going on, but knowing your mother, from the way she looked at you and Karen when you two walked in, I think I could put two and two together." Shawn gestured for his father to continue. "I think your mother is very concerned about how close you and Karen are. Now I'm not saying anything is wrong with it—"

A few minutes later Mr. Cook stopped talking. He was interrupted by the kitchen door, swinging open like at the OK Corral, but he wanted to make sure that it wasn't Karen coming in to get something to help out.

But it wasn't Karen, it was Shawn's mother. Apparently, she heard some of the conversation; at least, the point where Shawn's father said he didn't see anything wrong with it and that's where she picked up the ball. "Travis Cook, how can you sit there and say you feel that nothing is wrong? It's not only the idea that it's wrong. Shawn, it's not level headed business to have your executive secretary going out with you. What message are you trying to give? Plus, whatever happened to the young lady from your restaurant? Is Karen on the rebound or something? What is going on?"

Shawn looked at his mother with all seriousness. "Mom, Karen and I are friends. She's not on the rebound, and secondly, she and I have an understanding. She works for me. It's all business, plus, even if she was the one I chose to be with, it's my call, don't you think?"

Shawn's father stepped in before Shawn's mother could respond. From the way it looked, Roberta Cook was ready to rumble. "Ooo-kay," that was Shawn's father as he continued, "tell us about this young lady you met at the restaurant."

Shawn's expression changed like from night to day. He had such a bright smile. "Mom and Dad, you guys are going to like her. I mean she has the full package. She's smart, intelligent, beautiful, has a nice career job with the government, and independent and fine. I really like her. I feel a strong bond and connection like I never had before for any woman. Mom, I think this is the one."

Shawn's mother was very poised and calm. She said to him, "Shawn, how can you say all of this and you only met the woman a few times? And as far as I understand from a little bird, the first two meetings weren't smooth at all. I don't know about the others, and secondly, how can you check out the merchandise in one store and hang out in Karen's candy store?"

Shawn stood up and smiled. "Mom, like I said, I may be in Karen's candy store, using your metaphor, but I haven't tasted or tested the candy, and to be honest with you, I have no desire to do so. I wish you can understand that. What Karen and I have is special. I can't explain it. Karen is finer than fine. Look at her, she should be on the cover of your top magazines, but there is nothing here." Shawn touched his chest the area of his heart as he continued, "At least sexually, but I tell you the truth, she is the best friend a man could ever have. I wouldn't ruin that or mar that with sexual pleasure. No matter how fine she is, her friendship means too much to me."

Shawn's mother did not know what to say, but in a way, by the look on her face, she understood. Shawn noticed that the edge on his mother's face when she first came into the kitchen was slowly dissipating. He took advantage of the moment. "I wish I could explain what my heart really feels like. When it comes to Serenity, I never felt like this for any woman."

Travis Cook looked at his wife and said, "I think I know what you are talking about, Son. Your mother played hard to get also, but I never gave up. She made me jump hoops, but I would have jumped over the sun, stars, and the moon if I had the ability." Travis walked over to his wife and held her hand to his heart. Roberta just smiled with tears in her eyes as Travis Cook continued, "Son, if you love her, go after her and don't stop until you get the prize . . . that's what I did."

Shawn looked at his mother, who could only say to him to be careful. They all hugged, and his mother said, "Now come on, we have some hungry folks out there." Shawn and his father, at the same time, rubbed their stomachs and laughed.

Chapter 48

Sandra was going through Serenity's closet to find something for her to wear for her big date with Shawn. She wasn't looking for something that would make a statement, but something that would knock the socks off his feet—something that would cause him to want to grab her but realize that he can't touch the merchandise—something tantalizing and mesmerizing—something that would keep his Long John silver at attention, but she was having no such luck as she raked the conservative clothes from side to side. What started out as a fun task was becoming very frustrating.

Sandra said, "Why do you wait to the last minute to find something? I had a hot date tonight, well scratch that, the brother was tight with the Benjamin's, yet I bet he was going to want this Mary Jane."

Serenity was feeling bad. "I'm sorry, Sandra. I appreciate it so much. You are true blue." She hugged Sandra, who pretended she didn't like it, but deep down, she loved every minute of it. Sandra went back to the task of looking for something for her best friend to wear. She tried everything: combinations, mismatches, but it all resulted with the same conclusion—frustration. "Serenity, where are you and Shawn going? Look at your gear! All I see is business stuff and even those are dress suits or skirts that go beyond the knees. Hello . . . , come out of the ice age into show-a-little-skin age. No wonder I never saw you in something sexy or appealing. Remember, if you can't give honey, you won't attract the bees."

Serenity stopped looking for something to wear and looked at Sandra. "News flash, for one, I am a business career woman, and not a career slut, who works in a conservative business environment. I want to be referred to as the office supervisor, and not the office tramp, and if I wanted to show skin as you said, I reserve that for the beach, and not the office."

Sandra playfully reacted to Serenity tirade as if she was shocked by her words. "So, Ms. Powers, what are you saying or trying to imply? Are you calling me a slut or tramp or both?" Sandra laughed at her own voice makeover as Serenity continued, "Oh, by the way, what size shoes do you wear?" Serenity realized that one thing Sandra could not resist was a conversation on shoes. The girl's closet looked like an outlet store for DSM as she was eagerly prepared to discuss the answer, but Serenity cut her off before she could get going, "Well, I just wanted to say . . . if the shoes fit, then you shouldn't have a problem getting them on, and from what I can see, those shoes are fitting very well." Serenity laughed, and Sandra mocked the way Serenity was laughing. Serenity finally stopped laughing, not at her statement, but at the way her best friend was mocking her.

She calmed down to say, "Girl, you know I am only playing, but on a real tip, I have to admit you do wear some very interesting stuff, but then there are times when I just sit back and wonder, why does she bother to put anything on? You display all your stuff and leave nothing for the imagination."

Sandra waved her hand at Serenity and told her playfully that she was lying. Both women laughed, and Sandra added, "Just admit it, you are outdated."

Serenity said with her hand in a stop position, "Whatever hater, you just need to get in the game, girl." The two laughed like teenagers, but in reality, Serenity knew that Sandra was right. She really didn't have date clothes. It was all business attire.

Sandra seemed to have read her mind. "Look, Serenity, don't trip, girl. You know I am going to hook you up."

Serenity didn't know what to say. She knew if Sandra brought something, she better hold her applause until she saw what was in that bag, because anything could come out of that bag. So Serenity swallowed and braced herself.

Chapter 49

Sandra reached in the bag and pulled out a beautiful two-piece outfit. Serenity could tell that the skirt was going to be a little short, and the top, she could tell, was going to show off some cleavage, but compared to Sandra's wardrobe, this was superconservative.

Sandra looked at Serenity for a brief moment and finally said, "Well, what do you think? Go ahead and try it on."

Serenity looked at the outfit and back at Sandra and said, "Wow!"

Sandra smiled, knowing she had done well. "I decided on burgundy because red would have looked as if you want some. However, burgundy says, I'll give it, but you have to work for it, you know, earn it. I like to call it a tease color and, believe me, by the time the night ends you will have this man eating out of your hands. That's if you play this right."

Serenity nervously smiled and then turned a little more serious. "Why is it the things between male and female always seem like a battle to you? I mean you make this sound as if you are preparing me for war or something . . ." Serenity was now pacing her bedroom as she stopped, looking at her friend.

Sandra just blinked rapidly a few times and said, "Thud, so what's the problem?"

Serenity said, "What's the problem? Sandra, listen to me. I don't want to feel as if I'm in a fight. Why can't I approach this rationally?"

Sandra jumped up from the bed as if she had been shot out of a cannon. "Because men, these hunters by nature, think that we are game, and they are trying to score points—a notch on their wall. Listen, honey, it is a battle. It has always been and always will be a battle. That's their nature, to bag the game, and baby, whether you like it or not, you are in the game."

Serenity was speechless as Sandra continued, "Listen, I am trying to school you. I'm trying to teach you how to play the game."

Serenity feeling overwhelmed, put her head down into her hands, and shook her head as she thought that this was a bit too much, but then, on the other hand, she was more than aware that most, if not all of Sandra's experience with men had been negative. She had not found a decent guy and when she came across one or two, they were either married or they were not interested in a single mother of two—two beautiful children from two different daddies. Many would think she was loose and quick to spread her wings, but that wasn't the case. In each case, she had spent time and energy to make those relationships work, putting her emotions out there on empty promises—and the results—she was hurt, causing her heart to become hard in trusting men less and less, causing her to feel it as us against them.

Serenity felt Sandra's pain, not that she had experienced what Sandra was going through, but as her best friend, she felt her pain. But one day she would find the right one. God would make it happen. Serenity was convinced. She was lost in that thought when Sandra's voice brought through her thoughts, "Come on, girl, this is no time to be daydreaming. What are you thinking about? Are you nervous about this date? Listen, don't sweat it, you'll be fine. Now try on your outfit so we can make whatever adjustment that needs to be made." Serenity took the new outfit from Sandra, smiling as she headed to the bathroom to try it on.

The next day, Serenity arrived to work, feeling somewhat tired with a slight sniffle. If she had gone by her first impressions, she would have stayed in bed and enjoyed a day of me-hood, but she had to come in to finish up on some things. As she entered her workplace, she waved hi to no one in particular. The atmosphere was, as usual, upbeat. Serenity adhered to a strict yet fair policy of work expectations and work ethics of a set of rules she expected all her employees to follow—no exceptions. She knew that her employees viewed her as being tough and hard, but what they appreciated about her was her fairness; however, they felt sorry about how Serenity treated Sandra, but not sorry enough to complain or intervene on her behalf. They talked among themselves on how they felt Sandra was overworked, but little did they know, that all of it, Serenity's tough attitude, Sandra being overworked was all a front so Serenity could keep an air of respect and integrity in the workplace, and it had worked since Serenity started at her position.

Sandra watched Serenity sniffle and wipe her nose. "Excuse me, Ms. Powers, when you have a minute, may I speak with you?" Serenity already knew what Sandra wanted to discuss and tried to get Sandra to say whatever she had to say in front of the others. She knew Sandra would have to modify her question and come off sounding professional, instead of coming off behind closed doors letting all her ghetto behavior come out. Serenity wasn't in the mood to deal with it, not just yet, but she knew she will once she woke up, because in all reality, one thing Serenity loved about Sandra was her keep-it-real side—that street talk—Serenity was not raised around it. She had seen some of the kids from the projects behave in an on-the-edge manner, and it had always intrigued her. It had always piqued her curiosity, but she had never associated herself with that kind of behavior.

Sandra, keeping a few paces in front of Serenity, countered, "In private, please, perhaps in your office, if you don't mind."

Serenity countered, "Sure, but how about sometime this—"

Sandra cut Serenity off, "Pardon me for cutting you off, Ms. Powers, but my issue is urgent and personal." Sandra, with her back facing her coworkers, made a face at Serenity that could be summed up as a cocky smirk and had the nerve to wink at her as if to say top that. One of Serenity's rules was she would not see anyone before eleven o'clock, and Sandra knew this but decided to push the card, just to show she could, and on top of that, to use the excuse for personal reasons was cunning, crafty, creative and, of course, Sandra. Serenity realized that Sandra had won the battle as she gave a slight nod as to say touché. "Very well, come Ms. Beck, you have two minutes."

Serenity walked professionally in front of Sandra. Sandra humbly followed as she entered the office after Serenity and asked, "May I close the door, Ms. Powers?" Serenity, playing her role to the hilt for all its worth, said, "Ms. Beck, you have a minute and fifty seconds. If you want everyone to hear your business, then leave the door open. If you want privacy, then shut the door. You have a minute and thirty seconds."

Sandra, looking so grateful, closed the door as the other workers stopped what they were doing to see the drama unfold, thankful that it wasn't them in Sandra's place. They whispered among themselves *"Poor Sandra"* and other things, such as "She doesn't deserve such treatment," yet others said, "It comes with the territory. She makes enough money." Then one of them, whose name was Debra, said, "That's true. Oh well, better her than me. Do you know what I'm saying?" The others chimed in, "I hear ya" and turned back to the computers and started working again as if whatever sympathy that was expressed was so quickly forgotten.

Meanwhile, behind closed doors, Sandra had closed the door and turned to face Serenity with a serious look. She said, "Are you finished with your

Oscar performance, if they only knew?" Serenity gave Sandra a stern look as a warning to keep her mouth shut, and Sandra added, "Oh, stop it. I blow your cover. I mess up a good thing, but you sure know how to milk a situation."

Serenity, with those innocent eyes, said, "What happened?"

Sandra, mocking Serenity's voice in a cartoon like voice, said, "*What happened?* You know what happened. What was all of that stuff back there? You see, Serenity, you are taking this thing way too serious, and you know it—treating and talking to me like a second-class citizen—that wasn't cool, and you know it." Sandra acted as if she was serious, but gave in to a big smile when she looked at Serenity. Serenity sniffled and wiped her nose, while Sandra looked on with astonishment and said, "And what was that?" Serenity sniffled and walked past Sandra. Sandra looked at Serenity dumbfounded. "Oh no, you don't. Is there any sense of dignity in you? You need to stop it right now, Serenity."

Serenity looked at Sandra, did her sniffle, wiped her nose, and said with annoyance, "Stop what?"

Sandra said, "Don't even play it off, you know what." Sandra looked at Serenity with obvious suspicion. "Don't you dare sabotage this date tonight!" Serenity wiped her nose, looking at Sandra with a sniffle. "And stop doing that. You are not earning any sympathy points from me," said Sandra.

Serenity looked at Sandra and said, "Sabotage? I went to bed like this. I don't know what happened."

Sandra walked over to Serenity. "I know what happened . . . it's called chickening out, chicken. It's also called being a good actor, because when I left you last night, you were finer than fine, so stop it."

Serenity pouted and stomped her foot like a spoiled child. "I haven't been on a date in God knows when, and now with a high-profile sought-after brother. Come on, Sandra, I can't do it." Serenity sniffled, looking at Sandra with sad eyes.

Sandra waved her hand at her. "Listen, save it for someone that doesn't know you as well as I do. The only thing, rubbing your nose so much is going to do is make it sore. You better carry your Vaseline. You may need it to kill two birds with one stone."

Sandra laughed. Serenity made an unpleasant face, looking at Sandra and said, "You are so nasty, anyway, you could dismiss that thought. That's not going to happen."

Sandra said dismissively, "Whatever! Anyway, Serenity, you are going."

Serenity chuckled and said, "What are you, my mother now? Now I have two mommies."

Sandra replied with a sassy attitude, "Oh well, deal with it. However you want to slice it, look at it, it all boils down to the same answer. You are going out on this date, Serenity."

Serenity smiled at Sandra's rendition of being her mother, but despite the smile, she looked at Sandra and was ready to let off a barrage verbal retaliation when there was a knock at her door. Both ladies turned to look at the door. Serenity was getting ready to tell whoever it was to come back in ten minutes, because what she was about to say to her friend was going to only take two minutes, and the rest of the time, Sandra could talk to the hand or her backside, whichever she preferred.

However, Sandra, knowing her best friend like a close sister, quickly seized the opportunity to counter Serenity's move. "Come in."

Serenity, in total surprise, looked at Sandra and mouthed to her that this was her office. Sandra, in turn, stuck her tongue out at Serenity to rub in the victory as her office door slowly opened. Serenity whispered to Sandra, "This isn't over."

Sandra returned fire and whispered in a Valley girl vernacular with gestures and the whole bit, "Whatever!"

The door opened and a young man with some kind of delivery slogan uniform entered, carrying a long box with a very colorful card. The young man said, "I have a message for a Ms. Serenity Powers." The young man looked from Sandra to Serenity, trying to figure out which one was Serenity. Sandra took the box, looked at Serenity, and told her to tip the man.

Whether she realized it or not, Serenity's mouth dropped wide open, very briefly, as she dug into her purse and tipped the young man. The young man looked at what was given to him and was very happy. He thanked Sandra for the generous tip and went about his business.

Serenity looked at Sandra, shaking her head, and said, "You are unbelievable." Sandra looked at Serenity dumbfounded, and Serenity said, "Don't give me that 'I don't know what you are talking about look.'" Serenity walked over to her desk and picked up the nameplate on the desk. "See, my office." She picked up the envelope with the card inside and said, "Whatever is in there is my box, and whatever is in this envelope belongs to me. This is not a takeover." Serenity rolled her eyes and shook her head.

Sandra said, "You know you love me. You wouldn't have it any other way." Serenity knew deep down that Sandra, as much of a pain in her butt, was right. She was a friend to the end. She looked at Sandra. "Well, you took over my office, you took over my delivery, and you took over my purse, so you might as well go all the way and open my box. Why spoil a good track record!" Serenity acted as if she was annoyed, but Sandra knew better.

Sandra opened the box very cautiously and slowly, peaking instead of ripping the lid off the box. The excitement of wanting to know what was in the box showed all over Serenity's face. Sandra looked with awe at what was in the box. She was speechless. Serenity took the box from her and looked inside. She herself was speechless as she reached in and took out a beautiful gold necklace and a gold bracelet. Serenity placed her hand to her mouth as tears glistened from her eyes; the gold set was beautiful. Serenity wiped a tear from her eyes, and she said loud enough for Sandra to hear, "Who would send me such a gift? My parents would do something like this, but it's not my birthday, and Eric, well, as sweet as a little brother he is, he isn't that sweet." Serenity laughed as she stared at the present. Sandra chuckled as well.

Sandra picked up the card that came with the gold set while Serenity tried to figure out who sent her the gold necklace and bracelet. Sandra began reading the letter, *"Serenity, my darling."* Sandra made an endearing sound, while Serenity put her hands on her hips and gave Sandra a hard glaring look. Sandra said, "Well, I can't help it if this mystery man is a romancer."

Serenity looked at Sandra with a look of astonishment and said, "Now you are an expert on romance. If you can't read it, give it to me." She reached for the letter, but Sandra swat playfully at her hand and told Serenity in Oscar Hollywood fashion that she could do it. Serenity smiled and shook her head at her friend's crazy attitude. Sandra was looking on the letter where she left off, found the spot, and continued, "Let's see, OK." *"If I had to go to Africa in search for these diamonds, I would've."* Sandra once again, in Hollywood fashion, looked up at the ceiling as if she was swooned by the words and used the letter to fan herself. Serenity cleared her throat and that brought Sandra out of her overacting scene. Sandra continued with a big grin on her face. Serenity knew that she was really enjoying this, but who was this mystery person? "Let's see, OK, OK here we go." " . . . *go to Africa to have this ring placed on your beautiful finger and this necklace placed around your gorgeous neck, I would have made the journey until I would have accomplished my search. If I had to pick these roses from a special bush and endure whatever pain from their thorns, it would have been worth the sacrifice. Looking forward to Friday night. Please wear these items of my love. They are a token and a symbol of the start of our friendship. Until then . . . mi' amour. Shawn Cook."*

Sandra playfully collapsed in the chair, fanning herself frantically, and said to Serenity, "Call the fire department. I feel as if I am on fire. Girl, if you don't feel that, then you are either comatose or gay, because this man . . ." Sandra stopped, shook her head, and continued, "well, if that's his entrance, I wonder what else he has up his sleeve, and if the start is this good, homeboy's exit must be out of this universe and freak the world. Girl, let me say friend to friend . . . you better not mess this up, or I'm going to put my foot so high up your butt, not even the 'jaws of life' would be able to pull it out. Sen, this is a good man . . . with good money. Girl, this is your chance to get rich and . . ."

Serenity held up her hand, "Sandra, you and I know I'm not into that stuff." Sandra made a face as Serenity continued, somewhat a little more forceful, "Don't give me that look. You know how I am, so don't go there. I mean his money is not important to me, and if he's the stuck-up type, well, I could take it or leave it, no biggie."

Sandra smiled at Serenity and said, "Well, do me a favor. Make sure you let me know when you are done with him or whatever the case maybe. I don't mind eating the leftovers. I don't mind eating, in this case, period." Sandra had one of her horny smiles.

Serenity looked at Sandra and said, "You are so nasty."

Sandra, playing innocent, mouthed the words "who me." "Come on, Serenity, all seriousness, aren't you a little excited?"

Serenity thought about the question and then proceeded to answer, "Sandra, listen, I am excited, but you can't buy me with gifts and flowers and . . ." She picked up the necklace and rings and . . .

Sandra said, "Girl, you must have a serious brain defect, because if homeboy wanted to wine and dine me and shower me with gifts, homeboy could buy me anytime. Serenity, I may be poor at relationships, but I am good at other people relationships, and I am telling you, I feel it, girl. This man is the right one. I mean this guy is smooth. He's like secondhand smoke."

Serenity could not resist. "What do you mean?"

Sandra said, "I am feeling the affect."

Serenity rolled her eyes and playfully told Sandra that she was stupid. Sandra was on a roll, continuing, "Plus, the man speaks Spanish, the language of passion."

Serenity cut her eyes at Sandra. "Where have you been getting your info from, girl? How do you know the man speaks Spanish just because he said *Mi Amour?*"

Sandra shrugged her shoulders. "Maybe you are right. But let me tell you, if homeboy speaks Spanish, you have a multi-lingual lovemaking boyfriend, and if he's good, you can be on your way of learning another language—the language of passion."

Serenity didn't know why she was even dealing with Sandra. She knew in a funny way that Sandra wasn't wrapped too tight, but she figured what the heck. "For one, let's set this for the record. Mr. Cook is not my boyfriend, and number two, how can I learn Spanish by making love to someone who speaks Spanish?"

Sandra smiled said it all as if she was saying in her smile I thought you'd never ask, and Serenity knew what that smile meant. It meant she was like an insect caught in the web of a spider, and Sandra was that spider. Sandra smiled from ear to ear and said, "Well, before you know it, if he's that good, you'll be calling him Poppy, and if he's real good, you'll be saying it with passion, like Ooo Poppy, and if he's really at the right—"

Serenity held up her hand to cut Sandra off. "I get the point, my twisted sister." Both Serenity and Sandra laughed, and Serenity looked at her watch. "Sandra, oh my goodness, do you know how long you've been in here? Listen, I let you know my decision on Mr. Cook. The jury is still debating. We'll get together later. I am sure I will know by then."

Sandra, with playful pleading eyes, said, "Come on, Serenity. I am more than certain all of this is not this man's way of trying to buy you. I could feel it deep down that this is his style. This is his way."

Serenity saw the seriousness on her friend's face. "Well, so far I am not impressed. That's strike one . . . but I tell you what, I'll give Mr. Rich and Famous a chance. I am a woman of my word."

Sandra jumped up and down as if she was going out. That's what Serenity loved about her friend. She was always concerned about her happiness, instead of her own. *A friend to the end,* Serenity thought as Sandra gathered her things to head back to her desk.

Chapter 50

Shawn and his boys just got finished playing a couple of games of 3 on 3.

Shawn's best friend, Frank, said, "Yo, C-4 what's up? You played as if your life depended on it, what's up with that?"

Marcus jumped in, "Tell me about it. Yo, C you have the advantage. You work out every day, while we working folks work every day without such perks." Marcus playfully pushed Shawn's head, and they all laughed.

"Listen, we can't keep up with you." That was Hector.

Frank added, "He's right, Shawn." Shawn and his friends were getting dressed in the locker room as Frank continued, "You were unstoppable. You were a total monster, what's up? You can't be playing as if you are trying out for the Knicks. I am here to get in shape, but to deal with you on that level . . ."

Frank shook his head, and Marcus finished for Frank, "It's going to take me a few weeks, so have fun while you can. I am going to shut that jump shot down."

Shawn laughed. "We'll see." Shawn, fixing his tie while looking in the mirror, said, "I'm good. I just want to play hard, plus, well, I'm just a bit nervous about this date coming up this week. I want to make sure everything works out. This woman is . . . man, I can't even describe her."

Frank, standing next to Shawn, looking in the mirror while the others fixing their ties, said, "You nervous? Get out of here." Looking in the mirror that went from one end of the locker room to about halfway of the other side of the locker room, Frank and the others made a variety of male bravado comments. Shawn smiled.

Marcus said, "Now hold up. You're telling me that you C-4, aka Romeo, has met someone that has given you a run for your money? Oh, how the ties have turned!"

The others laughed and slapped each other with high fives.

James followed up with what Marcus said, "C-4, I hope this one is better than the last one. You guys remember that last one, right?" All the guys made an agreeable moaning sound.

Shawn thought as he put on his Windbreaker jacket and said, "Oh yeah, you're talking about Christina. Man, she was fine, but, man, did she have some issues."

James, coming out of the bathroom area, interjected, "Issues, come on, C-4, you are being nice. From what I can remember, I don't know about the others, but from what I remember, the girl was into every scam under the sun. She had no shame to her game."

They all shook their heads remembering, and Shawn said, "Yeah, you guys are right. I was blind sighted by her beauty and charm. If it wasn't for Frank catching her trying to run a scam on getting my money . . . I would have been in some deep-fry stuff."

Frank said, "Well, homegirl had a gig, working it 24-7 and nine to five and an extensive contract of five to ten." Frank started doing the music to the game show *Jeopardy* and acting like the host. "Does anyone know the answer?" Mike pretended to press a panel button to take a crack at the question, while Frank, still in the host character, said, "Yes, Mike."

Mike, acting like a nervous contestant, said, "Uh, what is Rikers Island?"

Frank said in that Alex Kubec voice, "Yes, that is correct."

All the guys laughed as they were fully dressed and ready to head out. They gave Shawn a dap-and-shoulder-to-shoulder touch and made plans to meet next week, the day after Thanksgiving and headed out. Frank, as usual, stayed behind with Shawn, just like it had always been ever since second grade in elementary school.

Shawn and Frank had met in the second grade, and the two had been like twins ever since even though the two were from different worlds, so to speak. Their vast differences did not interfere with the strong bond and connection they had formed. Shawn had grown up with well-educated, motivated parents who pushed all their children to excel at being the best at what they wanted to do or be in life. Travis and Roberta Cook would buy their children whatever was needed to help them form their dreams, and all of their children were expected to do at least five hours a week in the library. The Cooks had a no-nonsense policy.

However, Frank had experienced the darker side of negative parenting—that ugly side—the one you read about in the newspaper or end up hearing on the six o'clock news or the one that Child Welfare always seem to either miss or be at your door just a little too late, investigating rumors and reports of violent arguments and the sound of furniture being thrown, even threats of killing or hurting someone in the household. In Frank's case, it was his father that allegedly did all of those things. Nothing was ever proven, and his mother would always deny such rumors or reports—so-called protecting her children from being taken away—while the violence and nonsense continued.

Frank's father was one of those pop-up and pop-out dads. Whenever he wanted to pop-in, he would show up without any clue or idea, and he would just pop back in into their lives. He would come in like Santa Claus with all the gifts and surprises. Can you imagine Christmas several times throughout the year? Yet he would leave like Satan, and no one ever knew when he would return. However, one thing Frank remembered of his father was that he would always carry loads of cash and at least two handguns, which at the time Frank thought was cool. Frank's father would let him even touch and hold the guns while his mother would plead for him not to have their son do that. Frank's father would always say that Frank was a young man and had to learn what life was about. But his mother had to constantly tell his father that Frank was not a young man and that he was just a young child in the second grade.

Frank could recall how his parents used to have some big arguments about his father's lifestyle. There were nights when Frank would hear his mother cry and plead and beg his father to stop the things he was doing and get a regular job, and to that very day, Frank remembered his father's response.

He would say, "A regular job, woman, are you crazy? If I had a regular job, your ass wouldn't have all of this. You are never satisfied. You are such an ungrateful bitch, plus, I never see you complain when I give you money to buy whatever you want. Plus, I am in love with Franklin and Benjamin and the rest of my money train."

Frank didn't understand then what his father was talking about, but he understands now. He understood that his father did what he had to do to in order to not be held down by the system, but he went about it the wrong way. He knew the money he was making a regular job could not touch that, especially when most of it would end up in Uncle Sam's deep pockets. However, in the long run, Frank knew his father was no good, despite the fact he kept money in the house and also put all of their lives in danger.

His father may have been considered uneducated by society's standard, but in his world, where he had to hustle and bustle, he held a PhD in street-ology and thug-ology. He did not know how to accept or give love, but he knew how to get whatever he wanted by whatever means necessary. Frank remembered how beautiful his mother was when he was younger and how his father's popping in and popping out of her life put her social life on hold. She was a very attractive woman that whenever she walked outside, men, whatever they were doing, would stop to get a good look at that Nubian queen. She walked with such feminine class with her high heels and head held high, enough to give a sense of pride. She was not prideful, as in the case of being stuck up or snobbish. In the summer, she would show off those beautiful legs with her perfectly pedicured feet, and when the weather became cooler and colder, she wore outfits that would cling to her curvy hips. She had a beautiful olive skin with her shoulder-length hair and beautiful light brown eyes that would change color when the sun would reflect off them. She was enchanting, and even now some of that enchantment was still prevalent.

Frank could vividly remember how he and his mother walked down the street and how the men would stop and look. Some would even do their catcalls, just to be corrected by another brother. He would say, "Hey, are you crazy? That's that mad dog's woman." The person would apologize to no end, even volunteer to do whatever was needed, just to make sure word did not get back to Frank's father. It was ironic, but at the time Frank was impressed with that kind of power, but as he grew older, he realized that that wasn't power but a disrespectful fear. As Frank pondered it today, if that person was alone with his mother, he would have done what he wanted to do and freak the mad dog. But for his mother, that was how it was. Her existence was boxed in. She had no life and couldn't go anywhere. He had complete control over her. Every time Frank thought about it, he would cringe and wish to God that he was old enough back then to set that son of a bitch straight and knock his lights out. Even now if he knew where that low-life scum was, he would go and take him out of his low-life misery. He had his mother so boxed in that she didn't even have enough money to move and get away, start a new life, find someone who would treat her with the respect she deserved.

Frank thought that even if his mother had a chance to move, his father would only make it difficult by withholding the money. They had money—plenty of it. The house was full with the latest comforts. His father was good at that. Frank thought, *He treated us as if we were his dolls that went inside the dollhouse. What an idiot!* So the reason she could not move or get away was that he gave her enough money to only make it for the week, and the other reason, he kept her pregnant. Frank had two siblings younger than him, and as far as he could remember, his mother was always taking care of them as well as taking care of him. However, she did rely on Frank to be the man. Even at that young age, he would help his mother take his brother and sister for doctor visits and the works. His father had all the intentions to make sure she was not going anywhere other than where she had to go. He couldn't even remember his own children's names, and Lord knows how many other brothers and sisters those were out there. Frank often thought that his father would leave two things in between his visits: the first thing was gifts, and the second thing was his sperm. Frank remembered the nights of being up into late at night, listening to his parents go at it. He didn't know what to make of all the noise at the time. He just knew when they were at it his mother would call on the Lord. He had never heard his mother call on the Lord as much. She did it more than she did in the church, and his father would say a bunch of foulmouthed stuff, but it never failed. A few weeks later, his mother would have what she called morning sickness. Frank remembered that he had his share of materialistic comforts. That was one thing Frank could say about his father. He made sure Frank always dressed in style. His father used to say, "Son, remember, always dress to impress, no matter where you go. If you look sharp, the white man will respect you and so will the ladies."

Frank's father made sure Frank dressed to the hilt. Whatever was in style, he made sure Frank had the new styles a few weeks before they came out in the stores. So as early as the third grade, Frank wore things an adult could not afford, such as gold jewelry, gold bracelets, even rings and the latest style in sneakers and shoes—the top of the line, mind you. Frank did not quite understand the significance of the clothes, jewelry, and footwear even though his mother would be upset about it. But his father was happy and proud, and to Frank that is what counted. You see in his little second-grade, seven-year-old mind, if he could make his father happy, perhaps that would convince him to stay home. So Frank went along with the fashion show and whatever else his father wanted.

Frank recalled the time when his father picked him up from school in a big pink Cadillac with all the trimmings, you know, diamonds in the back and a sunroof top. Instead of the symbol of the horse on the front hood, he had a man and woman in a very erotic position. All the kids would gather around when Frank's father would drive up with his dark sunshades on and a pink suit. Frank's father used to get out of the car and greet the kids with money sometimes—a dollar for each kid—and tell them stories about making money. His conduct and speech was many times too advanced for their young minds. He had been reproached by both the principal and vice principal to tone down his message or they would get a court order, barring him a certain feet from the school grounds. Of course, he didn't want the po-po, into his business, so he cooled out somewhat.

    All of Frank's friends thought that his father was a movie star or something bigger. Frank would play along with the misconception and tell them that his father was a big-time producer and director and that he'd worked with big top names in the industry. Many of Frank's friends would say they wished that Frank's father was their father, that he was cool and that they didn't want to be like their own fathers, but they wanted to be like Frank's father. Frank would smile wide and big and take it all in, while inside he was confused and lonely because he wished he knew more about his father, and he wished he had a real father who spent real time with him every day, and not just a few times a year.

Chapter 51

All of this had started in the second grade, and now Frank had made it to the fourth grade. He had developed a little following, a little attitude, and a chip on his shoulder. However, he still didn't quite understand his father's ways or actions, but he had come to accept it and to get whatever he could from it, since his new crew looked up to him as their leader, and Frank was a prime example. He had the skill and qualities that he no doubt picked up from his father. It was funny how Frank thought he was a bad ass, but his mother knew how to keep him in check. She wouldn't threaten him and say wait till your father gets home because no one knew when that was going to happen, so she learned early on to handle that behavior herself. Momma did not play or took any mess.

The school did not appreciate the image Frank's father was giving him. Frank's mother would go to all the parents' teachers' conferences, and time after time she was told that Frank's behavior was satisfactory. However, what he was learning from his father was not healthy, and it may affect him later on in life. Frank's mother would agree with the assessment and even try to explain as best as she could and as much as she could, but she was limited to what she could say. Too much could get them in serious trouble, so she played the game.

Frank and Shawn met one day when Frank watched Shawn's father drop him off. He gave him a hug, a Black Power handshake, and told him that he would pick him at the usual time, so Frank knew that Shawn and his father had a regular thing. Frank watched the exchange and felt the pang in his heart. He wished he had that relationship with his own pops. He sometimes dropped him off, and when he did, he would let Frank let himself out of the car, and his father, without a wave, would take off, leaving Frank there, looking and feeling the emptiness in his heart. He wouldn't even come back to pick him up.

One day, as usual, Shawn's father dropped him off. Frank used to come and wait at the same spot, just to see the exchange. He could not understand why he would put himself through such pain, but for some reason, he had to see what it could have been like if his own father would do that. Even more interesting, he had to see what it felt like to pretend if Travis Cook, Shawn's father, was his father. Frank watched as the two went through their bond exchanges, or whatever it was called. He didn't know, but he thought it was cool. Frank noticed that Shawn's father had no shame in expressing affection, and Shawn had no problem taking it all in.

However, this one time, the exchanges were made and Shawn's father got into the car, waved at his son, and drove off. Frank looked on, and one of his friends said, "Here comes Mr. Softy." The others laughed, and Frank laughed too, but deep inside, he wished he had that. Frank was becoming very upset over the idea that with all the things he had at his fingertips, one thing he did not have was the love of a father. Frank looked at his boys and told them to watch what he was about to do.

Shawn met up with some more of his friends, talking about the new *Incredible Hulk* show with that bodybuilder that played the Hulk. As they were walking past Frank and his friends, Shawn ignored them, since they had already got into some heated exchanges with Shawn and his friends. Shawn would tell his friends to ignore them. They would call Shawn mama's boy or daddy's little fag, nasty names like that, but the names did not get to Shawn. He would continue to walk having a good time with his friends, but this one particular time, Shawn was walking with his friends past Frank and his boys and that's when Frank said to his boys for them to watch what he was about to do. As Shawn walked past Frank, he stuck his leg out and tripped Shawn. Everything went flying: his books, his lunch, and his pride . . . Shawn's hot chocolate spilled on his best friend, Pricilla. Poor Pricilla was hurting and in pain from the hot chocolate. Shawn got up off the ground and ran over to Pricilla to make sure she was OK.

He turned around, very upset at Frank, and said, "That wasn't funny. This could have been more serious than what it was."

Frank walked over to Shawn and pointed his little pointer finger in Shawn's chest and said, "Mind your business, mama's boy, sweet daddy's pet. You are nothing but a nerd." Frank pointed to Pricilla and said, "That little bitch is fine."

Shawn was at the boiling point; he was steamed. Shawn was upset with the way Frank had addressed Pricilla, not to say Shawn had virgin ears, but in his circle of friends and in his household such words were taboo. He looked at Frank very hard and said, "That's not nice. Please don't call her that, please."

While Shawn was talking, Frank's friend snuck behind Shawn and got down on all fours right behind him. Frank pushed Shawn, who graciously, just like a dancer, flipped over Frank's friend and landed on his feet. The move was so smooth and cool that everyone began to clap for Shawn. Shawn took it all in and smiled to the praise and applause.

Frank became infuriated as he thought that he wasn't going to let a mama's boy outdo him. Frank looked around at those who were there. He knew he was in a bind. To let it go would cause him to lose face among his peers, but to attack would keep him in the positive light that could earn him more respect as a tough guy, and word would get back to his father that he was no punk, so Frank stepped back a few feet contemplating his choices.

Then out of nowhere, Frank went after Shawn, trying to tackle him or spear him. Shawn saw Frank coming at a good speed. He stood his ground. Frank was surprised, and he began to have second thoughts when he saw Shawn standing his ground. He did not even budge and did not show any sign of fear, but for Frank it was too late. He was already in motion, and he had set some things in motion that he could not back down. Frank didn't know what to make of Shawn's frozen immobility. Then he thought that he had scared Shawn to the extent that the nerd was frozen, even to the point he could not move. *Now I got him,* Frank thought.

Shawn stood there like a deer caught, looking at a vehicle heading its way. Frank's confidence built up more and more as he put his all into the charge. As he drew closer, Frank timed his swing as he swung his fist at Shawn. Shawn timed the swing and, at the precise moment, ducked, stepped, and moved to his right, away from Frank while always keeping his eyes on Frank. The kids once again went wild.

Frank was even more infuriated. By now a little circle had formed in the shape of a boxing ring as the other kids were chanting and shouting fight, fight, fight. Frank's cronies wanted to jump in, but they feared the other kids jumping them, so they backed off and just watched. Frank felt like a complete jerk the way he had charged Shawn and missed, but that did not stop him. He, like a bull, came charging again. This time he thought he had caught Shawn off guard as Shawn was taking a bow to the girls who had immediately thought that he was bigger than life. However, Shawn, all along, had had his eyes on Frank, so when Frank went to grab him, Shawn spun like a dancer, and with his hands, he shoved Frank hard in his back, causing him to awkwardly stumble forward looking silly as he fell tumbling to the ground. The way he fell made everyone laugh, even the guys he hung out with. Frank was so embarrassed when he heard and watched the children laugh and pointing their fingers at him. In just about two minutes, he went from being the school bully to the school punk.

The other thing that Frank heard in his head was the voice of his father in one of those what his father called man-to-man talks. Mad dog would be drinking a can of beer while Frank would have a can of root beer, and his father would tell him, "Don't ever let someone punk your ass. You better do what you have to do, because if I hear you got punk, then I am going to beat your ass myself."

Frank may have played the role of tough guy, but inside he was a really confused and scared boy. In front of the other kids, he acted tough, talked tough, and walked tough, but what these same kids did not see was that behind closed doors Frank cried himself to sleep most nights hugging his teddy bear. However, outside he had to act like a bear, and here he was in a situation where the bear was facing a wise fox, and the fox was quicker and smarter than the bear. Then Frank, the so-called bear, got up from the ground and came charging at Shawn once again. Shawn could see Frank, but Frank could only see red. He picked up momentum as he came closer to Shawn. He was like a bull. At the right moment, Shawn quickly fell to the ground on his back and used Frank's momentum against him. He timed the move perfectly as he lifted both legs in the air, close to his chest, and at the right time, got under Frank's momentum, used his legs to lift Frank off the ground, took his hands, grabbed Frank's shirt, and used both his feet and arms to swing up and back, causing Frank to fly over Shawn and land hard on his back.

Everyone could hear the impact as Frank's solid body came crashing hard on the ground. All the children, that were out there, made sounds that described how cool the move was as they slapped each other high fives. Frank, shaken up a little, was seeing this from on his back. He slowly rolled over as his friends came over to try to stop him, but Frank, very angry pushed them away, and put up his fists in a boxing style motion. Still in pain, he hobbled his way toward Shawn.

Shawn, keeping still, just looked at Frank coming toward him. The confidence he had, at the beginning, was starting to leave, but Frank kept on coming. Then he continued to hear his father's voice in his head. Frank, without preamble, walked up to Shawn and swung wild with his right arm. Shawn quickly pivot and leaned slightly back and to the left. The punch missed by a whole lot. Frank desperately swung wild with the left with a cross punch, but Shawn, this time, weaved and leaned to the right. The same results: the punch missed, making Frank look stupid. Shawn saw the opportunity—the bull's eye. When Frank missed, he left his midsection unprotected and Shawn delivered a stunning blow, right in that area. The blow sent Frank crumbling to the ground. Frank tried to get up, but the blow was too devastating.

Shawn turned and looked at Frank's friends, who were stunned. When they saw Shawn looking at them, they took off running. When Shawn turned back around to Frank, he had already gotten up. Tears streamed down his cheek as some of the girls made fun of him and called him a big crybaby. Frank could not take the teasing from his schoolmates neither the disappointment he had brought to his father. Frank, with one last urge of dignity, lunged at Shawn, surprising him as the two boys crashed to the ground, trying to punch and grab each other. The kids went really wild. Mr. Towns, the gym teacher, came running over and pushed his way through the crowd as most of the kids dispersed, not wanting to be a part of the melee.

Mr. Towns grabbed the two boys by their collars and practically dragged them to the principal's office. Mr. Towns looked at Shawn and shook his head in disappointment. Shawn put his head down, because he knew he should have exercised better control and he would not be in the mess he was in right now.

Mr. Towns had called Mr. Cook and briefly explained, but not in detail, what had happened. Frank remembered that day as the day of truth and reality. Frank thought about it often. If it wasn't for that day when Shawn beat his behind and Shawn's father came to pick him up, his life would not have changed. It was on that day his life began to change for the better. If this had not happened, Frank knew he would have been a street thug.

Anyway, Shawn's father came down to the school. That itself was amazing to Frank that somebody came, but what was really amazing was when Shawn's father arrived he did not criticize Shawn in any form of way. He just gave him a look of concern, and then he looked at Frank and noticed the marks, bruises, and scratches he had. However, his heart, already connected to Shawn, made a strong connection toward Frank. For some reason, he just felt that Frank was alone. Mr. Cook motioned to Mr. Towns to meet with him outside the office in the hall.

When Mr. Towns got there, he said to Mr. Cook, "Listen, I know Shawn did not provoke that kid. Shawn is a good boy. In order for Shawn to do such damage that other boy had to have pushed Shawn to that point."

All the time Mr. Cook was trying to get Mr. Towns to stop for one minute, but Mr. Towns continued, "Listen, Travis, I teach my students, including Shawn self-defense karate, and from what I am hearing from the other kids, Shawn did not start this fight. He was protecting himself, so don't go blaming Shawn. He's a good kid and the best karate student in my class. But I tell you what, that Frank kid is bad news. His father, Victor, 'mad dog' Cole has been such a bad influence on the boy."

Travis cringed when Mr. Towns referred to Frank as a negative influence, or as he put it, bad news. Travis said, "The boy is fine. That can be fixed. It's his father that is trash . . . Do me a favor. Contact his mother, tell her what happened, and ask her if she could meet with me this evening at the community center."

Mr. Towns looked at Travis. "Wait a minute. Do you know what you are asking . . . what do you have in mind? I heard mad dog doesn't like anyone messing with his woman."

Travis looked at Mr. Towns with a smile and said, "Listen, I am not worrying about 'mad dog.' I am trying to save his son, plus . . . if Victor decides to act the fool . . ." Travis put his arm around Mr. Towns' shoulders like buddy-to-buddy and continued, "I'll have Xavier fifth degree black belt Towns right there by my side."

From that point on, Travis Cook took Frank in and said to himself, "Welcome to the family . . . son." And Frank and Shawn became the best of friends.

Chapter 52

However, things did not transpire as quickly as Travis wanted them to. Even though Frank spent most of his time at the Cooks, he was still in a troubled environment back at his house. Travis had already met with Frank's mother, and he voiced the idea that he would like to raise Frank. Frank's mother thought it was a good idea, but she had to sell the idea to her husband, Victor. Frank didn't know about it. He didn't want to get his hopes high just to see them come crashing down like a ton of bricks. So Frank still spent a lot of time at home, and the situation there was getting worse. Travis and Roberta could see the wear and tear and the stress it was having on Frank, but they held their tongue about the adoption.

Meanwhile, Victor "Mad dog" Cole seemed to be more and more on edge these days. He was quick to snap at Frank as well as at everyone in the house, but he seemed to zero in on Frank for some reason. Then one day Frank found out about that one reason. Somehow Victor heard about the fight between Frank and Shawn, and he was so upset he verbally attacked Frank, and once or twice he physically attacked him. If it wasn't for his mother, Victor would have done some serious damage. Frank within this time frame had developed quite a hatred for his father. He would daydream about hurting him by using different methods. Frank thought that as long as he got him away from his family that would be all that mattered. When it was only him and his mother, Frank would share some of the feelings of what he wanted to do to his father. However, although he thought he would have an ally in his mother, it turned out be that wasn't the case. Instead, Maureen Cole would try to cover up for his father. She had an excuse for every negative action he did. Frank would confide in the Cooks instead, who were very supportive, so at least he had an outlet.

One day what the Cooks feared would happen in the Coles' household happened. It was a day no child should have to ever see what Frank or his siblings saw, but on that day they, especially Frank, saw it all, and the emotional and mental scars are still very much embedded in his mind from that dreadful day.

Chapter 53

Frank remembered that day as if it had happened yesterday. Frank's mother sat him and his sister and brother down and told them that their father was a major drug dealer. The news rocked Frank very hard. He was in denial. His sister and brother were too young to understand, but Frank felt the impact even at that tender age. He had been under the impression all of that time that his father was a very important business man and his long absences from home were due to his busy schedule. Frank at one time, when he was younger, was very proud of his father despite his MIA status, but now he hated him to the very core of his soul. He had been angry even at that young age. He was angry how his father deceived him and had him thinking he was somebody important, but he had heard about drug dealers and how they ruined and destroyed families and even murdered the innocent, the helpless. Frank saw red when his mother told him. He blocked her out. He could not accept the idea that his father was nothing more than a loser. That was what he'd been taught in school about people who sold drugs. They were losers in fancy cars and clothes. Frank sat there in a state of shock while his mother, in tears, told them the truth.

Frank remembered it as if it had happened yesterday. It was a couple of hours after midnight. The front door crashed opened with a loud sound as if an explosive had gone off. The impact shook the house as well as Frank as he tumbled out of his bed in a hurry. His siblings were screaming and crying. The house was still in total darkness. Frank could only make out a few silhouettes. The whole thing went fast. The sound of loud voices mingled in together and over each other. The voices sounded angry and authoritative. They spoke fast and quick. Frank could make out the hand signals they sent to each other; their guns were drawn.

Frank heard his mother screaming, which added to the confusion. He wanted to run to her, not to protect her but to be protected by her, but one of the intruders had his knee in Frank's back, pinning him to the bed. Frank could feel the pain shoot up and down his body like cars on a freeway. He was helpless against the person who weighed three times as much as he did. He was a mere boy. He told and convinced himself that he was the man of the house, yet he was powerless. He could hear the screams of his mother telling them to get off him and that he was only a baby. Frank's brother and sister were in a corner totally terrified, screaming and yelling for their mother.

Frank felt helpless. He didn't know what to do. He did not understand what was going on, and he wasn't sure who those men were. Frank heard two of the men questioning his mother. They kept on asking her where her husband, Victor Cole, was and where was the stash. Maureen Cole retorted and yelled back that she had no idea of a stash. Frank was finally brought into the room with his mother; Frank knew that his mother was lying and that she knew where the stash was. Frank could not believe there were so many police officers or undercover officers. His father used to point out to him the difference between police officers and undercover officers when he used to drive him to school. There were so many undercover officers in his house.

Frank asked his mother in a voice filled with fear and panic what was going on. The other Neanderthal officer was screaming and yelling questions at his mother about where was the stash. When Maureen Cole did not answer him, Mr. Neanderthal became very aggressive and twisted her arm behind her back and jerked it up, causing a severe pain that made her scream in agony. Frank was helpless against the Goliath of a cop who held his arm real tight in a vice grip. Frank yelled at the officer to leave his mother alone. The officer looked at Frank, and for a minute he looked as if he had a change of heart, but the next thing Frank saw was his mother going airborne into the wall and slowly crumbling to the floor as she lay there like a rag doll.

Frank, panic-stricken, didn't know what to think. The first thing he thought, from the way his mother hit the wall, was that she was dead, if not dead then unconscious. Frank squirmed and kicked to break free from the Neanderthal. Somehow, he broke free and ran to his mother as his brother and sister, who were crying, looked on in horror. Frank approached his mother not knowing what to expect. He timidly called her. At first, there was no response, but when he called her the second time, Maureen stirred and slowly got up. It took every bone in her body, even the two broken ribs she sustained from the impact of crashing into the wall, for her to get up. She slowly got to her feet with the aid of her son, looked at the officer who threw her into the wall, and with a look of inner strength and integrity said to him and to all of them, "You will pay for that. Somehow, somewhere down the line you are going to regret what took place here. You have no right to come in my house and treat us as if we have some criminal connection with Victor. You have no right."

The officer who had slammed her into the wall walked up to her. Frank was afraid that he was going to hurt his mother again and was prepared to do whatever was necessary to protect her. Instead, the officer reached into his back pants pocket, took out a long sheet of paper, held it in front of his mother, and said, "No, bitch, this gives us the right, and because your boyfriend, man, husband, or pimp, whatever he is to you, is a dangerous man, we have a right to protect ourselves from anyone in this house, even that little punk of yours." The officer pointed to Frank and continued, "Do you know why? Because your significant other is also wanted for attempted murder of an off-duty police officer."

Another officer walked up to the Neanderthal and told him to back off. It wasn't a request but a direct order. The Goliath was about to say something but thought twice and backed off. The officer walked up to Maureen and Frank and apologized for what had taken place. He had just arrived and was in total surprise. He ordered another officer to take Frank and his mother into another room in the house, to make them as comfortable as possible under the circumstances, and to give them whatever they wanted until the search was completed. But the only thing that Maureen wanted was for those police officers to vacate her premises, although she did appreciate the fact that the officer was kind to her and her children, and that helped melt some of the anger and resentment she had. The officer gave her his card and suggested to her that she should consider pressing charges against the aggressive officer; Maureen looked down at the business card and thanked Officer Hendricks for his help.

As Maureen and her kids were being escorted to another room in the house, Frank heard one of the officers say something about finding the stash they were looking for. The only thing Maureen could do was put her head down. The nice officer who had rescued Maureen earlier gave her a firm squeeze and a reassuring smile that communicated to her to stay strong. Maureen shyly smiled back as she was led away. Frank and his brother and sister were escorted to the child welfare administration twenty-four-hour drop-in center. Frank could vividly remember the empty feeling as he and his brother and sister were separated from their mother not knowing where they would be taking her.

One hour later, Mr. Cook picked Frank and his brother and sister up with a court order. Mr. Cook reassured them that everything was going to be OK. He further assured them that their mother was doing OK and that they would be reunited with her soon. Mr. Cook explained the legal ramifications as best as he could so that Frank could understand it. He explained what bail meant and also that their mother would be coming home soon but would have to go back to court to deal with the charges of interfering and tampering with evidence concerning their father, Victor Cole. Travis assured them that her chances were very good of beating the charges. From that day forth, Frank knew he had an ally in the Cooks.

Frank always held the Cooks in the highest esteem for what they had done for him and his brother and sister. He would always remember the tears of abandonment he shed for his mother, tears of anger he felt toward his father, and tears of love he felt for the Cooks.

Maureen Cole made arrangements for the Cooks to become extended family members and help raise Frank. She felt that Frank had too much resentment toward her and raising him would be very difficult if not impossible, and she also felt that she could not concentrate on Frank's anger issues while raising his siblings; therefore an agreement was reached. The situation of the Cooks becoming extended family members was explained to Frank. At first, he thought the idea of sharing a room with his new friend was cool. Despite the fight they had, the two had become very close and now this. Yet, on the other hand, it also meant that he was going to be separated from his mother whom he really loved so much despite the trouble that she had allowed to come and stay in her life, which was his father. Yet Maureen Cole visited Frank at least two weekends out of the month and took him back home to spend time with her and his siblings.

As Frank got older, the weekend visits didn't work out. It just wasn't the same. Frank loved his mother and his siblings, but the visits just weren't working out. The gulf got wider and wider, and it became more apparent that Frank and his mother were turning the corner. The phone calls went from every day to four or five times a month, but Frank made sure he spoke to his siblings at least a few times a week. And Mr. Cook would bring them over to the house so they could spend time with him, or they would all go out to the movies or out to the park, but even that started to decrease due to the Cooks' schedule, which was becoming more and more demanding.

However, things began to improve; no one would have ever suspected what had caused the surprise turnaround, but the turnaround was because of Officer Captain Michael Henderson, the officer who was very comforting and compassionate toward Maureen and her children. Michael, after that night, never lost contact with the Coles, particularly Maureen Cole. As a matter of fact, rumor had it that between Travis Cook and Michael they played a huge part in getting Maureen's sentence changed from time in jail to a one-year probation. Michael had a strong feeling that night that not only Maureen was an innocent victim, but also he was falling in love with her, and from that night, he'd been involved indirectly behind the scenes so to speak. When the Cooks could not keep up with spending quality time with Frank, Michael saw his chance and stepped in. He picked up the slack and became a positive and productive part of the Cole family. Frank wasn't sure when or how it happened, but he was happy that it did happen. As young as he may have been, he was happy that his mother found someone who could love her. Frank realized even now that between the Cooks and Michael Henderson for the first time that was when life began for him. At that early age of ten, he started seeing life from a different and positive perspective, which shaped him into the man he had become today.

Every now and then, Frank would think of Victor Cole, the sperm donor. He still couldn't believe how anyone could cause so much heartache and misery in someone's life. But as a grown man now, one thing he had to admit, Victor had taught him, from his negative parenting and poor relationship skills with his mother, how to be a good husband and provider as well as a good father, just by doing the opposite of what he had done. Ever since that dreadful night, Frank hadn't heard from him. He could only imagine that if he was still in the game, he was probably a nickel-and-dime loser, or perhaps the game had caught up with him, and now he had to give an account of his actions to a higher authority.

Chapter 54

As Shawn and Frank finished getting dressed, while checking themselves out in the mirror, Frank couldn't help but think that he and Shawn had been together for a long time, closer than blood brothers in many ways. Shawn noticed Frank in deep thought and asked, "Looking sharp, Bro. What's up with that?"

Frank smiled. "What? Just because I am married I can't be the Mack daddy." He laughed.

Shawn rebounded, "It's kind of hard to be married and still be the Mack, my man. You gave up that mantel when you said I do. Now I am the lone ranger of Mack daddies." Both of them laughed. Shawn changed the mood and asked Frank about his son, "So . . . how's Bobby doing? Anything from this new doctor?"

Frank was looking in the mirror while fixing his tie that he had already tied but was now messing with. The subject of his son had always been uncomfortable for him to talk about, so he responded, "Well . . . you know he has his good days and not so good days." Frank chuckled and continued, "This is Jackie's new positive approach on the situation. She feels we need to speak positive no matter how things may be or may seem, hey, whatever works. Hey, if it helps her to hold it together, I'm cool with it." Shawn being a few inches taller than Frank stood a few inches behind him looking at his reflection. Frank, while looking in the mirror past himself at Shawn doing the final touch-ups and putting expensive cologne on, could not help but be reminded about the time when they were younger and how they would do the same thing when they would get ready for school, church, or party. *This was how it was then, and this is how it is now,* he thought. Frank noticed Shawn smiling, and he knew he was thinking the same thing.

Shawn said, "Yep, some things never change, my brother from another mother, and why should they? You remember, we were the Miami Vice of the Bronx. We would have our sunshades on thinking we were cool. Girls used to do flips for us. We had their heads turning, remember?"

Frank nodded in agreement. "Yep, we were hot, sunshades, our clothes were tight and right out of the Miami Vice wardrobe, nice haircuts, and fancy wheels."

Shawn laughed. "Yeah, stingray bikes, I mean we had them decked down. We had more accessories and stickers on the bikes than on a Christmas tree." They both laughed and high-fived each other.

Frank said, "Man, I miss those days." Shawn nodded in agreement. Frank and Shawn gave each other shoulder daps. Frank said, "Check it out, I hope your date goes well, if she's as good as you say . . . try not to let this one get away."

Shawn smiled. "Listen, I haven't staked out my territory as yet, but tomorrow, she will know how serious I am."

Frank gave Shawn a brotherly look. "Just let me know how it goes down."

Shawn gave Frank a solid black power handshake with another shoulder dap. "No doubt, no doubt, you are the first as always on my list, my man."

Frank said, "Yo, C-4, I'm out. Catch up with you later. Be safe." Shawn expressed the same sentiments and watched as his adopted brother made his exit, Shawn really cared about Frank. The two had developed such a bond for each other, one would have thought they were blood brothers, but Shawn felt deep down that something wasn't quite right with Frank. He had been meaning to ask him but he had brushed it off. He knew the situation with his son, Bobby, was putting a strain on Frank and Jackie. Bobby had a rare disease. The search for a cure was draining Frank and Jackie. Shawn was not aware that the cost to find a cure for Bobby was astronomical. It was draining Frank and Jackie financially. Frank had never mentioned it to Shawn, and so Shawn was under the impression that he had it under control, little did he know.

Frank had told Shawn that with his and Jackie's income they would have no problem financially, but such was not the case, and Shawn could see the wear and tear and the strain that Bobby's illness was causing on the family. Their marriage was slowly collapsing, but Frank was determined to handle his own affairs. But even on an equal scale, Shawn sensed that something else was terribly wrong with Frank. He sensed that whatever was going on or whatever was happening wasn't good. He had a strong feeling that Phillip Keys had something to do with it, but that was pure speculation. He looked at his watch and contemplated about his friend. He then tucked the thought on the back burner and decided to deal with the matter later. Right then he had to deal with another matter—Serenity Powers.

Chapter 55

Friday D-Day

"Let's keep up the good work." Shawn smiled and encouraged his staff, which consisted of at least two hundred workers as he continued, "Our stats for the quarter was excellent." Everyone hooted, hollered, and gave high-fives to each other as the air was charged with electricity. As Shawn continued, the applause died down a bit. "We tripled our profits thanks to all of you . . ." Someone started singing the Jefferson song "Moving on up." It wasn't too long before most of the workers started singing the same song, causing Shawn to chuckle. Shawn raised his arms to calm down the overly happy staff as he continued, "As I was saying, thanks to all of you for making Shawn Enterprise a success through your hard work and dedication . . . you should give yourselves a hand." The place erupted into loud applause. Shawn looked at his watch. He had to leave soon to give Serenity a call to see if she was ready, or maybe she had chickened out. The applause slowly faded. He lifted his glass of punch and said, "Thank you for coming. Enjoy the music and the refreshments . . . I wish I could stay and party with you, but I have another engagement."

Someone yelled, "Go get her tiger." The place erupted again with laughter. Shawn just smiled and shook his head, thankful for the men and women God had given him to work alongside him. Shawn did a general good-bye wave and headed out. The deejay pumped up the music as some of the people went on to the dance floor. The others watched and talked with each other. Shawn finally made his way out the door and headed to his office. He slowed his stride and listened to the music coming from the recreation room. He heard the voices of elation, laughter, and the noise of conversation. He could not help but smile at what was once a dream but now a reality. What many said could not happen, Shawn, with the help of God, made it happen. While other companies that had started when Shawn had started his company collapsed and folded, Shawn Enterprise was like the bird, the phoenix. No matter what or who tried to destroy it, somehow it would emerge into something better and stronger. He had started out with only a few employees, and now, six years later, there were two hundred employees and still growing.

Shawn enjoyed the brief memory of his success as he smiled to himself and kept walking toward the elevator. He got on the elevator and used his elevator key to bypass all floors to the basement. The elevator quickly came to a comfortable stop in the basement parking garage, where there was state-of-the-art parking area, state-of-the-art hidden cameras, and a well-trained team of security guards. The parking area was quite secure as it was designed for employees only. In order for employees to go upstairs or at the end of their day, they had to get double clearance, one from a security guard and the other from a state-of-the-art print booth. This was the area where the workers had to place their hands on a clearance monitor. As soon as the person would place his hand there, the computer within seconds would give feedback whether that person was an employee, and if so they would have clearance to go upstairs. And if the system would not recognize the person, the alarm would go off, and in a matter of seconds, armed security guards would be at the scene escorting the person off the premises. The system was considered 95 percent foolproof.

Shawn arrived at the booth and waved to his team of security guards, and they waved back. He went through the motions and placed his hand on the scanner in order to get through to the parking lot. The security guards noticed Shawn going through the motions and said, "Mr. Cook, go through. We've put the system on bypass." The guard, who was speaking, laughed and said, "We already know who you are, sir."

Shawn, however, was surprised. He waved at the guard and said, "Ted, don't worry about it. I appreciate it, but let me go through like everyone else. Thanks anyway. Good looking out." Ted felt he had made a basic and routine mistake. No matter who it was, even if it was the president of the United States, Shawn expected his trained team not to take anything or anyone for granted. He noticed the look of trepidation in Ted's eyes and eased up on his tone a bit. The scanner collected the information from Shawn and acknowledged and confirmed his status as the CEO of Shawn Enterprise. The gate slid open, and Shawn waved once again to Ted and his partner and walked to his car.

Shawn sat in his car for a minute or two and thanked God for getting him through another day. His car like his office held the state-of-art technology. He called his car "Complex." Complex was full of all kinds of gadgets. He smiled and said, "Good evening, Complex. Are all systems fully charged and ready to go?"

Complex answered with her sultry state-of-the-art voice mechanism, "Good evening to you, Shawn." Shawn could not help but smile to himself as he thought about Complex's designer T. J. Hawkins, who was considered one of the nation's top engineer specialists. She had once worked for NASA as the number two person who helped run the program. She had been next in line to take the number one spot but had declined and decided to leave the politics and the business to those who liked to brown nose and kiss butt. TJ walked away from a job that was paying in seven figures, and she never looked back. Two years later, she emerged with her own state-of-the-art company, making as much if not more than before, but what she really liked about it was that there were no politics or brown nosing or kissing ass allowed, as she would put. She had put together a team of professionals that were from the best engineer-dynamics schools in the country.

Tanya only dealt with wealthy folks and was a consultant for the government even though that was supposed to be one of the best-kept secrets, but word has a way to sneak through cracks and other crevices. The bottom line was that T. J. Hawkins was very much in demand. Her team right now were into designing cars on demand, and, give or take, T.J. and her team could put out about five to six cars a year all custom-designed, have it your way as the fast food slogan goes, and on top of that make a ton of money in the process.

Shawn met T. J. Hawkins at a workshop that she was giving on the latest technology in car dynamics. He was very impressed with the way TJ handled herself. He thought that her voice alone could make some of the male participants swoon. He thought that if Ms. Hawkins ever left that field, she would do great as a voice-over for one of those porn flicks or 1-900 . . . live sex talk call-ins, and if her voice could knock most of the men off their feet, her body would finish them off. The digits on her body had his eyes popping, 34-24-36. He thought of the lyrics of that song by the commodores, "She's a brick house." Shawn enjoyed the workshop. As a matter of fact, he enjoyed Ms. Hawkins even more. He went up to the front to thank Tanya for doing such a great job. There was a long line of mostly men trying to get to T.J. to ask their questions, but most of those men just wanted to get a better look at that fine-looking queen, using the guise of questions as a distraction. But no one, especially T.J., was a fool. How was someone supposed to ask a question looking at somebody's breast and how many times could someone keep asking the person to repeat their response because they didn't get all of it? Well, no doubt, a person would sense the person's eyes are on her breast or are transfixed on the person's full and juicy-looking lips. T.J. didn't mind. It just reminded her that she still was in demand in more ways than one.

However, when Shawn got his turn after looking at that fiasco of men tripping over their words, professional men, or asking the same questions two or three times or asking T.J. to repeat her answer as if they did not hear it the first time, he was ready. T.J. was writing something down on a piece of paper. When she looked up at Shawn, she had such a look of satisfaction. She was impressed with his demeanor. He was smooth and, as she would say to this day when they talk about that eventful time, that he was like silk. His voice was soft yet harsh with a deep baritone; his voice sent an SOS to those areas in her body that was calling for help. The two talked as the line of those waiting to speak with T.J. became longer. Shawn smiled and quickly looked at the folks behind him, and he made the suggestion that she should give her fans fifteen more minutes and then he knew a place where they could get away. The idea sounded good to her, and that was exactly what she did and that was exactly what they did.

The two went out for a light snack and coffee. Shawn and T.J. found a quick connection. He found her easy to talk to, and T.J. found Shawn deliciously fascinating. She was blown away by what she called his E-drive, his energy, while he was transfixed with her voice and sexy demeanor. When she walked into a room, she captivated those that were there, both men and women. Women's reactions were mixed. Some acknowledged with a smile of respect, while others either clung to their men they were with as if she was after them or poked or stared or even tapped their men on the head to snap them back into reality. If she would have wanted them, she wouldn't have a problem in getting them. Shawn sat across from T.J. smiled and said, "Do you always cause such a reaction?" T.J. put her head back and laughed freely as her shoulder-length hair fell back. Shawn was impressed that T.J. had no inhibitions, so it seemed.

As her laughter subsided, she looked at Shawn with the eyes of a young schoolgirl and said, "Well, ever since these developed." T.J. pointed and stuck out her perfectly shaped breasts.

Shawn was caught off guard with T.J.'s so-called freedom-of-expression attitude. He mouthed the word, "Whoa." He at that moment became self-conscious as he looked around in the small yet cozy diner. Some of the patrons who had caught the gesture were transfixed, and some who were in the process of drinking or eating started to cough. He looked at T.J.'s bodyguard, who smiled and turned his head; obviously he'd seen the reaction that T.J. had on others.

Shawn, who was considered a calm and collective guy, was just thrown for a loop as he turned his attention back to T.J., who took a sip of her water and said as if nothing had happened, "See what I mean, and of course the olive-colored eyes. My eyes alone can break a man down." She reached over and gently placed her perfectly manicured hand on Shawn's as she seductively said, "See for yourself."

Shawn deep down believe TJ. What man in his right mind can resist such a seductive woman. He looked at her with a smile and said with his own version of seduction, "I see."

T.J. laughed and Shawn joined in. When the laughter stopped, she said, "Well, Mr. Cook, I guess I met my match. I noticed you are a charmer yourself. I saw how the women stared at you . . . I can see why. I wish I had X-ray vision, just to see if the inside was as well packed as the outside." Her lips pouted slightly, showing another positive asset of her arsenal. Shawn thought that T.J. was dangerous, not because of her arsenal, but because she knew how to use each one effectively. He had to change the subject before he became a T.J. POW. The two talked as if they had known each other for quite some time. T.J. got to know how Shawn got started and he listened to her story of how a woman could become one of the most dynamic individuals in her field. He was impressed.

Both of them exchanged numbers and e-mail addresses. Shawn told T.J. about his community work at the Y. At that point, T.J. thought that that meeting was meant to be because she had for long wanted to somehow give back to the community, but she didn't know how to do it where it would make a lasting difference. While talking to Shawn, the idea hit her how it could be done.

As they said their good-byes, Shawn reached out his hand to shake T.J.'s hand. She pushed aside his hand and kissed him on the lips, a clean kiss that had a touch of appreciation. He was caught off guard, yet he wasn't surprised. He had learned that night that T.J. did what she wanted to do. Before they went their separate ways, he agreed to get her started with her give-back-to-the-community project by donating ten state-of-the-art computers for every center that she opened up. That deal included free maintenance as well as a six-month crash course once a year. In exchange,

T.J. agreed to design a car for Shawn every two years. Shawn would purchase the car and T.J. would transform it, maintenance included. T.J. looked at Shawn and threw in a condition—she and Shawn needed to get together at least every three months. Shawn smiled at the way TJ worked her way into things, but he liked her go-get-it attitude, and he agreed to the terms, even the extra stipulation or shall we call it manipulation. Whatever it was, it worked for him.

Shawn waited with T.J. until her bodyguard returned with the car. When he returned, Shawn opened the passenger door for her. She got in the car and purposely gave him something to think about as she allowed him a long look at her muscular and lean legs when she pulled up her skirt up to her thighs. He looked at T.J. and smiled, followed by a little chuckle, shaking his head. T.J. smiled at him and said, "Hey, what can I say, it's in the blood."

Shawn laughed. As he prepared to close her door, he asked, "Hey, by the way, what does T.J. stand for?"

TJ looked seductively at Shawn and said, "Tanya Jacqueline Hawkins." She winked at him and closed her car door, and her bodyguard drove off so fast she was in and then out. Shawn heard from her through e-mails every now and then, and then one day, she e-mailed him and told him to call her on her cell. Shawn did. Tanya said her sultry pleasantries and playfully asked him if he was being a good boy. He laughed and said he was being as good as she was. She told him that he was a naughty boy. Both laughed at the fun moment; in reality, neither of them had the time to go out, but the idea of pretending what could have been was fun.

T.J. asked Shawn whether he was outside. He confirmed that he was, but he didn't see anything different. "OK, T.J., what exactly am I looking for?" She told him to hold his cell phone outward toward the street. He did as he was told. The next thing he heard was a bunch of beeps and the cover on the car that was parked began to come off like a convertible top unfolding. The next thing that Shawn witnessed blew his mind, a customized, state-of-the-art car. He put his cell phone to his ear and said, "What is this?"

T.J. laughed and said, "Thanks for the computers, and happy birthday." She hung up, and Shawn felt like a kid on Christmas morning.

As Shawn sat in his car a year and an half later, he had established a tight relationship with T.J. to the point that that was his second customized car, and thus far he'd donated a good number of computers to what were called T.J. kids. The two had gotten together at least half a dozen of times, more to tease than appease one another. Shawn shook the thought off and looked at the control panel on the dashboard of his customized car. "Complex, are all systems fully charged and ready to go?"

Complex responded, "As full and as charged up as I ever going to be. I'm at my peak, baby."

Shawn laughed, thinking that Complex was no doubt designed by T. J. Shawn could sense her personality. He became serious, "Complex, I need for you to be on your best behavior. I will have a guest this evening, and I need for you to be polite."

Complex responded, "Oh . . . you are bringing a female. What is this, a threesome, big boy? I will try to be careful and watch what I say to the little . . ."

Shawn contemplated what she was going to say and then said with precise calculation, "Complex . . . I hope you are on your best behavior. Do I need to put you on manual control?"

He waited for Complex's response. "No, Shawn, please don't do that. That would not be necessary. I promise to behave myself." Shawn smiled and thought, *OK, that is done.*

He said to Complex, "Bring up my control buttons." Complex did so without a confrontation; Shawn knew that Complex wanted to say something because that was how her designer was, and if Complex was designed after TJ the fight was not over yet. Complex brought up the buttons 1-100. Shawn asked, "Complex, find me something modern and mellow to listen to with an edge of romance." Complex took some time responding to the request; Shawn picked up on a little resistance. "Complex . . . what is taking so long?"

Complex sounded a little agitated. "Shawn, I am working on it. Now you want me to be Dr. Joyce Brothers."

Shawn with an edge to his own voice said, "Complex, I am warning you."

Complex put on soft, romantic music. He said, "Now that's much better." He pressed number 43. A mist silently filled the air; the scent was soft and sexy. He said to Complex, "Thank you, Complex, for your cooperation. Switch me to manual mode. I will switch you back when I drop her off . . . I promise."

Complex protested, "Shawn, I thought we agreed that if I will be on my best behavior, you will let me stay on auto."

Shawn wanted to keep Complex on auto mode, but he could not take that chance. He thought that if Complex was like her designer it meant she had unpredictability written all over her program. Complex was still talking, trying to convince Shawn. He insisted, "Manual mode, Complex . . . now please." Complex made an aspirated sound as if to say she had surrendered. Shawn noticed Complex's AI lights dim out slowly.

Shawn sat there for a few minutes listening to the music. The song was about some guy who was madly in love with this girl. Yet the girl he was madly in love with did not feel the same way about him. After a few more seconds, he slowly drove out from the parking garage, even though the building where Serenity worked, the Federal Plaza, was in walking distance. He wanted to see Serenity as she walked from the building. He wanted to take a sneak peek at her beauty as he watched and observed her waiting for him. That was the deal. Shawn and Serenity agreed that he would meet her in front of her building. However, there was one catch. Shawn smiled to himself. He had not said how he was going to meet her.

Chapter 56

Shawn pulled up across the street from the Federal building. He pressed a button on his panel and the music went into surround sound. It was as if every instrument could be heard and every note could be felt. He smiled at the fact that Complex was designed to perform. TJ's design of Complex was years in advance.

Shawn sat there and waited for Serenity to come out as he went over his plan for the night for him and Serenity; everything seemed in place. He checked his watch. The time was 5:45 p.m. He decided to give Serenity a call. On the second ring, Sandra picked up and gave the quick protocol greeting, asking how she could direct the call. He cleared his throat and said in his deep baritone voice, "Good evening, Sandra, how are you?"

Sandra on hearing Shawn's deep voice almost dropped the phone. She became uncharacteristically tongue-tied. She was glad all her coworkers had left, saving her the embarrassment of seeing that other side of her. She recovered quickly, but Shawn heard it and thought he may be able to use it as an ace up his sleeve.

Sandra mustered up enough confidence to say, "Good evening, Mr. Cook."

He returned the greeting, but also added a little incentive to the pot, "Ah . . . look, Sandra, I spoke to my friend Marcus. He would like to meet and hook up next weekend with you. Is that cool with you?"

Sandra, returning to her old self, stated, "Next weekend, why? What's wrong with the brother? Why next weekend? Don't tell me he's getting cold feet!" Shawn knew at that point he could not afford to lose Sandra as an ally; he had to make sure that she knew that he had everything under control. He laughed at Sandra; the two had never met, but he could tell that she was a good person, and Marcus was the coolest cat he knew besides his boy, Frank.

As Shawn tried to make light of the matter, he said, "Naw, it's not like that. Marcus has a few projects he's working with, and he will be out of town this weekend, but he is more than excited about next week . . ." Sandra did not respond as quickly as he had hoped she would, so he poured on the gravy, "Listen, Sandra, Marcus is very upset about this, and he can't wait to meet you."

Sandra smiled and gave a seductive response, "Oh really, well, I take your word, Mr. Cook. I know you wouldn't try to play me."

Shawn felt a sense of relief as if he had just avoided a major train wreck. He did not want to say something that would cause her to go backward, so he changed the subject as he added, "And please call me Shawn." Sandra thought that Shawn Cook was Mr. Suave, slick and smooth, and as far as she was concerned, there was only one animal that hisses, and it usually hides in the grass waiting for its victim. She did not know Shawn on a personal level, but she wasn't new to the game either. She did not know what to think of him; the jury was still in deliberation. In the meantime, she would let her own street suaveness be her guide. Shawn interrupted Sandra's plan of thought and said, "Listen, you and I will talk later. May I speak with Serenity if she is in, please?" Sandra said with a smile for Shawn to hold on.

A few minutes later, Serenity came to the phone. "What in the world did you say to that girl? She's acting as if she just hit lotto." Shawn laughed; he was so happy to hear Serenity's voice.

He said, "I don't know. I was just being myself. Is that a crime . . . is it?"

Serenity enjoyed listening to Shawn's baritone voice and responded with a nervous chuckle, "No . . . I guess it's not a crime." Serenity wanted to back out of the so-called date; she was having second thoughts. She found talking to Shawn Cook was easy. He was a man that she could see would get underneath her defenses, and that sort of scared her. Serenity had always been an arm's-length person, but she was starting to let Shawn enter into a no-fly zone so to speak and that could spell trouble in the long run. She came out of her reverie. "Uh . . . where, I mean are you outside . . . ?" She laughed at her own question and continued, "Well, of course you are outside . . ." She sounded somewhat flustered, "I'm sorry, just exactly where are you? Outside could be anywhere, right? Silly me . . ." She was feeling like it was her first date. Well, in a way one could look at it that way since it had been so long since the last time she went out, but she said to herself, "Girlfriend, you better stop tripping and pull this thing together."

Shawn tried to control the laughter that was bubbling deep down inside of him, and for the most part he did, but he could not help but release a chuckle. He said, still chuckling, "Listen, meet me on the east side of the Federal building." Shawn chuckled a little bit more.

Serenity wanted to ask him whether he had finished, but instead she asked him, "What exactly are we going to do, and where exactly are we going?"

Shawn smiled to himself. He knew he had to score a point or two, and he didn't have to work up a sweat to do it. He said, "Whoa, slow down, not so fast. You see, I would rather show you than tell you . . ." His next line came in his sexy, baritone voice, "It takes the suspense away."

Serenity felt goose bumps shoot up and down her arms and back and that feeling at the pit of her stomach. She thought, *Oh, oh, mayday, mayday, Houston, we got a problem.* She continued, "No, I am sorry, I just wanted to know . . . is that a crime?"

Shawn smiled and thought, *Oh yeah, we got ourselves a live one.* He said, "It will all be explained. I just want you to sit back and enjoy the ride . . . this one is on me."

Serenity wanted to laugh at that line. She thought about her friend, Sandra. If Sandra ever heard that line all she would see would be dollar signs, and she would yell at the top of her lungs, "Jackpot." But Serenity was of a total different breed. She responded, "Thank you, but I must put my cards on the table so there won't be any misunderstanding . . ." She paused for effect and continued, "You can take this anyway you choose, but I hope you take it the right way. My first few dates with someone I'm just meeting, I like to go Dutch . . ." She paused to see how Shawn's ego was going to handle this. She was surprised that Shawn was quiet as if what she had just said did not in the least affect him. Then she said, "I know your pockets reach deep, but I am not fazed by that since I am not trying to be impressed by you. Just get a meal and have a nice time, therefore, don't worry. I can keep up."

Shawn normally was turned off by women who liked to lecture, but the way Serenity handled her business turned him on as if she was manipulating the whole thing. The way she said her words, the softness of her voice, and the way she had framed this conversation caused a sensation to hit Shawn right in his groin area. As he thought about Serenity keeping up with him and not necessarily in a monetary way of speaking, the thought sent a feeling on an emotional scale of 9.5. Shawn tried to gather himself together as he coughed and continued, "Uh, no offense, Serenity."

Serenity came back with, "None taken, I am just laying out the ground rules. I like to know that everything is clear and up front."

Shawn made a sound that registered as saying OK as he continued, "Well, I appreciate your viewpoint. I'm not sure what part of the neck of woods you are from, but where I'm from and the way that I've been raised, the man pays the cost." Serenity was happy she was going out with a gentleman, but she had to make this idea crystal clear before anything took place. She knew that this was the time, and whatever power play Shawn had under his sleeve, which he may use on his clientele and on perhaps some of his little gold digging mamas, she would not become a part of his harem, so now she was more than determined to set the boundary lines and the ground rules in the sand, figuratively speaking.

Serenity's mood became serious. "Shawn . . ." She paused for effect, and in Shawn's mind she had an effect. He before this had strongly thought that he had made a positive impression on Serenity as he kept on adding points to his account. Now Shawn not knowing what was about to come was taking those same points back and placing them in the red column as he listened intently to Serenity. "I do appreciate your gentleman attitude, it's very sweet. I appreciate your intentions and your generosity." He felt good as he was in his mind moving those red points out of the red into the black as she continued, "But . . ." He imagined his hand stopping as she continued, "Two things."

Shawn thought, *Uh-oh. Incoming.* As he was preparing to hear the two things before moving the points back to the red column, she continued, "Number one, in case you haven't noticed, I am a full grown woman, working woman at that. I am independent, and I handle my own affairs and take care of my own business. I don't need anyone telling me when, where, or how, and I don't have to give an account to anyone about why I do or what I do." Serenity made her voice sound carefree and sweet as she said, "I'm sure you understand where I am coming from . . . don't you?" Shawn did not know what to say; he was still reeling from the first set of blows and now he was bracing himself for the next incoming attack. Here it came, "Number two, no matter how rich, wealthy, or famous you are, I don't want to be in the position where I owe you anything. That's why I pay my own cost because I am my own boss. Furthermore, Mr. Cook, the only boss I really have, his initials are not SC it's JC. I think those are the ground rules. You have anything you would like to add?"

Shawn coughed to clear his throat and said with a bit of trepidation, "Uh . . . no . . . I think you covered all the bases."

He was caught off-balance. He was like a person who had been spun around at top speed and then left to walk blindfolded while he was still reeling and staggering from the sensation. In one sense, he felt totally out of his element. He wasn't used to being treated as such by the opposite sex, but he appreciated that there was someone who did not care about his money or fame and would challenge him. It was not someone who would "yes" him to death, but someone who was not afraid to tell him where to go and how fast, with a can filled with gasoline and a match. While Shawn was thinking, Serenity repeated, "So is everything clear?"

Shawn couldn't recall anyone ever speaking to him as such as he responded, "Crystal clear."

Serenity responded, "Good." She felt good. She had stood up to one of the most powerful men in New York City. She was now ready to meet Shawn.

However, Shawn being the fighter that he was broke the silence and countered, "Ms. Powers, first of all, let's clear the air of something. If we are going to play, let's make the ball field equal, shall we?" Serenity, caught off guard, made a sound that sounded like she agreed, as if her mouth was full and she couldn't say the word yes. "First, I think you are right on target. I don't want any misunderstandings between us, but hello . . . I am the good guy. I don't know what you or who you dealt with in the past, but you need to relax and sort of keep in mind that not all guys are out to mess with you or are out to hit it and get it. I'm not here to score, baby. There are still a few good guys out there, who want one thing, just time to spend with the woman they want to get to know, so deflate the hate, baby." Serenity tried to interrupt, but Shawn cut her off, "Please let me finish. You had your chance." Shawn continued, "I never for once had given a minute of thought you were that type of woman, the loose, easy, sleazy or cheap and cheesy. I know you have class. I don't know where all of what you said came from, but I could tell you, if I thought you were that type of woman, we wouldn't be having this conversation. I don't date loose women, and I am looking for more than a piece of ass. Women throw themselves at me every day. That's not what I am looking for. I want someone with a good heart. Now if you don't fit the profile, let's not waste each other's time . . . Ms. Powers . . . I just wanted to make the crystal a little clearer."

Serenity felt as if someone had knocked the wind out of her as she scrambled to recover from that rapid fire of verbal bullets.

She thought, *Why did I listen to Sandra?* Serenity in her mind mocked at Sandra's words that she had spoken to her, *Be tough and stand your ground.*

Don't give an inch or he'll take a yard. I know about these things, trust me. Serenity didn't realize that she was talking loud enough for Shawn to hear but not quite make out what she said, "Yeah, trust me, yeah, right."

Shawn said, "Excuse me, what was that?"

Serenity caught by surprise did not realize that Shawn had heard her. Quickly she made up something, "Ah, nothing, I was just thinking out loud." She thought, *Wait until I get that no frills, dear abbey wannabe.* Serenity was attacking a man for the second time, who did not do a single thing to her; she had to listen to Sandra's paranoia ass. She further thought that she had to be out of her mind to go toe-to-toe with someone like Shawn Cook, who was an expert in verbal warfare. He had gone up against the best deliberators and cognitive minds and come out unscathed. His motto, she remembered reading somewhere, was, "Don't just win, but win at all cost." Serenity felt way out of her league. The only thing she could do now was to not back down and remember that in love and war one should not show his hand or in this case not show the damage your opponent has caused. Serenity cleared her throat and continued as if what Shawn had said had no effect on her, "Well . . . Mr. Cook, it seems as if we do understand each other after all."

Shawn felt as if he was in one of his karate tournaments against a tough opponent. He felt a sense of relief when Serenity did not continue the verbal volley. He felt he did not have any strength to keep the verbal confrontation going on as he put his hand to his forehead and mouthed the word, "Whew." He then looked up in a prayer kind of gesture and mouthed the words, "Thank you." He knew the scoreboard read Shawn—two, Serenity—zero; however, he also knew this was the second battle and that there would be a lot more of them to come; that was how good combatants were—relentless.

But, in reality, Shawn knew that Serenity was a fighter and that he had met his match. He knew deep down if he was going to win anything, it wasn't going to be a verbal battle, for now he would take whatever he could get. Although Shawn was aiming for a higher prize, a more meaningful prize, a more enduring prize, he was determined to aim for the highest prize, which was the heart of Serenity Powers.

Chapter 57

Serenity hung up her phone in her office, put her head down in her hands, and moaned, "Why did I listen to Sandra? Why did I just now attack that man? That man never did a single thing to me . . . not yet . . . but I could at least give him the benefit of the doubt. Why did I listen to her?" As she raised her head from her hands, she said, "What have I gotten myself into?"

At that precise moment, Sandra walked in and said, "Honey, you have gotten yourself into something nice and profitable if you play your cards right . . . I like to call it a pay-for-life situation. It's called a sweet farewell, and if you are sweet you can fare very well and not worry about welfare."

Serenity's eyes burned into Sandra like daggers. Sandra stepped back with a look of apprehension and concern. She did not bother to beat around the bush but cut right to the chase, "First of all, let's deal with office basics, shall we?" Sandra with an unsure look on her face prepared to answer the question, but Serenity cut her off, "Don't bother, zip it. Sandra, I don't know when you were growing up if you guys had doors or lived in open huts." Sandra was about to answer the question, but Serenity just gave her a stern look that said "if you say one word." The look was enough for Sandra to zip it as Serenity continued, "Let me remind you. When a door is closed you are supposed to knock and wait for the person inside to say come in, or did you guys did the opposite, when it's open, knock and close it?"

Sandra looked at Serenity with a bit of confusion, then back at the office door, waved a hand dismissively at it, and said, "Girl, what's wrong? Are your panties too tight or what?"

Serenity stared hard at Sandra. "I tell you what's wrong. I just got finished listening to your advice about how to treat men, one in particular, Shawn Cook." Sandra smiled and walked to Serenity's office refrigerator and opened it up.

Serenity just shook her head, looked up, and went through the motions of mouthing a prayer, begging for patience and strength, patience to deal with Sandra and strength to beat her silly, as Sandra continued, "So how did it go?"

Serenity's voice was in a high pitch. "How did it go? I'll tell you how it went. I attacked a man who never did anything to me, but listening to you I made myself look stupid."

Sandra did not know what to say, "OK, damage control, that's all, Sen. But play your cards right and you can be a rich woman, and of course I will be your financial adviser."

Serenity looked at Sandra and said, "My financial advisor, when hell freezes!" Sandra pouted her lips.

Serenity got up from her desk, straightening out her clothes, and then realized that she would be taking off the outfit and wearing another one. *So why was she straightening them out? This girl got me going nuts.* She said, "Sandra, no more advice. I don't want damage control advice. Enough damage has been done already, and I feel out of control. I keep telling you, and I don't know why it's not sinking in. I'm not after this guy for the money. That is such a ghetto mentality. A woman needs more than that. I make money. Why would I need a man to give me money?"

Sandra looked at Serenity as if she had been offended, "Well, Mrs. Rich and Famous, speak for yourself. I need all the money I can get. I'm so desperate I carry around monopoly money just to make myself feel rich."

Serenity looked at Sandra with an incredible look and said, "Unbelievable." Sandra watched Serenity look at her watch, make a flustered sound, and scurry past her to change into her outfit in the bathroom.

Sandra said to Serenity as she passed her, "That's right. I may be unbelievable now, but when I strike it rich by finding Mr. Rich, I'll be unforgettable."

Serenity came out of the bathroom totally transformed. It was as if she had stepped into a makeover machine, like that show that used to come on television where women would go in looking as if they'd been in a train wreck and come out looking better than Hale Berry, Beyonce, and J-Lo all put together. Doctors from all over would do a number on them, like the six-million-dollar man and the Bionic woman. *We can rebuild them.*

Serenity was glowing. She looked radiant and sparkling. Sandra said, "Now that's unbelievable." Serenity's long locks that were hanging down her back were shining and beautiful and the outfit accentuated her hips. Sandra thought that Serenity would have every man in the place wishing they were the one, the man, her man, holding her waist. Serenity's skirt was till midthigh, showing off her voluptuous legs, legs that a man could only dream, which would wrap around them and do some crazy things to them.

Sandra convinced Serenity to go bare legs. Serenity didn't want to, but when she looked in the mirror she could see where Sandra was coming from. Serenity's bare legs looked sizzling hot. She looked straight up untamed, fantastically wild, and erotic. Sandra knew most women could not get away with that, but she was more than certain that Serenity could do it. Serenity's blouse was designed to make her cleavage stand out, not that her breasts needed any help; they were already the perfect size. Sandra knew one thing for certain concerning Serenity's breasts, and that was that Shawn was going to have problems keeping his eyes off those mountains of joy. By the time the night would be over, Shawn was going to want to climb those bad boys.

Serenity did a quick modeling turn for Sandra and walked the length of her office, making her hips in that skirt do a dance as she walked with a smile. Sandra looked with awe as Serenity twirled around, playfully winked at Sandra, and said, "Well I guess from your reaction and the fact that you haven't closed your mouth yet, I look good."

Sandra closed her mouth and said excitedly to Serenity, "Girl, good is what Halle Berry looks like, but you look fabulously radiant. You are going to drive this man crazy. I just wish I could be a fly on the wall and get all the juicy grit."

Serenity, not looking at Sandra, responded, "It is not that kind of party, girl. If the brother becomes hot and bothered, I would suggest that he take a nice cold shower." Serenity laughed and turned to face Sandra and noticed that her eyes were misty. Serenity went over to Sandra and hugged her, "Sandy, come on, what's the matter? I thought you would be happy for me."

Sandra and Serenity let go of embracing each other. As they looked at each other, Sandra said, "Don't be silly, I am happy for you. You know how I get." Sandra wiped her eyes.

Serenity said, "Yeah, I know, tough as nails on the outside, soft and mushy on the inside." Both women laughed.

Sandra jokingly added, "You better not let out my secret."

Serenity did the scout's honor signal. She said, "I know we have our disagreements about men, but I must admit you are better than a best friend. You are like the sister I wish my parents had. I mean Eric is cool."

They both laughed at that as Serenity continued, "But I'm glad you are more than a friend." Sandra agreed and felt the same way.

Serenity looked at her watch and was surprised how time had just flown. She said, "Oh my goodness, I have to go. I can't believe the time."

Sandra being nosy asked, "Where are you guys going?"

Serenity wanted to tell Sandra to mind her business. Instead she said, "I'll talk to you later." Sandra wanted to say something but decided that something was better than nothing. As Serenity was walking to exit out of her office, Sandra called her and Serenity turned toward her. Sandra gestured to Serenity and mouthed the words, "Call me." Serenity, in turn, made the same gesture while looking at Sandra and mouthed the words, "No way." The two laughed. Serenity was nervous. She walked with a determined step to meet up with Shawn, but deep down she had a feeling that going out with Shawn Cook may be more than she could handle.

Chapter 58

Shawn was about a half block from the side entrance of the Federal building as he sat in his customized car. His windows were tinted. He could see outside, but those on the outside couldn't see on the inside. Legally, Shawn's tinted windows were against the law, but due to his special relationship with the mayor, he had been allowed several perks, and tinted windows were one of them. In addition, Shawn gave a large donation to the NYPD at least twice a year, and the mayor, in turn, had given Shawn an immunity sticker to put on the windshield of his car as well as keys to the city.

Shawn watched the workers coming out of the building to their means of getting back home—trains, buses, cars, carpools, taxicabs, motorcycles, whatever means of transportation they had it planned out from the time they sat down that morning at their workstations. Some were going from one beast of burden to another just to try and keep up with the cost of living. Many left the place of work like horses let out of the gate to race, while others moved like turtles, a sign of a rough and exhaustive day. Many quickly said their "see you later and see you next week," while others were too exhausted to say anything other than to lift a hand to wave. Some had spouses or boy—or girlfriends waiting for them, while others had no one, but most of them seemed content. Shawn could not clearly make out the faces from the angle his car was parked in. He pressed a button on his panel, and the lights on his panel came to life. He smiled and said, "Welcome back, Complex."

Complex responded with her usual greeting, "Ooo, Shawn, you really know what buttons to press to turn me on. What can Complex do for you?"

Shawn could not get over the fact that Complex's computer chips were so sensitive. She was able to hold an intelligent conversation on the highest level of understanding as well as complexity and flexibility. He responded, "Yes, you see, I told you I was going to bring you back."

Shawn waited for Complex to respond, but she did not. Instead she said, "Yeah, right, what can I do for you, Mr. Cook?"

Shawn knew immediately that he was in the doghouse but chose not to deal with the matter at this time. Instead, he cleared his throat and said, "Activate the viewfinder . . . please." Complex told Shawn that it was no problem, but she still referred to Shawn by his last name. The next thing Shawn saw on the control panel was a clear picture of people coming from the places of work or going to work; the picture was so clear and the zoom was so powerful that it seemed as if the person caught in the viewfinder was standing right by the car. The viewfinder was a gadget TJ threw in just because she liked Shawn. It was her way of thanking him. Since she could not thank him the way she wanted to, this was the next best thing.

Shawn programmed the viewfinder toward the Federal building. He wanted to get a close shot of Serenity coming from the building. The Federal building was surrounded by several other buildings, and people were coming and going from all directions. He could not make out anything with the natural eye. There were too many people bunched up and moving, sliding, too close to each other, volleying to get a position to head out and head for their homes. In addition, the time of the seasons, which was early fall, had brought with it daylight saving time. The shadows were coming in quickly. Shawn told Complex to set the zoom to a certain magnification. Complex complied. He looked through the screen on his panel and that was when he saw her. He instructed Complex to zoom in more, which she did, and the picture was so clear he could make out the look on Serenity's face. He thought that Serenity was a beautiful woman. His eyes became fixed on her as she walked toward the area where they had agreed to meet.

Shawn took control of the viewfinder and zoomed in on the way she walked and the way she moved. Her hips swayed from side to side in a hypnotic movement as if in a dance that left him in a trance that enthralled and captivated his full attention. He couldn't swallow, and he did not want to blink as he just could miss something. No, he wanted to remain transfixed on that rare gift of beauty.

Shawn wasn't about to end his appraisal as he continued to zoom in on the finest of details, the way she looked at her watch with such femininity. He studied her further. As he looked at the length of her locks as they flowed down over her shoulders, perhaps to the middle of her back as they bounced and kept the rhythm of her swaying hips, he thought he was looking at a concert in progress. He zoomed in even further on her lips,

lips that were full and sensual, lips that showed her African heritage, lips that he could not wait to touch with his lips and feel and slowly lick with his tongue. He was beginning to feel a weight in the groin area. He caught his breath as he viewed her legs. Serenity's coat was slightly opened, and Shawn noticed the short dress she had on, but what really turned him on was the fact that Serenity was not wearing stockings and he could see that her bare legs were strong and firm. They were long and beautiful, a dancer's legs, the kind that any man in his right mind would love for those legs to be wrapped around him in a tight embrace. Anyone may start out in their right minds, but when legs like those are done with you, they could drive you out of your mind. He admired the firmness of her legs, legs that could endure the ride or take you for a ride. In either case, Shawn thought it was a win-win situation.

Serenity arrived at the curb, looking at her watch and then looking around. By that time, the area was clear. People had gone to where they were going. The shadows of the fall sky had given way to a quiet nightfall. Street lamps lit up some of the area, but where she stood the night engulfed her. It was a strange feeling. Anytime during normal working hours this place was like an ant farm, but on a Friday, this area became like a ghost town, desolate and isolated, which was strange for New York.

Serenity never hung around after work, so she was starting to feel uncomfortable as she looked up and down the street like a lost child. Shawn thought it was a look of pure innocence. She wanted to kick herself. She should have asked Shawn what would he be wearing or better yet told him to call her when he got there, instead of her waiting for him to get there. *What was she thinking?* she thought. *Anything could happen.* She took another look at her watch and nervously touched her hair. Her face had a look of concern as she looked at her watch again, not knowing that the car with the dark tinted windows was where her date was, looking at her, watching her, enjoying the view of her, and admiring the way she became flustered, no doubt because she had come to the conclusion that he was late. She looked at her watch again and quickly looked up and down the street . . . again. Normally, she would have gone straight to the car garage, got into her car, with a smile she would have said, "See ya," and drove home. However, she had left her car at home, thinking that Shawn would drive her home, but now it looked as if he wasn't going to make it. She took out her cell phone and checked for messages. There were none. Now she had to walk in either direction to the corner street and hopefully catch a cab. If not, she would have to find another means to get home.

Shawn noticing Serenity's frustration said out loud that the game was over and that it was time to rescue the gorgeous beauty in distress. Serenity turned to walk to the corner. As she was walking, she noticed a car moving slowly along the curb of the street. She did not know what to make of it at first. Her panic button kicked in, and all types of thoughts began to flood her mind. She began to regret for the first time the outfit Karen gave her. Now that she thought about it, perhaps she looked like a lady of the night, a whore. *I mean I have on a short tight fitted skirt, bare legs, and what have you. What does that sound like?* Serenity thought. *It has prostitute written all.* She began to walk faster, and the car began to move a little faster, tapping its horn. She thought about turning in the opposite direction and run like the wind down the block, since the street was a one-way street, but then on the other hand, she thought that maybe if she could haul it, she could make it to the corner. *I'll just toss these shoes to the side and run like the roadrunner.*

However, little did she know that there was another car parked a few cars back from the tinted car. The person inside that car was watching her every move. As a matter of fact, he'd been watching her all week, trying to get down her routine, but now the watcher had his zoom camera out, taking and snapping pictures of her with such precision and speed, as the camera whipped and whirled with airlike sound. The watcher put down the camera, picked up his cell phone, and dialed the number he was instructed to call. This was the part of the job the watcher did not like and often times wondered how he became so entangled in such a web as this. On the second ring, a voice spoke as if he was expecting the call. The watcher could not make out the gender of the voice. It was obvious that whoever it was using some type of device to alter and manipulate his real voice. The watcher told the voice that the young lady was alone, apparently waiting for someone. The voice told him to take advantage of the moment and grab her. He added that she may know too much. The watcher tried to reason with the voice as pertaining to the role of this woman, that she did not know anything.

"If she had," the watcher stated, "she would have gone to the police." The voice did not say anything, but he did realize that the man had a point. The watcher did not know how to take the silence; a part of him felt that the voice was rethinking his plan while the other part of him did not know what to think anymore. The voice finally spoke, and he agreed with the watcher. However, he said he could not take that chance of having a loose wire somewhere. He thought that all loose ends must be dealt with and taken care of. The watcher for the first time since the craziness started disagreed reluctantly. The voice reminded the watcher in a firm tone about what was at stake and who came to whom for help. The watcher remembered his situation, and the reality hit him like a ton of bricks, which was that he was trapped. He was in too deep. He should have read the so-called fine print. He should have realized that people like the voice don't give freebies. They just take whatever freedom that one has. He should have realized that one can't play with fire and not get burned.

Chapter 59

The watcher weighed the matter and came to the conclusion that his situation was direr. So he made his move, pushing the gears into drive and pressing down perhaps a little too firmly on the accelerator as he focused his attention on the target. However, the car with the dark tinted windows, which was several cars in front of him, sprung to life, and apparently whoever was driving had the same intentions as him, heading toward the woman. The watcher did not understand what was going on. *Perhaps this was all a setup,* he thought. *Perhaps the voice wanted to have his cake and eat it too. He wanted to eliminate the girl and then get rid of him.* The watcher thought that that wasn't going to happen. As he quickly assessed the situation right before his eyes, he also noticed that the woman was doing her own assessment of the situation and realizing that she was in danger had made an attempt to run.

The watcher watched with respect how the driver with the dark windows reacted with quick precision and reflexes. He had never seen anyone drive like that before. He was impressed, yet he was angry as well because it could have been all over, and he could have done what he needed to do and get his life back. However, this new situation created some new problems. As he watched the driver cut in front of the woman to block her path, the watcher looked at the woman. She was totally stunned as if the wind was knocked out of her. As he watched her, she looked like a trapped animal, her eyes darting, moving, and looking for an exit, another escape route, something to make her escape, but she was too stunned to move. She looked as if she had been glued to the sidewalk.

A part of the watcher felt a sense of relief. He wasn't a murderer, and this was no doubt out of his league. In another sense, he had to find out who it was in order to deal with the matter from all angles, but if that person had been hired by the same mystery person that approached him, then this was going to be more complicated than he ever anticipated. The watcher did not want himself to be seen or the type of car he was driving. He quickly pulled out as he drove past the tinted car. The watcher tried to see who was the driver, but due to the dark tint he couldn't, so in frustration he continued at a fast speed down the block to the corner. He stopped at the stop sign. He looked up into his rearview mirror to see what was going to happen to his target. If she was in trouble, he would call some of his friends he knew at the police station for help while he would try to distract the person. But what he saw in his rearview mirror shocked him even more. The sight hit him like a blow to the gut, a sucker punch. Now he knew for sure he had to get out of this. The watcher looked through his rearview mirror at his good friend, Shawn Cook.

Whatever you are going to do, girlfriend, you better do it now, Serenity thought. In one fluid motion, Serenity bent down to take her shoes off and run and fly like the wind. *All those muscles in these legs better kick in*, she thought. Shawn in the meantime could not believe that he could have frightened her to the point that she was ready to run. He quickly requested for an emotional assessment from Complex.

Complex said, "What? That she is scared like a deer and that you scared the crap out of her, and she is about to . . ." Shawn quickly accelerated the car and cut right in front of Serenity's path. Now she knew she was in trouble as she turned to go the other way. He at that moment saw a look of panic and fear, as if Serenity was an innocent animal caught, trapped, and doomed. It pricked his heart, and from that moment he made a vow and said under his breath, "From this day forward, I'll never let anything or anyone harm you or hurt you, Ms. Serenity Powers."

Serenity, who was still in a state of panic, was about to turn in the other direction when the window on the passenger side of the expensive car began to come down. She did not know what to make of it. If whoever it was had a gun, she wasn't going to get too far anyway, but she had to take a chance. Serenity turned to run when she heard a familiar voice coming from the car, "Well, are you going to stand there or are you going to get in? Perhaps you are looking for someone else." Serenity felt as if a weight had dropped from her heart. She was so happy to see Shawn; she didn't know whether to laugh or cry. Serenity smiled, a smile that took the express route from Shawn's heart to his groin area. Shawn got out of the car, came around it from the back, and went to open the passenger door. Serenity loved the way he moved. He moved with such fluidity and grace as if he was walking on air. Serenity was so relieved that she fell into his arms and gave him a kiss on the cheek. Shawn was caught off guard. He smiled with that million-dollar boyish grin.

The two stood there as if frozen in time as Serenity broke the ice, "I am so glad that you are here."

Shawn held Serenity's hands and said, "I am so sorry. If I would have known this would be the result . . ." He paused, put his head down, and continued, "I would have never done this to you. I just wanted to surprise you . . ." He paused. "That's all . . . sorry."

Serenity felt that there was something concerning Shawn that she could not put her finger on as she responded, "Well, let's say you did more than surprise me, a job well done." Both Shawn and Serenity laughed, then Serenity's adrenaline was back to normal. She playfully hit Shawn on the arm. It was a tap, but Shawn made it into something bigger as he reacted to the hit by rubbing his arm. Serenity said, "You know that didn't even hurt you, big baby. Don't you ever do that again." As she playfully hit him in the arm again and got the same reaction, she smiled and shook her head as she got into the car. Shawn made his way back over to the driver side and got in.

Serenity noticed his long legs and his wide chest and shoulders. She wanted to fan herself. Even though the weather for October in New York was downright chilly, yet she could feel the heat rising from sitting next to that man. She immediately could smell the soft mist of air freshener, and the romantic surround sound that engulfed the car was downright smooth and sexy. She had to say something or she was going to do something. So she cleared her throat and said, "Uh, so . . . so where are we going?" Shawn smiled, showing his pearly whites and those deep dimples that Serenity thought she could get lost in them because they were so deep.

Whatever defenses were put up by her own ignorance or by Karen's craziness Serenity felt them slowly melting, layer by layer. She wasn't expecting that from Shawn, especially after their heated head-bashing conversation earlier. By any right, she wouldn't have been surprised if Shawn told her where to go and how fast, but she was totally surprised by the gentle giant of a man, a man with a soft and compassionate heart. She was starting to feel something, but she shook it off and thought, *This could never work, the prince and the pauper.* But deep down she really liked her prince.

Shawn thought back about the car that had pulled out and gone down the street and how at the same time he had moved toward Serenity. He quickly dismissed it because his focus was on what was happening then, but he made a mental note of it. He sensed that something was about to go down tonight, and Serenity was the target. It was a good thing he had been there to spoil their plans. He could not put the pieces together: Why? He did not know. Whom? He would find out. And when he did that the person was going to regret the day he or she was born. In the meantime, Shawn said to himself that he would make sure to keep close tabs on the woman he was falling in love with.

Chapter 60

As they sat in the car, Serenity was impressed with the customized design. Shawn from the corner of his eyes caught Serenity staring at him, not that he didn't want her to. It just made him feel self-conscious as he looked down at himself to make sure the bulge he had been feeling earlier wasn't so obvious now. He said, "What?"

Serenity, realizing that she was caught, wanted to kick herself as she quickly tried to recover, and taking a chapter out of Sandra's "How to recover when caught" she commented, "Ah, no . . . nothing. I was just thinking. All this time I stood on that dark sidewalk, you was there all the time . . . What were you doing? Don't tell me you are a peeping Tom." Serenity laughed.

Shawn loved the way Serenity laughed. He waited for her to compose herself, and then he responded, "What was I doing?" He looked at her and with compassion coming from his dark seated eyes continued, "I was watching the next best thing to a sunset. I was watching the most beautiful woman I've ever set my eyes on."

Serenity's laughter slowly died away as she blushed and responded softly, "Well . . . thank you, coming from a man of your stature and reputation with women I take that as a high compliment." Shawn looked at Serenity before he burst out into loud laughter. It was a type of laughter that held no inhibitions. Serenity who had missed her own punch line asked with a confused look, "Are you finished? What is so funny?"

Shawn, controlling himself, looked at Serenity with a smile and said, "People misjudge me. They think because I am successful I got game. I have women. I have whatever I want, whenever I want, but in reality, believe it or not, it's not like that. You see, I can't drop it like it's hot, and it maybe, but I have to protect my heart against those who just want me because of my Benjamin's and not for Shawn Cook . . ." Shawn was getting ready to start the car when Serenity put her hand on his arm and apologized. Her touch caused his heart to skip a beat as he nodded his head as if to say, "Apology accepted." As he turned to express what he felt, Shawn caught a glimpse of her cleavage. Now it was his turn to stare, much longer than he really wanted to. As Serenity looked down to where Shawn's eyes fell, she looked back up at him with innocent eyes, made a sound, took her hands, and moved her blouse to show less cleavage. She put the tip of her pointer finger in her mouth, blushed, and said sorry. The gesture sent a flood of sensations to Shawn's groin from different directions. The feeling sent both hot and extremely hot chills to every vein in his body. Serenity playing it for all its worth decided to turn up the heat as she asked him in a soft throaty voice if anything was wrong. Shawn tried to express himself, but the words would not come out. All he could do was shake his head and drive.

Serenity quickly ran through Sandra's checklist as she did a mental report and checked off in her mind what was working and what was not. She sat back in her seat and thought about how well things were going and that everything was working. But as she quickly glanced over at Shawn, she realized that she had better not count her eggs before they are hatched because deep down she knew that Mr. Shawn Cook when it came to the dating stuff could run circles around her. So she had better stay on her toes or she could find herself on her back, giving the gorgeous man whatever he wanted. Especially after that night, Serenity was starting to have a newfound respect for Mr. Shawn Cook.

Shawn continued to drive through Manhattan streets, but deep down he felt like a three alarm fire. Every part of him felt as if he was on fire. He felt such a deep sense of passion that although his eyes were looking at the streets, the rest of him was looking and thinking about the woman who he knew he was falling in love with.

His thoughts were interrupted by Serenity's soft voice, "So where are we going?"

Shawn had to clear his mind of Serenity in order to answer her question. Clearing his throat he said, "I want to surprise you, so do me a favor. Please sit back, relax . . ." He made his voice a little more sensual and said, "And enjoy the ride . . . ," as he winked at her and concluded, "OK."

Serenity could feel her body react to Shawn's wink; the three-alarm fire was now totally out of control. She tried to sit back and enjoy the soulful love ballads that played in the surround sound H/D. She was starting to feel uncomfortable. *You ask a man three or four times where we're going and he doesn't respond, and when he does, his answer is to do a dance step around the question. Wouldn't that make someone curious or suspicious or plain old stupid because your dumb behind should have known the answer to the question before stepping into this man's car who has one thing on his mind, and that is to give you the best ride you've ever had?* Serenity was thinking these things as she nervously played with her locks, twirling them and pulling on them, while biting her bottom lip and biting her fingernails. They were all signs of a person who could be experiencing some form of anxiety. She was feeling uneasy, even fidgety. She knew in her heart that she was being ridiculous, but after the earlier situation, she was still shaky. She was trying to figure out all the time from where had the other car come, but she was stumped for an answer. She rationalized that perhaps it had been someone wanting to show off. She brushed the thought away, but deep down she knew something was amiss.

Shawn, sensing Serenity's uneasiness, thought that if he had been in her shoes, he would have liked for someone to be so mysterious or even ambiguous. He sometimes took for granted the idea that the playing field for the average person versus his playing field left him with a huge advantage. For one who was a master at Ka-we-do, it simply meant that anyone who tangled with him on that lopsided playing field could find himself eating out of a straw for the next several months. However, as he continued to drive and at the same time slanted a look at her, he knew that it did not take a rocket scientist to come to the conclusion that Serenity was fragile and tender and furthermore did not have that quality of self-defense under her belt.

Shawn stopped at a red light and looked at her with compassion and tenderness to relieve some of her fears. He said to her, "I want you to do me a favor . . . I want you to keep in the center of your mind and in the tenderness of your heart that I would never let anything or do anything to hurt you, and secondly, I would never do anything you don't want to do. I am a firm believer in the 'no means no' concept, plus . . ." As the light turned green, Shawn looked at his rearview mirror and the side mirror and noticed that it was safe to pull over which he did. Serenity admired the way he handled the car. He had a soft touch, or rather a right touch about him, as Shawn continued, "Now, where was I . . . ? Oh yeah, as I was saying, Serenity, I want you to know this. I am not a hog or a parasite. Understand this, I will not violate your space. I know when to back off. I know how to walk out the same way I came in. I am not like a lot of guys who can't seem to find their way out of a relationship once they get in. I know how . . ." Shawn once again made his voice low and sexy, winked again, and said,

"OK, baby." Serenity's heartstrings began to flutter as she began to nod her head up and down in agreement; any verbal words would have made her sound like a babbling jerk. She thought about not what Shawn had said, but more so about how he said it. *And that signature move at the end, that wink. Oh my goodness, homeboy must have practiced that in the mirror for years. Now he has it down to a science because the man has me hotter than Phoenix.* Serenity felt an attachment to Shawn Cook not because he made her tingle, but because he made her feel something no man had been able to make her feel and that was . . . safe.

Shawn pulled into the garage and waved to the night crew. The crew smiled and waved at him and looked a little too long at Serenity. Shawn wasn't offended. He knew that any man in his right mind who could let that woman walk past him without admiring such beauty was blind, dumb, or gay.

Shawn found a space and pulled into it. He got out and went around to help Serenity out. He opened the door, and she made a move to climb out. However, her skirt began to inch up her legs. Shawn was speechless. He was looking at legs that were bare, strong, firm, and shapely, Serenity made an attempt to climb out but forgot that the seat belt was still clicked on. She then realized the seat belt was jammed. She reached up to undo the belt, but when she did so, Shawn saw what appeared to be two beautiful mountains. He found himself face-to-face with a cleavage that was beyond description. The only thing he could say to himself was, "Lord have mercy." All the while, Serenity tried her best to remain ladylike. With one hand trying to open the seat belt latch, she tried to prevent her skirt from going higher with the other hand. Unfortunately, she was losing the battle, but her efforts of trying to remain ladylike turned on Shawn even more. He thought that it was cute that she was more concerned of remaining ladylike than trying to get free. He tried his best to concentrate on getting her free from the seat belt, but he could not help but look at her deep cleavage.

Finally Shawn reached inside to where the belt was jammed and he felt around for the emergency release button. In doing so, he came close to Serenity. He could smell her perfume. He could see that because of her breathing her breasts went up and down. The next thing he could feel or rather hear was her shallow breathing. He listened carefully all the while trying to find the release button, and then it dawned on him that the shallow breathing wasn't just hers. It was both of theirs. Their eyes met. Shawn wasn't sure what that did for her, but he knew what it was doing to him, as he tried to peel his eyes from Serenity and said, "I just don't understand this. This is the first time this has happened. I am so sorry."

Serenity could smell Shawn's cologne; it was a turn on. Her garden was starting to get wet. She half listened to what Shawn was saying. The other part of her was somewhere else. She tried to stay focused by concentrating on Shawn's strong hands trying to undo the latch. She could not help but see his long, thick, strong fingers trying to open that little latch, but his fingers were too big, and at the thought Serenity was hit with such a heat wave she thought she was going to explode. Shawn didn't make it any better because now he was so close to her face she could smell his minty breath, and she was sure that he could smell her breath. A brief moment of satisfaction came over her and she was happy that at lunch time she had passed up on the burger with extra onions and garlic. She wanted to laugh because Sandra went to town on that thing. Now she was probably killing everything around her. Serenity was brought back to reality when she felt another wave starting at the base of her garden.

Shawn could smell Serenity's breaths. He could not detect the smell, but whatever it was it was soft and sweet. He thought that Serenity could breathe on him all day. The sensation shot straight to Shawn's stomach. He tried to say something to Serenity, but it came out more or less like a moan. The two lips appeared to be on a collision course, two ships in the night. Both were about to throw caution to the wind, and whatever was going to happen was going to happen. What had started out as a rated PG night was about to turn into something hot and steamy. As the two lips came closer, there was a hard knock on the driver side. Both Serenity and Shawn were somewhat startled as they turned to see who was knocking. Their lips quickly but lightly brushed against each other.

"Uh, Mr. Cook." That was Omar the one who was knocking on the driverside window as he continued, "Sir, is everything OK?" Shawn quickly pulled his head out of the position he was in and told Omar, the night guard, as he stumbled and stuttered over his words that everything was fine. Omar stood there and looked at Shawn long, trying to pick up any nonverbal clues or gestures, but there were none. Omar once again smiled at Shawn and tipped his cap at Serenity who also gave Omar an "I'm OK" cheesy smile. Omar continued on his hourly rounds. Shawn was pleased to see that his security team was doing their job and were on point. However, he wasn't too happy that he was the one who got his hands caught in the cookie job, but at that moment, he had some more serious concerns to deal with, one being that woman who had made a deep impression in his heart. While he was thinking about Serenity, she was still trying to unlatch the seat belt.

Then at that moment, something strange occurred. The panel of the car with all of those buttons went on and a sound as if someone was exhaling came from it. The latch on the seat belt clicked open, and Serenity was free. She was so elated she said in a jubilant voice, "I finally got it." Serenity continued jokingly, "Thank you for rescuing me for the second time tonight. You are a super hero."

Shawn was still halfway in the car. As he was trying to get out, he stopped, looked at the control panel, and said, "Well, I am sure I am no super hero. It was probably a malfunction in the controls. This car sometimes acts as if it has a mind of its own." Shawn added in a stern tone, "I will deal with it later." He helped Serenity out of the car. She brushed her skirt down and made an attempt to pull it down. Shawn draped his light jacket around her.

She was more than grateful for the gesture as she said, "What are we doing back here in your office building? Did you leave something?"

Shawn smiled and said, "You have more questions than Colombo. Come on, I want to show you something."

Serenity hesitated; Shawn gave her a look that said, "We've been over this already." She still had a look of reservation. He urged her forward by lightly placing his hand in the small of her back. Serenity appreciated the gesture and found herself liking Shawn's style more and more. He looked at her and noticed some resistance. He said, "Please, it would mean so much to me . . . please."

Serenity did not respond to Shawn in words but with a nonverbal nod of her head, and that was the green light he had been waiting for.

Shawn led Serenity to the elevator. She noticed his steps were full of purpose. She quickly thought back to the time when they had first met in the restaurant. When he had left her sitting at the table, his steps were full of purpose and direction. *I should have known something was special about him then,* she thought. Serenity walked a few steps behind Shawn, and from her perspective, she really liked what she saw. She thought, *No wonder the papers have named him Shawn Cook, the King of Swing.*

They arrived on the main floor where Shawn ran his multimillion dollar business; he was extremely excited, almost like a child on Christmas Morning. Serenity was taken aback by this side of him. She was used to hearing or reading about the seriously rich and powerful Shawn Cook, but this side that she saw had a childlike quality, such innocence. She was immediately drawn to him within her soul.

Shawn noticed Serenity in deep thought. He got her attention by whispering in her ear. He said, "Before we go out to dinner, I want to show you me, not that person you read about in the paper or in the tabloids or any other profile place . . ." Shawn paused to think about the next few words he was about to say. He wanted to make sure that his words came out right. H continued, "Not to say that is not me, but this is the real me, and if I had a chance to reveal who I am, I'd rather have you see the real me."

Serenity didn't know what to say. She felt special that that man wanted to reveal his real self to her. She thought, *He's not trying to impress me. He's trying to set the record straight.* She felt privileged. *I know a lot of guys would probably show off what they had or what they have done, you know hang out all their accomplishments, because in reality they felt insecure. So they'd hide behind these smoke screens so that their real selves can't be seen, but this man has not said any such thing. This man was not trying to run some game.*

Serenity put her head down briefly and came to the realization that she was wrong all along. *She had prejudged this man, a good man, even though she still had a little bit of reservations. The jury was still out so to speak, yet the more she was with him, the more she liked him.*

Shawn took Serenity's hands into his, looked her in her eyes, and said, "I have never allowed anyone to get this close to me or to know the real truth about me!"

Serenity stood still as if she was frozen. She thought, *Why was this man telling me all of this, all of his business?* But in the back of her head there was a faint and fading thought. *He'll probably treat me like his other women, a disposable chick, used and disposed. I bet Mr. Cook has women coming from every hole and every direction, and I bet my thong that he delivers the same line to them all.*

Serenity remembered the conversation she and Sandra had. She could clearly recall Sandra saying, "Don't be fooled by the hype. The man has a solid smooth game, but listen to the woman of experience because I would not guide you wrong, girl. Don't be fooled."

Serenity stood there and felt she was being pulled, perhaps hoodwinked, but deep down in her soul she felt something was right, something felt right. Shawn urged her to walk down the hall with him. The lights were dim, and she could not see but a few steps ahead of her. But Shawn walked on as if the lights were on. He held her hand and led her to a corridor where he flicked on the light switch. The place lit up. Serenity looked around and was amazed by the huge offices and state-of-the-art computers. She looked at Shawn with a sense of confusion. He smiled, stretched his arms out, and turned around in a circle. "I just wanted to show you where

I work . . . I just feel . . ." As he drew closer to her, he said, "I strongly feel that when you like someone, you just want to shar . . ."

Shawn stopped and paused, and he quickly diverted the conversation to something a little safer. Serenity could tell the quick shift in the subject matter and had a deep curiosity to know what he had been about to say, but from the way it looked she had to settle for reading between the lines. But she had to know, so she pushed aside the passive thought and pursued and urged Shawn to continue, "I'm sorry, but what was it you were going to say?"

Shawn shook his head and said, "It wasn't important. Here, come on . . ."

Serenity refused to move as she said in a strong yet tender tone, "It's important to me . . . please finish."

Shawn looked down at his shoes and then back up at Serenity and said, "Let me show you around, and then we can talk about it. How about that?"

Serenity did not like when someone who had something to say started and then stopped without finishing what was on his mind. She was from the old school that if you had something to say, get it off your chest and say it, but she did not push the issue. She just reluctantly agreed to put it off for the time, but she told herself, as she followed Shawn back in the elevator, that she and Shawn would discuss the matter at a later time.

Chapter 61

Shawn gave Serenity a complete tour of the five floors that he owned. They started on the seventeenth floor and went up to four more floors. They were all huge, and all were for a different purpose. Serenity was more than impressed. She had thought before that tour that Shawn was all work and no play, but after the tour, she had come to realize that he was a man of balance. She thought about the twentieth floor, a floor that was converted from offices into a state-of-the-art gym, basketball courts, and tennis courts. The nineteenth floor was also impressive; that floor had been turned into a weight/aerobics room, where self-defense classes were also held, and the eighteenth floor had been designed for the students of employees as well as some of the community kids that were from poor background. Those were the ones Shawn and his team targeted. It was his baby. Shawn working with the board of education was able to get three computer teachers and volunteers among some of the students who were doing well in high school and college. It was a community outreach effort. The program had been a success to the extent that community leaders and politicians had started a scholarship program. The program had been featured on several talk shows as well as in top black magazines. Shawn refused to take the credit. As a matter of fact, he always directed the credit to his team players, despite the fact that he was the brainchild and founder of the program.

Serenity was taken aback. She could not believe all of what that man was doing for the community as well as for his employees. Even though Serenity was starving, she had to admit Shawn Cook was truly all what was said about him and more, but what impressed Serenity more than any of these things was the idea that he was a humble man. Yet he carried himself with an air of confidence and assurance. He looked at Serenity as they got on the elevator. He pressed the button for the solarium and asked, "Hey, a penny for your thoughts." Serenity was brought out of her reverie.

She smiled at Shawn and responded to the question, "Oh nothing, just thinking, that's all." She continued to feel a bond being formed between her and Shawn, and she was scared. *This was strange, for one she hardly knew the man, and yet she felt she'd known him like an old friend.* As she leaned against the wall of the elevator, she thought about how a bit earlier she couldn't express her thoughts to Shawn the same way he couldn't express his thoughts to her. She smiled to herself and thought, *Two peas in a pod.*

The elevator stopped on the thirty-fifth floor, the last floor. Shawn led Serenity out of the elevator straight to the solarium, which was an indoor-outdoor facility. It was absolutely stunning. She thought that the twentieth floor was the most impressive. It had to be by far the cream of the crop. She was quite stunned at the beauty of all the plants and flowers. The place felt like the Garden of Eden. Everywhere Serenity turned, she saw the awesomeness of beauty of all kinds of plants. She said, "Wow, who takes care of this place?"

Shawn, who at the time was looking at one of the plants, responded to the question, "Oh well, I do. I try to get up here at least a few times a week. If not, I get one of my students, who's been trained, to come and take care of the place." Serenity's eyes became moist. Shawn noticed the moist gleam in her eyes and had to hold down the lump that was forming in his throat.

He was glad when Serenity spoke, "My goodness, this is beautiful. This place is enchanting. I bet your employees enjoy this on their breaks or lunch breaks. What a place to come and relax and shut out the crazy things going on in their lives, I could only . . ."

Shawn cut her off with a smile, as he stood just a few feet behind her taking in her scent, and responded, "I share practically everything with my staff, but this is one thing I call my own. This is my domain. This is where I come to when I need to think or when I just want to get away or even just to relax or even when I'm feeling burned out or when I botch a multimillion dollar deal. This becomes my solace." Shawn paused for a brief moment and continued, "When I am about to make a major decision, I come here before I go to my board." Serenity had an inquisitive look on her face as she wrinkled her nose like she always did when she did not quite understand something. Shawn thought the look was endearing as his heart continued to be drawn closer and closer to hers. He continued, "This place feels pure. It has a tranquility that words cannot express . . ." Shawn was so caught up in what he was saying that it seemed as if he blocked everything out as he continued with a look of awe on his face, "When I am here, no matter what

I am going through, this place . . . I can't explain it . . . but this place seems to melt away everything and anything that does not belong. Sometimes I spend hours here just meditating. I call this place God's sanctuary, God's paradise When I am here, I feel it's just God and I."

Serenity was speechless as she thought, *Here is a man who could have taken her to the most expensive restaurants. He could have really tried to impress her by spending money as if it grew on trees. He could have done a number of things, just to prove that he is Shawn Cook, but instead he brings me to his humble hideaway getaway.* Serenity felt a lump in her throat as she thought. She recalled Shawn saying that he had never invited anyone up there before. *But here I am in a place he has reserved for himself.* Serenity put her head down because the feeling overwhelmed her. When she lifted her head, she looked straight at Shawn. He was looking with concern at one of his plants. As she watched him, he with tender hands and fingers touched the roots of the plant, picked up the dirt, and rubbed the dirt between his fingers. He then looked back at the plant and moved it to a special place on the side where there was artificial light. Serenity watched as Shawn made room for the plant. He turned and looked at Serenity, who was staring at him. At that moment, they both stared at each other. Shawn smiled and at that moment she felt it. It hit her like a bolt of lightning, but she felt it. A connection had been made, or maybe it was continuing, she did not know. The feeling frightened her and at the same time reassured her that what she felt was right. All the way down to the bone, it was right—no inhibitions, no restraints or constraints, no restrictions. At that point, she felt as if she was a bird, free. She'd never felt this way before. The cage door was open. She was free to be free.

They stared at each other until Serenity nervously walked to the other side where she saw a telescope. She looked through the viewfinder and her breath got caught in her lungs. She was speechless; the night was clear and the stars beamed with such brightness. Shawn heard Serenity say a quick statement in awe about God. As she continued to look through the finder, she saw the majestic beauty, and her eyes began to water and teardrops slid down her cheek. Shawn wanted to capture every drop and bottle it. He noticed Serenity shivering. As he approached her, he took his coat off and wrapped it around her shoulder. His hands stayed on her shoulders a little longer than normal and he said, "Isn't it beautiful, so majestic, and awesome?" Serenity nodded her head. She was too caught up emotionally to respond, as she wiped the tears from her face.

When Shawn put his coat around Serenity, she protested and said, "No . . ." She made an attempt to take Shawn's coat off her shoulders and give it back to him while continuing to protest, "How about you?" She looked at him with a look of wonder and continued, "I don't want you to get sick. You're not superman." She smiled and then continued, "Or are you? You have really impressed me tonight. Thank you anyway."

Shawn stopped her from taking off the coat and said, "I'm OK. Please leave it on. Don't worry about me. I've trained my mind and body to deal with the most extreme conditions." He looked at her with a confident smile and said, "And, no, I'm not superman, and the night is not over." He was referring to what she had said about being really impressed that night.

Serenity removed her hand from the coat, and in doing so, she brushed it against Shawn's strong hand. The gesture may have been minor, but what it did to and for Serenity's heart was major as she blushed and said, "Just a few more minutes, then we can go, OK?"

Shawn shrugged his shoulders in a way that said it didn't make any difference to him, but in his heart he was thinking about how he wished he could bring her there every night and just watch the expression on her face as she looked through the telescope. It was a look that went deep down in his soul. Serenity finished looking through the telescope. She shook her head, and the only words she could say was amazing. Shawn looked at her and gave a smile that confirmed what Serenity was feeling. As the two walked back to the elevator and stood there without pressing the button, Serenity said, "I can't believe you take care of this place by yourself."

Shawn responded with a chuckle, "Why do you find that so hard to believe?" Shawn continued, "What? You think only women and feminine men can do this?"

Serenity smiled and playfully held up her hand as if to say, "Don't get excited."

Shawn continued, "And as you can see, or at least you will find out, I don't fit in any of those categories."

Serenity blushed a little at Shawn's prediction and began to twirl her locks. She felt like a schoolgirl. She was speechless as he continued, "When I was growing up, all six of us, really seven . . . but that's another story. Anyway, we were taught both male and female responsibilities, so I don't have a problem doing dishes or cleaning up. It was expected of us." Serenity nodded her head; the more she found out about Shawn, the more she liked him and the more that armor protecting her heart melted. Neither of them had summoned the elevator to come. Both were enjoying the moment of getting to know one another.

Serenity still twirling her locks asked, "So why did you ask me to come up here?" Shawn moved closer to her, towering over her by a couple of feet, looked down at her, and responded as he held her hand, "Well, I made a promise to myself when I had this part of the building changed over to a greenhouse/observational tower that the person that I will invite up here will be the one I would love to spend my time with, someone that I will want to be a part of my life."

Serenity's eyes drifted to Shawn's massive chest. She was nervous as she bit her lower lip, which she did every time she would become nervous, and said in a low whisper, "But how do you know if I am that person? How do you know that I am the one? I am sure there are many out there who can please you as well as keep up with you financially and . . ."

Shawn cut her off as he placed his pointer finger gently on her lips and said, "I know that you are the one. The first time I saw you I went home and destroyed my black book. I knew you were the one. I can feel it deep down in my gut. When I sit down to eat my mind is on you. When I am conducting business at these business deals, I see you. You are in my dreams, my thoughts, my feelings, my emotions. I am locked in on you. I don't have any interest in any other but you, Serenity Powers . . . that's how I know that you are the one." Serenity did not know what to say. She had never been put in such a situation. Men found her attractive, but they wanted only one thing and that was control. But this man was about something totally different. Shawn was saying these things as he drew closer to her to the extent she could smell his nice minty breath as her hands went to his massive chest. His chest made her hands look like a child's hands. As she blushed and smiled, he continued, "I am not looking for a one-night stand, I am looking for someone who will stand with me, not in front of me or behind me, but beside me. So if you don't fit the bill, you might as well get to stepping because I am not into playing games. That's for boys. I am a man." Serenity felt as if she was melting as Shawn bent down slightly and brushed his lips against hers just to see if she was on the same page. He found out real quick. She pulled him closer to her, lifted her head up, and stood on her toes as she wanted to give him a little more of herself. She wanted to devour those juicy lips. She opened her mouth slightly for him to go from a little sampling to a complete surrender.

Her cell phone chimed; the music broke the love trance and brought them both back to the present. Serenity quickly grabbed it and answered it without looking to see who it was. Then she heard a familiar voice say, "So how is it going? Did you rock his world yet, girl?" Serenity turned slightly away from Shawn because Sandra was talking so loud in her wild ghetto self as she continued, "So what stage are you on? Remember the ones I taught you."

Serenity had a look of surprise on her face. Then again she shouldn't have been surprised at Sandra's timing or her questions. The woman had no manners. Serenity, with her mouth barely open, responded to Sandra, "We will talk later . . . no, not now . . . no, it's not like that . . . no, not tonight . . . yes, I will be home tonight . . ." From the corner of her eye, Serenity could see Shawn smiling as she continued to get Sandra off the phone. "Yes, tomorrow . . . no, don't call me, I'll call you . . . It's not like that . . . listen, I have to go . . . Yes, I will . . . no, I don't plan on spending the night . . . Bye, bye, I will call you later." As Serenity closed her cell phone, Shawn could faintly hear Sandra yelling something.

Serenity looked at Shawn, blushed with a smile, and apologized. Shawn waved it off and told Serenity that he thought that Sandra was a cool person. Serenity at first was surprised that Shawn knew it was Sandra. Yet, on the other hand, he had probably heard her big mouth. Serenity smiled and agreed with Shawn. Her girl could get on her nerves at times, but she was a friend who had proven her worth time and time again.

While Serenity had been at it with Sandra, Shawn had taken the liberty to call for the elevator. She was surprised when it came. She was so caught up with silly Sandra she hadn't realized that Shawn had called for it. He looked at Serenity and asked, "How about you and I go and get something to eat?"

Serenity liked that idea. After a long day at the office, she welcomed the idea of a nice place to relax and eat, and she said, "So where are we going?"

Shawn thought about it for a minute and then had a big smile on his face. Just about the time when the elevator doors were closing and Serenity was about to get on, Shawn remembered he had left something in his private quarters, which he was supposed to get earlier to bring to his mother. "Listen, I forgot something in my P/Q room I was supposed to bring to my mother. Come back with me. It will only take a minute."

Serenity agreed as he led her in the direction of the greenhouse. She being curious asked, "What does P/Q stand for?"

Shawn smiled and said, "Oh, I am sorry, that's the other area where I go to relax. It's on the roof. Do you remember seeing a small building, which looked like a shed? You know one of those that people have in their backyard to keep tools? This one's a little bigger. Remember seeing that?" Serenity nodded her head. She had seen a small kind of shed but didn't bother to inquire what it was. She assumed it was a storage room. They both walked toward the area they had just left. From there, he took her hand and walked across the roof to what looked like a little shed or something.

Serenity had come to the conclusion that the little thing was not attractive looking and that it looked as if it was put together by glue. It did not seem strong or sturdy, and the closer she drew near to it, the more she believed that the big, bad wolf would have a field day in this place. She smiled. Shawn caught her smiling and said, "What's so amusing?" Serenity, who for the second time that evening had got her hands caught in the cookie jar, knew she could not brush that inquiry off like she had done earlier.

She responded this time, "I think . . . it's cute, but it doesn't look like . . ."

Shawn cut her off and said, "What? Strong or attractive . . . ? I know, but never judge a book by its cover."

Serenity didn't want to offend Shawn as he'd been so sweet and kind to her. However, she hesitated and nodded her head sheepishly. Shawn noticing her ambivalence assured her that she wasn't offending him and said, "Like I said, never judge a book by its cover. Things may not seem the way that they look." As they walked up to the shack, Shawn said under his breath, *What was that code again?* He looked at Serenity, who was holding back her laughter, and he smiled and continued to pretend that he was having a hard time remembering the code. He said, "I know what you are thinking. Why have a code for this thing? Well, no code, no go." Serenity chuckled as Shawn began to say the code out loud and at the same time press the buttons on the pad. Serenity playfully tried to stop him, but Shawn brushed her off and said, "Shhh, I'm trying to concentrate."

Serenity said jokingly, "Just wait for a big wind to pass. It'll probably tear down this whole thing."

Serenity laughed out loud and watched Shawn as he put his finger to his mouth playfully and told her to hush. He said, "I can't think. Silence, please, while the great Shawn tries to remember the code." Serenity laughed so hard she thought her stomach was going to burst open. She smiled and turned her back away from the door. Shawn smiled and started over. When he was finished, he opened the door slowly with his arms stretched out like magicians do. He stepped aside and urged Serenity to enter. She entered slowly as cautiously as a cat, afraid that something may drop down on her head or pop up to hit her in the face. She kept her eyes on Shawn to see if his expression would give anything away. She could not detect anything, and so she took a deep breath and stepped into a dark room. Shawn flicked on the light switch, and the sound of electricity connecting at first made Serenity jump a little. As she grabbed onto Shawn's arm, he could not help but laugh. Then, suddenly like magic, everything came to life, and Serenity could not believe what she was looking at.

Chapter 62

Serenity put her hand to her mouth as she was totally surprised of what she saw.

Shawn stood back smiling at Serenity as she walked in and tentatively touched the items that looked so unique.

Serenity was amazed that the outside of what she had thought was a shed turned out to be a well-furnished studio with all the amenities; there was a bathroom that was small but looked cozy, a small island kitchen, and a medium-size living room. Everything was state of the art. The place had all the entertainment anyone could ask for; you name it, the place had it.

Serenity noticed there were no windows, yet she could feel a nice, comfortable kind of mild heat. She looked at Shawn, and he already knew what she was thinking.

He countered, "Haa, ha, you see, you are probably thinking, no windows, so how do I see what's going on? But who needs windows?" Shawn went over to some buttons on a wall and began pressing them, and just like magic, the walls slid apart and behind it were five large monitors. They took up the whole side of the wall. Shawn pressed another button, and the monitors revealed the solarium as well as the lobby. He said, "I have cameras stationed in different locations: two outside on the roof, one in the solarium, and two downstairs, one in the garage and one by the security front desk. So sometimes when I want to relax or just get away for the weekend I come up here, and if someone comes to see me I know who it is. And I can relay a message to my head of security through the earpiece in his ear without anyone suspecting anything." Serenity smiled and shook her head in amazement. "But if I want to just relax . . ." Shawn pressed another button and two out of the five monitors showed the stars of the night. Serenity's breath caught in her throat as she was looking at the stars and planets. Shawn continued, "Or, during the day, I can program this special camera to show the main buildings and other aspects of New York. The magnification on this camera is awesome."

Serenity nodded her head with a smile. She was more than impressed; she was excited. Shawn noticed her smiling and thinking. He asked, "What are you smiling about now?" Serenity did not miss the "now" in Shawn's question. She thought she must have looked silly all night with that silly grin on her face. She thought about that fast food commercial where that king has that silly grin on his face throughout the commercial. That's what she felt like. Yet, on the other hand, it made her feel good that Shawn had been paying attention to her throughout the evening.

She responded, "No, I was just thinking that you are amazing and a man of many surprises. You have surprised me over and over again." Serenity blushed and smiled and then began to twirl her locks while nibbling on her bottom lip as she continued in a soft tone of voice, "You . . . you also seemed to know what I'm thinking before I could get it out of my mouth. I find that also amazing."

Shawn stood there just a few feet from her. He decided to stay put. He did not want to push it, but deep down he had a deep yearning to go to her, hold her, and kiss those full and juicy lips. Instead, he made a decision to play it safe as he responded to her statement about reading her mind, "Does that bother you?" Serenity looked at him with those big, brown eyes and wrinkled her nose, indicating she did not understand. He had fallen in love with that look. He made an attempt to clarify what he meant, "You know, me reading your mind."

Serenity blushed and said, "It doesn't bother me. In a way it scares me. I mean what does that mean. We've only known each other for a short time, and most of that time, I had so many misinterpretations about you, I . . ."

Shawn felt a knot in his groin area. If he was hearing what Serenity was saying that meant she had taken a step closer to him. He responded, "Well, the only thing I can say is I want you to be in my life. I am not a mind reader, but I know when there is a connection, I feel it right here." Shawn pointed to his heart as he continued, "Whenever you are ready, I'll be waiting. I found what I've been looking for. There is no need to look any further."

Serenity caught the intensity and seriousness in Shawn's eyes. His voice was so strong, and his eyes were kind of penetrating past all of her excuses and procrastinations. They were ripping down her defenses and getting rid of her misconceptions. Serenity had to turn slightly away. There was nothing else she could use to hide behind. Shawn tore them down. This was his moment to move in. She was vulnerable and she was ripe at that moment, but he told himself he did not want her like that. He wanted her when she was ready, not when her emotions were playing guilt trips with him.

He realized that he was coming on strong. He backed off a bit, as he changed the subject, "Listen, I know you have to be hungry. I don't know about you, but I can eat a bucket of whatever or a pizza pie with anything on it." Shawn was rubbing his stomach. Serenity had to laugh looking at Shawn's boyish behavior and how down-to-earth he was, but she also knew fully well that his eyes was probably too big for his stomach. Yet again she could not blame him. So was hers, as she interjected, "OK, so where are we going?"

Shawn looked and responded to Serenity as naturally as drinking water, "How about if we order out?" Serenity did not care for the idea. She had worked all day dealing with nonsense, getting ready for tonight. All she wanted to do was relax, have some space, and kick back. The thought hit her that they could probably go back to Shawn's office to eat. That did not go to well with her. Shawn noticed the look of disappointment on Serenity's face. He asked, "What's wrong?"

Shawn had been so good to her she didn't want to seem like a spoiled brat, so she responded, "Well, I was hoping to get out after being in the office all day. I just wanted to relax, and it is such a beautiful night, a place where we can listen to some music and eat until we can't eat another bite."

Shawn contemplated what Serenity had said and stated, "Well, I don't mind going out. I just figured we both had a hard day, and the last thing we would want is going out looking for a place to eat and dealing with the wait and the crowds . . . but if you want to go out, that's cool with me."

Serenity felt the same way as Shawn. She didn't want to deal with those things, but she concluded that it was better than eating in his office . . . Serenity's thoughts were interrupted by Shawn, "Or . . . we can eat right here." Shawn went over to the panel of buttons and pressed one, and the monitor showed the night sky, the stars, and the moon as he continued, "We can eat at peace under the stars, so to speak." Shawn pressed another button, and music started playing, soft, soulful hits that penetrated the surround sound of the place. It was as if the music was coming from everywhere. Shawn continued, "And the good part is, there is no wait, and it's just you and me, and I could get them to deliver the food in a matter of minutes, since I own the restaurant . . . so what do you think?"

Serenity smiled and said, "You mean right here?"

Shawn chuckled and nodded to Serenity's question while responding, "And if music is not your thing, I have the latest DVDs or we can order a movie. We can relax and not rush because we both have off tomorrow, and I will make sure you get home at a decent hour, or we can leave from here in the morning."

Serenity felt a sensation in her garden area when Shawn made his subtle pitch. She twirled her locks and bit her bottom lip, thinking about the choices. Shawn looked at his watch and said with excitement, "The night is still young. What is there to hold us back?" Serenity laughed as if she was ten years old again. Shawn smiled, enjoying every minute of it. She was excited about the idea of eating under the stars and planets. It was such a romantic idea. It was perfect, but she didn't want to give Shawn the wrong impression. He went over to his desk and pulled out the menu to his restaurant and asked Serenity what she would like to eat. She came over to him and looked at the menu. Shawn looked at the menu and then back at Serenity.

Serenity was so hungry she had a hard time making up her mind. The way she felt she wanted everything. She said in playful frustration, "I can't choose, I am so hungry. I want everything." And she laughed.

Shawn laughed and said, "OK, I tell you what, let's look at the menu and you can chose three of your favorite dinners and then you can break down the three through the process of elimination. How about that?"

Serenity looked at Shawn, shook her head, and added, "Even in choosing a meal you approach it from a business perspective."

Shawn shrugged his shoulders and said, "Life is all about choices and the process of elimination. Only the strong survive, baby."

He did not take it any further as he reminded himself that it was a date and not an educational field trip. They settled on the beef BBQ place down the street. Shawn called downstairs to his security team and let them know that the order would be coming within the next ten to fifteen minutes. He asked Omar to bring it upstairs when it arrived. Shawn used a special air chute that looked like a pipe to send down the money. He placed the money in a canister and sent it down.

Then Shawn went over to Serenity and stood behind her as she watched the large screen of the stars. He said, "Our food should be here any minute. I took the liberty to order some wine."

She blushed and twirled her locks and said, "Thank you."

Shawn continued, "If you want you can freshen up in the restroom. It's not big, but it has all the amenities you would need." She agreed to do so as she wanted not only to freshen up, but also to see how the number one bachelor lived.

Serenity took notes of everything. She wanted to give Sandra a full report. She could not believe that his place was so organized and orderly. Serenity thought, *There must be someone that comes in here to clean up at least once a week, probably a female.* He made her place look like cluttered R us, and she always referred to herself as a cleanliness freak. But she had to step aside and hand over the mantle to Shawn, and if that was the case with her, then he made Karen's place look like something as if the hurricane twins had gone through that place.

She went into the bathroom, and the first thing she did very quietly was to open the medicine cabinet. Sandra had told her that that was the first thing to check in a man's house. It revealed a lot about him. To her surprise, it was stocked up with first aid kits, toiletries, and condoms . . . She blushed when she read on the condom, "Extra large." She fanned herself playfully. She then took out her cell phone and called her best friend, Sandra. She could not wait to let her know what had taken place up to now, but mainly what she had found in his medicine cabinet. She dialed, and Sandra who of course had caller ID picked it up on the first ring and said, "OK, let me have the 411. All of it."

Chapter 63

Shawn wondered what was taking Serenity so long. *It's not like the restroom is huge. How long does it take to wash your hands?* Shawn knew from personal experience of growing up with sisters that a clean restroom is a girl's favorite friend. *But this is ridiculous,* he thought. As he was thinking, Serenity came out of the restroom, looking refreshed.

Since she didn't wear makeup, Shawn was taken aback by Serenity's natural beauty. She looked better than some women who wore makeup. He, still thinking about Serenity, thought that at the end of the day she took nothing off her face, no makeup, no touchups, and no cosmetics. It was all natural. What you see was what you got from sunrise to sunset. He liked that in a woman, no surprises of looking good one day and the next day looking like a hit-and-run victim. He dealt with women like that, and those were the ones who in his opinion had multiple personalities; they had a personality for every look. Shawn chuckled to himself and thought about his friend Rick, who was probably a player of players.

One day he said to Shawn that he'd been shocked so many times to wake up and find a total stranger laying next to him, compared to the person he went to bed with. He remembered Rick saying, "Yo, C-4, I could recall going to bed with a princess and waking up to the Bride of Frankenstein. You don't know how many times I had to sneak out of houses and change my cell phone numbers."

Shawn stifled a laugh as Serenity said, "You have such a cozy bathroom. You have an eye for decoration." Serenity's eyes seemed to have a mind of their own as she quickly looked at Shawn's midsection and nervously looked around, hoping that Shawn did not catch her trying to get a quick peep. She did not know what had come over her that moment to make her look in that general area, but then it dawned on her that it may have been those extra-large-size condoms she discovered, and after talking to crazy

Sandra for a quick minute, within that time she had put all types of ideas in Serenity's head.

Serenity, feeling nervous, twirled her locks and bit her bottom lip.

Shawn smiled and thought, *No wonder she took her time. I hope she found something to talk about. Some women going into a new place are like putting a kid in a toy store.* He brought his attention back to Serenity and said in a nice tone, "Thank you. Like I said, my parents taught us that there was no job in the house a man or woman could avoid. That is, just because you are either a man or a woman you could do or not do certain jobs. Not in our household, my sisters would take out the trash, while my brothers and I did the dishes."

Serenity smiled and agreed with him. She'd mainly thought that a lot of parents, especially people of color and mainly the single moms, would treat their sons like men, young boys, still pee pots. They would talk to them as if they were the men of the house, and yet they didn't even know their left from their right. These young children turned out to be adult children with no sense of direction or purpose or responsibility, and then they would go out and try to hook up with someone who would treat them like the way their mother had.

Serenity smiled. She was grateful that she had never become involved with some of those men, those who were men on the outside but acted like little boys on the inside. However, she couldn't say the same thing for her friend, Sandra. That was all she came into contact with. She found these "little boys" in these adult places.

Serenity could not help but shake her head. She then looked up at Shawn, smiled, and thought, *But here is one that went in the proper order of growth, from a boy to a man.*

Shawn noticed Serenity staring at him so intently. He had to ask her what was up with that. She smiled, showing those wonderful full lips and white sparkling teeth, her cheekbones chiseled to what looked to be like perfection. Shawn saw her as the essence of beauty. He just wanted to grab her and make hard, passionate love to her for hours. Her look seemed to burn right down to his soul.

Serenity responded, "Uh, pardon me, I'm usually not this rude. I just find you such a very interesting person." She blushed a little and thought whether she should say what was about to come out of her mouth. She battled with the thought, then she just threw caution to the wind and came out with it, "It's just, I never met anyone as together as you. Your parents raised you right. Wow, kudos to them."

Shawn like a dry plant drank in every word. He loved to hear her voice, the way she pronounced her words, the way her hands moved while she spoke, and the eye contact as if to say "it's just you and I, everything else is shut out."

Shawn at first felt emotionally overwhelmed. He was speechless. Then he slowly nodded his head as to say "thank you" and then he verbalized it, "Wow, thank you. No really, that means more to me than any certificate of recognition that I could hang on the wall in my office, but what you just said is sealed in my heart."

They both stared at each other with looks of raw passion, just ready for the scales to tip, but Shawn once again aborted the mission and said with a bit of sexual tension, "We have to save our boys, boys that grow up into the weak males of our society. On the outside they are tough, but on the inside they lack what it would really take to survive. Eventually, if we don't do something to save what we can we are a people that will be added to the list of extinct animals. Do you know what I mean? This is one reason I started the mentor/defense program. It's a program that we try to holistically teach our boys stages of passage." Shawn continued, "When you complete the program, you just don't sit around with nothing to do. No, you become the teacher."

Serenity found herself mesmerized just by listening to Shawn. She agreed with what he said. Then both of them got into a deep philosophical discussion. Both were impressed with each other's knowledge of what was going on in their community, how programs were being cut back, such as summer programs, or etched out such as certain educational programs or art such as music. They talked, shared, and laughed, agreed as well as disagreed, but one thing that they both knew but would not admit it was that they both had etched a deeper level of emotional connection with each other.

During their talk, their food had arrived. Shawn asked Omar to bring it up. He was up there in a matter of minutes; Shawn thanked Omar for bringing up the food and gave him an extra tip, more than what he had sent down the first time to give to the delivery person.

Shawn brought the food that came in several containers toward the table. Serenity removed the items that were on the table. He instructed her to toss them on the side.

Serenity placed them on the nightstand. Shawn placed the containers lined up on the table like a salad bar setting. As Serenity watched, her stomach made sounds. When Shawn was finished, it was like an Indy 500 race.

"Get on your mark, get set, go." The gun sounded, and the cars, that is, the two of them, took off out of the starting gate. Shawn, in between serving, stopped to put on some jazz music with his surround sound. Serenity had her plate full, totally unladylike, starving like Marvin, full to the tilt. Food was falling off the side, but at the speed she was going, there would be room. She tried her best to behave like a lady, but seeing that she had filled her plate to the max, she threw that concept out the window. And if that didn't do it, this did. She tried to pick the meat off the beef ribs with her fork, dainty style. She used the knife to hold the tasty meat in place. When she saw that she wasn't satisfied with the results, she chucked that idea, picked up that beef rib, and bit into it with a vengeance. She thought as her eyes looked and darted from side to side, *Whatever he's going to think about me, it's going to happen tonight, about . . . right now. No matter what was said earlier, after this, this will be the deciding factor.*

She continued to rip the meat off the beef rib. Shawn on the other hand could care less how Serenity was getting the job done. He was busy getting his grub on, and the way he was doing it would not have earned him a clean and neat star. The two ate like they hadn't eaten in days. There was no talk between them, just the sound of good food being thrown down and chopped up. It was a familiar sound of satisfaction. They were like human garbage disposals.

Serenity did not say it while she was devouring her food, but she had to admit that that setting was better than any restaurant setting. She was swept away with the whole atmosphere, the music, and the stars on the big screen, and a nice not too warm and not too cool air was coming from the vents. She really felt the sensation of being outdoors. *She could not remember the last time she felt like this on a date.* She smiled to herself. *This was special.* It wasn't that she didn't date because of the way she looked; on the contrary, most guys found her extremely attractive and intelli . . . *Wait a second, stop right there. Yes, most guys did find her intelligent, but those were the same ones who also found her intimidating due to her intelligence, while others found her intelligence as a challenge.* Most men she dated had to prove to her in some way that they were more superior, like "me man, you woman." Or another way to put it, they were the smarter one of the two because of their male status.

One night, she briefly remembered, her date ended in a total disaster just because she beat her date at scrabble. Mr. Harvard-PhD had an asinine attack because he lost not once, not twice, but three times, but now she was with someone who as far as she could see did not have any problem with her intelligence or anything else.

The two had finished eating, and Serenity felt as if she had eaten for an army as she tried to find the most comfortable position without compromising her womanhood. She finally settled in. Shawn looked relaxed as he lay back on the couch with his hands folded on his full stomach. The nice R&B sound flowed through the surround sound as the two enjoyed watching the large monitor which was displaying the sky. The mood was quiet; it was a nice moment. Serenity felt very comfortable. She asked Shawn, "You mentioned about your siblings. Can you tell me more about your family? They sound so wonderful."

Shawn nodded as he thought, *If anything will get her to see what type of person I am. My family is the strong point.* Shawn went into details about how his parents, he, and his siblings went from rags to respect and riches. He talked about all his siblings and how successful they were. He talked about his nephews and nieces and how he took out time for them and spent time at the movies, arcades, and museums. Serenity not just listened. She was seeing another side of the man many people hadn't seen before, especially the media. She had a deeper appreciation for Shawn as she added, "How did you do it? Being one of the youngest, busiest, and wealthiest men in the city."

Shawn laughed holding his stomach. Serenity looked at him confused. He controlled his laughter and explained, "Please forgive me. I laugh because, and don't get me wrong, I appreciate everything you said about me, but in reality, it's not what you have on the outside. It's what comes out from the inside. Even if I wasn't all those things you mentioned, I would still treat my nephews and nieces the same because I love them." Shawn continued, "People get confused about what does it mean to be rich and wealthy in the eyes of the world?" Serenity was captivated and waited for the response as he continued, "You are put on top of the world one day and in their trash the next. I take what I read about myself in the papers or how many talk shows I'm invited to with a grain of salt. They don't make me who I am. I don't care how much time of fame they are giving me. I give God public glory and let everyone know. He's the reason for Shawn Cook's success, so if you have a problem talk to Him." Shawn smiled that billion-dollar smile.

Serenity was full not only from the food, but also with Shawn's attitude and his concept of life. She could stay there all night and listen to that man. *No wonder, he has won the hearts of women. Oh yeah, she was impressed.*

Serenity did not know where that other idea came from, but it was there, and that was that Shawn Cook was a man that her parents always told her to go for and to look for. "They are one in a million," she remembered her parents telling her. She remembered how her father would sit next to her and say to her, "Make sure you have your shopping for the right man grocery list." Then she remembered how after he went through the list, he would say, "Look for someone with integrity, dignity, pride, character, an education, and most of all someone who loves God." That he would say was a good package, and Serenity had to admit that Shawn had the full package in more ways than one. As she was hummed a jazz tune, Shawn was just looking at her as if she did not have a care in the world. *What a difference,* he thought, *compared to the first few times they met. The battle of the sexes.* Shawn smiled and shook his head as he stared at her.

Serenity opened her eyes and caught Shawn staring at her, and he didn't make any bones about it. He wanted to get caught. He wanted her to catch him watching her. Serenity smiled and ignored him as she continued to hum to the music, feeling it in her body, while her body moved to the flow of the beat. She didn't care if he was watching. She thought as a wide smile spread across her face, *If you want to watch, keep watching and enjoy the show.* Shawn loved the way she moved. She touched all the right point zones in his body and caused all the right reactions. Serenity sat back as the music faded out to make room for another jazz hit, but she had to make a comment about Shawn's family, "I want to thank you for sharing your family with me. It sounds like you guys are really close."

Shawn chuckled and responded, "Yeah, we are. We are very tight, but I failed to mention that my parents also raised my best friend, Frank . . ." Shawn paused and continued, "It's a long story. I'll just say Frank came to us when he was around nine or ten, and the two of us became inseparable. And to this day, he's my road dog, my best friend."

Serenity could only shake her head in amazement as she commented, "Wow, it's one thing to raise your own kids, but I give anyone extra credit who takes the time and energy to raise someone's child, especially that of a stranger. It tells me that your parents are special people."

Shawn shrugged and said, "Well, they are cool parents, always have been, but Frank is cool too, and we are very proud of him. He's come a long way. He wanted to work in law enforcement. He went to West Point and graduated with honors. He did six years in the Reserves and went back to school for a couple of years, and now he works for the government as the FBI top notch drug enforcer on the East Coast." Shawn paused and his eyebrows went up as it usually did when an idea came to him as he continued, "As a matter of fact, he works in your building." Serenity looked surprised, but shook her head as if to say she didn't know him as Shawn continued, "He's about six foot two and 230 pounds with caramel complexion. Him and his team handle all packages that come in or go out."

Serenity tried to picture Shawn's friend but could not. Shawn noticed her struggling to remember and tried to help her, "He's very distinguishing looking." She looked at Shawn and thought, *Yeah, just like you.* Shawn noticed Serenity drifting off. He pulled her back to the present moment, "Serenity to earth, Serenity to earth, come in."

Serenity quickly focused her attention back on Shawn as she stated, "I'm sorry, I was trying to visualize your friend. Sorry, I can't say I've seen him."

Serenity in her mind wanted to slap herself for getting caught, but on the other hand she could not come out with the truth and say something like, *Hey, Shawn, I didn't know Frank, but I wouldn't mind getting to know you.* She could not believe that she had just thought what she had. That wasn't her, but there it was. She was floundering over that man. Shawn looked at Serenity and asked her whether she was OK.

Serenity responded, "Uh, yea, I was still trying to . . ." She continued her Oscar performance as she waved her hand in frustration.

Shawn interjected, "Well, it's no biggie. Don't sweat it, but believe me, you will know him when you see him. He works in the immigration department, the top gun."

Shawn dismissed the conversation regarding his buddy Frank. Meanwhile, the music had switched back to soft R&B. Shawn wasn't pulling any stops. He wasn't taking any prisoners. *This may be his last good chance to win Serenity.* He programmed the music to concentrate on one part of the body—the heart.

Serenity was feeling the results as her heart felt it was melting. She felt something odd. She had felt it earlier, and she could not put her finger on it. So she dismissed it, but . . . there . . . she felt it again. She was trying to find the words that would describe what she was feeling, then it dawned on her. She felt a . . . yes, that's what it was a . . . connection.

Chapter 64

Serenity tried to shake off the feeling. *This wasn't the place or the time.* Well, she was wrong there. *This was the place, and this could be the right time, but in reality that couldn't happen, two different worlds . . .* Her thoughts were interrupted by Shawn's question, "So how about you?"

Serenity looked at Shawn and crinkled her nose. "What about me?" she asked.

Shawn looked at Serenity for a brief second and noticed that she looked a little tight. He responded, "Are you OK?" Serenity nodded with perhaps a little too much energy pumped into the nodding as Shawn continued, "No, I was just asking what about you? You know, your family."

Serenity felt like a complete moron. It was a simple question that she took far more seriously than what it was as she responded, "Well, I don't have the number of siblings as you. It's just my brother and I. I am the eldest. My parents are retired. They've been working what seemed like forever. My father has his own law firm. I don't know if you ever heard of Jason Powers Sr.?"

Shawn perked up, "Yeah, of course I have. Wow, this is a small world. Your father and I have done some work together . . . on a small scale."

Serenity was surprised, but then she thought, *Why should she be? Anyone who has any kind of affluence in this city would know Shawn Cook or at least cross paths with him one way or another.* Serenity continued, "My mother retired as a top official for the board of education. She worked practically every position, climbing the ladder, finishing up on her own schooling with a PhD . . ." Serenity paused, took a deep breath, and let it out. She was very proud of her parents. She also cherished the tranquil moment she was experiencing right then as she continued, "My brother, Jason, was a copartner with my father at the firm. He now has a chance to take over the firm. He's young but very smart and he has the experience, and he will always have my father in his corner."

Shawn read in between the lines and looking inquisitive added, "But . . ."

Serenity smiled at how quick Shawn was when it came down to reading between the lines as she added, "But he feels he may not want that responsibility, so he's opted to have someone run the firm for another few years while he keeps working for the firm gaining wisdom, knowledge, and confidence."

Shawn nodded at the choice that Serenity's brother had made. He felt it was a good move. "It showed that he has patience and he's not worried about any takeover . . . that's good."

Serenity shrugged her shoulders and, while twisting her locks, said, "Well, that's about it. I completed my studies at Spelman College and Morgan State University."

Shawn nodded his head, looking very impressed. Serenity blushed and looked down at her watch. "Oh my goodness, I didn't realize it was this late." She could not believe how fast time had flown as she looked at the clock on the wall and mumbled something along the same lines as "Oh my goodness!"

Shawn had a coy smile on his face as he responded, "Well . . . do you work tomorrow?" Serenity shook her head to say no. Shawn looked at her and said, "Well, what's the rush? Do you want to check out a DVD? Or we can play a board game . . . I'm good at . . ." He got up and Serenity had no idea what was on his mind. He went to the small music center and opened up the bottom shelf and took out a monopoly game. Serenity briefly for a minute got lost in those days in college when she and her friends would play until the wee hours of the morning, cop some sleep for a couple of hours, and then go and take a test half exhausted and still pass. She giggled and then looked at her watch. It was around 11:00 p.m.

Serenity knew that monopoly wasn't a close and shut game, but she had to hand it to Shawn for picking a challenge that got her attention despite the late hour. It could take a while and she knew it. And she was already getting herself mentally ready for the long haul, plus she could not back down to a challenge such as this, as she playfully stated, "As long as I get the shoe."

Shawn looked on with glee and playful amazement as he inquired, "Why the shoe?" Serenity felt that Shawn had walked right into this one and was eager to say what she had to say, "Because when I get finished walking and stomping on you, you are going to hang up your monopoly shoes, so you better pick the dog to lick your wounds, buddy."

Shawn laughed a hearty laugh, rubbed his hands together, and said, "Well, I was planning on taking the car, so when I am done with you I'll leave you in the dust with your old granny shoes." Serenity laughed to the point that she had to hold her stomach. Shawn's childlike behavior touched her to the extent she felt another piece of armor breaking off and another piece of her heart surrendering to Shawn.

Two Hours Later

Two hours later, Shawn and Serenity were still going strong, laughing and yelling every time something went in their favor or when they felt the other person did not do something right. Serenity had the edge and Shawn knew it, but he was mounting up a defense as he was starting to use some of his business savvy to come back aggressively against her. Serenity's turn came up. She took the dice, shook them in her hands, and let them roll out. The dice clashed into each other and tumbled, and one rolled a three and the other a four—a seven. She happily started to count off the spaces, and slowly her expression changed as she realized she was about to land on one of Shawn's major properties, which was Atlantic Avenue and where he had also built a few houses as well.

She knew she was in trouble, so she put on her poker face. She thought Shawn wasn't paying attention because he was counting his assets, and she quickly said, "Here roll your turn. Let's not slow down the game, Shawn, wake up."

Shawn, who at the time was also biting into some of that good leftover chicken from dinner, took the dice from Serenity and said, "Oh, thanks. OK, I'll roll." Serenity had a look of satisfaction on her face as she laughed to herself as she thought, *Mission accomplished.*

Shawn was shaking the dice in his hands and getting ready to let them go when he stopped, turned to look at Serenity with a smile, and said, "As soon as you pay me for landing on my property with your granny shoes."

Shawn laughed, but Serenity didn't think it was funny. *This is where the game got complicated.* She had to pay and pay big. Shawn laughed that crazy, robust laugh as she reluctantly gave up the money. Shawn smiled. Serenity noticing his cocky smile said, "Don't worry. I'll get paid. I can't wait until you land on my property." Shawn's infectious laughter continued to the point that he fell on his side.

Serenity, who had a mean look on her face, started giggling as well; she then looked down at her watch and said, "Ooh, it's almost one in the morning." The reminder of the time brought Shawn to a sense of calmness. He did not want Serenity to leave.

He had not had so much fun in quite some time.

"Well," he said, "I tell you what, let's stop right here."

Serenity felt a pull in her heart. She didn't want to stop. She wanted to spend more time with Shawn. She was falling for him, and the armor continued to come off. She wasn't good at this, but from the way he had looked at her all night she would have thought the same thing. Shawn continued to speak, not knowing Serenity was too much into thinking whether Shawn liked her. But she was able to put together some things as she picked up on what he was saying, "So how do you like that idea?"

Serenity at first looked befuddled and did not know how to respond. Her heart was someplace else. She responded, "Ah, uh, yeah . . . that sounds good to me." She smiled faintly.

Shawn realized that she was in another zone. He smiled as well and responded, "On what part sounds good?"

Serenity felt like a deer caught in the headlights as she fumbled and stumbled her way to a clearer response but with difficulty. Shawn came to her rescue and bailed her out, "OK, we'll put the game aside and play a couple of hands of Uno." She laughed because firstly she knew exactly what he was doing and, secondly, she never saw a man with so many games, even a PlayStation II.

The two played a couple of hands of Uno and then Serenity reminded Shawn of the time. Shawn looked at his watch, whistled, and thought, *3:30 a.m.* He said, "Well, thank you, I had so much fun tonight."

Serenity looked at Shawn with bloodshot eyes, and Shawn thought she still looked beautiful. He said, "Yes, it was fun. You are crazy. Thank you for keeping us indoors. I wasn't sure how this was going to turn out, but I must say I wouldn't have had this much fun in a restaurant . . . Thank you."

Shawn smiled that billion-dollar smile and said, "Listen, you are welcome to come by and stay anytime you want. And as long as you want, I could let you spend the night, and I will come back in the morning and we could go and do something." Serenity blushed and bit her bottom lip.

She appreciated Shawn's gentlemanly attitude, something one rarely saw in guys these days. She had to decline, but she told him thank you nevertheless.

Shawn went to get Serenity's coat and helped her put it on. He then called downstairs and asked Omar if someone could have his car ready for him. Both Shawn and Serenity left the small building that looked like a storage house. As Serenity walked in front of Shawn she felt a sense of infinity. She did not want to leave, but she had a strange feeling that she was going to be back one day, one day very soon.

They both arrived downstairs where Shawn's car was waiting. Shawn waved his doorman off who came forward to assist Serenity into the car. Shawn knew that was his responsibility as he opened the door for Serenity. The early morning air was crisp and brisk, the way that time of the year was supposed to be, but the car was nice and warm.

Serenity knew that she could have stayed, and she believed that Shawn would not have had a problem with that, but she was looking at the bigger picture. *What image would she be projecting if she stayed? How would Shawn look at her? Maybe as easy.* That wasn't the image she wanted to convey. She liked that man, and she knew she had to play this one by the book, which was her style anyway. Sandra wanted her to take a different approach—a get it, hit it, don't quit it approach. That wasn't her style, never had been and never would be. Shawn quickly rushed around to the driver's side. Shawn adjusted his seat since he was much taller than Omar. He had already gathered the information from Serenity where she lived. He programmed the info and put it in into the navigational system rather than have Complex speak and perhaps insult Serenity from that earlier incident with the seat belt. *No, this was best,* he thought. *Later he'll deal with Complex.*

Serenity started to give Shawn directions, but he put his hand up and told her he knew where she lived, and he told her to just sit back and enjoy the ride.

Serenity tried to engage Shawn into a conversation, but realized she was losing the battle against the sandman. Her eyelids betrayed her, and she fell asleep leaning on Shawn. He looked at Serenity and thought she looked like a princess. He smiled to himself, thinking about how the evening and the morning had gone. He thought, *If this was a basketball game, this would be an all net three point shot. If this was football, it would be a kickoff return, and he may go all the way . . . If this was baseball, this would be a walk off homerun into the playoffs.* But this was Shawn scoring big with Serenity; everything seemed to work out like clockwork. It was a flow, no tricks.

Shawn was pleased with himself; he thought the evening went well as he sat back in his designed car content and satisfied. He was feeling good until he noticed there was a problem with the navigational system. He wasn't sure what was going on, but he knew he needed the information in order for the system to direct him in the right direction. He knew it wasn't a major problem, but at that time it was a nuisance because in order for him to use the backup system he would have to activate Complex and that may not be the best thing under the circumstances.

Shawn had no other choice as he drove within the speed limit. The roads were clear; the Cross Bronx known for its congestion during the day and its quietness in the late wee hours was living up to its reputation. He looked over at Serenity and noticed she was breathing evenly and softly. *She was out cold,* he thought. He didn't think a fire truck that would pass them with its sirens blasting would wake her up, but he found it hard to keep his attention on the road and the distraction that lay next to him. He loved the way her nice-size round, shapely breasts went up and down ever so quietly and consistently without missing a beat so to speak. He was amazed at that. He was amazed after all these months, from first watching her, then sitting across the table from her and debating with her, then practically begging her for a date, sending her tons of flowers and notes, bribing her secretary and pleading with Marcus to this.

Yet he knew he had to do what he had to do. He knew the Bronx pretty well but Bronxdale was another tale. Shawn put the code in. The dashboard lights flicked on and came to life. The sexy voice from within it spoke, "Hello, Shawn, baby."

Shawn shushed Complex and asked her to lower her volume. Complex briefly protested, and Shawn said in a stern voice, "I don't have time for this, Complex. This is not negotiable. Do it now. Keep your voice level down." Shawn waited to get some indication that Complex had followed the directive. At that stage, there was no confirmation. Finally, the dashboard indicators responded and the bar went to a lower level. Shawn thanked Complex and added, "I really have to find out why TJ set you up to resist the way you do."

Complex responded, "Well, as I understand, you said you didn't want something that had a maid mentality. You wanted spunk, spirit, nerve, bold, and sexy. Well, here she is, partner."

Shawn wanted to respond, but it wasn't the time or place, so he presented the problem at hand, "Complex, the navigational system is not working properly. I am not sure—"

Complex cut off Shawn, "Shawn honey, it is working, all of that flickering and stuff . . . it's working." Shawn was about to protest because he knew firsthand it wasn't working, but then it dawned on him that Complex had something to do with it the same way she had something to do with the seat belt the night before. He should have known that Complex was designed to overrule certain functions. It was in case if Shawn was not able to convey the information for one reason or another.

Shawn cleared his throat, took a deep breath, and continued, "I need GPS direction for Serenity's address. It is—"

Complex cut Shawn off, "Shawn, I have it. I picked it up from the so-called malfunction navigational system. It's all program. We should be there in approximately twenty minutes. From what I gathered from traffic and weather sources, we are expecting no surprises. Is there anything else, baby?"

Shawn was speechless for a minute and then he asked, "When was this information going to be given to me?"

Complex responded, "After I noticed a little panic and sweat."

The only thing Shawn could do was shake his head at Complex's boldness and just say, "Wow, unbelievable."

Complex changed the subject as she continued, "So our friend is going home. Now that is where the 'wow' should come in. Wow, Shawn baby, you must be losing your touch. What? The stud is turning into a dud?"

Shawn responded with a nervous laugh as Serenity somewhat stirred. Shawn's ego caused him to respond as he looked over at Serenity, "Complex, don't be rude. You know that was never my lifestyle, and if you're talking about those women that stayed over, they were given separate quarters, not that this is any of your business. To tell you the truth, I wish I had time to put you in your place. What you did last night with the seat belt . . . don't deny it. It wasn't a malfunction. It was a complexity name Complex, and now tonight, I will deal with you later, but for now all I need for you to do is get us to Serenity's house, *comprende.*"

Complex responded, "Ooh, la, la, Shawn baby, you know what you do to my circuits when you talk Spanish and dirty." Complex was making all kinds of erotic sounds like the ones on those 1-900 numbers, just to rattle Shawn's nerves. Shawn quickly turned to see if Serenity had stirred. He turned back and waved his hand at the dashboard for Complex to stop the sounds as Complex kept going on and on. Shawn finally realized that Complex didn't respond to movement, only to voice commands from only Shawn and her designer TJ.

Shawn quickly said, "OK, Complex, that's enough. We will talk later."

Complex still in that sexy voice mode responded, "You promise, Big Poppa."

Shawn said with clenched teeth, "Yes, we will."

Complex said, "Shawn, relax, why so uptight? Your little friend according to my environment reading shows she is resting. She is really out. You must have put a little extra something, something on her . . . , Big Poppa."

Shawn wanted to smile, but he was too upset with Complex, although he wished that whatever she had said was true. Instead he said, "Complex, just get her home, please."

Complex sensing the serious tone responded, "No problem, Shawn." Complex took the quickest route, saying, "Shawn, not even a map quest can do that. They should be called map adventure instead of quest." Shawn was still a little upset with Complex, but he was easing up as he laughed at her joke. As Serenity stirred again, Complex continued to give directions, "Shawn, make a right at the next corner and a left after that." Shawn did as he was instructed. Complex said, "567 should be the fourth house from the corner." And there it was, a nice, little, cozy-looking private house with a porch.

Shawn smiled and said, "Listen, Complex, thanks. I do appreciate you very much, even though you get on my nerves, but in the long run . . . it's all good. You always come through for me."

Complex said, "Thank you, and I know I can be a handful. That's how my girl designed me, but my main purpose is to serve you, just bear with me."

Shawn nodded and said, "Fair enough." He then added, "Well, with all that behind us, you may go on silent mode."

Complex protested of course with deductive logic regarding what had been just said as she stated, "Shawn, I will be on my best behavior. No rude remarks, promise."

Shawn was feeling bad when he stuck to his guns but left Complex with that as he said, "Look, I promise this week I will introduce you to her."

Complex sounding a little jealous asked, "You plan on seeing her again, Shawn?"

Shawn responded in a firm tone, "Yes, now silent mode."

Complex huffed and said, "Use a woman, then kick her to the curb." Complex's lights slowly dimmed and then were out.

Shawn smiled and thought that Complex was a major asset in his life. *She may be a pain in many ways, but her positives supersede her negatives.* He turned his attention to Serenity. He shook her lightly. She did not respond; she was out cold. He shook her again, but this time called her name.

Serenity slowly turned, half stretched, and then shot up like a bolt. "What . . . Where are we?" she inquired in a cute, raspy voice.

Shawn smiled at her, more at her voice, as he responded, "You are home, baby." Serenity got her bearings together. Once she did, she recognized everything and slowly slumped back to her side. "I had the most craziest dream," she stated in between yawns. Shawn just wanted to hold her, cuddle her, and never let her go, but he resisted the temptation and let Serenity continue, "I dreamt that you were talking with a woman . . ." Shawn froze for a brief second or two, which was hardly noticeable. Serenity continued, "I know that sounds crazy, right . . . ?" Shawn was getting ready to respond but realized that it was a rhetorical question as she continued, "But it seemed so real. She sounded intelligent, smart, quick with wit and humor, and, oh yes, very feisty."

Shawn listened and responded while clearing his throat, "Oh really, wow, anything else?"

Serenity thought, *It was as if a lightbulb went off.* "Yes, come to think about it." Shawn knew that this was it, the missing link as he listened to Serenity blow his cover. She continued, "She had one of the most sexiest voices I have ever heard." Shawn slowly let out a breath of relief as Serenity slowly stated, "Oh well, it was just a crazy dream, I guess to add on to the magical night I had . . . thank you."

Serenity looked at Shawn like he'd ever seen anyone he'd taken out look at him. *It was with such sincerity. I mean women have expressed it verbally, but never the complete package of verbal and visual acknowledgement of sincerity.* Shawn got out, walked around, and opened Serenity's door. Serenity looked at Shawn as if she needed help with the seat belt, and without any help she made an attempt to unlatch it herself. The latch gave way and released the belt without any problem. She made a sound of satisfaction. Shawn had a look of surprise as he helped her out of the car and walked her to her door.

Serenity, feeling a little nervous, mumbled in a raspy voice for Shawn to come in for some milk and cookies. Shawn, while thanking her, declined nevertheless and said he'd take a rain check, knowing that as long as he knew the offer was there he could claim his prize anytime. Serenity felt as if her feet were glued to the steps of her house. She was fumbling inside her purse for her keys. Then she finally found them, held them out, and shook them with a slight giggle. She opened her door and stood there as if she did not know what to do next. She looked up at Shawn who moved closer to her, and she moved closer to him, still looking up at him. Shawn bent his head down toward her mouth. Serenity's lips were slightly open, waiting for his arrival. He noticed her juicy, full lips as he continued to bring his mouth toward hers. Serenity could feel the heat of his face as he came closer and closer. *This was the moment of truth,* she thought as she saw those wonderful lips approaching. Serenity closed her eyes and waited in anticipation.

Shawn noticed that Serenity's eyes were closed and her juicy, full lips pouting out, calling out for that connection. It did something to his manhood, but at the last minute Shawn made a detour and kissed Serenity's cheek. Serenity felt his lips but not in the place she thought it was supposed to be. She opened her eyes in surprise as she watched Shawn pull back and stood back to all of six feet and 3 inches of himself. Shawn saw the look on Serenity's face and knew it would not have been the most popular move, but it was still ranked as an act of respect. Shawn walked Serenity into her house, made sure she was OK, and headed back out. Serenity knew she behaved like a big doofus as if she did not know what to do next.

Shawn looked at her as he stood outside the door and said in that nice, soft baritone voice, "Serenity, I'm leaving now. Come close the door." Serenity smiled and shook herself free from the heavy, romantic fog Shawn left her in. She came to the door, smiled at Shawn, and mouthed the words "thank you." She then closed the door and locked it.

Shawn smiled to himself and was already thinking about his plans for both of them the next day. He got into his car, whistling, "Complex, welcome back. You may speak. We have to talk, don't we?"

Complex's lights on the dashboard came on. She responded, "What is there to talk about?"

Shawn made a smug sound. "Plenty, and you know it. First of all, I want to . . . thank you for not jamming the seat belt when Serenity was getting out, and I want to thank you for bringing her home, even though you set that one up."

Complex responded, "Wow, thank you, babe. You are welcome. Shawn, I must say, I really like her. I heard the things she said about me. If I would have been human, I guess I would say I would have been touched. I must admit, she is one smart chick."

Shawn responded, "Well, I am glad to hear you say what you are saying. Sounds like you are sincere."

Complex responded, "My actions earlier were not productive. I do apologize, but, Shawn, please understand. This is my domain. It's like having two chicks in the kitchen. Only one is going to rule. The same applies here."

Shawn thought about it, and he smiled and responded, "I never looked at it that way. OK, truce. From now on, I will let you know in advance who is coming into your domain, OK, fair enough?"

Complex retorted, "Well, that's not going to work, Shawn."

Shawn got fed up and said, "Why not? What now?"

Complex's tone became soft, "Because I don't think, and I might be wrong, but I don't think there will be anyone else in my domain except for Serenity. I think you picked a winner, and like I said, I like her. She has excellent judgment."

Shawn laughed that hearty laugh and shook his head. Complex continued, "Shawn, I think you should take her home to meet your parents."

Shawn got all excited. "You think so? I mean I thought about it, but now that you mention it, yes, I will set it up."

Complex's voice expression went up, "It's been a long day. Do you want to go back using auto pilot? Just sit back and let me take over the controls."

Shawn smiled and said, "Sounds like a good idea. This is your domain. Take us home." Shawn kicked back and relaxed, and Complex did the rest.

And she responded, "Yes, sir, Captain, I mean, Shawn baby."

Shawn shook his head, smiled, and said, "Wow, unbelievable." This time Shawn meant it in a good way.

Chapter 65

Serenity was exhausted. She could feel it in her bones. She was so exhausted she became giddy. Little senseless giggles came from her as if someone was whispering a joke to her. She would get giddy and get the giggles. It lasted for about two minutes, and then it was back to feeling bone-tired, but it wasn't tiredness from pure exhaustion. It was a tiredness that was a result of accomplishment and fulfillment; she felt full.

Serenity sat on the edge of the bed ready to topple over, but she felt good. It was such a good but odd contrast. She looked over at her answering machine which displayed fourteen messages. She sucked her teeth in frustration because she had no other choice but to listen. She was tempted to put it off until the next day. Then she thought, *Today is tomorrow, or rather yesterday is today.* She stopped herself from the brain twister and faced the music. There was no other choice as she thought, *I mean, suppose it's an emergency or some pertinent information.* Her conscience told her that she would never forgive herself. She reasoned. She stomped her foot and agreed to listen, and if it was not important she would erase it. Serenity pressed the button; the answering machine started up in its robotic voice, "You have fourteen messages . . ." Beep . . .

"Hi, baby, this is Mommy. I just want to remind you . . ." Serenity pressed the save button. The machine responded, "Message save." Beep . . .

"That's it, girl, ride that cowboy off into the sunset. Remember rawhide? Uh, no pun attended, move them out, round them up, and move them out, hee ha. Girl, you better call me and don't spare the details. I want it all." Serenity was laughing at Sandra's stupid rendition of *Rawhide*. There was a long gap of silence, well, at least for about five seconds; Serenity did not know what could have happened, so she got ready to erase the message when Sandra cowboy's voice on the machine came out of nowhere, yelling, "Yeah, rawhide." Then Sandra laughed like a space nut and asked

Serenity to call her. Serenity smiled and shook her head. The rest of the messages were business. Except out of the twelve, seven of them belonged to Sandra, who was thirsty and wanted to get the 411. Serenity quickly brushed her teeth. She looked at her bloodshot eyes in the mirror, and she knew the shower was calling her like that man in the Ricola commercial; well, in this case the shower was doing the same thing. Serenity passed on the shower and promised herself she'd take one first thing in the morning. She changed her clothes, just dropping them at the foot of the bed, and threw on whatever she could grab as nightwear to sleep in. She jumped in bed and hoped she'd sleep until . . . until . . . until . . . She was out like a light with a smile on her face.

Serenity woke up to the sound of someone going off on her doorbell. She got up in a huff, and she staggered in a circle. Then she went into her closet and came back out with something that no home should be without. She came back out with a New York special which she had received on bat day at Yankee Stadium. All the Yankee players signed the bat, which meant the bat had a lot of good swinging power to get the job done that morning. Before she stepped out of her bedroom, she looked back at her bed clock. It said 11:00 a.m. She wasn't interested in the time. She just wanted to make sure that when the police questioned her about the time, she would know what time she had batting practice on whatever insensitive, finger-pressing jerk. That would be her defense.

Serenity held the bat in one hand and used her other hand to look through the peephole. She could not believe who she was looking at. Big as day and with a nerve to have an attitude, it was Sandra, looking all impatient. Serenity thought as she looked at the bat that it wasn't big enough or long enough. She wanted one so long that if Sandra made the attempt to run, the hit would be like one of those in Tom and Jerry cartoons. She needed one that she had to only swing once. *That's it or one that could reach around corners. No matter how far or how fast, the bat will find you and tap you good.*

She unlocked the door and grabbed the doorknob, pretending it was Sandra's little neck. She opened the door so fast, even Shaft would have been impressed. The door flew open, and Serenity was ready to swing for the fences when Sandra brushed right past her in her diva style that only Sandra could do and said, "I would have thought you got enough wood last night, girl. Put that toy away before you hurt yourself."

Serenity was seething by that time as she responded, "I have one place I would love to put it right about now."

Sandra kept on walking toward the kitchen with a bag in her hand, which made Serenity even more madder, as she responded, "No, baby, I'm not into artificial wood, and is this how you treat your best friend, who was concerned about you and brought you your favorite breakfast for us to eat and just spend a nice quiet Saturday morning?"

Serenity perked up. She could smell the pancakes, sausage, and homemade hash browns. *Only one place can make such a dish,* she thought as she closed her eyes for another whiff, *and that's Sonny's Soul Food restaurant. Mouthwatering food that just dissolves in your mouth. Food so good it makes you scared to eat it.*

As fast as the hunger mood had come on, a stronger need overcame it, and Serenity said, "Thank you so much, but, Sandra, I'm exhausted."

She smiled. "Ah, hit it, get it, homeboy must have run a marathon on your ass."

Serenity looked at Sandra and became serious, "Homeboy, Shawn that is, did not run any marathon on me . . . and watch your language."

Sandra retorted, "Well, he put something on your . . ." She looked at Serenity and checked her language as she continued, "He put something on you. Look, you must have dropped it like it was hot. It's 11:30 a.m. and you're still in bed. That's not the Serenity I know. Usually you are up and out, hitting the streets, running your crazy miles, doing your exercises, and then getting out to the malls or whatever."

Serenity had to admit it was different as she walked into the kitchen, pulled down some plates, glasses, and some silverware for her and Sandra, sat down at the table, and said, "I got in around . . . listen, I can't remember, early in the wee hours of the morning."

Sandra looked at Serenity and said, "Girl, you are an animal, a beast. You partied all night. Where did you guys go? To that new club in the village. I understand they know how to jam, so where? The Image? Girl, to be honest, I didn't know you had it in you, so you have one of those double personality things, during the day a mild—mannered supervisor and at night a super freak. You go, girl, this is between you and me, OK?"

Serenity shaking her head looked at Sandra and stated, "You are as usual jumping to conclusions, but if you must know, Miss 411 Wins, we played . . ."

Sandra cut her off and stated, "You guys played strip poker." Serenity looked at Sandra sternly, who gestured an apology and urged Serenity to finish.

Serenity rolled her eyes at what Sandra had said as she continued, "We played monopoly practically the whole night. Before that we had dinner, and before that we looked at the stars through his telescope. It was the most romantic thing I've ever experienced."

Sandra smiled and said, "Wow! I never heard of monopoly strip. It must be something new. You land on his Atlantic Avenue and have to rip something off, or he lands on your Park Place and has to, like I said, 'drop it like it's hot 'n cool.'" Sandra was going through the motions of having her clothes ripped off, a little bit here, a little bit there. She continued, "Ooh, oh, you landed on another one of his properties, there goes the panties, your . . ." Sandra was waving as if she was waving at a friend going away. Serenity was ready to verbally tear into her. Sandra seeing Serenity's anger stated, "Chill, girl, I'm only playing. Wow, that sound really . . . ah . . . boring . . . monopoly, oookay."

Serenity said her blessing, started eating, and stated, "Sandra, not everyone views a date like you . . . a screw fest. The only time words are spoken is when you ask whether the person has a condom. Anyway, that wasn't right. I'm sorry. Where are your babies?"

Sandra said her blessing and then responded to Serenity's question, "That was low, but I'm not mad. Anyway the babies are at my mother's place. I told her I will send her a postcard, and I left." Sandra laughed at her own joke.

Serenity was laughing as well; she said to her, "You are so stupid. I'm going to ask your mother if you were ever dropped when you were small."

Both laughed, and then Sandra retorted, "Sometimes I think she was dropped on her head. Every time I ask her to take care of the girls she always says, 'No problem.' I really believe she was dropped on her head." Serenity laughed. Sandra could tell that Serenity was happy, and she said, "In all seriousness, I'm happy for you, Serenity. You're doing it right . . ." There was a brief pause as she continued, "Oh, guess what, you will never guess who called me."

Serenity's mouth was so full she just gestured to Sandra to continue, who dismissed Serenity with a "don't bother wave" and said, "Marcus." Sandra had a big smile on her face. When Serenity gave her a "who is that" look, Sandra continued, "You know Marcus. Come on, you know Mr. All night long, Homeboy."

Serenity thought and said, "Who . . . Mr. All night long, who's that?"

Sandra like a teenager playfully hit the table with her hand and said, "Omigod, you know Mr. Rich and Famous."

Serenity swallowed and said, "Don't call him that. His name is Shawn."

Sandra put her hand up in defense and said, "Whoa, honey, go ahead and defend your man, girl."

Serenity became defensive as well and said, "For one, he's not my man, and you know how I am, Sandra. Don't label people. You know we are constantly labeled."

Sandra got testy, "OK, OK, just chill, Ms. Panther, relax. I didn't mean anything by it. I got the message. His name is Shawn . . . or can I call him homeboy or will you get offended over that as well?"

Serenity waved at Sandra playfully and asked, "So what's up?"

Sandra smiled at the street vernacular hood talk as she responded, "Well, he wants to meet me."

Serenity squealed like a teenager. She smiled and was as excited as Sandra as she stated, "That's wonderful, Sandra. From what I hear, the brother has class."

Sandra jumped in, "And his own business, Black Enterprise Consultants." Serenity did not know that little piece of information. She was happy that Shawn didn't seem like the type that loved the spotlight or limelight. He was a well secure black man who had that inner confidence. He was not into being the center of attraction or one to use his power or prestige or money to be in the limelight. From what she could see, he was a man who would rather avoid all of that other stuff and be himself. Serenity became lost in her thoughts. Sandra playfully said, "Houston, we got a problem. We have a victim that is madly in love, even though she may not be aware of it. All external signs are pointing to it. She hasn't heard one word I said. Do you read?" Sandra laughed, and Serenity blushed and apologized for being rude while Sandra went on and on about Marcus.

Serenity's smile turned into a serious look, and she said, "Listen, San, you know I am the last person to try to rain on your parade, but do me a favor, please . . . please go slow. This is a good brother with promise. This guy could be good for the girls and really good for you."

Sandra was all seriousness, which Serenity had seen once or twice since the time she'd known her. However, the Sandra before her was very serious. Serenity listened very intently. "Serenity, to tell you the truth, I'm scared. You know me. I've kicked it with losers. I know that. That way I could say I'm smarter than them because to be real, these brothers can't even hold down a nine to five, and they look at me as a queen with a good job with the Feds. That says a lot to them, but I've never went out with a brother like Marcus. His head is on straight. He has his own business. He has a postgrad education. His compass is pointing south, and I don't mean south as in down, but 'S' as in successful, a brother with a vision and not just dreams. Am I scared? Hell, yeah, I am afraid I'm going to sabotage this thing before it gets started because I can't walk in his steps."

Serenity caressed Sandra and said, "Hey, San, don't try to walk in his steps. Just make your own."

Sandra smiled and continued, "Sounds good, but I have to look at myself every day in the mirror and tell myself that I am beautiful, I am attractive, and I am intelligent because you know my track record. Losers R us. Losers are attracted to me, and I also know how to pick them. I accept their losing attitude. I've dealt with that kind for so long, I was convinced that was the hand I was dealt. Big cocks, little brain, know how to turn you out to the extent you are screaming your head off, but have no idea how to treat a woman like a lady. I am tired of being f/u, if you know what I mean. I want to be made love to. It's the same thing over and over again, déjàvu, different brother, same crap. I know this is not the case with Marcus, and that's the thing that scares me."

Serenity grabbed Sandra by both hands and looked into her eyes. "But look now, you have been tossed a couple 'of aces. Use them wisely. They're yours. It can change the hand that you've been dealt." The two women hugged like sisters until Sandra broke the embrace and wiped the tears from her eyes, tears of having a friend like Serenity.

Sandra composed herself and said, "So what are your plans for this afternoon?" Serenity giggled and said, "Jump back in bed and stay there all day. Get up and eat and go back to bed."

Sandra laughed and said, "I hear you, girl. Well, I am going to the mall to pick out an outfit that would knock the socks off Marcus. It's funny we've never met, but the few times we've talked on the horn getting to know one another, I feel like I know him already . . ." Sandra looked at Serenity and added, "Do you know what I mean?"

Serenity smiled and responded, "Yes, I do. You feel you have that connection."

Sandra nodded her head excitedly in confirmation, smiling. She continued, "But I am going to buy something that's going to have Marcus's eyes glued on me the whole night."

The two women gave each other a high five. Serenity said, "I know what you mean, girl. That outfit you picked out for me . . ." Serenity just shook her head. She was speechless as she raised her hand in the air as if to say "I declare."

Sandra was practically on the edge of her seat, so excited to get all the juice as she encouraged Serenity to finish. "What, what . . . what happened?" Sandra shouted in excitement.

Serenity got some control over herself and continued, "Girl, that outfit. Shawn looked like he had three legs."

Sandra responded, "Ooo, girl, you are so fresh."

Serenity continued, "Yep, I saw him when he tried to cover it up, but it was too late. It was already transforming from Bruce Banner into the Incredible Hulk. I mean, at one point I thought it was going to burst through his pants."

Sandra, who was really into it, folded her legs Indian style in the kitchen chair she was sitting in with her chin cupped in her hands. She responded, "What? Get out of here, girl."

Serenity just nodded. The two girls were like school pals in the girl's locker room. Sandra asked, "Serenity, tell me the truth . . . Is homeboy packing?"

Serenity put her hand to her mouth in astonishment and said, "Girl, from what I saw in the bathroom, you know the extra-large condoms, and from what I saw that was trying to break out of those pants, that thing needs to be listed as an illegal weapon." Sandra acted as if she had fainted. She had Serenity rolling.

Sandra, recovering from her fake fainting spell, said, "Well, like I always say, if you don't know how to use it, it ain't worth, Jack. You just have a weapon and don't know what to do with it, you can end up hurting yourself." Serenity and Sandra laughed, even though for Serenity the conversation was helpful because she was a novice to all of this stuff. She went on dates, and the guys always acted as if they knew what was going on, but nine times out of ten, the guys knew as much as she did, so this was new to her. Anything she could learn would be helpful, but deep down she felt that when that time came between her and Shawn, even though she did not know as much, she had a strong feeling that Shawn would be what he had shown her all along to be, a nice considerate gentlemen, soft, passionate, and gentle.

Sandra got up from the table, stretched, and asked Serenity in the midst of her stretch, "Are you sure you don't want to hang?"

Serenity, yawning and stretching, responded, "Yeah, but I will take a rain check." Sandra nodded and was getting her stuff getting ready to head out when the phone rang. Serenity had to run to the bathroom, so she asked Sandra to see who was on the phone. Sandra said OK, picked up the phone, and put her phone etiquette to work. One would have thought that Sandra did not have a ghetto bone in her body from the way she answered the phone. Serenity from the bathroom asked Sandra who was on the phone. She did not respond.

Serenity came out of the bathroom into the living room, where Sandra was sitting on the couch with this silly grin on her face, just saying things like "yeah, no, yeah, yeah, yeah, no, yeah," as if she was under some sort of hypnotic spell or something. Then Sandra realized that Serenity was standing there and pointing to her to let her know that the phone call was for her. She thought, *Well, my house, my phone, no really?* Serenity raised both hands and mouthed the words, "Who is it?"

Sandra didn't want to come out straight and say Shawn's name because she knew Serenity made it perfectly clear that she didn't want any calls and that she wanted to rest today. So Sandra looked around, found a long candlestick holder, and put it down by her crotch area as if it was that part of the male organ. Serenity wrinkled her nose as if to say, "What are you talking about?"

Then Sandra asked Shawn, "So what are some things that Marcus likes?"

Serenity at first looked as if she was going to faint with excitement, like a schoolgirl, then she quickly sobered up and snatched the long candlestick that Sandra was absently still holding down by her crotch area. Sandra took the phone away from her mouth and whispered, "I'll tell him you are sleep, OK?" Serenity motioned to Sandra not to do that and to find out if he wanted to speak to her. Sandra said to Shawn, "Do you want me to see if she is awake?"

Serenity gave Sandra a look that translated, "If you do, you die."

Sandra quickly said to him, "Oh wait, she is awake. Hold on." Sandra still playing her part handed Serenity the phone, saying, "Oh, I thought you were sleeping. You said you were tired. You were snoring, sounded like a . . ." Serenity snatched the phone from Sandra, who gave her two thumbs up. Serenity wanted to give a message with her fingers as well, specifically the middle one on both hands, but thought otherwise.

She calmed down and spoke nice and soft into the phone, "Hello, Shawn, thank you and a good morning to you as well. Yeah, a little bit, but I'm OK, yeah. No really, I'm good. Yes, I am sure. OK, yeah, all right, bye."

Sandra looked at Serenity and said, "Hum, all those OKs and yeahs don't sound too good, I wonder why. Perhaps you would like to shed some light on the matter."

Serenity carefully responded, "Well, he wants to pick me up, and he has a surprise to show me."

Sandra looked at Serenity with narrowed eyes and asked, "I thought you were so tired. I mean you even said, 'I'm so tired.'" Sandra mocked Serenity in an over exaggerated way as she continued, "What happened? You're not tired anymore, ump . . ." She paused for a second or two and continued, "Girl . . . go for it. Let that man be your energized bunny." Both women hugged each other. Sandra left while Serenity was getting ready for her knight in shining armor.

Chapter 66

As the days and weeks went by, Shawn and Serenity became inseparable; yet they were very much independent of each other. When you saw one, you saw the other. They went out every weekend. They would have dinner either at his house or at her house. Sometimes they would be bold enough to cook together, working side by side, making each other their test dummies. The more they hung out with each other, the deeper they got to know one another. They even started going to each other's churches. Serenity would go to Shawn's church on the second Sunday, and Shawn would go to Serenity's church every third Sunday. Shawn got a chance to meet her pastor, Bishop Samuel T. Jones of the renowned Ebenezer Baptist Temple. He was also the famous author of many self-help books and other entrepreneurial endeavors.

Shawn and Serenity were very happy. They probably spoke to each other perhaps five to six times a day during the week, during working hours, in between meetings and even during meetings. They would excuse themselves just to speak to each other. Serenity still wasn't convinced that it was love, but she knew that she liked him a lot. Sandra used to say to her, "Stop fighting what your heart has already said yes to." She loved being around him and hearing his voice, and it was the same for Shawn, but with him he really did love Serenity. There was no doubt in his mind. He knew it from day one. He'd always said that she was the best thing that had ever happened to him besides getting his life straightened out by God. She had been the next big thing.

For example, during a multimillion-dollar meeting with a very famous director and the film company that would be shooting the film, Shawn had this strong urge, this strong desire, to speak to Serenity. He could smell her scent in the room. He casually looked around and realized none of the women in the room had put on that scent. It was the scent of his woman. He could not resist any longer as the words of whoever was talking were drowned out by the compelling thought and scent of his lady. Even though that deal would have placed Shawn's team in a wonderful financial spot for months to come, in that instant, in that moment of time it did not matter. What mattered was finding a way to get out of that meeting and call the woman he had spent the previous night with at the Garden watching the New York Knicks. Shawn could still see Serenity screaming and yelling, and after the game he had been able to make arrangements for her to meet some of the players up close. He could still see the thrill on her face. He could not take it any longer. He raised one finger and looking at his phone with a distressed look he said, "I have to take this. Please give me a minute." The executive of that film company was already running very close for his next meeting. When he saw Shawn getting up, the executive wanted to bolt as well. Then he noticed the seriousness and the stern look in Shawn's eyes, and the executive agreed to wait. He respected Shawn, and he patiently waited, giving Shawn extra time.

Shawn went down the hall to his office and dialed Serenity's direct cell phone number; she picked up on the second ring, "Hi, baby." That came from Serenity as she continued, "Your big meeting was canceled?"

Shawn melted at her voice, still sounding raspy from the game last night. The raspy voice hit its target in Shawn's heart, and it did an express route to manhood boulevard as Shawn responded, "No, baby, it wasn't canceled. I snuck away to call you."

Serenity, who was having her midmorning coffee, almost spit it out as she raised her voice, "Shawn, are you nuts? Even you said how important this meeting was for your team and that this guy has the patience of an ADHD kid. What are you doing, baby?" Shawn loved it when Serenity bent over backward to show concern about the things that were important to him. She was so supportive in that way. It was a quality that he adored in her, and she did it so naturally.

He said, "Listen, baby, I had to hear your voice."

Serenity sounded grateful yet upset. "OK, you heard it. Now go back to your meeting, you silly lovable bear." Shawn laughed, kissed Serenity bye, and told her that he would pick her up in front of her job like he'd been doing for the past several weeks.

Shawn went back into the meeting, feeling energized. The big executive looked like he was about to cancel everything. Joe, Shawn's assistant, looked like he needed CPR, and Shawn looked like he was madly in love. The meeting went off very well, and Shawn landed his biggest contract ever.

After the meeting, the two groups shook hands and said that they looked forward to working with each other. Mr. Executive came up to Shawn, shook his hand, and said, "Son, she must be mighty special for you to walk out of a multimillion dollar meeting contract. Tells me either you are nuts or you are madly in love." The executive with his entourage behind him chuckled and continued, "Son, I met mine thirty years ago, and she is still the center of my life. All of this stuff means nothing compared to what I have." The executive smiled, still holding Shawn's hand. He placed his other hand on top of the hand he was shaking and said, "Son, I would have made the same decision about making that phone call." The executive tightened his grip on Shawn's hand, smiled, and then he and his entourage walked off.

It was just an example of the bond that those two had for one another. Many were curious; even the media was curious of who this mystery woman was, but Shawn kept everything in perspective as he was still able to effectively create contracts and maintain a healthy relationship with Serenity.

Serenity had a good idea that she was now falling in love with Shawn. He was a 100 percent man and such a respectful and positive brother.

The big test was when Serenity met Shawn's family for the first time; she was a bundle of nerves.

Serenity did not know how she should conduct herself; she was meeting not only the parents of the most influential man in the city, but also one of the wealthiest as well. Shawn's parents also packed powerful reputations as well. So many times she tried to make up some kind of excuse, but Sandra talked her out of it. Then one day while she and Shawn were watching a movie, he sensed something wasn't right. He said, "Why are you so coiled up? You feel like a spring getting ready to bounce . . ." Shawn looked at her. Serenity tried to deny that by saying that nothing was wrong, but she knew she could not fool this man. *This man had such a tap on her heart that it's hard to fool him.* However, Shawn had always told her that her heart was a part of his heart, and whenever she felt something he felt it too. This was one of those situations. Shawn lifted up her chin and kissed her ever so lightly; yet it was such a powerful peck.

Serenity felt its effects and said, "Listen, what's up with you? You are in my heart, my mind. I can't hide anything from you." Serenity folded both of her arms as if she was in a huff, but she loved the fact that Shawn was so in tune with her. *With all the business day-to-day transactions that take place, this man is zoned in on her.* He responded, "Your heart, your mind, and your soul, that's because you are my soul mate. When you hurt, I hurt. When you rejoice, I rejoice. I just know. Now we went over this before. Stop stalling and come out with it, the thing that is bothering you."

Serenity was making circles on Shawn's broad chest. He enjoyed the softness of her fingers and that look of concentration as Serenity spoke, "Listen, it's just that . . . it's just that . . . listen, forget it. It is so anal." Shawn held her hand, the one that was making the circles, and began to kiss each finger. The act turned her on as the sensation shot to her stomach and traveled further south of the border. Serenity getting caught up into the movement turned herself more toward Shawn. He could see her face was flushed and her breathing had changed, but that wasn't what he wanted to accomplish as he pulled back so she could finish what she had started to say. Serenity knew that the party was over, and she had to get back to the subject as they both took breaths to compose themselves. Serenity said through the hot flashes, "Shawn, I don't know what it is."

Shawn happily volunteered, "Let me see if I can help. Perhaps this has something to do with you meeting my parents tomorrow."

Serenity's eyes opened up wide, and she smiled, shook her head, and said, "I think you are in the wrong field. Well, at least when you leave this field there will be something else waiting that you are good at. Yes, that's it. I don't know how to approach them, what to say, when to say what. So there it is."

Shawn rubbed her face with the back of his hand; her skin was so soft. He said, "Well, just make sure you call me master and fetch whatever I ask you to. That will make a good impression on them."

Serenity looked at Shawn half-frightened, half-surprised as she responded, "What? Are you out of your mind . . . ? Forget it. I'm not going. I can't do that . . . I'm not going. Call me when you are back home." Shawn was laughing so hard while Serenity was becoming upset.

Shawn held his hand up and his laughter slowed down. He said, "Baby, I am only kidding . . ." Serenity playfully hit him on the shoulder. He caught her hand, brought her closer to him, and kissed her generously. She took in every bit; the two let go the embrace and Shawn continued, "Just be yourself. They are really cool people. Don't worry, they will love you."

The next day, some would call it the D-day and to Serenity it felt just like that, Shawn took most of the sting out of the bite, and Serenity felt a little better as they walked up to his parents' door and rang the bell. Shawn had a panicked look on his face and looked like he was getting ready to run. Serenity did not know what to do. She looked like she was about to defecate, in her panties. As Shawn laughed, smiled, and stated that he was only kidding, Serenity playfully hit Shawn in the arm and told him, "Never do that again." Shawn stifling a laugh could not speak and just nodded his head in agreement.

Shawn's parents opened the door, and in that moment of time Serenity felt a connection with them, a sense of endearment, a strong sense of support and love, and a sense of belonging as Travis and Roberta welcomed her with such genuine love. Serenity could feel their sincerity as she beheld Mrs. Cook, who was a strikingly attractive middle-aged woman with a strong positive aura, and Mr. Cook, who appeared to have ardent eyes of youthfulness, raw zeal, and energy with an air of intelligence and confidence. He was not the snotty kind, but the natural kind, and she could see where Shawn got all of his attributes from. He had his parents written all over him. Serenity took to both the Cooks, but she really liked Mr. Cook. He had such a sense of humor, and that dimple reminded Serenity of Shawn. *When he gets to become that age,* she thought, *he's going to look as distinguished as his father.* Well, it was over, all that anxiety and fear melted, and Serenity felt comfortable. As the day and early evening went on, she had a chance to meet all his siblings, and they all seemed to like her. That evening they played Uno and other card games, but for Uno, Shawn's sister Alicia teamed up with Serenity, and they were an unstoppable team, bulldozing their way past the competition.

Serenity had so much fun. If that wasn't enough, Mrs. Cook announced dessert. They all gathered in the spacious living room, looking at old photo albums and telling mostly Shawn stories. Mrs. Cook made sure the ones of Shawn were singled out. Serenity every now and then would look over at Shawn as he would have different reactions for every story; sometimes he would flinch with embarrassment, the other times he would beg for a story not to be told, but it was told anyway out of fun and enjoyment. That night was the first time she saw Shawn turn two shades, especially when a photo was showed of him with his fro uncombed and eye glasses too big for his face.

Shawn had his head down, but when he heard them say, "Take a look at this," he knew immediately what they were talking about. He made a failed attempt to prevent Serenity from seeing the photo as his two brothers and two brother-in-laws held him down. Mrs. Cook walked past a struggling Shawn, who tried to break free, to hand Serenity the photo. It was too late. Serenity was laughing so hard she was holding her stomach.

Mr. Cook came to his rescue, "OK, you made a point. That was a funny photo. I have to admit it myself."

Shawn still being held down playfully said, "Thanks, Dad, or is it Benedict Arnold?" Everyone laughed. Mr. Cook responded, "Hold up, Son. You know, I always have an ace up the sleeve. Don't doubt me now." Shawn nodded in agreement as Mr. Cook continued, "Like I was saying, my son, Shawn was a late bloomer. That was him then, but once he started there was no stopping. Here is a picture of him when he was in his late teens, and let me say, it seemed as if every single girl within a ten-mile radius was calling here." Serenity took a look at the photo, and her laughter felt like someone had tossed a bucket of cold water on her as she felt a twinge of jealousy when she thought of how good Shawn looked as a late teenager and of those young girls blowing up the Cook's home phone. She quickly brushed off the feeling. Shawn was let up by his brothers Malcolm and Jonathan and his two brother-in-laws David and Will as he gave his father two thumbs up. Shawn stuck his chest out at the victory while celebrating.

Jonathan said, "But did you guys forget about this one?" Jonathan took out the photo and held it up. Everyone looked, and the laughter started up again. Shawn looked over at his father, who grabbed his sleeves and pretended to shake them, and nothing came out.

He said laughing, "Son, I don't have any more aces up the sleeve. You are on your own, Son." His father and mother left the room laughing. Serenity looked over at Shawn, who looked at her, shrugged his shoulders, and laughed as well. At that moment, Serenity felt something shoot deep down in her heart. *This was it. The last doubt just broke like an iceberg.* She felt it as it crumbled. She knew deep down in her soul that she loved Shawn Cook.

Chapter 67

Shawn and Serenity had taken off three days to prepare for Thanksgiving and an additional two days to relax afterward. Both of them knew that that was going to be a busy holiday; however, both of them seemed to be ready for it, at least emotionally. Shawn called Serenity. She answered on the fourth ring; the phone had been ringing off the hook, Sandra, her crazy self, asking for instructions on how to make certain dishes. Serenity at one point had asked Sandra whether she looked like *Rachelle Rae*. Sandra was desperate, even though she was at work. It was the last day of work before Thanksgiving, and Marcus was coming over the next day for Thanksgiving dinner. So far whenever he'd come over they had eaten takeout, so the next test would be the next day at the front door. "Can you burn in the kitchen?" Serenity asked. Sandra with her crazy self told Serenity that burning was her specialty and that cooking was her fantasy. Both women laughed. But seriously speaking, so far that morning alone Sandra had called at least twelve times.

Serenity wondered how Sandra was getting her work done, but the calls were mainly to be nosy and to brag about how she and Marcus were getting along just peachy; that was Sandra's new word. She said that she and Marcus would call each other at least seven times a day. Serenity was very happy for her. Finally her best friend had met someone who respected her and she respected him, and as for Sandra's girls, Ashley and princess, were concerned they adored him and wished he could live with them. Ad in any single mom's eyes, stability and consistency were a major plus and a must.

But Sandra with her horny self wanted to know, since it'd been about a good year and some months since Serenity and Sir Shawn had been together, whether she had given it up yet and how well did she handle Mr. Big Stuff, or did he have to use a machete to cut the weeds to get to that thing? Sandra would say in her back in the day way. Serenity, sounding like a broken record, explained to Sandra that was not the case. It wasn't that kind of party as she explained to Sandra over and over again. She told Sandra that she and Shawn had decided to wait till after marriage. Sandra made some kind of comical negative sound that only she in her crazy self could do.

Then Serenity flipped the script and asked, "Well, how about you . . . ? Have you broken off a piece of the pie? Given Marcus some of the milk, and if yes how was it?" Sandra paused; Serenity could feel Sandra was contemplating the response. Serenity held her breath and prayed that Sandra had not. She was hoping that her best friend would have learned from her past. "You want a man who can deliver more than sex; if sex is the first thing, then he doesn't have anything else to give. It became a humping and a dumping. He humping you and then dumping you, if not literally then emotionally," she said.

Serenity had this discussion with Sandra several weeks ago before she had started going steady with Marcus. She didn't want to come off sounding like an expert, which she knew she was far from that, but she also knew a little bit about guys who were out to score. At the time, she wasn't sure if Marcus fit the profile, but she just wanted to make sure her friend was well prepared. They would get into heated discussions over the matter. Serenity remembered telling Sandra, "San, listen, Marcus or any other guy for that matter may be . . ." She was using her fingers to count off the attributes as she continued, "Smart, intelligent, well educated, has a good income, drives a nice car, owns a home, and hangs well, but you better look past all of that superficial stuff, girlfriend, and understand this reality. Are you listening?" Sandra nodded her head as Serenity continued, "Once you break off the piece, a woman has really very little to give that person something to look forward to. To say it in your language, once you let the kitty cat out of the cage, then you have lost your most powerful bargaining chip, girlfriend, and do you know why? It's because he's taken a peak at your cat and the hunt is over. Now it's time for the hunter to move on because what you just gave him, he can find anywhere."

This was a discussion that Serenity and Sandra had weeks ago. Now Serenity waited on pins and needles for the answer to the question, "Have you given it up yet?"

Serenity was holding her breath as Sandra responded, "I don't think anything is wrong with giving up a little taste. It keeps the hunter hunting for more." Sandra winked at her friend and continued, "On the hot scent trail, if you know what I mean."

Serenity responded, "No, I don't know what you mean, Sandra. Why repeat the same mistakes?" She covered her head with her hands. Sandra reached over and touched Serenity's shoulder. She reluctantly looked up.

Sandra continued, "No, Serenity, I have not. I thought about it one night when it was getting hot and heavy and the girls were over at my mother's place. I mean it was hot. Even the windows were getting fogged up. Girl, I was so wet even the little man in the boat was drowning, but Marcus didn't push me, and that gave me a window of opportunity, one that wasn't fogged." Sandra laughed and continued, "You know my crazy thinking of the past. Give him some and he'll stay. Well, not this time. This time I put on the brakes and said no, but the strange thing was that he understood, and he stayed anyway."

Serenity was more than relieved. She could relate to the hot and heavy stuff. She and Shawn had a few of those close calls as well, but so far the kitty cat was still intact. Serenity and Sandra talked a little while longer. Serenity gave Sandra instructions about work since she would be out for the next few days. She hung up on Sandra, and as soon as she took her hands off the phone, it rang again. This time Serenity did not bother to look at the caller ID. She knew it was crazy Sandra. She'd been doing that all day, so she picked up the phone and said, "Listen, I told you once and I told you three times, I did not give it up to Shawn, even though . . ." Shawn on the other end said, "Even though what?"

Serenity thought she was going to faint as she hemmed and hawed her way for an explanation; she finally said, "Oh my goodness, Shawn, I . . . I thought you was Sandra. She's been bugging and hounding me all day."

Shawn was his usual self, very calm and cool; he said, "Come on. You are not off this hook, even though what?" Serenity was blushing turning two shades; Shawn let her off the hook and said, "Listen, do you want to go shopping for the Thanksgiving dinner later on when I get home or tonight?"

Serenity thought that he must have forgotten. She said, "Sweetie, you forgot, we're going to your parents, and then we are going to my parents."

Shawn responded in a matter-of-fact way, "And then we are coming back to your place where I could relax and taste my baby's cooking. No, I did not forget. I just figured that since we are going to be off for two days after Thanksgiving, I think we should lock ourselves in and watch movies and eat."

Serenity thought about it and really liked that idea. She said, "So what will be on the menu?"

Shawn jumped right in, "Well you know nothing overboard. Let's see: turkey, rice, black eye peas, cabbage or collard greens, macaroni and cheese, ah, and some type of pie or cake of your choice."

Serenity shook her head. "Wow, my choice, how nice of you . . . but we won't go overboard, right, babe?" Shawn nodded with a grin. Serenity continued with her hands on her hips, "Shawn Travis Cook, where and when and how do you see us doing all this cooking and cleaning, and by the way, slick, who is doing what?"

Shawn had a smile in his voice. "Come on, baby. I know you can burn in the kitchen. That is not a problem." Shawn was smiling, Serenity was not as she thought, *Well, at least one area is covered now let's see about the other half. Let's see what Mr. Cook has to say.* Shawn, still rambling on, said, "Now I know what you are thinking, and, baby, we are a team. Even though football will be on, my boys will be looking to hook up, but we are a team. Now about burning, I may not know how to burn like you, but I know how to start a flame."

They both laughed as he continued, "Plus I figure the morning of Thanksgiving I usually turn the restaurant into a soup kitchen and serve the poor in the community. This is our first Thanksgiving together, and I want you to be a part of that and many more to come, Serenity." Serenity had tears in her eyes. *This man was letting her in every crevice in his life. He didn't care. He wanted her to be in it and a part of it.* Serenity was amazed and wasn't sure how Shawn would be able to feed all the poor in the community as she made a feeble attempt to protest, but Shawn came back even stronger and said, "Honey, listen, I've done this ever since God made a way for us to open up the 'Just as You Like It Diner.' It is my way of expressing what God has given to me. Now I could at least share it with others, especially those that don't have." Serenity was totally blown away about the man's generosity. Just when she thought she knew him and had him pinned down, he always seemed to show a deeper side of himself. *How can she deny such a wonderful man?*

In reality, she knew that day was going to be busy, so she'd put up a fuss and a fight, but she knew one thing. She was going to be where her man was going to be, no ifs or buts about it. *But it wouldn't hurt to put up a fight, now would it?* she thought as she began her argument, "Shawn, we already have so much to do, then we have to cook dinner for ourselves and for the community, then go visit our families. It's so much, plus wouldn't your establishment take a hit."

Shawn loved the business side of her. She was drop-dead gorgeous even over the phone, so Shawn was aware he had to be on his "A" game in order to sell his idea. "Honey, listen, the business will be fine. I have volunteers from the community and other organizations who made commitments to help out since early as May. They will come in and start the cooking. Other organizations and individuals including myself have donated food, dessert, and drinks, so as you can see, everything is taken care of. We will only be there for about three or four hours and then we can go and get our visits done. Don't worry if we don't have time to cook. I am sure from all the leftovers we will be fine. How about that?"

Serenity could not fight against those terms of agreement, plus she was already sold on the idea. She gave a few more sounds of resistance, for good measure, then finally gave in.

Serenity and Shawn agreed on cooking the turkey, one vegetable, and a starch over at his house; the rest they would get from leftovers. So by late afternoon, their dinner was ready. Shawn asked Serenity to pack a little bag of clothes and women toiletries. Serenity enjoyed packing her bag as she liked spending time at Shawn's Mount Vernon mansion.

She had been at Shawn's place several times already, and each time she fell more and more in love with it. The mansion was a huge but cozy two-story house. The house had seven large bedrooms: three downstairs and four upstairs; three bathrooms: two downstairs and one upstairs; four walk-in closets that were as big as some average-size bedrooms; and two attics turned into fully equipped playrooms for his nieces and nephews and even his siblings with such things as the PlayStation 3 with the newest games. You name it, and Shawn's place was prepared.

The basement was Shawn's domain; a part of it was his bedroom with a small kitchen and bathroom and the rest of it was his state-of-the-art office. The size of the basement was huge from one end to the other with state-of-the-art computer gadgets. Shawn had everything at his fingertips. If he wouldn't have been a people's person, he could work from his basement. He also had hi-tech surveillance that was set up with hidden cameras at different locations on the outside, and the monitors were placed in certain rooms in the house. This was for privacy and protection.

Serenity loved the setup. The exterior of the mansion had three garages that housed three of his cars, a huge pavement driveway that went on for at least one-fourth of a mile before reaching the house, a huge half-pavement, half-grass backyard with a basketball hoop, a six-foot-round pool, and a play jungle gym. Serenity had never thought that places like this existed in New York City. Shawn explained to her that the original house was ordinary and nothing spectacular, but when Shawn bought it he had made it extraordinary. He added on everything and even purchased the land they were going to build another house on, so there weren't too many houses like that in New York.

Whenever Serenity spent the night, she spent it in Shawn's master bedroom while Shawn slept in the basement apartment. Serenity did not like the idea of moving Shawn out of his bedroom, but he did not look at it that way. Now the two stood in the kitchen, finishing up on the Thanksgiving dinner. Shawn looked at Serenity; her locks were tied up and she looked every bit like the cook she was, with that apron tied around her waist and sweat coming down from her pores. The look turned on Shawn; as a matter of fact, any look that Serenity displayed turned Shawn on. He drew closer to her, reaching out to tenderly and gently hold her waist, not breaking eye contact. The CD track from *Dirty Dancing* was playing. Yes, the first one, the raw one, the one in which Patrick Swayze got everyone in an uproar. Shawn came closer. Serenity was twirling her locks and biting her bottom lip, looking like an innocent virgin. The look shot straight to his loins. It bypassed every other exotic nerve.

Shawn looked down at her. His baritone voice caused a sensation of ripples to vibrate her garden of Eden as he said, "You're not putting me out. I enjoy with such a deep pleasure of satisfaction putting you in. This is a future investment of where I want you to be for the rest of our lives. Do you understand?" Serenity was so mesmerized, the only thing she could do was nod her head. He was in control, and she knew it. He was her narcotic stimulus that made her trip out every time she got a taste of him or stood at a certain radius around him. He bent down all six foot three of him to her five-foot-five height—five feet and five and a half inches when she went up on her toes then. The two lips collided like two trains in the night. The collision could only be described as electrifying and intoxicating. The kiss sent chills through their bodies as their tongues continued in the ritual dance of submission. First Shawn's tongue was on top of hers, and then Serenity's tongue was on top of his. Then both did the catch-and-dart-and-duck dance. Serenity bit Shawn's lower lip lightly, and he pulled away and found the E-spot on her earlobe as he nibbled at it, teasing it and passionately tormenting it. Shawn continued to love assault it as he made a pathway of sweet kisses from the base of her collarbone to the soft budding flesh of her earlobe. They leaned hard into each other to the point it seemed as if they were holding each other up. Serenity could see and feel the results of his love assault as Shawn's manhood wanted to burst out of the pants that were confining it. She rubbed against it and teased it, setting off every sensitive nerve in that area. Shawn was intoxicated with Serenity to the point that his head was spinning, spiraling out of control. He thought, *Mayday, mayday, we are going down.*

Serenity, feeling that Shawn was about to lose it, decided to give him an overdose of that good love as she firmly placed her knee in his crotch area, moving to the rhythm of the music. Shawn, in turn, began to nibble on her neck as he held her buttocks firmly in both hands, squeezing. Serenity felt the nipples of her breasts become erect, standing out there like two search light beams; her breathing had become shallow as little whimpers came from her. She was reminded again that Shawn's manhood was pipe-hard and pipe-large, and she wondered how long could his sweatpants hold such a powerful force. *How long can a dam hold the force of the water behind it?* She couldn't resist; she had to get a firsthand account of the size as her hands slipped down to the suspected area. She could not tell where it began and where it ended. Her hand touched the area and realized that it wasn't a little storm. It was a Mark 5 storm, huge and dangerous.

The touch sent Shawn into a world where he could only see bright spots. She knew she was in a red zone. They both knew she had entered a danger zone, especially when you don't have a hard hat or the proper gear. They both heard the warning bells, but it felt too good to stop. They were about to turn the corner of no return as Shawn took her blouse off over her head and was about to remove the bra that confined those two huge-sized breasts when he had to use every ounce of strength not to go further, and she as well. They both held each other tightly just to avoid letting go and picking up where they left off.

The panting and heavy breathing that came from both of them was slowly returning to normal. They had escaped the storm once again, but each time it got harder and harder. However, they knew that one day the storm would win. Shawn hoped that would happen on the honeymoon night when he wouldn't care whether the dam broke or not. He spoke first, "Wow! Are you OK?"

Serenity, barely talking, nodded her head. Speechless, she finally was able to put some words together. She said, "I . . . you . . . we . . . oh . . . my . . . god, oh . . . my . . . Shawn, you are a bad boy . . ."

Shawn came back with his own line, "And I suppose you were an innocent schoolgirl, but let me tell you something you are a closet freak, girl. The things that you did with those hands, only a bonafide freak can do that."

Serenity blushed and denied the accusation, but they both knew that if that was a taste, they could only imagine what the main meal would be like. Serenity knew that Shawn was experienced. She could tell by the way he found her exotic or E-spots. It seemed as if he had one of those finders that you see people using on the beach to find gold or other metals. She came to the conclusion that he had something like a zone finder. He had her so wet, and she knew he was pipe-hard to the point she wouldn't be surprised if he went off to the bathroom to take a shower to finish the job.

They both looked at each other and seemed to know what the other person was thinking. Serenity elbowed him in the ribs and told him he was a bad boy while Shawn smacked her on her firm and shapely butt. The love tap started a spring in her garden as she cut her eye at him and told him he was a bad boy. Shawn looked at her and smiled.

Shawn and Serenity got up early to head over to the restaurant; they agreed to stay for about four hours and then head out. As they arrived at the restaurant, Serenity was surprised to see the line that stretched around the block. The doors had not been opened yet, and the people were there anxious and hungry. Serenity could imagine that when those doors opened a stampede would take place.

Chapter 68

Shawn led Serenity to the front door and knocked on the door. His second in command at the enterprise along with "Just As You Like It" diner workers, Beatrice and Candy, all three were so happy to see him as they unlocked the door. "Good to see our fearless leader on time as usual." That remark came from Joe while the girls laughed and made room so Shawn and Serenity could get in.

Shawn said, "This is all right. It looks like we have more people this year than last year." They all agreed as he continued to say to no one in particular, "All my helpers and volunteers are here like they said they would be?" Shawn looked around.

Joe answered that question, "Yes, sir, I made confirmation calls two days ago, and they are all here except for your crew boys."

Shawn gave a not too concerned wave of the hand and said, "I am not worried about them. Those guys will be here." He looked at his watch and continued, "As a matter of fact, give them fifteen more minutes, if not then call Marcus and tell him to get his butt down here." Shawn smiled with that and looked at the ladies who would be in charge of serving and packing. "Ladies, are you ready? Did I get all my volunteers as promised?"

Beatrice the leader of the group said, "Everything is everything."

Shawn nodded as to if to say, "good," as he continued, "Listen, everyone, you guys remember Serenity, my girlfriend, right?" Everyone greeted Serenity with smiles, hugs, and handshakes as Shawn continued, "She will be working alongside of most of you, so be patient with her. She could be slow at times, you know hard to understand things." Serenity was nodding when she realized everyone was laughing, and it dawned on her what Shawn had said. She playfully hit him in the arm. The others were still laughing. Serenity chuckled at Shawn's crazy self and playfully hit him again.

Beatrice walked up to Serenity and said, "You see, he's not that bad, right? A little drama here and there, but not that bad, right?"

Serenity laughed and said, "Not at all." Both women laughed remembering their first conversation about Shawn. Serenity blushed a little; Shawn caught it but was too busy orchestrating and navigating the day.

Joe said, "Ah, Shawn, a couple of politicians would like to help out."

Shawn thought about it and said, "Anything for a vote, sure. Even the poor have a voice, but when you know the event is going to be on the news, they want to so call 'help out.' Is it the poor vote they want or just the fifteen minutes of fame . . . ? Sure as long, and, Joe, let them know this, as long as they keep their issues to themselves, that is, including my guy as well."

Joe agreed and acknowledged he understood as he took brief notes, then he remembered, "Oh yeah, Shawn, we have a DJ coming as well, DJ Turnout, one of the locals."

Shawn agreed, "OK, cool, as long as you let him know to keep it mixed, more of the 1990s and up. No profanity. If it happens once, Joe, he's gone. Let Teddy that big guy at the door know. No gangs or colors will be allowed inside. If they want to come in, they have to remove their flags, and beef with anyone, take it to the meat market not here, or they could come down to my martial arts class and go a few rounds. Give them that option as well." Shawn looked at his watch. It was about time to let people in. He yelled over at Teddy, "Teddy bear, it's about that time. Listen, I want this thing done in order. Anyone that gets out of hand, they have to leave. If they can't behave for a short time for a free meal, then let them take their tin cup and get out. Give them one warning, then they have to go. Most if not all know me, and they know I won't put up with the nonsense."

Serenity all the time was looking at another side of Shawn, a tougher yet gentle side. Once again, he had proven to surprise her and keep her on her toes. As she walked up to him she said, "Hey, Captain, you run a tough ship."

Shawn winked at her and said, "Always, baby. I don't have time to play with people's lives, and I don't have time for them to play with me. I don't have time for sob stories." Shawn looked at Beatrice, "Bring me two aprons and a hairnet and serving rubber gloves, and let's knock out hunger for the day and hopefully for a lifetime."

They all clapped and cheered, and Serenity stood back and took it all in. She was so proud of Shawn. The music started up. The DJ must have come in when Shawn had been talking. He had everyone so entranced no one noticed the brother, but he was getting down.

Shawn looked at Teddy and said, "Yo, Teddy bear, unlock those doors and let them in." The people streamed in. No one was pushing. They knew that Shawn always fed them very well and gave them enough that they did not want seconds.

Serenity watched as the poor of the community came streaming in just for a hot meal for one day. She became emotional as tears streamed down her cheeks. As she served the undeserved, Shawn stood at the other end, serving and watching her. Even his eyes became moist. He looked up briefly and said a little prayer to God for the woman that he had allowed to come into his life. At that moment, Shawn felt an urge to look in her direction, and she was already obeying her thirst as she was looking at him. They both mouthed the words at the same time, "I love you."

As the Thanksgiving festivity went on, the place was packed and people were still coming in. The DJ was jamming and putting together a string of hits that gave the atmosphere a mixture of a relaxed and party atmosphere.

Shawn gave clear instructions to Joe Johnson, his second in command, that no one should be turned away. He said, "Joe, I don't care if you have to put one extra chair at each section, just do it. If you have to, pull out those folded tables and find a spot for them so we can fit families at them. Is that understood?" Joe nodded.

Shawn looked at Joe and said, "I can't emphasize it enough, Joe. I want these people fed. I want families to go home or back to their shelters with their stomach full, satisfied."

Joe nodded and Shawn walked off.

Shawn went up to Beatrice, who was directing the crowd to volunteers who were waiting for them to help them to be seated to keep some form of order. He said, "Bea, listen, I want you to make sure that everyone gets a job application for the restaurant. I want you to announce this in a few minutes. I want you to set up the interviews with me starting next week. Let's see . . ." Shawn was rubbing his chin as he continued, "Ah, Wednesday, Thursday, and Friday from 10:00 a.m. to 4:00 p.m. Let them know to come dressed. If they don't have, there are nonprofit places that would set them up. No outs or excuses. Those who want it will do it. Those who don't won't come. Anyone who has been clean for a year or more, they may qualify for the program. You know the one I got Karen into." Shawn looked around at the people and said to Beatrice in a low, frustrated tone,

"You know, Bea, some of these people at one time had it working for them. They had it right at their fingertips, and then one day boom or the rug was snatched from under them, and they lost everything and for some I mean everything, even their sanity. Here one minute, gone the next. On top of the world one minute, the next, the world is on top of them. I want to change that, Bea. I know the only thing some of them need is a chance."

Shawn was still in deep thought when Serenity came up from behind him and touched him. He was a little startled and turned toward her, looking a little out of sorts. Serenity said, "Baby, I'm sorry, I didn't mean to startle you. Are you OK?" Serenity still looking at Shawn with concern asked, "Baby, what's wrong?"

Shawn, looking at her with the pain of conviction written all over his face, said in a tone she had never heard before, "This is wrong, Sen. This is wrong. This whole thing is wrong, a Band-Aid. It's like putting an ACE bandage on a broken bone. Looks impressive but doesn't do jack for the broken body part, you understand?"

Serenity was like a ship in a storm. As a matter of fact, she thought she had walked into a storm as she said in confusion, "Shawn, you are not making any sense. What are you talking about, baby?"

Shawn looked at her for a brief second or two, shook his head in frustration, and said in the same frustrating tone, "This. What impact are we making? I want to make a difference, Serenity. I don't want a tax write-off for this. I want to write off hunger and homelessness. How can this be happening in the society we live in? It should not be . . . it should not be."

Serenity, still confused, could not understand why Shawn was looking at the glass half-empty. *Yes, this was a big problem, but they were making progress. Every little bit helps.* She said to him, "Baby, this event is successful. You are doing something no one has come close to do. Look, baby." She showed him the latest stats. "Look, baby, you set a new record of feeding the poor and homeless. You are making a—"

Shawn cut her off and in frustration snatched the paper from her hands. The move startled her as he responded to her latest statement, "Do you really want to know what this stat really means? They may fool some people, but remember, baby, I deal with stats. I live by numbers. No, this doesn't mean we are making progress because we are feeding more of the poor. It means that there are more homeless people coming into the area. That is not what they want you to know. They want you to buy into the smoke screen. No, baby, there are more people every day losing their homes or apartments because they can't keep up with this freaking rat race." Shawn waved his hand agitatedly and said, "Do you want to know why things are the way they are or at least one of the reasons, Serenity?" He grabbed her shoulders firmly and turned her to the table where the politicians were sitting. When he grabbed her, she flinched a little because of the pressure he was applying. He realized he was hurting her and let up on the pressure. Nevertheless, he stuck to making his point, "Look around you." Shawn was saying in her ear. Serenity could not figure out what he was talking about as she looked at him with confusion. He said, "The politicians, those guys right there that are supposed to represent the community. Look at them. Not one got off their butts to sit at a table with these people. It's the needy versus the greedy, not one time, Serenity."

Shawn found himself pleading with her as he continued, "They're not looking at them as citizens, but rather as Third World folks, nuisances, society's backwash." Serenity told Shawn to stop and calm down. Shawn ignored her and said, "How could you understand them if you don't get to know them? Like I said, you can't judge a book by its cover. You see that man over there by the DJ." Serenity nodded. Shawn continued, "He used to be the number one surgeon in the nation. Now he's public enemy number one. He lives in the shelter down the block. People fail to recognize that those same hands that pick up bottles and cans out of the garbage used to save lives at one time."

Serenity didn't know what to say. She had never seen Shawn like that before, but she knew it was a part of his frustrated passion as he tried to continue, "Serenity . . ."

Serenity had heard about enough from him. Now she was upset, "Listen, why do you go through all of this then? Why the charade? Why the game if what you are saying is true? Then why waste your time and energy along with those who believe what you believe? That is your problem, Shawn. It would be an ideal world if everyone was like you." Shawn made an attempt to say something. Serenity cut him off, "I'm not finished. Don't be so rude. I understand what you are saying, but you have to understand that every little bit count, plus this is not the time or place. Let these people enjoy a nice, warm quiet meal. Deal with your issues later. This problem didn't happen overnight, and as super as you are, not you or one or two people will get rid of it overnight. Look, if it takes a village to raise a child, then it will take a nation to come together and get rid of homelessness and poverty. Keep doing what you are doing. Don't only keep the faith, but spread it and share it with others. What else can you do?" She was holding his hands the whole time while she was talking to him.

Shawn looked at Serenity and said, "Oh, I'm going to show you how I'm going to deal with this matter, right now and not later. This is a perfect time."

Serenity tried to grab his arm without making a scene, but he was too quick and too evasive. He was quick like lightning as he moved toward the table where the politicians were sitting. He approached them like a panther approaching its prey.

As she looked around, she spotted Joe Johnson. She yelled to him, "Joe, please."

She pointed in Shawn's direction. Joe knew from the look on Serenity's face that there was a problem, and when he saw Shawn's face he knew who the problem was. Joe knew that look. It was that same look before his martial art tournaments.

Joe thought whatever was going on it wasn't the time or place, especially not with the media around. He took off toward Shawn without drawing attention to himself. There was a short distance between where Shawn was heading and where Joe had to get to. From the way it looked, he wasn't going to be able to avert disaster. Shawn was just a few feet from the politicians' table, and Joe was still en route, closing in but not fast enough. He knew that when Shawn's passion hit that level, there was no telling what C-4 would do. C-4 was the nickname Shawn's close friends such as Frank Hall gave to him. Shawn was about to get to the table, and Joe was about to take off in a sprint and explain later. But just when he was about to reach the table, several homeless folks whom Shawn knew from the hood walked up to him to thank him and tell him they were coming out for the interview next week. Shawn was happy about that, so was Joe because it gave him enough time to catch up with Shawn just at the time the conversation with the homeless folks was about to end.

Watching the whole thing, Serenity was on pins and needles and then breathed a sigh of relief when Joe was able to reach Shawn before he reached the table. Serenity noticed Joe putting his arms around Shawn, and at first Shawn seemed to put up some resistance. Then after Joe said a few words to Shawn, which grabbed his attention, he just turned to go. Some of the politicians waved to him, said a few words of thanks, and made verbal commitments to him. Shawn smiled, and he and Joe headed back toward Serenity. Serenity said she was going to serve for about another hour and a half, then she was going to take a break. In actuality, she and Shawn had been going to head out at least thirty minutes ago, but things were so busy they weren't worrying about the time.

A couple of Shawn's friends then walked in, Marcus and Frank were still missing. Serenity was happy as the two who came out seemed to cheer Shawn up.

Shawn was calm with his apron, net cap, and serving gloves on as he stood behind Serenity while she was serving. "Can I speak with you for a minute?"

Serenity heard the apology in his voice but wasn't going to give in so fast as she said to him, "Baby, this line is long. I can't stop serving right now. I am on a mission." She winked at him. The gesture sent goose bumps up and down his arms. Shawn thought that she was looking sexy in her outfit. It was really doing something to him. He rubbed his hand down his face. From the corner of her eye, she could see what she was doing to him, and it made her smile. Shawn called for someone to take Serenity's spot. One of the girls came over.

Shawn took Serenity toward the back of his office where there was some privacy but not much. The restrooms were back there as well, so the traffic wasn't constant but consistent. Shawn opened his office door, and they went in. He closed the door, but knew it wasn't even a deterrent, so whatever he had to say he'd better say, "Listen, I want to apologize for my actions earlier. I know I was way out of line and I should be at least grateful for the progress that has been made from year to year. You were right . . . I guess I want things to go faster." Serenity was rubbing her shoulder to make a point. That was the one Shawn had squeezed. He saw what she was doing and flinched. He said, "As long as we are together, and I plan going the long haul with you, baby, I will make sure that would not happen again . . ." Shawn pointed to Serenity's shoulder and continued, "I promise."

Serenity looked at Shawn. At that time, he looked like a big kid who had been sent to the principal's office. She felt a deep sense of love for him as she said, "Honey, your passion is so awesome. I have never been with anyone with that level of passion." Serenity smiled, flirted with him, and said, "Does that passion cross into all areas?" She smiled and kissed him hard and passionately; she pulled away as she continued, "Shawn, I want to be a part of that passion, but you have to allow me to come in. I won't be a sideline wife. That's not me, so I leave it up to you. The cards are on the table. Deal wisely."

Shawn was still stuck at the part of wife. He smiled and said, "You said—"

Serenity interrupted him as she pulled him close, placed little kisses around his lips, and said, "You heard exactly what the future Mrs. Cook said, Mr. Cook."

Shawn beamed from ear to ear as he passionately kissed her. They were interrupted by Beatrice as she opened the door without knocking. She said, "Oh, I am sorry. Can't you guys rent a room? Listen, we need you guys back in there."

Serenity looked at her watch and put her hand to her mouth, "We are so sorry. We did not realize we were back here for twenty minutes."

Beatrice smiled, looked at her watch, and said, "Well, either your watch stopped or you just forgot how to tell time. It's been thirty minutes. Now you two lovebirds, come on." Shawn smiled at Beatrice. No one could get away with the stuff she said and did but her. No one could get mad at her. She was loud at times and other times rambunctious and talkative but with a heart of gold. He wouldn't trade her for nothing. Shawn and Serenity headed back to their stations. The time right then was 1:00 p.m. Serenity felt more love for him than she had ever felt before. She realized that she and Shawn were meant to be together, soul mates, and nothing humanly possible would be able to stop that.

Chapter 69

Meanwhile an Hour Earlier on the Other Side of Town, There Was a Dark Sinister Presence

The electronic voice on the other end was conversing with Frank Hall. The voice was the only name it went by. Frank could not tell whether it was a woman or a man. He just knew that he was way over his head as the voice said to him, "So, Mr. Hall, I understand from my informants that you know where Ms. Powers is at this precise moment."

Frank knew that he had made a big mistake when he got involved with the group that referred to themselves as "The Alternative." He responded, "Of course, I know where she is at, but I could tell you from what I have learned, Ms. Powers doesn't know much of anything. You are making a huge mistake." Frank tried to steer them down a more congenial path, but the voice was not buying it. Frank concluded that the voice was a seasoned player who had been around for some time.

The voice ignored Frank's strong statement and stated, "Mr. Hall, last month a package that was meant for me somehow by mistake was sent to Ms. Powers. Later, I learned the common breakdown. The person who committed the flaw was located and was eliminated. Mr. Hall, some child did not see his parent that night. I hope that the arrangements that you and I agreed on, that you plan on keeping the end of your contract, I would hate to—"

Frank cut off the voice and said, "Listen, I am not impressed by your ability to carry out a hit. Please keep your subtle threat to yourself. I, for one, am not intimidated, so save it."

The voice continued, "Mr. Hall, I am not trying to intimidate you. I am trying to save you a lot of pain and suffering. Now as I was saying, I hope you realize in that package there was top secret information regarding

'The Alternative,' and every single person or politician, who believe in our vision, was on a list in that package. Someone may now have that list or maybe not, but I have a strange feeling that we may have to do some collateral damage. I would suggest damage control, but the situation if it is true can bring down a lot of people including yours truly. And that's not going to happen, Mr. Hall. Are we on the same page, Mr. Hall?"

Frank made a reluctant sound that he understood and made his plea again to get Serenity, his best friend's girlfriend, off the hook. "So I don't understand how Ms. Powers fit in this equation. She doesn't know anything!"

The voice was starting to become perturbed. "Whatever, Mr. Hall. The point is when the box came to me it had been opened. The contents were tampered with therefore, as you know, you were assigned a few weeks ago to take care of that problem. I even made it easier to bring her to you, and if you would have listened, we wouldn't be having this conversation."

Frank was becoming ticked off with the whole situation. He said, "You know damn well why I didn't go through with the plan, and I keep repeating myself. She is not the one. You got the wrong person!"

The voice was becoming agitated with this cat and mouse game, "Then you tell me, who the hell you think it is, Mr. Hall, since you already know, and by the way, I find that interesting, that Ms. Powers is innocent? Are you certain you are not screwing her brains out? I heard she is one fine black whore."

Frank, becoming offended, responded, "Hey, watch your mouth or this conversation is over."

The voice just laughed that sinister laugh and continued, "You know, Mr. Hall, why would you defend her so? What is really going on?"

Frank, who by now had about enough, said, "What is going on? Nothing other than the fact that you have this paranoid behavior."

The voice said, "Or maybe it's not that. Maybe it has nothing to do with Ms. Powers, well, not directly, perhaps more so with the association she has with Mr. Shawn Cook, your best friend. Mr. Hall, I do have a question. Where is your loyalty? You rather put your best friend in harm's way rather than save your family. Boy, are you a piece of work."

Frank had reached the boiling point. The voice had touched on an area that had been bothering him since day one as Frank retaliated, "Shut up, I mean it. You don't know why I did what I did. One more word about anything other than business I walk. Is that clear?"

The voice gave a sinister laugh and ignoring the threat said, "You are in no position to question or threaten me, sir. I have your ass in so many compromising positions, you can't even crap right. So don't mess with me, boy. You are right. Let's stop playing games. I had about enough. I know all about you and Ms. Powers and Mr. Cook, your childhood chum. Now do as you are told, and you will collect your money as promised, and this will be over quick and easy." Frank tried his best to repeat that Serenity did not know anything and that they were making a serious mistake, but it fell on deaf ears.

The voice went back to becoming that ice-cold bloodcurdling and chilling voice. Frank realized he was dealing with a psychopath as the voice continued, "Mr. Hall, my sources tells me that the box we are talking about was seen on Ms. Powers' desk a few days ago. She was looking at the tape job as if to see if she had done a good job sealing up the box. Now you may be right. Maybe she is innocent. I want to know where she is right now! At this moment, we just want to speak to her. We want to see how much she knows . . . and if she knows nothing . . . well, no harm, no foul." The voice gave a sinister laugh as he continued, "Now, Mr. Hall, we know fully well or rather we've learned that you are not a killer. I thought you had guts, but I was wrong. So that's why I just want to know where is she at right now, and if you can't help me, sir, the deal is off. You do not pass go and you do not collect the money, and of course your poor son remains in a dangerous predicament. And from what my medical sources tells me, his doctors were so close to a cure, but . . . poor Bobby."

Frank knew he was way over his head as he rubbed his face with his hand. He knew that they knew they had him by his balls. Frank tried to sound strong, but the force of the words came out very weakly as he said, "Don't talk about my son as if you give a damn, you psychopath. You can care less about him. No, I know what you are concerned about. You are not concerned about this box and those names, for some reason, Mr. Psycho, but you are concerned that a trail could be led back to you and the takedown of a major operation, whatever that is that the so-called Alternative is working on. And if that is so, I assume some big names would blow even your most daring reporter out of the water, so cut the crap, who's BSing who?"

The voice still sounding as calm as ever and as cold as ice said, "Mr. Hall, this conversation is over. Good luck to your son . . . bye, Mr ." . . ."

Frank desperately pleaded for the voice not to hang up, "OK, OK, I'll keep my end of the bargain, but I want my money up front."

The voice laughing that sinister laugh sent chills up and down the spine of Frank Hall while it said in a cold, calculating, and chilling manner,

"I am a person of my word, sir. The deal and arrangements will remain the same, the same way. Half of the money was dropped off in an account only you had access to. The same rules will be applied. The money will be in your account immediately after the task is accomplished. Not that I don't trust you, Mr. Hall, but human nature could be, let's say, very sinister and sneaky. Even the Bible says that the old nature can't be trusted. Now if God feels that way about his own creation . . ." The voice laughed that sinister laugh again.

Frank realized that he had been outdone. He tried to buy time, but the voice paced him and played him like a toy. Everything he tried, the voice was two steps ahead of him. He had no other choice. Well, he did have one more ace up his sleeve, but he wasn't sure if the prodigal son was going to be accepted back. It was a gamble. After what he had done he wasn't sure if his best friend would ever accept him back. Frank made one more plea to the voice, "I don't want anyone to get hurt. You gave me your word."

The voice laughed and said, "That was then. This is now, Mr. Hall. The situation has changed somewhat not due to me, but blame yourself. But I will try to make sure there are no casualties as long as she cooperates. There shouldn't be a problem, sir. My men will be in place. Now, Mr. Hall, the three-million-dollar question, which is also your final pay. Where is Ms. Powers?"

Chapter 70

Thirty Minutes Ago

Joe came to Serenity on the serving line and whispered in her ear that she had a phone call. Serenity playfully lifted her hands with the serving glove and said, "This is just a fashion statement, Joe . . . Please take a message. People are still coming. Does it ever end?"

Joe's smile turned into a serious and sober look as he said to her, "I see, but the person is persistent. She says it is urgent, ah, somebody named Sandra."

Serenity blew out an aspirated breath, shook her head, and thought, *Sandra probably wants to blame me for burning her turkey dinner. Well, me no speak English.* She looked at Joe, who was caught in the middle of that war, and said, "Joe, thanks, I know what it is all about, but let her know that I will call her as soon as I get a break." Joe looked at the long line and back at Serenity with his left eyebrow raised questioningly. She looked back at him and said, "Exactly, just tell her I'll call her back as soon as I can. Thanks, Joe, sorry you are in the middle." Joe shrugged his shoulders and walked away to talk to Sandra.

Shawn watched the whole interaction between Joe and Serenity and was curious about what was going on. He asked Beatrice to find someone to take his place. As he took a walk down to Serenity, he asked, trying not to sound jealous, "Is everything OK? What was that all about?"

Serenity smiled and said while serving, "Oh that, that was crazy Sandra. She wanted to speak to me. She used the panic button, saying that it was urgent."

Shawn looked at Serenity with a serious expression and said, "Well, what's going on with her? And where is Marcus?" Serenity still serving while talking to Shawn shrugged her shoulders. She had enjoyed the whole day. She was exhausted, but she really felt like she was doing something for the community. She felt she was making a difference as she continued, "Honey, one thing you will get to know about Sandra if you don't know already, and that is, Sandra is the queen of drama." Shawn still wasn't convinced. He thought, *Why would she call just to say it wasn't important?* But what could he say. She knew her friend better than he did. Serenity assured Shawn with a "don't worry" look and said, "Baby, believe me, it's nothing urgent. What could have happened was that she probably burned her Thanksgiving dinner, and now she wants to blame me since I gave her instructions how to prepare and cook the turkey, watch." Shawn laughed and walked back to his place in the line.

Sandra, looking dumbfounded, stood there stunned and said to Marcus, "I can't believe she refused to talk to me. I have to get her this message, Marcus." Sandra started to pace the floor. Marcus was relaxing, enjoying his day off with his new girlfriend; he'd worked hard for the past three days, more than looking forward to spending the day with Sandra.

Marcus responded, "Honey, relax, you may be taking this thing a little overboard."

Sandra was upset at Serenity, but she wanted to smack some sense into Marcus's head because he wasn't taking that thing seriously as she repeated his insulting statement, "A little overboard, maybe, perhaps. I know I've been called drama queen, Dear Abbey, Wendy Williams, but I am right nine times out of ten, and this is serious, Marcus." Marcus looked at her, not totally convinced, as she continued, "Listen, first I find this package on Serenity's desk. You know me, a little inquisitive. So I opened it so I could call her and tell her what came in the mail, but something was strange about this mail."

As Sandra was thinking about it, Marcus jumped in and interrupted her thoughts, "What do you mean by strange?"

Sandra looked at Marcus and said, "There's no forward address, and I've been working in this building for some time. And, Marcus, I may be wrong, but I have an eerie feeling that this package came from within somewhere in the building. This is an inner-office mail, Marcus. Do you understand the implications of this?"

Marcus was not in the mood to play cloak and dagger or detective, so he said in a very impatient tone, "Sandra, please get to the point. I don't see anything wrong with inner-office mail in a Federal building, save a stamp. What is your point?"

Sandra slammed her hand down on the wooden coffee table, looked at Marcus as if he was from another planet, and said, "You don't see anything wrong with the contents in the box such as the blueprints of the building and how to get past secret codes and where the security will be at certain times, and oh, passwords and the schematics of other Federal buildings with codes and dates. Well, I didn't think anything of it either. All of it was, you know . . . was gibberish to me, so I thought Serenity will know something, seeing that she holds a high position. So I called her and left a message for her to call me at her office."

Sandra was looking at Marcus without saying anything, so Marcus spoke up, "So what happened?"

Sandra shook her head to clear it and get back on track. She said, "Marcus, I picked up the phone, expecting to speak with Serenity instead I heard something out of a horror flick." Marcus made a gesture for Sandra to get to the point as she continued, "It was this electronic voice, and it said, 'You have something that belongs to me, bitch, and I want it. You have a package. Drop it off in the mailroom the way it is already sealed. If I don't get it by tomorrow, you are one dead chick.' Then the person hung up. I thought it was Serenity playing with me, knowing the package was coming, so I laughed it off. But then I thought that how would she know unless someone from the mailroom would have called her cell if she was expecting the package. I know Serenity, and she is so organized. If that was the case, she would have called and asked me to put it up until she returned, but that wasn't the case."

Marcus sat up at the edge of his seat. He was shocked and surprised about the phone call. "Wait, baby, hold up a second. Let me see if you and I are on the same page. What you are saying is that the contents in that box are contents to blow up Federal buildings on the East Coast and the dates represent the time frames. Is that close?" Sandra slowly nodded her head very soberly. Marcus was on a roll as he continued, "Oh, sugar, the Federal building, the one you work in has a date for next Thursday. Oh man, Sandra, we can't sit on this, oh, sugar."

Sandra was stunned. She was speechless, then the words came out in a struggle, "Next week, Marcus, next week. According to this, we have another 9/11. Omigod, Marcus, hand me the phone."

Marcus, who looked in shock, hesitated with Sandra's request, "What are you going to do, Sandra?"

Sandra still emotionally shaken was able to get the words out, but this time she had a shake in her voice, "Marcus, let me try again to get in touch with Serenity. I have to get through."

Sandra called and spoke to Joe again and went through the same song and dance. Marcus heard Sandra practically beg Joe to speak with Serenity, but once again he told her that Serenity was busy.

Sandra hung up; Marcus looked at her and said, "So what are we going to do?" Sandra's face took on a serious, alert look, "Marcus, we have to get down there ASAP. She has to know about this, Marcus. Serenity may be in danger. If not, next week we all will be."

Marcus looked at her and said, "Listen, I'm with you, baby. Those are our friends, especially C-4. You mess with him, you might as well mess with the crew, and I'll let you know right now, we are not taking any prisoners. We are there for one reason, not to talk but to kick some butt." He was curious about one thing though. He asked, "So what did you do with the box?"

Sandra, who was getting her stuff on, pretended she did not understand the question.

Marcus stopped in the middle of getting his coat on, "Sandra, what did you do with the box?"

Sandra shoved her arm in the sleeve of the coat, turned, looked at Marcus with a look of frustration, and said, "I sent it to where I was told."

Marcus replied in an incredulous tone, "You what? That was your only evidence. I can't believe you . . ."

Sandra held up her hand with a calm look and said, "Honey, calm down, I may have sent back the box, but thank God for cell phones and the power of the pen." Marcus just looked at Sandra with curiosity.

Thirty Minutes Ago

Shawn was told by Joe that he had a phone call. Shawn called one of the girls to take his spot in the serving line. Serenity was busy like crazy, so he didn't bother to tell her where he was going. He took the phone in his office. He spoke into the phone, "Hello, this is Shawn. Who is this?"

Frank Hall had mixed feelings about speaking with Shawn; a part of him was relieved while another part of him felt like a heel, a Judas, a turncoat. He was hurt about what he'd done. He had sold out his best friend, his brother, and even though he had a good reason, he knew that he had done wrong. He knew he was way over his head. He wished he had never spoken to the voice about his problem. It had happened so quickly. One day he put the word out he was looking for some extra work to make some extra cash. The next thing he knew he received a phone call from the electronic voice.

At first, he did not know what to make of it, but he knew that he was in serious trouble. The bait was out there, and his son's situation was getting worse, so he took the bait. The job was very simple at first and the money was good and consistent. The only thing he had to do was make sure certain packages from inside the building that were marked "Priority" with a red "x" were sent to the mailroom. Those boxes had no destination, but Frank was supposed to pick them up, and the voice would tell him who to send the packages to and so forth. At least two packages came in a week. Frank would pick up the packages, follow the instructions, and deliver the packages to wherever he was asked. Frank had no idea what was in the boxes or to whom he was asked to drop the boxes to. He didn't care. His main concern was to make the money because his son's medical bills were astronomically expensive, but once he started doing this side job it made it possible to pay not only for past bills, but also for current ones as well. In addition, Frank whose house was about to go for foreclosure was now able to pay his mortgage and have some money left over for a family that was under stress, going through a serious crisis, and was at the point of collapsing.

Frank was happy once again. His wife was ecstatic. The Halls were once again a family with promise and hope. Things were looking better then. They were back to the prominent family they used to be. Everything seemed to fall into place. Treatment for Bobby was going well, and Bobby's doctor was pleased with the results, but he cautioned Frank and Jackie that the treatment must be consistent. To fall back on the treatment would put little Bobby at risk, and it was very possible that it would make his illness more resistant to treatment.

The Halls received the news that a cure for Bobby was possible. That was all Frank wanted. The storm was over, or so they thought.

One day, something went wrong. The box was sent to the wrong department. It was sent to Serenity Powers' department. Frank got word from the voice where the box had been sent to. Somebody had made a blunder, and Serenity found the box and didn't know what to make of it. She called the senior vice president, Mrs. Fry, who, in turn, reported the matter to Frank's office that was in charge of items coming in and going out. Frank removed the box himself. He brought it to where he was told. Later that evening, the voice called him and told him that the box appeared to have been tampered with. The box had been taped up as if it'd been opened. The voice came to the conclusion that Serenity had opened the box. Even though all the contents seemed to be untouched, the fact that the items in the box had been exposed had changed the playing field drastically. The voice could not be sure if that was the case. He could not take any chances, so that was the night when Frank was to put a warning hit on her. He was to make it look like an accident as people are generally careless and are hit by cars on a daily basis. That's what Frank was supposed to do and let the voice's team do the rest.

The voice knew all along that Frank did not have the guts or the heart to do what he was supposed to do, plus the voice soon learned that there was a conflict of interest. He found out that Serenity Powers was seeing a wealthy multimillionaire Shawn Cook and that Frank Hall was Shawn Cook's stepbrother, so to speak. Now the web was very much tangled, but things calmed down weeks ahead, and the voice was convinced that Mrs. Powers did not know anything about that box despite the evidence of tampering. Perhaps that may have happened in some other fashion. So Frank's blotched hit turned out to work in his favor, but a few weeks after that, another blunder occurred. That time the voice did not dismiss it. It was too risky. The voice asked Frank where was Mrs. Powers. Frank hesitated for a while, but then he was threatened that the money would be cut off from him as soon as the phone was hung up. Frank was in a bind. He had to make up his mind whether he was going to sell out his best friend's girlfriend or count his loses and deal with the situation with his son's life. He knew if he told Shawn what was going on, he would be pissed off to put it mildly. The worst-case scenario would be that Shawn would kick Frank's butt like he did in elementary school. This time it would be on an adult level. That meant he was going to rip Frank's heart out of his chest, shove it down his throat, and watch it come out his ass when Shawn scared the crap out of him.

Frank heard Shawn in the background, asking who was on the phone. Frank was too much in his emotional pain to respond. Shawn asked again who he was speaking to; again there was no sound but the pain of inner turmoil. Frank knew he had done a bad thing. He sold out his best friend, but he knew he had to warn his best friend . . . well, his once best friend. After this, Shawn was going to become Frank's worst nightmare. Frank knew it.

Frank knew he had to warn Shawn of the danger to Serenity. Frank said, "Hey Shawn."

Shawn was surprised to hear Frank's voice on the other end. He said, "Hey, my road dog, why didn't you respond when I was asking who was speaking?"

Frank still sounding dull and broken said, "Sorry, there must have been a bad connection."

Shawn thought that was strange, but he let it go. He was just happy to hear from his buddy, and he said, "Wait a minute, yo, why aren't you down here? You was supposed to have been down here helping me out, so are you coming?"

Frank put his head down and slowly lifting it up said, "Shawn . . . there is something I need to tell you." Frank was sounding distant and remote.

Shawn knew something was wrong, terribly wrong. "Frank, what's the problem? Are you OK? What happened? Is Jackie OK . . . ? Please tell me that Bobby is OK." Frank's pain intensified. Even then his best friend thought something was wrong with him and showed concern about the matter. *Who am I? Just a no good heel, a piece of crap, a blackguard, a miscreant,* Frank thought. He was all of those things because how he turned on his friend/brother like a dog with rabies turning on its owner.

He felt that low as he responded, "Shawn, listen to me. Everyone is fine, but I did something awful, man. I messed up big time."

Shawn said, "Whoa, hold up, bro. Come on, man, we are boys. What in the world could you have done that is making you sound so bad . . . ? Come on, we are boys, talk to me."

"Shawn, I got myself into some trouble, deep trouble, man. Things started out cool, but now, yo, this crap is out of control."

Shawn didn't know what was going on exactly, but he knew whatever it was, wasn't cool. He said, "Frank, straight up, what's going on?"

Frank tried to get the words out; he said, "Shawn, I don't know how to say this, but I'm too deep in this mess . . . and Serenity is involved."

Shawn froze; his world felt as if it was crashing down. He felt every impact of it, and he said in a desperate tone, "Frank, what the hell are you talking about, man?" Shawn did not give Frank time to respond as his tone became harder and more forceful, "Frank, what the freak is going on? What Serenity, how . . . what . . . *talk to me, Frank!*" Frank knew it was useless to try to calm Shawn down. He explained the whole situation from the beginning. The more Frank talked, the more Shawn's world was spinning. He could not believe it. *It had to be a mistake. Perhaps Frank meant someone else. He could not have meant his Serenity, no way.* Shawn was caught off balance as he emotionally struggled and wrestled with the news. His mind reeled and spun, trying to come to grips with the truth. He fell against the filing cabinet, bounced off that, and crashed into his desk chair. He had mixed feelings, a part of him was trying to come to grips with the truth, the other part of him wanted to take out every bit of his frustration on Frank Hall. He blamed him, and he said, "You no good son of a . . . how could you get Serenity involved? You are a low life bastard . . . wait until I get my hands on you. By the time I am finished with you, they wouldn't have to worry about doing an autopsy, I'll have most of the work done already." Shawn deep down knew he did not mean any of the things he was saying because he knew it wasn't Frank's fault. As a matter of fact, ironically, it was probably Frank who had kept Serenity alive up to this point. Shawn said, "Who are these people? What am I up against?"

Frank had to find the heart to speak, "Shawn, I don't know."

Shawn, who was totally frustrated, said, "What do you mean you don't know? What the freak does that mean? Didn't you get money from them?"

Frank who did not back down was now frustrated, "Like I said, I don't know. I never met them. I can't tell you if it's a man or woman. The voice was electronic. I have no idea, really, Shawn, plus I don't care what you say or what you do. This is not going to be a you. This is an us. I got Serenity into this, and I'm going to get her out."

Shawn was still livid; he felt like a volcano. "I don't want your help, and I don't need your help. You did enough damage already. If you've come to help, I might make a mistake with friendly fire. I don't believe you. You could have come to me for the money. Why didn't you?"

Frank was yelling now, "Why? So Frank once again could be bailed out by Shawn Cook? I'm tired of you playing super hero. I wanted to do this. I needed to do this! I didn't think things would come to this. If I did, do you think I would have put Serenity at risk?" There was silence.

Frank, seething now, said through clenched teeth, "You arrogant, pompous, no good son of a bitch, oh, you think because of who you are you are the only one that has the means to do the right thing. Well, Mr. Pompous, I don't."

Shawn yelled back, "Hey, Frank, watch your mouth or you are going to need dentures, my man." Words were exchanged at the same time. Both men were yelling at each other. Frank wasn't backing down even though he knew that Shawn being an expert in martial arts could rip him apart, but he felt that if it came down to it, Shawn wasn't going to come out scratch-free. *This wasn't public school anymore. That was then. This is now.*

Both men calmed down. After a brief moment of silence, Shawn asked, "Where are these men? How soon?"

Frank shook his head and said, "Shawn, I don't know? As far as I know, they may be there right now. I don't know what they look like. I don't know if they are male or female, black or white, Chinese or Japanese. I don't know. They may come in suits or they may blend in with the homeless, I don't know."

Shawn was shocked. "Wait a second, are you telling me that these people may be here right now?"

Frank said, "Yes." Shawn tried to think of everyone who had come in the restaurant. There were too many people, too many . . . Shawn stopped. His thought process kicked in. His mind went back to the three men who had come in wearing old clothes. Shawn at first hadn't thought anything of it. *A lot of homeless folks hung out together, but those three,* Shawn thought, *were different. They had put on old clothes. But who wore old clothes with nice shoes, clean-shaven faces, nice shape-ups, nice manicured nails, and good expensive cologne?*

Shawn got up real quick from his desk chair. He seemed to have received new energy from an inner reservoir, no doubt from the years of martial art training, as he said to Frank in a rush, "Listen, you are still my road dog. We will deal with this, but I have to go. I think these guys are here. We'll talk later." Frank was relieved that at least there was some hope for him and Shawn. *That was his main boy.* He'd made a mistake, and now Frank Hall was going down to the restaurant to take care of business. It was like playing hide and go seek. He had no idea who those people were, but he would be on major alert. Shawn hung up. Frank tried to say something, but it was too late. Shawn hung up, and Frank went to his desk drawer and took out his Dirty Harry special. He packed it in his waistband.

As he was doing so, his wife, Jackie, came in and saw what was happening. She in a panic asked, "Frank, what are you doing? What is happening?"

Normally, Frank would never ignore his beautiful wife, but he had no time to explain. He just said, "Baby, I have to do something, something that I should have done long time ago." Frank kissed his wife and said, "Wait up for me, I will explain everything." Frank quickly rushed out of the door to his car.

Chapter 71

Shawn hung up on Frank and came running out from his office. He ran straight into Joe. Shawn looked at the serving line and Serenity wasn't there. He wanted to panic, but he couldn't. He had to stay calm. He looked around the restaurant for the three men; they weren't there. He grabbed Joe by the shoulder. "Have you seen Serenity?"

Joe was looking at Shawn as if he had lost his mind as he pushed his hand off his shoulder, "Shawn, what is up with you? Are you OK?" Shawn looked at Joe with a look that prompted him to answer the question, "Yea, she is right over there in the serving line." Joe pointed in the direction of the serving line while looking at Shawn. When he looked in the direction he was pointing and did not see Serenity, he said in surprise, "She was there a few minutes ago."

Shawn cut him off, "Do you know what direction she went in or did she leave with three men? And I am not talking wise men, but rather wise guys."

Joe thought about the question and responded, "Of course not. Come on, Shawn, what is going on?"

Shawn looked at Joe as he headed toward the serving line. "I'll explain later. Call 911," Shawn said quickly and firmly.

Prior to Shawn going to his office to answer the phone when Frank had called, he had gone around to the other tables to see how everyone was doing; so far the luncheon had been a huge success.

Shawn had been at one table where some young boys were playing table football. This was the game where someone had four tries to move either his paper triangle or his penny to the very edge of the opposite end of his end zone, so to speak. If a person got his paper triangle on the edge without causing that paper to fall off the edge, that person was awarded six points and a chance for a field goal, which consisted of the opposite player forming with his fingers what looked to be like a goalpost. The player who scored had to kick that triangle through the uprights, which was counted as a point. If successful, the team was awarded seven points, and then it was the turn of the opponent. He or she would go through the same steps and so forth. Shawn had collected about five of those hard triangle paper footballs. They were made out of two or three layers of construction paper. By the time one was finished making the triangle, it could be used as a weapon. Shawn said to the boys and girls that were playing, "Listen, you guys, I warned you earlier about playing with these triangles. Someone could get hurt, therefore, I will hold on to them until you are ready to leave."

The group was very upset, yet they knew they were in the wrong. Secondly, they knew that Shawn was firm, but he played by the rules.

Now getting back to Shawn, he was heading toward the serving line. The crowds by now had died down. Some folks were heading home, wherever that was. Shawn quickly walked over to Beatrice and gently led her away from the serving line. He asked her, "Beatrice, have you seen Serenity?"

Beatrice was getting ready to answer when she saw Sandra and Marcus were headed their way. Beatrice said, "My goodness, that man is more than fine. He's fine with all capital letters. Move over, Denzel, there is a new heartthrob in town." Shawn looked at her with all seriousness. She apologized and attempted to answer the question when Marcus and Sandra quickly walked up. Marcus and Shawn gave each other power handshakes.

Marcus noticed the look on Shawn's face. He knew something had gone wrong. He asked what was going on, but before he could answer, Sandra did, "Shawn, where is Serenity? She's in danger. The box that I opened."

Shawn looked at Sandra and with a loud, hard tone said, "You were the one that opened the box. Well, it put Serenity in danger."

Sandra nodded her head and said, "Shawn, we don't have time. We have to locate her. I'll just say that the contents in that box Shawn are going to cause some key power figures to be exposed. That's why she is in danger."

Shawn looked around in frustration and said, "That's why I am trying to find her. We have to get her into a safe zone, then we can find out who is behind this in the meantime." Beatrice was eyeing Marcus until Sandra made it clear in some crazy way that Marcus was hers, and she wasn't into sharing.

Beatrice looked at Shawn and said, "Oh yeah. Serenity was here a few minutes ago, but she needed to get away for a few minutes. That girl—"

Shawn cut her off, "Bea, just tell me where she's?"

Beatrice pointed to the back door and said, "She said she was going out to get some fresh air."

Shawn looked at the back door and back at Beatrice. "How long ago?"

Beatrice looked up at the ceiling to think and then at Shawn, "About four minutes ago." Shawn told Marcus and Sandra to stay put and make sure everybody was OK, and he told Beatrice to make sure no one left by the back door. He also told Marcus to let Joe know that when the police arrived he had to send them out back.

Sandra with panic in her eyes said, "Police, why the police? What the hell is going on and where is my best friend?" Marcus tried to calm her down, but Sandra was too livid.

Finally Marcus said, "Listen, Sandra, if Shawn knows where she is, don't worry. He is well capable of handling this situation, trust me." Sandra nodded her head and said that he hoped that she was. Marcus said to himself, "I hope so too."

Chapter 72

Shawn rushed out of the back door and saw Serenity standing by the fire escape totally exhausted. She had her head down, and when she heard the noise of feet rushing toward her, she looked up to see Shawn with a serious look on his face as he approached her. Serenity said, "Shawn, what's wrong? What's going on? Talk to me, baby."

Shawn grabbed her and hugged her, and he said, "Look, baby, we have to get you out of here. Something was discovered at your office. I can't go into detail, but we have to get you to a safe place." Serenity looked at Shawn and laughed, hoping that he would laugh as well and that all of that was one big joke, but Shawn wasn't laughing. He wasn't even cracking a smile. That made her panic, and it quickly engulfed her face. She said, "Shawn, what's going on?" Shawn told her that he would tell her later and that once they got her safe, he would explain everything.

Serenity was nervous. She wanted to know right then, but she forced herself to try to remain calm and trust Shawn that he would explain everything. Shawn and Serenity were a good several feet from the back door entrance, but that was the best way. Shawn knew he had people in there, who could detain anyone, so he lightly took her arm and headed for the door. Coming around the corner was Frank Hall. By the look on Serenity's face he did not have to ask if everything was OK. He knew it wasn't, but he was there to redeem himself and to be that ace his best friend always referred to him as. Frank with some trepidation greeted Shawn.

Shawn without hesitation grabbed and hugged Frank, like Esau hugging Jacob in the Old Testament. As they were letting go of the embrace, three men came walking down the alley toward them. Each had their hands in their inner coat pocket, stalking, clean cut on the outside and bad intentions on the inside. Shawn reached in his pocket and slowly took out those five hard thick-layered construction paper triangles. Frank looked at Shawn, and Shawn looked at Frank. Shawn nodded his head as he pulled Serenity behind him to shield her. Frank stood next to Shawn. They looked like two bodyguards protecting the main prize, two cowboys at high noon, as they stood there fearless and bold, being taken over by pure determination.

The men walked a few feet toward the three and stopped. Frank was slowly moving his hands toward his waist when Shawn quickly darted his eyes at him and unnoticeably shook his head. Frank slowly put his hand back down to his side. The three men looked young and nervous. Shawn got a good look at them and the memory clicked in. These were the three he had noticed back in the restaurant. One of them said, "Look, we just came for the chick, that's it."

Shawn moved Serenity closer behind his back in a protective way and said "Well, fellas, you guys wasted a trip because the woman, not the chick, perhaps your mother is a chick, you know hoe, perhaps even bitch, but this is a woman, and you go back and tell your leader, this is not going to happen today."

All three young men moved closer to Shawn and began to circle them. Their hands were still in the inside of their coats. Shawn could tell that these guys had as much training as those kids in that movie The Bad-News-Bears baseball team, but he did not underestimate their trigger-happy attitude. One of the men said, "Look, we don't want to hurt anyone. We just want the girl."

Shawn looked at the young boy and said, "Where she goes, we follow. We are a package deal." From a good distance, Shawn could hear the police cars. He thought, *If I can hear it, no doubt these guys also.*

One of them said, "Oh well, like the boss said if there's going to be collateral damage, don't worry about it."

Frank said, "Yeah, he's such a sweetheart. I've dealt with your boss before, yeah the electronic voice person." The three young men tried not to look obvious, but Frank and Shawn caught them darting their eyes at one another, a dead giveaway. Frank continued to stall, "Ah, so you and I, well, I used to work for the voice, and now it's your time to get burned like he burned me. Watch, you'll see."

The three young men looked at each other without hiding it. It was more evident now as Shawn took a look at their stance. He noticed that they were becoming a little more lax, until the one who looked like the leader said, "Enough with the small talk, we are taking the girl."

The three came within striking distance for Shawn. One of them told them to get on the ground. They both slowly moved toward the ground when

Shawn made his move. He struck quick like a cobra as he hit the leader in his throat with the heel of his hand. The man crumbled like a potato chip. The two inexperienced wannabe gangsters watched their friend crumble to the ground with a busted windpipe. The few seconds they watched gave Shawn the opportunity that he needed. He quickly struck, using the hard triangles made out of three layers of construction paper. He used them the way the ninjas use the ninja star as he threw three at one of them and two at the other, hitting their targets. Once it hit, Shawn knew he had to move fast as he quickly gave a sidekick to the midsection, causing the punk to release the gun and hold his stomach as he crouched down on both knees. Shawn with lightning speed gave the one that was catching his breath a hard heeled ax kick to the back of the head, knocking him out instantly. In that quick moment, when Shawn went to attack the third gunman he knew that Serenity's protection would be compromised. The third gunman, who had been hit in the eye with the triangle, started shooting. He managed to get off three shots before Shawn disarmed him and snapped his shoulders out of place; however, when he shot, Frank saw the direction he was shooting in, and he jumped in the way to protect Serenity. Frank was hit as he fell to the ground hard. By that time, the gunman, even though he had a dislocated shoulder, went after Shawn. Shawn showing no mercy gave the man a hard chop to the throat. Both his hands went up painfully in shock to his throat. Shawn quickly kicked the side of his knee cap, shattering it. The young man collapsed in pain, screaming and yelling.

Shawn noticed that Frank was down and was barely moving. Marcus came out and used the medic skills he learned on Frank. Shawn got up and ran over to Serenity, who was shaken and leaning against the wall.

Shawn said, "Baby, it's over. Frank's been hit. I don't know the seriousness, but Marcus is good. I think he'll be OK. EMS is on their way." Shawn looked at Serenity and could clearly see she was shaken. Serenity, who wasn't saying much, fell against the wall. Shawn looked at her and noticed something wet. He opened up her coat and noticed blood. It then hit him. *She's been hit.* Panic came upon his face as Serenity struggled to breathe. Shawn was trying to find out where she'd been hit, but there was so much blood. Then he noticed she was hit in the upper neck area. He tried to apply pressure, but the blood would not let up. Sandra came running out. She saw Serenity and started screaming and running to her and Shawn as she almost knocked Shawn to the ground. Sandra was screaming, looking at her best friend and begging her to get up. Marcus came running over after he got Frank stabilized and pulled Sandra away.

Shawn looked at Marcus and said, "I can't stop the bleeding, damn it." Shawn heard the ambulance perhaps a block or two away. He could not risk it. He could not wait. The blood was coming out fast like a faucet. He went to his car keys and pressed a button. Complex responded. Shawn told Complex to meet him in the back of the restaurant. Complex was programmed to know that without going into the GPS. Shawn picked up Serenity and headed toward the street to the back of the restaurant. Complex was there as soon as Shawn got there. He got in the backseat with Serenity and directed Complex to go on auto pilot, using the sub-driver decoy. In the driver seat was an inflated lifelike driver. Shawn said, "Complex, I need for you to take us to the Northeast Bronx Hospital. Use police sirens and warning lights. Get us there, Complex. Hit fifty miles with cautionary driving safety methods employed." (In other words, haul ass and get us there.) Complex took off. Shawn was in the back, trying to stop or slow down the bleeding. He finally got it to slow down, but she had lost so much already.

Serenity opened her eyes and said weakly, "Who were you talking to?" Shawn put his finger on Serenity's lips and told her he would explain everything. Complex was about ten minutes away when he asked her to give him an open line to a doctor friend he knew was working. Complex did so.

"This is Dr. Wilson. How can I be of assistance?"

Shawn quickly told his buddy, Dr. Wilson, what had happened. By the time Complex pulled up, there were several doctors and nurses already out there. Leading the charge was Dr. Wilson, the head of emergency surgery. Complex pulled up, and the driver decoy had already been deflated and slipped back into the square compartment in the driver's seat. The doctors and nurses were amazed that no one was driving, yet they got there in record time compared to where they were. Dr. Wilson met with Shawn as he told the doctor that he could not stop the blood flow, but could just slow it down. Dr. Wilson always as far as Shawn had known him spoke positive, no matter what the case may be. He used to say, "I have my opinion that my god has the answer."

Dr. Wilson told Shawn that he did well by slowing down the bleeding and that they would take over from there as they placed Serenity on a gurney with an oxygen mask and an IV and wheeled her into the surgery operating room. Shawn rushed with them by her side, looking at how helpless she looked. As they came to the door and went into the operating room, Shawn could not go in. He knew that it was going to be a long wait as a tear dripped down his cheek.

Shawn stood at the window of the Northeast Bronx Hospital, which housed the best trauma unit in the city. He appeared to be looking out the window, but in reality, his mind was elsewhere. He could not believe what happened today. It happened so fast. One minute, three armed dudes surrounded him, Serenity, and Frank, and the next was a blur as Shawn shook his head.

Shawn stared out the window. Serenity had been in the operating room for about three hours. No one had come out to say anything. He knew, from the way blood was coming out, the situation did not look good at all, but he'd been taught to never give up, never quit, and to keep believing, but it was hard.

Shawn's mind went back to that alley, and he thought hard about how everything had gone down. He looked at it in his mind, frame by frame. He had to bring closure with himself about doing everything possible. Shawn stood there. He clenched his fist and jaws, and he punched the bulletin board, causing a serious impression in the board as he thought, *If I would have hit one of the other guys first, maybe . . . two people would not have been shot.* Shawn put his hand on his face and dragged it down. He hardly ever second-guessed himself. Once he made a decision, it was a calculated decision. He had already looked at the situation from all sides, all points of view, the best that he could give or take whatever information he had to go by, and he knew it had been quick. But he had done the same thing in that situation. *He had evaluated the situation and then acted based on whatever he knew, so why was he second-guessing himself? Was there a better solution?*

Joe Johnson, Shawn's second in command at Shawn Enterprise, walked in. He looked as if he had been in a fight. Usually a neat dresser, he now looked like a victim of a mugging. He asked in a raspy whisper, "Any news?"

Shawn just shook his head as he continued to stare out the window. He broke the trancelike state for a minute, looked at Joe, and said, "The doctors have been tag-teaming, trying to stop the bleeding. They finally stopped it, but they said she lost so much blood and her body has gone into shock a couple of times . . ." Joe shook his head as Shawn continued, "The doctors said that the bullet went into her neck and did a pinball number throughout her body, causing a lot of damage, and now the freaking thing is lodged near her spine. They said they needed to remove it if they could, or chances are questionable whether she . . ." Shawn put his head down. Joe put his hand on Shawn's shoulder, squeezed it, and gave him some words of encouragement. Shawn took it in, but he could not face the grim truth about the situation with Serenity. *It was do or die, anyway you look at it. The scales can tip in any direction as despair stood over him like Ali stood over Sonny.*

Shawn said to Joe, "I don't know what I will do if . . . this woman is my heart. She is the essence of my soul. She is the key to my heart, man . . ." Shawn stopped to see what the noise at the door was. He saw all his family and friends come in; some were with blood-teary eyes, while others looked as if they were going to collapse from exhaustion.

Marcus went up to Shawn and gave him a power grip handshake. He said to him, "We are praying. It's going to be all right." Shawn smiled and hugged his friend. As they were letting go of the embrace, Frank walked in. His arm was in a sling. He stood at the door and did not move. He looked around at everyone, trying to read them and trying to understand whether it was safe to enter or had it become enemy territory.

After a few brief seconds, Shawn said, "Well, are you going to come in or are you going to stand there?" Frank eased on in and walked straight into Shawn. He hugged him and apologized for the mess he had caused. Shawn looked at him and said, "Nah, man, if it wasn't for you putting your life on the line, Serenity may have been worse . . . I just wanted to say thanks." Frank didn't know what to say. He nodded, gave Shawn a high five, and sat down. Sandra walked up to Shawn and handed him a list and a photo. Shawn looked at the list and photo inquisitively and then back at Sandra as if to say, "What is this?"

Sandra explained to Shawn that that was the list and photo she had got from the box that she found on Serenity's desk. Shawn now looked at the items from a different perspective. He said, "So this is from Pandora's box? This one box has caused havoc and hell in a matter of minutes . . ." Shawn looked at Sandra, still upset. "So what do you want me to do with this?"

Sandra wiped the tears from her eyes and said, "I did not touch the contents inside. As a matter of fact, I sent the box to where I was told. Everything was intact, even the names of those who I thought may be involved in this mess or maybe the targets to get rid of. I don't know . . ." Shawn looked at it, still unsure what to do with the box. He didn't want to turn it over to the police or FBI . . . not yet. Sandra continued, "Oh yeah, I saved the recording of the voice. Maybe you can look into it." Sandra, wiping the tears away, said, "Listen, Shawn, I gave you the box because I know right now you are the only person in this room who can bring justice to this whole matter. You know people and people know you. I just want you to nail the bastards for what they've put you and us and Serenity through. Nail them, Shawn, nail them to the wall. Let them know they hit hard, but you will hit them twice as hard." Shawn fully understood her point. He would start tomorrow, but now his main concern was Serenity.

Chapter 73

Shawn walked softy into Serenity's private hospital room; Shawn had made a special request to Dr. Wilson whether he could make that happen. Shawn eased in and peeked at her; she was resting on her side with a couple of IV's going into her. Shawn thought that, from the way she was lying there, she looked comfortable while, amazingly, only a few hours ago he had been trying to stop the bleeding and was losing the fight. He had almost lost her; she had been the best thing that had ever come into his life.

Shawn stood there very much thankful as he stared at her and thought how scared he had been. He laughed to himself as he thought about the years of martial arts training and came to the conclusion that his training had been helpful, but he really had to depend on God to see him and get him through this one. And no amount of training could have done that.

Shawn smiled and shook his head from side to side. He looked up and said a prayer of thanks as he turned to walk away. He was beginning to feel the strain and stress of the whole day. It was as if exhaustion hit him all at once; yet he knew if he went home he wouldn't be able to sleep. He'd stay up worrying about Serenity.

Shawn decided to go over the contents in the box. As he turned and headed for the door, Serenity, still lying on her side, said, "My hero, who was that handsome man . . . ?" Serenity chuckled to herself and then became serious. "Please don't leave."

A lump formed in Shawn's throat as he said to himself, "As long as I have health and strength, I'll never leave you, sweetheart."

He was happy to hear her voice as he drew closer to her bed; ever so careful, he said, "Hey, back to you." Shawn held on to her good hand. *She felt good,* he thought. She felt normal compared to when she was feeling cold, but now he could feel the bud of life in her making a comeback. He was thankful for the way she was feeling, and he said, "I'm not going anywhere. I will not take that chance of losing you again. Do you realize that you scared me, waiting for somebody to come out and bring me good news? Man, I thought I was going to lose you. I don't know what I would have done without you." Serenity smiled because of Shawn's passion. She also smiled because she felt the same way about him. When that shooting had taken place and she had been hit, Serenity had thought, *I don't know whether I am going to make it or not, but I refuse to leave this man.* She kept on fighting and fighting. She didn't know where that strength had been coming from, other than from God.

Serenity looked at Shawn and said, "The doctors were able to remove the bullet. They said it was going to be risky. I told them to go ahead. I want to live to see my grandchildren grow up . . . I want us to grow old together. I love you so much, Mr. Shawn Cook."

Shawn chuckled and said, "My love for you, Serenity, is unbreakable. I will always love you. You are the woman of my dreams."

Serenity smiled and then becoming serious she asked, "Oh no, I've been meaning to ask you, but with all so much is going on, it slipped my mind. But how is Frank doing?"

Shawn smiled and said with confidence, "My road dog is doing OK. The two bullets he took exited. Doctors are expecting a full recovery. He was here earlier."

Serenity closed her eyes for about a minute, then opened them up, and said, "I know I love you so much, but when I got hit I knew then and right there how much I am madly and crazily in love with you."

Shawn smiled; her words were like butter. He felt a warm sensation all over, and he commented, "I'm never ever going to let you go. You mean the world to me."

Shawn kissed her hand lightly as Serenity changed the subject, "How about the three young men? What's going to happen to them?"

He snorted and said with indignation, "What men? You mean those boys, the ones without a decent role model to follow, so they follow after the almighty dollar and come into contact with a psychopath who tells them how to make a quick dollar. That's not a real man. Those are boys in men's bodies." Shawn felt himself getting worked up which he did not want to do, so he calmed down and answered the question, "Well, these so-called men will be sentenced today. As far as I understand, they are being charged with attempted murder on all three counts. That should make them nice and gray perhaps with dentures when they come out."

Serenity just shook her head slowly and said, "What a waste of time! What a way to squander your life! These men could have been something and made something of themselves if they would have made the right connections, better decisions. I thank God that my brother Eric did not squander his life. I mean, there was always someone around to make sure that he stayed within the lines. My mother used to tell us, 'Don't color outside the lines. No matter how beautiful the color, going outside of the lines always makes the grand picture ugly.'" Serenity smiled and continued, "But she used to say, 'If you stay within the lines with those same colors, you will see how beautiful and creative a picture would become. You could see the potential.'"

Serenity winced when she heard the charges.

Shawn shook his head and added on, "The sad thing is that they worked for a person, who employed them but never bothered to show them his face or help them to become the men they needed to become, absentee parents, especially fathers and an absentee boss. They just wanted to make that quick dollar at any cost, but how about building up that self-worth, that self-concept, we are so used to building on the outside with our fancy cars and clothes and name brand this and name brand that. We sadly neglect to build those things on the inside like self-worth and integrity. It's a damn shame."

Serenity added, "Yeah, that self-esteem. They have to learn how to take care of themselves before they learn the power and value of a dollar and how to get it and invest it."

Shawn agreed with her as he added, "As long as they could see the faces of Benjamin and others, they did not care who got hurt. Like I said, those are not real men. They are boys in men: bodies, punks, wannabes."

Serenity nodded slowly and agreed, "Yeah, I guess you're right. Look at them now. What do they have? Nothing, there is nothing to show." Shawn continued, "And if they did, they can't enjoy it. Now they are going to find out how tough they really are. When they come up against someone in jail with the first name of bend and the last name of over, they are going to soon find out how tough they really are."

Serenity wanted to laugh, but she didn't think those three young men were going to survive the everyday harsh life of jail. She felt bad for them, especially on learning that all three young men came from single parental homes where the mothers had to work two jobs just to make it work. But in the meantime, somewhere in between job one and job two, they missed their main job, and their kids fell through the cracks of the system. Now they would have three jobs, making that journey to see their sons to lift their spirits. Serenity shook her head and thought, *What a shame! If only these kids would have found Shawn's program of the rights of passage, their chances would have been much greater. I mean, at least they would have been given something to fight for and strive for.*

Shawn noticed Serenity in deep thought and asked her, "Hey, what are you thinking about in far faraway land?"

Serenity chuckled; she hadn't noticed that she had drifted out so far. She said, "Just that if those boys would have discovered your program, perhaps disaster would have been averted."

Shawn nodded, kissed Serenity on the forehead, and said, "Perhaps." Shawn stated, "My parents used to say, 'If you make your bed hard, you have to sleep in it.'" Serenity nodded her head, yawned, and covered her mouth. Shawn knew she was tired. She had to be exhausted after a day like that. He asked, "Are you tired?" She nodded and yawned again. He said, "Sleep well. I'll see you in the morning." He bent down and kissed her on the forehead; he let his lips linger there longer than usual. He was thinking at that moment that the nightmare was over.

Shawn didn't want to tell Serenity that a policeman would be guarding her room door 24-7 until she was discharged or when the information regarding those names as well as the mastermind behind that was got. That was the hard part. Giving in the names and seeing where it led was easy. Finding out who was the mastermind behind it was going to be a pain in the rear because of the electronic voice. Shawn knew that no one in the NYPD had the technology to figure out who it was. Not even the government technology was that advanced, but he knew who would be able to figure it out.

Chapter 74

Shawn walked to Serenity's door to leave. She called him to come back as she had something that she wanted to say to him. Shawn went back to her bed to find out what she wanted. He had that million-dollar smile on his face, the one that at first she hadn't wanted to have anything to do with, but now she thought she could not live without it.

She knew why he was smiling. *That was a smile of getting another chance, that was a "thank you, God" smile, and that was because we both still have each other's smile, unbreakable hearts.*

She looked at him with tears in her eyes. Shawn became concerned as he reached out to her, "Baby, what's wrong? Why are you crying? Are you in pain? Do you want me to call the nurse or the doctor, what?" Shawn was reaching for the call help button that was connected to her bed. Serenity held his hand and started laughing and crying. Now Shawn was really concerned. He thought she was about to blow a gasket.

She saw the startled look on his face and said, still holding his hand, "I don't need a doctor. I don't need a nurse. I don't need a social worker. Do you remember that song by Diana Ross?" she said. "Don't call the doctor or lawyer. Well, I don't need those people."

Shawn asked out of concern, "So what is wrong?" She looked at him as she asked him to help her sit up; he did so.

She continued, "Shawn, there's no cure for being madly in love with someone that is madly in love with you. You are my doctor and lawyer and social worker. You are all them wrapped up in one. Remember that song by Heather Headley called 'He is'? That song reminds me of you." Shawn smiled and was getting ready to say something when she cut him off, "Sorry, but I am not finished. Now I have a question. Well, I really have two questions." He nodded and encouraged her to go for it, and that is exactly what she did. "First of all, I know this is not the way it should be done . . . but . . . this is the way I'm going to do it . . . Shawn Cook, would you marry me?"

Shawn stopped as if he was frozen and looked at her with a twinkle in his eyes, and he said without blinking, "No."

Serenity was shocked and speechless.

She was about to burst into tears when Shawn said, "I'm a traditional man when it comes down to this." So Shawn went down on one knee by her beside and said, "Serenity Naomi Powers, would you marry me?" Serenity was so excited she really didn't know whether to laugh or cry. Shawn pulled out a small box and opened the lid, and inside was a beautiful set of similar diamond rings.

Serenity looked at Shawn with tears of surprise and asked, "How did you know this was going to happen?"

Shawn smiled, got up to kiss Serenity lightly on her lips, and said, "Well, I didn't know, but I knew this moment will come because you can't keep unbreakable hearts from each other. You are my soul mate, my best friend. You are the twin tower of my heart. You are my peanut butter, and I am your jelly." Serenity laughed at that one as Shawn continued, "Now answer the question, would you marry me, woman?"

Shawn smiled, waiting for an answer. Serenity smiled and said with excitement, "Yes."

There was a loud applause at the door; family, friends, and staff had been there the whole time listening. They stayed for a little while longer, giving Shawn and Serenity their blessings. Then they filed back out into the waiting room. Shawn was still smiling when Serenity said, "Before you jump the broom, I still have one more question. This will determine if I am jumping this broom with you or not." Shawn looked at her strangely, as if to say, "Woman, what are you talking about?" He had never thought this relationship would have more twists and turns, pit stops, pitfalls, and surprises than a soap opera.

Serenity had a smile that faded. She asked inquisitively, "I want to know who is the other woman." Serenity looked at Shawn's expression to see if she had caught him off guard. The only look he had was a look of confusion as he thought, *What the heck is she talking about?*

Shawn looked at Serenity with all seriousness and said, "Girl, what the heck are you talking about? What other woman is there?" Serenity looked at Shawn and he could see the frustration building, which he did not want to happen.

She said with a sarcastic smile, "Oh, so now we play the dumb game, duh. Which way did she go? No, Shawn, the one that drove me or rather us to the hospital because I may have been born at night, but it wasn't last night. There is no way you could have attended to me and driven at the same time and doing all that from the backseat, no way, and I heard her sexy voice . . . who is she . . . ?"

Serenity thought Shawn was going to confess. He looked as if he was at that point. Instead, he looked at her and started laughing, that bear kind of laugh. Shawn laughed so hard, he missed his laugh, and so did Serenity, but right now she had no time to evaluate how much she missed his laughter. Shawn looked at Serenity and started laughing again; he could not believe she went there. He said, "When I tell you who it is, you are going to be surprised."

The Next Day

Shawn got up early. He knew he had certain things on his list that he had to accomplish in a timely fashion. He quickly showered and came out drying himself off. His clothes were already ironed. Shawn looked at his agenda. At around 9:00 a.m., he had to call to see if Captain Moore was in. In the meantime, Shawn went out to his garage. He checked his security cameras. Everything was OK. *He wasn't expecting any surprises, yet again you never know,* he thought. He got into his car, clicked on all the buttons, and then he finally turned on the ignition, and the car came to life. Shawn said, "Good morning, Complex."

Complex responded, "Hey, handsome, you are such a turn on." Shawn always felt that Complex had a way to make him blush; he coughed to clear his throat, but before he could speak, Complex asked, "How is Serenity?" Shawn was happy to report that she was doing much better, that she had a good night, and that her therapy was going very well.

Complex was glad to hear the good news; she responded, "Good, Shawn, I really like her. I know you will do right by her."

Shawn was glad that things had started to look up with Complex and Serenity; things had not started out that way. He said, "Well, good, because from what I understand from her . . . she likes you too." Complex made a sound of confirmation. Shawn continued, "When you were driving us to the hospital, she heard your voice . . . again. She said your voice is very sexy, and she thought you . . ." Shawn did not finish the sentence.

Complex was curious and asked in an inquiring tone, "She thought what, Shawn . . . come on."

Shawn chuckled. "She thought you were the other woman." Complex was silent, which set off a red flag in Shawn's mind because Complex was never silent. Shawn continued, "Isn't that crazy?"

Complex responded in a serious tone, "Shawn, I am the other woman."

Shawn noticed Complex wasn't playing around, and he could feel trouble brewing. He had too much on his mind to add this to his plate. Shawn continued very cautiously, "Complex, you are the other woman, but . . . not in that sense." Complex was still very serious. He made what he hoped would not be a futile attempt to explain the situation, "Complex, you are very important to me. Sometimes I don't know what I would do without you. I mean, you are resourceful, intelligent, but you are not human. If you were, I would probably be swept off my feet. TJ has done a wonderful job with you, but . . ." Complex thanked Shawn for the kind words, but she still was in a funk. The lights on her computer board lighted up. Shawn was concerned, "What's the matter? I've never seen you like this before." Shawn said out of concern, "Complex . . ."

Complex's lights were flashing bright. Shawn asked, "What's wrong?"

Complex's lights slowly dimmed as she responded, "Shawn, as you may know, TJ made me to be as close to human as possible. Well, my lights flashing, I guess you can say I am what you humans call laughing." Shawn looked confused as Complex continued, "Shawn, I'm only pulling your leg. I know that there is nothing between us, so you can tell Serenity she has nothing to worry about. Now let's get back to business."

Shawn nodded his head in satisfaction and said, "Well, one thing for sure, you are my best friend, and I appreciate you very much, and the way you got us to that hospital . . . tells me how much I really need you . . . thank you." The only thing Complex could say was thank you, and after that there was silence until Shawn said, "Complex, I have a recording of a voice in electronic mold. I wanted to know whether you can decipher it."

Complex told Shawn she would give it a shot. She added, "It'll probably take an hour. Is that OK?" Shawn told her that it was no problem. In the meantime, he said he would call the precinct to speak to Captain Moore.

Captain Moore picked up on the third ring. Both men exchanged pleasantries. Shawn had known Captain Moore for quite some time; the two had met each other during a "Reaching out to single parents" conference. Shawn found out that Moore was in charge of the conference; the two were introduced, and from that point on, they had been doing favors for each other.

Shawn and Captain Moore discussed the situation. Shawn went over his plan with him. Curt Moore was concerned about the whole matter; the situation was a delicate one. Moore said, "Shawn, you realize that this case should be handled by the FBI. If what you are saying is true, you will be uncovering the biggest terrorist plot on this side of the home turf."

Shawn immediately gave credit where it was due. He protested, "Hold up, partner, I wish I could take the credit but I can't. My fiancée girlfriend did this."

Curt Moore briefly continued to talk and then stopped in mid-sentence, "Back up a minute, partner. Did I hear you say fiancée? As to say, you are getting married?"

Shawn laughed at Moore's expression as Moore continued, "Do you mean to tell me that someone has lassoed your butt? Get the freak out of here. This young lady must be special." Curt Moore was five years older than Shawn and had always considered Shawn a young man because of that. He continued, "Oh wow, congratulations are in order." Shawn smiled and thanked Moore. The two men talked for a little while longer about the plan they were going to put into effect.

Shawn was asked to fax in the list he had received from Sandra, and Curt Moore said he would get in contact with someone he knew at the FBI in order to cut through the red tape of bull crap. In the meantime, Serenity had not been able to put all the pieces together. She still didn't know about the box or the list made up by Sandra, along with the photos taken. Shawn did not want her to be concerned with that. He told her to just concentrate on getting better and that it was better that she knew as little as possible.

Shawn went back out to Complex to see what she had come up with. It'd been over an hour. Shawn got in the car and said, "Complex, anything your data files came up with?"

Complex's panel brightened; she said, "Yes, Shawn, I've analyzed the voices, and I've come up with two identifications."

Shawn was surprised. He wasn't expecting "culprits." He said to Complex, "Complex, I am not doubting your analytical analysis, but I thought there was only one voice."

Complex responded, "Rightly so, Shawn, because your ears are trained to listen to one, plus the human ear would not have been able to notice the change in the breathing or the other subtle changes I picked up on . . . You see, that's why one day computers will rule, but I will reserve a spot for you, baby."

Shawn cackled at that remark, but overall he was more than surprised. Now there were two people involved. He responded in astonishment, "Wow, that is amazing, Complex! Do you think Captain Moore's crew or the FBI have the technology to analyze this stuff?"

Complex snorted and stated, "Shawn, are you on crack? Come on, baby, I am light years ahead of the game and get a face-lift twice a year. You just insulted my intelligence. Next question." Shawn apologized and explained to Complex that he was concerned about the Feds getting their hands on that stuff and what would be the repercussions. Complex retorted and, in short, told Shawn that the results would be a lot of sleepless nights and headache medications. Shawn laughed at that. He then asked Complex for a printout of her findings and the names of the culprits. Complex was one step ahead of Shawn. She explained to him that the printout was in tray one on the passenger side. Shawn was impressed. Complex always seemed to surprise him about her capabilities. Shawn looked at the printout and the names; one of the names stood out like a sore thumb, and he was shocked. He looked at Complex and was on the verge of asking her if she had made a mistake. He put the thought aside, folded the paper, put it in his coat pocket, and then instructed Complex to drive over to Sandra's apartment. He had to get to the bottom of this. Shawn reached into his pocket, took out the folded paper, and looked at the name again as if it had changed. He then shook his head and said under his breath, "Wow!"

Shawn looked at his watch; visiting hours was almost over. Whatever he was about to do, he had to do it fast. He called Curt Moore at the police station and told him everything about the list and the photo of the items that were in the box. He explained that he did not understand what the names meant or what part they played in all of this, but it was something to go on. Shawn told Curt he would call him back in about thirty minutes. The next phase after hanging up with Curt was to work with Complex and see if she could duplicate a voice to make it sound like the electronic voice. Once she had that down pat, she was instructed to contact every contact person that was on the list, and then after that, they'd sit back and see if the rats would take the bait . . . Let the games begin.

Chapter 75

Thirty minutes later, Complex had the electronic voice down to a T. She told Shawn that she had already started contacting those on the list; so far she was batting a thousand, and she had three more names to go. Shawn had explained to her before she started contacting those on the list to make that initial contact and then instruct them to stand by for further instructions. That was something Complex would be working on by herself; in the meantime, Shawn would go and visit Serenity for the remainder of the visiting time left.

Shawn walked to Serenity's room and noticed the two police officers that Curt had assigned to stand watch outside her room, just in case word got out where she was staying. He understood from Curt that the FBI was now involved, which made too many cooks in the kitchen, but Shawn had made it clear that he wanted it to stay at a low profile level. Everyone in Shawn's camp was hush-hush with the media. The media was aware that the young lady Shawn had been seen with around town had been shot as a result of a mugging attempt, but they were bumping heads as to which hospital the young lady was brought to. They assumed from diligent searches that the young lady's injuries were more serious than what they had heard or that she was under a pseudo name to avoid any news coverage. Shawn had to find more and more creative ways to duck and dodge the bloodthirsty reporters, but so far so good. He understood reporters weren't dumb; the pendulum could go against him anytime.

Shawn walked in and was surprised to see Serenity sitting full up; she looked like a million bucks and she sounded like one also. Her confidence was coming back in her voice. Prior to arriving at the hospital, Shawn had gone over to speak with Sandra; however, she wasn't home at the time. He also knew that she had taken off for the week due to everything that'd been happening. Shawn wasn't worried that she wasn't home. He knew that he would eventually run into her, and when he walked into Serenity's room Sandra was there along with Marcus. Shawn nodded in their direction but kept his stare a second or two longer on Sandra. He went over to Marcus and gave him a brother-to-brother hug. Shawn knew that time was running out, and he needed some answers fast. He suspected that Complex should be about completed with her assignment. He hoped that everything had gone well. He hadn't heard from her, so he kept his fingers crossed.

Shawn asked if he could speak with Sandra alone for a minute. Marcus at first had a look of curiosity on his face. He looked at Serenity and she shrugged her shoulders, and he did the same.

Shawn pulled Sandra to the side in the waiting room and explained to her what was going on. He showed her the printout and the two names that were involved. Sandra was stunned. Her breath caught in her throat, and she shook her head and said to no one in particular, "This is impossible. There must be a mistake."

Shawn and Sandra went back into the room. Sandra looked as if she had a case of food poisoning. Serenity looked at Sandra and saw the same look, and then she looked at Shawn as if to ask, "What the hell is going on?" Marcus knew Shawn well enough to know that his friend C-4 had a reason to do what he had done. He'd get the 411 later from Sandra; in the meantime, he had no doubts about his boy's motives.

Shawn looked at Serenity and told her he would explain later. Shawn kissed her on the forehead and headed out to see what Complex had come up with. He had his fingers crossed and a prayer to God that his plan was coming together.

Shawn got into the car and asked Complex whether she had able to make any further progress on the assignment. Complex took a few seconds longer than normal to respond and finally told Shawn that she had indeed made progress with all the names on the list and that the meeting place was set for that evening at six. Shawn felt a weight fall off his shoulders. He asked Complex, "What was the hesitation with the response to the question?"

Complex's panel lights flicked on and off, which meant that she was having a moment of fun. She responded, "Well, I wanted to be like some of these reality shows that make the person wait for a response that will determine their success or failure. The person is at the point of doing either number one or no doubt number two or both. Which category were you in, Shawn? Underwear number 1, 2, or 3?"

Shawn was still relieved and chuckled at Complex's humor. Complex continued, "Shawn, I set it up the way you had instructed. From the way it is looking, you should have 100 percent attendance. They all know what is at stake."

Shawn called Captain Curt Moore and told him about the setup; Moore told Shawn he would alert his friend at the FBI. Moore asked Shawn, "Do you really think these people will take the bait?"

Shawn thought about what Complex had said and responded, "They have everything to lose if they don't show up. There is too much at stake for them not to show up." Moore agreed and hung up. Twenty minutes later, Moore called Shawn and told him that a plan was in effect; everyone was on the same page. Moore asked Shawn about the ringleader. Shawn explained how that was going to go down. He requested for some of Moore's men to be present at the Federal building. He said he would contact him sometime after the operation evening. Moore agreed and told Shawn that whenever he was ready his men would be on standby.

Showtime

Shawn gave instructions to Complex and the cue as to when to switch her voice to the electronic voice. Shawn had Complex's system hooked up to the PA system in the warehouse.

Shawn knew that the chances of the plan failing were slim, but nevertheless there was a slight possibility that something could go wrong. However, Shawn knew it wouldn't be because of Complex. If anything it would be a human error, but he had confidence that everyone was on the same page, and as long as there were no hotshots or hotdogs trying to make a name for themselves things would go well, plus Curt Moore had requested his FBI friend to send the best and the most experienced and competent agents.

Shawn parked Complex near the curb of the entrance, where he could get a good look at those who were coming or going; however, due to Complex's dark tinted windows no one could see any movement from within. So for the normal observer, Complex looked like a regular parked car. Shawn had already instructed Complex to bring up the viewfinder-zoom mode. He wanted a close-up photograph of each person going in and coming out. Just like clockwork, cars started coming in. The viewfinder started taking pictures—photographs of license plates and individuals getting out of their cars. The viewfinder could amazingly take so many pictures per second. The viewfinder zoomed in, whirled, and moved. The finder also had the ability to show on the monitor in video style what was happening. The monitor was located on the dashboard. It was a medium-size screen that picked up everything. There was also a record button that Shawn could either press or have Complex to work within her command system.

Shawn didn't know where the FBI agents were, but he knew they were out there. He could have had Complex to locate them just by their body heat, but that wasn't necessary.

The warehouse down in the Hunts Points area of the Bronx was huge; the owner of the warehouse gave permission for NYPD and the FBI to use it, of course, for a small fee and to get on their good side for future references if needed. The meeting was about to take place; all six men and four women were all accounted for. Shawn was surprised to see even women, but he dismissed the thought and said to himself, "Everyone seems to have an ax to grind these days." The warehouse was wired, and hidden cameras were placed in different locations. After Shawn took the photographs of everyone, including video shots and sound bites, he instructed Complex to drive inside the warehouse's garage so she could be hooked up to the PA system. While everyone was busy talking among themselves, trying to make sense of what was happening, Shawn was able to hook up Complex to the system. Everything was in place; even agents and NYPD undercover officers were at certain locations within the warehouse. The sting operation was ready to keep the freedom of others the way it was supposed to be . . . free.

Chapter 76

The group of men and women were talking among themselves when the PA system came on and the electronic voice began, "I want to thank you for coming on such short notice. As you know when we recruited you, you were aware of last minute changes. The Alternative organization would like to thank you. However, the reason you are here today is due in part to some disturbing information we have received from the central headquarters. Our current plans to show this government that they can and will be overthrown not by a Jihad but by their own citizens have been compromised." The men and women reacted to the news as whispers and murmurings buzzed and hissed throughout the place like a forest fire. The low voices became louder and louder until the electronic voice had to intervene, "Yes, we may have a dirty operative among us, a double agent."

The buzz started again. There was a lot of speculation and finger-pointing as the voice called for order, "Do not worry. Our central intelligence have an idea where such treason originated from, but due to this mishap the current plans to bring rightful results of condemnation upon those who dare to defy this new world government must be put in effect immediately. They must be dealt with and used as an example for others who would dare attempt the same fatal mistake." The men and women broke out in loud applause.

Then the meeting took an unsuspected turn. Some of the men and women had questions. It was not in the game plan. It was to simply state the postponement and to keep the cause alive despite the setback, but it was unexpected as a question came from the middle of the small gathering, "Yes, we would like to know when will we be able to carry out this plan."

The voice did not respond right away, which could have been a problem if anyone had been paying attention, but, fortunately, the level of anger was so high they missed it. It sailed right over their heads as the voice responded, "This setback will not deter us. This government with all of its hypocritical laws and biases must be overthrown." The gathering broke out in applause again, and the voice continued, "We will closely look at the signs of the times, and as soon as we are able, we will bring the traitor or traitors to justice. This may have been a tragedy, but I promise you, we will get the victory. They may have won the battle, but we will, ladies and gentlemen, win the war."

The gathering stood up with loud applause, and then they broke out with a chant, "Victory, victory, victory." Apparently everyone was satisfied. There were no more questions as the voice said, "In the meantime, to show we mean business, each of you will be given an assignment to show these so-called leaders of our downtown areas that we mean business. The Alternative central intelligence will be contacting each of you within the next week or so. Please be ready to travel." The group pledged that they would be true.

Shawn felt he had seen and heard enough, and with the hidden cameras and everything that'd been said, they would have enough evidence to bury those folks under the jail. He instructed Complex to let the gathering know that each would be contacted when things calmed down. The gathering got up to leave as they did a secret handshake with each other. The voice's last assignment had been to have the group go through a brief commitment to the cause, an evaluation test. Each person was instructed to go into the booth that was made like a voter's booth, where a person casts his vote, and then the voice would ask them regarding their prior assignment and they would be given new assignments.

Each person went into the booth and answered the questions accordingly. Each person also stated their last assignment and was given his current assignment. As each person completed the task, finally, they were asked to wait for their comrades before leaving. The concept as explained by the voice was that they should leave as a unified team. They all agreed. When the last person completed the questions, they were thanked again for their presence. The lights in the warehouse had been already dimmed, but as the group started to make their way to the exits, the warehouse lights came on in full blast. It was enough for the group to shield their eyes. They did not know what was going on. Then all of a sudden, a voice boomed out of the speakers, announcing, "FBI. If you have weapons do not attempt to draw them. You are surrounded . . . lie face down on the floor with your arms out in front of you." The group of men and women complied as the law enforcers rushed in and made the arrests.

Shawn said to Complex, "OK, that's done. Let's close the curtain on this thing."

Complex was ready, but she had some concerns, "Shawn, before we put the next phase into effect, what took place a few minutes ago, doesn't it bother you?" Shawn already knew where that was going; he also knew that Complex was not designed for treason, so the concept may not be comprehended. TJ had not put a chip in her to comprehend treason. She was designed to follow the principles and ethics of right and wrong, not necessarily the constitution, but the idea of the concept of ethics. So in other words in her world, 2+2 would always equal 4, but 4 could be got by different ways.

Shawn responded, "Ah, yeah, this is a tragedy. These were once good men and women, who believed in the system, but something went wrong. However, the answer is not to destroy the system, but to try to improve it. I don't like what this country stood for two hundred years ago or even twenty years ago. I don't like war, but you have a president that would go down as the worst president in the history of this country. I don't like poverty and hunger and homelessness. I can see why people get all freaked up, but you don't buck the system. You challenge it, you confront it, you object it, and you question it. I mean, that's the way we were raised, and you vote for the ones who think like you and want the same things you want. That's what makes this country different from everyone else. You can do something positive about it, and then you hope change will come."

Complex responded, "Thank you, Shawn. I don't fully comprehend, but I want to thank you. Maybe the next time I am with TJ, perhaps she can put that in my program."

Shawn chuckled sarcastically and said, "Complex, you are perfect the way you are. If you change, you may get all screwed up like these folks. Live by the famous wise saying."

Complex asked, "And what is that, Shawn?"

Shawn smiled and said, "KISS. It simply means, 'Keep it simple stupid.'" Complex's dashboard flashed with different colors, Shawn knew she had caught the joke.

There was a moment of reflection which seemed to come from both of them, then Complex asked, "OK, baby, what do you want me to do? I am hyped, I am fired up, and I am ready to kick some ass."

Chapter 77

Shawn looked at his watch and said to Complex, "Let's go to the Federal building. Give me an open line to our perpetrators to make for certain that they are there."

Complex using her built-in phone system dialed the number according to her directory and got the receptionist. Shawn asked if the two individuals were in. He was told that they were. He thanked the receptionist and disconnected the line before the receptionist could ask any more questions.

Shawn called Officer Moore and told him that they were both there. Moore told Shawn that his men were nearby, staying out of sight yet making sure that neither one of the perpetrators left the building. Moore informed Shawn that his men would start getting in place. Shawn agreed and made a request, "Listen, Curt, instruct your men to back off the one you and I discussed. That sucker is mine."

Officer Moore had no problem with turning the other way when it came down to blind justice and righteous vengeance, especially when someone had the nerve to send thugs or, in this case, punks to snuff out your soul mate. He didn't have a problem with the outcome. He said, "Hey, do what you need to do. I don't see nothing, hear nothing, or say nothing. As a matter of fact, this call never happened."

Benita Fry wasn't looking too good. She seemed a little anxious, nervous may be a better description. She looked at her watch and cursed under her breath. The time when she end her day could not come quickly enough. Her phone rang. She looked at it and wondered who would be calling her at that time. She picked it up and spoke in codes as if she was expecting someone else to be listening. All of a sudden, Benita Fry's face turned red with anger and frustration. She said to the other person on the line, "How the hell would I know where is everyone? I tried to get in contact, but no one's cell seemed to be working. Yes, I am aware that they were supposed to call me an hour ago. How would I know? Well, I don't. I gave up my crystal ball long time ago. Well, don't ask me stupid questions. I'm in the dark about this whole damn thing as you are. No, I did not contact them . . . not yet. Why? So we may seem incompetent? You better watch your mouth. Remember who you are talking to. Yes, yes, I'll meet you at the same place in an half an hour . . . yeah, yeah."

Benita Fry hung up the phone, but she did not like the feeling she was getting . . . *Something wasn't right. She never second-guessed her feelings. She didn't think anyone messed with the box. It was sent back to her, but someone did tamper with it.* But everything was intact, untouched.

She stood there, contemplating. It didn't make sense; the whole thing didn't make sense.

What the heck was going on? She began to shut things down as she thought that she had come this far, this close, and she would not let anyone or anything get or stand in her way. She would get revenge on the hypocritical circus of a government. *The nerve of them putting me on the back shelf, stating that I am too old. I will show them. The only thing I asked for was a position I put in for two years ago. They say yes to me and promise me, and then snatch the rug from underneath me. Well, let's see how they are going to handle this old, disgruntled witch. They all will pay* . . . As Benita Fry sat there thinking all of this, there was a knock at the door. She did not like what she was feeling, but she brushed it aside.

Chapter 78

Benita Fry wasn't expecting anyone. She became agitated over the interruption of her thoughts. She calmed herself down and reasoned that it was probably her staff letting her know that they were leaving. *Such plantation idiots, they come here and sweat their butts off just to make it up the ladder of opportunity knocks, while their government takes every opportunity to knock them down. There goes your opportunity knocks, right on your butt.* Benita began to seethe because she was just like them. *Look where it'd landed her.* Benita tried to gather her composure before answering the door, but that attempt failed. She was not in the mood for pleasantries. She told in a gruff voice for the person to enter. The person entered Benita's office. She saw who it was, and she became even more frustrated. She said in an indifferent tone, "Oh, it's you. Didn't we just get finish speaking to one another? And I thought we had an understanding where we were going to meet." The person did not say a word; he just stared at her and listened. She said, "I don't have time for you. I have to find out what is going on! A little damage control."

The person continued to stand there, watching her, and said to her, "I think it is a little too late for that, you stupid old bag."

Benita Fry stopped gathering her belongings to go home and looked at the person. She responded in an impatient tone, "Look, I don't have time for games. You better watch that smart mouth of yours . . . We are in a middle of a crisis that can blow this whole operation apart. So what is it that you want? If you would just learn how to follow orders, perhaps we wouldn't be in this situation. I asked you to meet me where we normally meet, and you can't follow such simple instructions?"

The person very calmly said, "There has been a change in plans. Yes, you are correct. Time is up, well, at least for you that is. I received a message from Central. You have failed in this mission, and as much as you would like to blame me for your blunders, we all are aware that you are . . ." The person reached into his jacket and pulled out a gun with a silencer as he continued, "The weakest link . . . as they say . . . good-bye." Benita Fry tried to reach her desk drawer for her weapon, but she was too slow and too frail. As the person lifted the weapon and fired two shots, there was a "whiff" sound that came from the gun.

Shawn heard the sound, and then he heard a loud thump, as if someone had fallen. He knew both distinct sounds. He immediately got into his fighting stance and slowly walked on the balls of his feet. It was as if he was gliding and not walking. His eyes were focused like a cat, his muscles were tight yet flexible, and his ears were attuned to any sound. He knew where he was headed. He was like an arrow. He was ready to defend or attack. He had no plans to bring anyone back who wasn't willing to surrender. He was the judge, jury, and executioner.

Shawn walked as a cat, looking at the numbers on the door and listening for any sudden movements. *If his suspicions were correct, then apparently Mrs. Fry was no longer a part of this world. Hopefully, God would show her mercy in order for her to make it into the next.*

Shawn knew Curt and his men would be up there soon. They'd find Mrs. Fry and continue to follow the blood trail.

Shawn was then more determined than ever to find the ringleader and put a stop to the madness. He had been wrong about Mrs. Fry. He had thought she was the head honcho, but after what had taken place there that night, he knew that was not the case. Shawn had a strong feeling that his target had gone back to the office, and when questioned by the authorities, he would pretend he knew nothing of the hit. And to add insult to injury, he would say that he hadn't heard any gun go off. *Pretty smooth.* But Shawn knew better, and like an arrow he bolted toward his target.

Chapter 79

Shawn didn't bother to knock on the door; he wanted the element of surprise to be in full effect as he walked right in. Sitting behind his desk was a man Shawn had seen before but could not connect where. He stared at him long enough until it connected. That's when he remembered him from the restaurant during lunch where he and Frank had met for lunch to hang out. Shawn's mind played back that moment like a movie. That guy had come over to them, and Frank had said "Shawn, I want you to meet my colleague . . . Mr . . . . Mr . . . . what . . . that's it, Phillip Keys."

Mr. Keys looked up when Shawn entered his office. If he was caught off guard, he didn't show it. He didn't even look concerned. He just looked back down, doing whatever he was doing before Shawn came in. Shawn was more than surprised; this whole ordeal was a labyrinth. He had an idea that Keys had seen the look of surprise on his face. At that point, he did not care as he said, "Phillip Keys a.k.a. the voice and Frank Hall's so-called friend and helper."

Mr. Keys was impressed. He said, "Wow, what a memory! We only met once and that was for a few minutes . . . That is impressive, Mr. Cook. I knew you were a formidable foe, but you have gone beyond my expectations." Keys was still sitting at his desk while Shawn was watching his every movement. Keys responded, "So I see Mrs. Fry was right. The items in the box had been tampered with . . . so, Mr. Cook, please satisfy my curiosity. How did you do it, I mean, track down this whole thing to this?" Shawn looked at the distinguished-looking gentleman. By all appearances that man could have gotten away with the charade: clean cut, Caucasian, well-educated, well-spoken. Shawn was focused as he looked at Keys without blinking.

Shawn knew that his reflexes were at their peak as he responded to Keys' question, "It wasn't me since you would like to know, but—"

He was cut off as Keys retorted, "Ah, that's right. It was that nosy bitch of yours . . ." Keys smiled; he knew he had gotten to Shawn as Shawn flinched and his muscles flexed when he heard the derogatory term.

Mr. Keys added gasoline to the fire, "Mr. Cook, why continue to be on the losing side. Join us. The Alternative will one day take over. We could use your skills and talents. Join us."

Shawn looked at Keys with a look of disgust and said, "You and your washed-up losers are going down. The process has started already earlier today. That list that was in the box, well, all the king's horses and all the king's men were sent to the pin." Now it was Shawn's time to smile as Keys face turned two shades. Shawn continued, "Plus, you used your colleague's situation for your own gain, which was low and dirty."

Keys countered with a dismissal wave of the hand, "Who, Frank? Yeah, anything to get a foothold, him and his pathetic son, him walking around here looking like woe is me. He fitted right in the plan. I knew he needed the money, so we set up the means. What was so bad about that? He wins, we win . . . You don't have a problem with winning, do you, Mr. Cook, eh?" Mr. Keys was back to that stupid-looking smile.

Shawn, if his skin shades could be seen, right about then would have been in the pissed-off category as he responded, "I like winning, Keys. That's why I am going to beat you like your momma should've for using my boy, Frank Hall, and calling my girl the 'B' word. I am going to wash your mouth out with my fists, so when it's time to rinse, you will be spitting out your teeth." Shawn continued, "So this is what this so-called new order is about. Play upon the weak and frail."

Keys laughed, saying, "We are no different than what this country did to the native Indians. We are just using their technique." While Keys was laughing, Shawn was scoping, looking around to see what he could use to take Keys down. He counted four things he could use as a weapon, and being an expert in martial arts with emphasis on weapon warfare, Shawn was ready to put that thing to test. He knew that Keys, the jackass, would try to make a move, and when he did, he'd be on top of him like flies on poop.

Shawn did not like violence, but this one time he hoped that he could open up a can of kick-ass on Keys as he pushed the provoke button, "Hey, Keys, it's over. Your ragtime group has been captured. The plans of bombing all Federal buildings have shut down, and your second in command was killed by the first in command. Man, you guys are unraveling like a cheap suit."

Shawn knew he had gotten under Keys' skin as Keys responded with a sneer, "Mr. Cook, you are good, very good, but as they say, all good things must come to an end." Shawn with a purposeful overconfident smirk said, "I hate to rain on your parade, Keys, but the only thing that is going to end is when I put my foot so far up your butt, it's going to come out your mouth." Keys did not appreciate those who went against him and was breaking down. Shawn knew that Keys was slowly having a meltdown; it was now a matter of time before he made a move. Shawn watched his hands and body language very carefully.

Shawn had already noticed the wooden coat rack to his right. He would have to be quick to grab two of them and use them as a one-way boomerang weapon. He also saw two solid ashtrays on the desk, a fire extinguisher to the left behind Keys, and a bookshelf full of books. Getting hit with the corner of a book is no joke, especially when it's thrown with force. Shawn was peeved off, but he could not allow his anger to distract him. He had to remain poised and under control. It was hard because all he wanted to do was put his fist down Keys' throat.

Mr. Keys after he had returned from Mrs. Fry's office had put the gun back in his desk drawer. He knew Shawn wasn't a novice; therefore, he had to be quick and precise in order to get it. In that split second, he lunged for his desk drawer. Anyone else would have been flatfooted and would have had a late reaction, but Shawn was in attack mode, he was ready. He had been on the balls of his feet in patient anticipation and with what seemed to be lightning speed went for the coat rack and snatched two wooden hangers from them, one in each hand. Keys was reaching in his drawer. He was a split second or two behind Shawn. Shawn used it to his advantage as he flung both of the hangers with such force and accuracy, striking Keys in the face. The impact was hard enough for Keys to react by removing his hands out of his desk drawer and holding the area of his face that was struck with the hanger. He cursed and yelled in pain; however, it did not stop him from making another attempt to go into the drawer again for his weapon.

Shawn was ready as he dove on the desk, and with such quickness, he took both hands and slammed the desk drawer on Keys hands. He yelped in pain. Shawn said, "And you called my girl the 'B' word. You sure do a good impression of one."

Keys snatched his hands out from the desk, still with no weapon in his hand, and said while still in pain, "Oh, you like to make jokes. Tell me if you think this is funny. This should really crack you up." While Shawn was getting up off the desk, Keys took a golf club from the side of his desk and came down hard on Shawn's ribs. Shawn heard something crack.

Keys was coming for another strike, but Shawn in pain quickly rolled off the desk. The blow nearly hit him, and the impact that it made on the desk, if it would have hit Shawn, it would have done some considerable damage. Shawn was now probably fighting at 80 percent. He knew that his ribs were cracked and he would have to change his fighting style.

Keys, like a bull, came toward Shawn with the golf club swinging wildly. Shawn, who in his defense stance looked like a cornerback in football, timed Keys' swing so that when he swung, Shawn ducked, leaving Keys' rib cage exposed. Shawn, not missing a beat, came up and hard with four quick blows, two on each side of Keys' rib cage. When he was hit, Keys dropped the club and stumbled toward the door. Shawn like a shark smelling blood went after him.

Keys, still in pain, saw Shawn coming turned and did a crazy version of a roundhouse kick. The distinguished-looking Keys looked like a clown. Shawn wanted to laugh as he ducked, slid to his right, came up with the palm of his hand, and struck Keys with such force on the bridge of his nose that Keys yelled, "Arrr, you broke my nose you son of a—"

Shawn quickly slapped Keys in the mouth like a mother would do a child for saying a bad word and said, "Didn't I tell you to watch your mouth?" Keys, beaten and humiliated, lunged after Shawn. His aggressiveness caught Shawn off guard. As Keys grabbed Shawn by the throat, both of his hands squeezed and constricted Shawn's neck. Shawn, reserving the little energy he had, put both of his arms by his side and swung upward with such force, hitting Keys' arms. The blow knocked Keys' hands off Shawn's neck into the air. Shawn quickly took both hands, and with a thunderous impact, he clasped both hands on either side of Keys' ears. Shawn felt something crush when he delivered the blow; he knew it was Keys' eardrums.

Keys was now a little off-balance, but he was still swinging, and then he came at Shawn and speared him with his shoulders right into his cracked ribs. Shawn flinched from the blow as he was driven backward. Shawn, while being driven back, used the edge of his elbow and came down with quite hard consecutive blows on the back of the head and neck of Keys. The blows caused Keys to let go of his grip as he staggered and was dazed.

Shawn slowly came toward Keys with darkness in his approach. *Keys was done for. If this would have been a boxing match, his manager would have tossed in the towel.* But Shawn wasn't finished with him yet as he approached a battered and badly beaten and bruised Keys.

Shawn, without a second thought, came swiftly with a chop to the throat. Keys bent over in pain, holding his throat. He was choking and coughing, trying to catch his breath. Shawn still stalked him slowly as Keys, still bent over, raised his hand to indicate he had enough. But Shawn ignored the request and said, "You wanted to change your voice. Well, after that blow you won't have a voice to change." Keys slowly stood up, staggering like a tree blown by the wind, smiled, and raised his middle finger in both hands. Shawn just shook his head and turned to walk away, but he quickly pivoted and delivered a six foot three, two-hundred-and-something-plus-pound roundhouse to the jaw of Keys. He spun like a top, snapping his neck and collapsing to the floor. Shawn stood over him and said, "Game over. Didn't I tell you to watch your mouth!"

Officer Curt Moore and his men came rushing in. Moore surveyed the damage and made a whistling sound. He looked at Shawn and his eyes alone asked the question as to whether he was all right. Shawn responded with a wink and two thumbs up. Moore said, "Now I see why they call you C-4."

Shawn, still a little winded due to his cracked rib cage, responded, "The murder weapon he used against Fry is in his top desk drawer."

Shawn squeezed Moore's shoulders and slowly walked out of Keys' office, holding his rib cage. Moore said, "I hate to do it, but you're going to have to come down to the station." Shawn turned, looked at Moore, and nodded his head.

Two Hours Later

Shawn was at the police station, finishing up on a police report. He had submitted all evidence pertaining to the group who called themselves, "The Alternative."

Captain Moore shook hands with Shawn and said, "You are a hero. Do you know how long the FBI have been trying to track these guys down and bring them to justice? And here you go. You do it in a few days, very impressive." Captain Moore paused and said, "Hey, would you like to join the force?"

Shawn looked at him as if he was out of his mind and told him in a very polite yet firm way, "No, thanks."

Captain Moore quickly said, "No, wait, hold up. I'm sorry I didn't fully explain myself." Shawn just looked at Captain Moore with that look that said, "I was born at night, but I wasn't born last night," as Captain Moore continued his pitch, "Look, Shawn, or C-4, I am talking about joining not as an officer. No, sir, I was thinking more on the lines that we use you for our special cases unit." Shawn was still looking at Moore with eyes of "who is trying to sucker who" as he continued with his hands raised like a club scout leader, "That's it, nothing more. I'll make sure that the pay is worth your while. I know that was dumb as if you need the money."

Shawn noticed that Moore looked as if he fought a hard battle and lost as he said to him, "I'll tell you what, Curt, I'll think about it. How about that?"

Captain Moore shrugged his shoulders and said, "Hey, I gave it my best shot, and thanks, I can't ask for more than that. At least I have my foot in the door." Shawn could only smile and pat his friend on the back. As he was walking out of Moore's office, Moore called to him, "Hey, Shawn, how about being our self-defense instructor? After what I saw what you did to Keys . . . hey, the pay is top notch, I know, as if you need the money."

Shawn with a look of confusion said, "I thought you guys already have an instructor." Moore waved his hand in disgust and said, "Listen, he's the commissioner's son in law. The guy sucks. Whoever heard of using ballad as a warm-up. Do you know how that looks when I see grown men of 250 pounds doing an open-leg squat bend? It turns my stomach. Listen, my ten-year-old could beat him. We really need someone, Shawn. Send us one of your students. We'll start them out with three days a week, and if they like it, we will increase it to four days. How 'bout it?"

Shawn was in thought, and he looked up at Curt, nodded his head up and down, shrugged his shoulders, and said, "We'll see. Listen, I have to run. I'll keep in touch, Curt. I am glad things worked out . . . later."

Moore said as Shawn turned to go, "We busted a huge operation, I mean huge, but we are still after the mastermind, although we do have some good leads." Shawn stopped, turned toward Curt, and walked back toward his office with a look of surprise on his face. Curt Moore urged Shawn to come back inside his office and closed the door. Curt was sitting on the edge of his desk looking down at the floor. When he knew he had Shawn's attention, he said, "I bet you thought Fry and Keys were the ringleaders?" Shawn was getting ready to respond when Moore cut him off and continued, "They were the little fishes in a giant pond, just paws moving up the ranks . . . well, at least Keys was. Fry was bent mainly on getting back at those who stiffed her out of a position she wanted."

Shawn looked at Moore and said, "How do you know all of this?"

Moore nodded his head with pride and said, "Aha, this is good detective work, but the truth is we searched her office and her home and found two diaries at her home, which basically told us everything we needed to know about this operation, Keys, whatever . . . And by the way, she could not stand Keys. She thought he was an arrogant bastard, who made it as far as he did because of his highly qualified master's degree in business. She had some plans for him but . . . Anyway, it's a big organization. They've been around for years but very much hidden, waiting for the right moment to move and strike. In the meantime, they were recruiting and had their secret meetings and things of that nature." Shawn just nodded and listened as Moore continued, "But they are all over the USA. Shawn, these are people like you and I. They may look like you and I, go home after a hard day of work just like you and I, vote just like you and I, and even sit up in church praising the same God just like you and I, but they are twisted upstairs. The elevator is not making it to the top, if you know what I mean. They feel they have a higher calling from God to destroy the beast and bring the true divine reign, justice, righteousness, and equality to the new world. Oh yeah, what I read in her diaries confirmed that Fry's brain, no pun intended, seemed really fried." Shawn just shook his head and walked out of Moore's office.

Thirty Minutes Later

Shawn told Complex everything. She understood everything due to her well-advanced intelligence, but she did not have any answers as they pulled up to the hospital.

Shawn got out, walked to the front desk, and showed his ID. The security at the desk told Shawn that wasn't necessary as his reputation had spread that quickly. He thought that Moore had worked fast and appreciated his competence even more.

Shawn got up to the floor, and the two officers were still present, in anticipation that any residue might have been left over from the scum. He walked inside the room and saw Serenity looking as beautiful as ever. He stood there as she was surrounded by friends and family, but he only saw her. Serenity looked toward the door and saw Shawn standing there. What made her look that way could only have been the bond, the connection, they had for each other. Her face lit up like a bright light bulb as if she was so happy to see him. Shawn walked toward her bed as family and friends parted like a flower opening up. They were so happy to see him as well. Serenity was so excited she could not wait to tell him how well she had done on her first day of rehabilitation. She was going a mile a minute while the others listened and laughed at her animated expressions. She told him how rough it was, but she kept on seeing him in her mind and that gave her the inspiration to push herself until she was able to take a few steps. She said, "Shawn, everyone was excited. I felt as if I was in one of those movies where the odds were against me, like Rocky." They all laughed as she continued, "But, baby, when I took those first steps, everyone in the room was clapping. Even my therapist had tears in her eyes, but I did it, baby, I did it."

Shawn was excited as his parents stood alongside him excited as well.

Mr. Cook said, "Shawn, you have a good woman here, I mean it." Mrs. Cook agreed with her husband and kissed and hugged Serenity. Serenity's parents had tears in their eyes as well. They were so proud of their daughter. The parents did a conversation detour from Serenity's first steps of rehab to marriage and the sound of little feet invading their lives. Everyone started laughing while Shawn blushed.

Serenity pointed at Shawn and said, "Oh my, look, he's blushing. Someone take a picture, no doubt a priceless moment." Everyone laughed.

Shawn relaxed and said, "Come on, you guys, she is just learning how to walk again. You know how us guys like to get those legs high." Everyone laughed; now it was Serenity's turn to blush as she playfully smacked him on the arm. Shawn, in turn, pointed at her as payback for laughing when he had been blushing.

Shawn's mother said, "Now don't make me get the soap. Don't be so fresh."

As she playfully nudged his head, Shawn's father was laughing and said in a chuckle, "Now that's what I'm talking about, Son." Shawn's mother was the one blushing now as she playfully hit her husband in the arm; everyone laughed.

Shawn had a chance to meet Serenity's brother, Eric, again, and he came to the conclusion that he was a cool dude. *He would have been a good brother to have, but yet again he wouldn't trade his blood brothers Malcolm and Jonathan for anything, even though they were a pain growing up, like they're still a pain as grownups,* he thought playfully.

Malcolm said, "Hey, big brother, Frank said to give you this." He handed Shawn an envelope. Shawn opened it and inside was a "thank-you" card. Shawn read the card to himself. In the card, Frank said that he wanted to thank him for everything and that he hoped that their friendship could remain strong. He said that he and his family were going away for about six months to work on their marriage and to get Bobby the help and treatment that he needed. He thanked Shawn for the money. He also mentioned that it was more than enough for the treatment. Shawn smiled to himself and thanked the voice. Complex had been able to hack into his account. Shawn still doesn't know how she did it, but he had helped himself to his cash. He figured if he didn't take it, his uncle, that is the government, would have. He would make sure that it would go to good use.

Shawn asked if everyone could leave the room as he needed to speak with Serenity alone. There were a few protesters, but everyone complied. Shawn was now all alone with his woman and she with her man. He smiled at her, thinking that she had come a long way. She smiled back at him, thinking about what the young lady had said in the restaurant when she didn't like him. Beatrice had told her that Shawn was a good man, and a year and some change later, she could say without a doubt that Beatrice was right. He was a good man, the best she had ever known.

Shawn opened up to her. Now was the best time. He told her everything about her life being in danger, about the three men in the alley and that it hadn't been a robbery but a hit on her, and about her vice president, Mrs. Fry, and Frank's coworker, Philip Keys. He told her about the plot and the organization. He told her everything, even the two officers, which she did not know were outside her door from the time she came in the hospital.

Serenity was overwhelmed. All of it was too much to swallow in one gulp. The amazing thing that for her was hard to believe was that all of it had been happening right under her nose. She shook her head in awe, and she did not say anything for a few minutes. Finally she said, "Well, I thought I would never come to say this, but I'm so glad Sandra is nosy. If it wasn't for her who knows what may have happened." Shawn kissed Serenity with passion on her lips, and their tongues did an erotic tangle. When he stopped and moved back a little, Serenity smiled. Shawn inquired why she was smiling, she said still smiling, "I missed that. Ever since I've been in this hospital you've been kissing me on the forehead as if I was your little sister or something . . . It feels good to feel your lips and taste you all in my mouth."

Shawn smiled that million-dollar smile and said, "Oh, really?" Shawn bent down, and he kissed her again with all the passion he could muster up. Serenity felt as she was melting.

Shawn started to plant little love kisses all over her lips, neck, and face, and she said enjoying every minute of it, "You just haven't forgotten what turns me on, have you?" Shawn pulled away reluctantly and said, "Never." And continued with the passion he had missed for long.

Shawn was more than happy. He thanked God for his mercy and Grace. He had one more thing to do, and he would need Serenity's help with that. He knew she would not have a problem with that. He smiled and looked at Serenity and she looked at him, and they both said the words "I love you" at the same time, and then they both smiled and said together, "I know." They laughed and hugged each other with passion.

Final Chapter

Six Months Later

Shawn and Frank stood in the mirror. Shawn being a little taller had to bend down a little so that Frank could pin the lapel on his suit jacket. Frank was getting frustrated, "Come on, C-4, why are you moving? Keep still. Every time I get it, you move." Shawn replied, "No, Bro, you think you're getting it, but you keep getting me, sticking me with that pin. Can't you tell the difference between material and flesh, and that thing hurts I want you to know."

Frank made fun of Shawn. "Ah, the poor six foot three, two-hundred-plus-pounds baby can't take a little stick."

Shawn looked at Frank go through his poor acting performance and responded, "Oh yeah, let me stick you and show you how it feels."

Frank flinched back a little and cleared his throat, "Ah, no, that's OK, you are doing fine."

Shawn chuckled and said, "Yeah, I thought so." There was a knock at the door.

Frank, who almost had the lapel pinned, was distracted and he asked, "Who could that be?" He pressed the pin too hard into Shawn's tuxedo and into his skin again. Shawn let out a loud "ouch." Frank looked at the door and back at Shawn in frustration and said, "I almost had it."

Shawn said, rubbing the area where he had been stuck, "Yeah, you've been saying that for the last half an hour." Frank, still looking very frustrated, told Shawn to hold the lapel in place while he got the door. Shawn, holding the lapel pin in place, was still making sounds of pain from the last stick.

Frank snatched the door open, startling Macon, Shawn's sister; she looked exasperated and said, "Come on, you guys, what is taking so long?"

Frank, still upset, said, "Blame the big bear with the tack in his foot."

Shawn said out loud, "I heard that, Frank."

Frank and Macon chuckled as Frank let Macon in, shaking his head and saying, "Man, your brother is a trip."

Macon walked over to Shawn and said, "People, who made this trip from the South and who knows from wherever else, are going to be pissed." Macon looked at Shawn holding the lapel in place and looking pathetic and said, "You mean to tell me that two grown able-bodied men can't put a simple lapel on. That is sad."

Frank jumped in, "No, not me, him." Both Macon and Shawn told Frank to shut up at the same time.

Macon took the lapel from Shawn and said, "Let me see this." Shawn tried to kind of help her, but she playfully smacked his hand away. "Move, move, oh, now you feel inspired to help, move." Frank, turning his back away from them, was covering his mouth, laughing. Macon took the pin, covered it with her hand, and jabbed at his butt. Her nails were the thing that touched him, and Frank practically jumped three feet in the air. When he looked back, Shawn and Macon were laughing so hard. As Macon showed him the finger that she poked him with, Frank waved his hand at them, smiling, and walked over to the other part of the room. Frank came back over to observe Macon putting the lapel on. He was very close to her, to the point she turned, looked at Frank, and said, "Excuse me, would you please stop breathing on my neck. You sound like Darth Vader."

Shawn laughed and Macon pretended she had stuck him; he flinched and said, "Ouch."

Macon laughed and said, "Dog Shawn, I didn't even touch you."

Frank feeling vindicated with justice said, "See, that's what I had to deal with."

Macon looked at Frank and said, "No, Frank, from what I could see of his skin, you were using our brother as a pincushion, so don't go there." All three started laughing, just like when they had been growing up. Frank was considered and accepted as a brother in the family.

Macon touched the lapel here and there and said, "There you go, my handsome big brother." She kissed Shawn on the cheek and turned to walk out the door.

Frank acting as if he was jealous said, "Hey, how about me, sis?"

Macon said, "Yes, Frank, you too." She rolled her eyes up to the ceiling and kissed Frank on the cheek. She then said, "All right, Mutt and Jeff, let's go."

Shawn said, "OK, give us a minute, I promise, at the most three, OK. I need to speak with Frank." Macon was getting ready to protest but saw the look of seriousness in her big brother's eyes and chose wisely not to challenge the request as she quietly nodded and turned to go.

Shawn and Frank stood looking in the mirror. Frank was adjusting his bow tie while Shawn was fixing his shirt collar. Frank said, "Hey, just like old times, right, C-4?"

Shawn did not respond right away and finally stated, "Listen, Frank, I want you to know, and I know we talked about this briefly when you came back, but I understand, or at least I think I understand, why you did what you did, you know with the voice, I—"

Shawn was cut off by Frank, "Shawn, I still can't believe that Philip was the person behind the voice. I trusted him with my situation."

Shawn jumped in, "And he took advantage of you. He knew where to hit you and how hard, and you did not know he was the one." Frank just shook his head, still looking in the mirror then at Shawn to see if there was any giveaway expressions, but as usual Shawn dealt with a clean hand, no hocus pocus stuff, as he continued, "That's what I wanted to say. You are cool in my book, always will be, especially the way you put your own life in danger to protect Serenity . . . thanks."

Frank's eyes was moist, and he wiped them and said, "Listen, I am the one who is grateful. If it wasn't for you, they would not have found a cure for Bobby, and for your information, he's doing great. And if it wasn't for you, my marriage would have been history. I will always be in your debt, my brother." The two men gave each other a shoulder tap and a hug. Frank once again reminded Shawn of the special day.

Shawn in turn responded, "Yo, Frank, I wouldn't trade this day for nothing." Frank nodded, understanding his buddy.

Frank said, "Hey, congratulations, my brother. You are a blessed man." Shawn and Frank once again shoulder tapped and embraced one another.

While they were still in the embrace, Macon walked in. "Wow, one last minute fling."

Shawn and Frank laughed. They both pulled Macon into their circle and they hugged each other.

Shawn stood next to Frank. He was nervous as he whispered to Frank, "Now you sure you have it right. No screw ups, right?" Frank playfully patted his pocket on his jacket and then made a face as he was patting the other pockets on his jacket and pants, his face becoming more serious by the minute. Shawn, in turn, made his own face of panic, more like controlled panic.

Frank finally patted his side jacket pocket, smiled, and said, "Hey, I got your back. I'm only playing. It's right here." Shawn wanted to see it. Frank asked Shawn whether he trusted him. Shawn thought about the question and then insisted that Frank should show him the item in his pocket. Then it happened.

The doors opened up and everyone stood on their feet in the direction of the open doors. There were the nonverbal sounds and expressions of "exquisite" and "elegant beauty" as everyone's breaths got caught in their chests. Women covered their mouths as tears of joy and amazement ran down their cheeks. Even some of the men were wiping their eyes as the nonverbal expression of awe continued and the flashes from cameras went off at a rapid pace. Serenity after six months was walking again; her arm was locked in with the first man who had ever loved her and taught her what a true man really was. He held his head high as he walked with her. They slowly stepped to the perfect and familiar tune of the music. She looked a little nervous as she made her way down to the second and only man who would ever love her while the train of her white wedding gown seemed to go on forever as her bridesmaids, all eight of them, followed. Sandra, her best friend, was the first of the eight; she was so happy for her friend she could not contain her tears.

Shawn watched in awe as his bride-to-be made her way down the aisle to meet the man who was everything and meant everything to her. Frank nudged Shawn as he watched two of his closest friends about to become one. Shawn was so nervous he hoped that he wouldn't be like one of those guys who fainted during the ceremony due to nervousness. *But this is what he wanted from the first day he met her. This moment, in his eyes, was preordained by God. This is his soul mate, his Eve.* For him it was a dream come true. Nothing on earth could compare to it. He had captured his prize, and his prize had captured him, and now he was letting everyone in that place know it with his million-dollar smile.

Frank had tears in his eyes. Sandra had tears in her eyes as she looked at one groomsman in particular, and that was Marcus. He looked at her, and she mouthed the words at him, "You're next." Marcus played around and put his hands together as a gesture of prayer, asking for mercy. Sandra gave him the eye with all seriousness. Marcus smiled and mouthed that he looked forward to it. The parents were very happy. The Cooks knew they were getting a fine daughter-in-law, and the Powers knew they were getting the best son-in-law that any parents could ask for.

The ceremony was being performed by both Shawn and Serenity's pastors. Both Shawn and Serenity wanted their pastors to perform the ceremony, so they came to a solution to have both of them.

The Reverend Dr. Elijah Collins who was Shawn's pastor started, "We are gathered here today . . . Who is the person that is to give this wonderful woman to this wonderful man?" Mr. Powers stated that he was. He united his daughter to his future son-in-law and he stepped back and sat down with his wife. Dr. Collins continued with the familiar opening of the ceremony. As the pastors went back and forth with those famous words of matrimony, Pastor Bishop Samuel James, Serenity's pastor, finished up the vows by saying, "Is there anyone who would object to these wonderful folks getting married? Speak now or forever hold your peace."

Bishop James waited for a few minutes before the Reverend Elijah Collins said, "Bishop, the only ones that will object would be the haters who had their chance and blew it and the wannabes, who wanna be up here." The congregation erupted with laughter.

As the ceremony came to a close, Shawn and Serenity wanted to express their own version of their vows. Each one took their turn to express what that moment meant to them. Dancers of all ages came out and danced gracefully around them as they said their vows. The timing and the meaning of the dancers doing their dance was a momentous and captivating event. The congregation looked on in awe, some with their mouths open, others with their eyes fixed on the dancers, refusing to blink in fear they would miss something. There were others who concentrated on the words that Shawn and Serenity delivered to each other, refusing to be distracted by anything that could cause them to miss one single word, while the others held their breaths, unable to exhale because of the stupendous moment, what some could call a perfectly choreographic art of beauty, bliss, and a joyful wonder to behold.

The meaning was not abstract. It was clear as Shawn and Serenity continued to state their love and commitment to each other. The dancers signified the angels of God in affirmation of the fact that God was pleased, and the angels or dancers confirmed the Creator's confirmation as if those two were highly favored and blessed by God. As Shawn and Serenity came to the close of their personal vows, the dancers also came to a close as well. And as that part of the ceremony ended, the people stood to their feet and gave a standing ovation to the dancers and to the creativity of Shawn and Serenity. They also gave glory to God for the great things they had been a part of that day; the air was filled with mirth and praise.

As the dancers completed what many had entitled *The God is pleased* dance, someone began to sing the song, "The wind beneath my wings." As both Shawn and Serenity faced each other, looking into each other's eyes, while the song ended, Bishop James asked Frank if he had the ring. Frank with all seriousness reached into his jacket pocket and gave Shawn the ring. Shawn was then asked to place the ring on Serenity's finger with the traditional vows being repeated by him, "With this ring . . ."

Then Pastor Elijah Collins had Serenity repeat after him the marital vow of commitment, "Do you, Serenity Powers . . ." Then both pastors at the same time pronounced them husband and wife. Frank and Sandra retrieved a broom from one of the aisles and held it down on the floor. Shawn and Serenity jumped over the broom, and Shawn was given permission by both pastors to kiss his bride.

As the two shared a tender and deep kiss, someone from the congregation shouted, 'Hey, save some for tonight.' The congregation erupted in laughter. As the music played and the dancers led the way out to an upbeat tune, Shawn and Serenity followed and quickly dashed to the limo that was waiting while Rose pedals were tossed at them. They jumped in, closed the door, and shared yet another deep and passionate kiss.

Shawn's father, Travis, said to his wife and Serenity's parents, "We won't have to wait too long for grandkids from these two." All four of them laughed with tears of joy in their eyes.

The reception was held in Northeast Bronx at a new place built just around three months ago. The wedding planner had heard about the good service and the affordable prices just for renting the place for three to five hours. Both Shawn and Serenity had wanted a place where people could get to if they didn't have a car as well as a place that wasn't expensive. Shawn had told her not to worry about the price, but she did. She knew for Shawn the sky was the limit, but she had seen days where a couple of dollars would be her limit. She looked at herself as not being tight, but a wise spender.

Shawn was more than impressed with the choice Serenity made. The place was eloquent with marble floors and nice tables spread out, where one did not have to rub their behinds on someone as they would try to get past. The walls were mirrored all around and the lighting was just perfect, low but not low to the point where you could not see who you were talking to and not bright enough where you wished you couldn't see who you were talking to. As you entered this wonderfully designed edifice, one of the two hosts would greet you and direct you to the event according to your invitation. There were three different-size banquet halls on the main floor. People would rent according to the occasion and how much a person was able to spend. In addition, there were two more halls upstairs as well. Shawn and Serenity had the hall on the main level, which was the one to the left. It was larger than the other two.

There were two restrooms for men and women on both floors. Each restroom had someone to assist them with a towel after they got finished using it. Before you entered the hall, down from the hall was where the coats were dropped off. It was simple, no hassles, no confusion. You dropped off your coat, you received a ticket, and the coats were placed in numerical order so that there weren't any mistakes when it was time to pick up your coat. The other unique thing about the coat drop-off was that it was so organized. You had those who took the coat and made out the ticket and you had those who would put the coat up, while most places had the coats piled up and each person had to identify their coat by a particular mark or something. This place that Shawn and Serenity had rented was huge and beautiful. As one entered the banquet hall, on the far right and straight back was the kitchen area. There was an area for a small band and a DJ straight at the back of the hall. The tables were on both sides, and dividing the tables straight down the middle was the catering line where in this case it was all you could eat. Shawn and Serenity chose the soul food menu. The huge marble floor a few feet from the tables was where one could go and dance the night away. The eloquence and the beauty of the banquet hall gave the appearance of a fairy-tale story; everything was so captivating and marvelous.

Shawn and Serenity didn't want to keep the people waiting. They knew by then they were hungry enough to start nibbling on each other, so they got there a little shortly after most of the people. The music was pumping. Some people were sitting around talking, introducing themselves, while others were nodding their heads to the live music, and there were others who were already on the floor, dancing, club addicts. You could tell that those were the ones who no matter where the party was, they had to get on the floor and show their stuff. And there were some characters tonight. The place was jumping. When the DJ took over, he set the place on fire with his mixing. Shawn thought that Marcus had told him the guy was good, and Shawn had to agree. *This dude was smoking.*

The master of ceremonies slowed things down a bit as he called the bride and bridegroom to the floor. The M/C said, "This comes from a special request from Shawn to Serenity with love." The lights went low as the colorful lights scrolled and moved around them while the DJ played the song at Shawn's request, a song written and sung by one of his favorite artists, called "Unbreakable." It was considered the wedding song about ten years ago, probably also the "making a baby" song as well. Serenity had tears in her eyes as she listened to the words, the words of a man giving and pledging his life to make the one he was marrying pleased, content, and satisfied. As Shawn hugged Serenity tight, he bent down and started singing the words to the song. He continued to dance and hold her so close to his chest she could feel his heart beat. Then as a surprise like no other, the DJ faded the music out, and the band started playing it.

And then Shawn was handed a mike who started singing the song as the people, who were sitting, got up to take a closer look, and the ones who were already close came even closer to watch and listen. And Shawn went on describing his love as he sung the words to "Unbreakable," the first dance love song, with passion. "This day has finally arrived. I didn't think I would survive. My love for you is stronger than hardest of steel. It's genuine. It's the real deal. This day has finally arrived. I didn't think I would survive." As he placed her hand to his heart, he continued to sing, "I want to share every inch of me. What I have is now yours. It's no longer a separate thing. I don't see a I or me, but this love have become a we, for I'm your Adam you are my Eve. It is your love I desperately cling. This day has finally arrived; I didn't think I would survive."

Serenity felt full as the tears of joy streamed down her cheeks. He went down on one knee, as the women in the place went wild, as he continued, "Everything I do, everything I say I want you to be a part of it in every way. Everywhere I go, I want you there. My love for you I do declare." Shawn continued as he circled her and hugged her from the back, breathing softly on her neck, and in between lyrics showered her with sweet kisses on her neck and collarbone. As he prepared to sing the final stanza, still holding her from the back, he said, "You are the milk in my coffee, my jelly on the side. Without you, I am incomplete. How would I survive?" The women went wild and the men applauded as he continued, "I have found the piece to the puzzle I've been looking for. There is no need to look any further. It is your unbreakable love I most adore. I surrender my body, heart, soul, and mind for this unbreakable love God sent right on time. This day has finally arrived. I will survive."

Shawn turned Serenity around to him and kissed her with such passion her feet started too tingle as goose bumps raced up and down her arms and spine. It felt like a low-grade electric shock. It seemed as if everyone in the place surrounded them and applauded, even those that were in the kitchen, as he hugged her and whispered in her ears that he loved her more than life itself. Serenity believed it too as she succumbed to the emotions and broke down in tears of joy, for she knew that there was no other man on the face of the earth who could demonstrate such love and compassion than the one who was holding her right at that moment. Through tears and gulps of breathlessness she expressed to her husband how much she loved him.

Shawn and Serenity made their way around as many tables as they could, thanking everyone for coming. It was a day that they would always remember, and as a token of their love, everyone on the guest list received a glass with their photo on it, kissing one another.

The reception was still jumping. The M/C, who was doing a great job, kept the people moving with things like the "soul train line" and the "electric slide" and on and on. The people were having a great time. As the party was still in full swing, Shawn and Serenity announced that they were getting ready to leave, but they encouraged everyone to continue and party. However, Shawn had one more task to perform.

Shawn signaled for Frank to bring a chair to him. No one knew what he was up to. Shawn had been a man of surprises throughout the whole celebration. He kept the people thinking "let's see" and on their toes, not knowing what would happen next. He placed the chair in the middle of the floor in the big banquet hall, and then he looked at Serenity with those eyes that told her that he was up to something. Shawn pointed at her with his finger and beckoned her to come out onto the floor. All the guys caught on and began to clap, hoot, and make animal sounds like barking dogs. Shawn, in response to the male calls, raised both arms in victory, stuck out his chest, and slapped it, as if to ask his male cohorts, "Who was the man?" They shouted back, saying, "You are." He repeated two more times the same phrase, and they responded each time that he was the man. And then Shawn raised his arms again in victory, nodding his head with an overconfident look on his face as the place burst forth with a testosterone of energy.

Serenity, who had never seen that side of him, loved it. He reminded her of a child on Christmas morning, full of energy, but, on the other hand, she knew that that energy was up to no good. As she slowly made her way up to the middle of the floor and stood in front of Shawn with a nervous look on her face, twirling her locks and biting on her bottom lip, he motioned for her to have a seat in the chair. Serenity was blushing and looking nervous as she pointed to the chair and asked, "You mean this one?"

The place erupted with laughter. Shawn nodded his head to her question. The women were shouting and encouraging her not to back down, all the time telling her to stand up to the challenge. Serenity at that point seemed to have a shot of encouragement as she lifted her chin in defiance toward Shawn. Shawn, in turn, raised one of his eyebrows and looked at her, and she, in turn, put her hands together in a prayerlike fashion and playfully begged for mercy. Everyone laughed. Some of the women told her to be strong and playfully told her not to be afraid of that bully and to do something. Serenity bashfully stretched out her arms and shrugged her shoulders as if to say she didn't know what to do. The women were shouting more words of encouragement, such as, "Don't let us down," "Come on, girl represent, you can do this. Stand up and be strong." But Serenity knew she was out of her element. She was stuck as the men continued to shout that Shawn was the man and he like a king took it all in; the more he heard, the more confident and cocky he became.

Sandra ran up to Serenity and whispered something in her ear. Serenity's eyes opened wide and her hands went to her mouth, and everyone laughed at her animated expressions. Some of Sandra's friends didn't know what she was saying to Serenity, but they knew Sandra. That was enough said. The women began to chant to Serenity the words "Do it, do it . . ." over and over again. One of Serenity's friends who was also Sandra's friend shouted, "Do what she says."

Serenity looked up at Shawn, who gave her that same look with the eyebrow, which the wrestler, the "Rock," used to do. Sandra whispered in Serenity's ear, and she, in turn, nodded her head. The guys were still encouraging Shawn, who looked as confident as ever. Shawn knew that Serenity wasn't the type of girl who would follow her friend's advice, so he felt confident that she was going to back down from whatever request Sandra was suggesting to her or so he thought as he raised his arms in victory. Serenity looked at Shawn as she slowly inched her wedding gown higher and higher to the claves, higher to the knees, higher, nice and slow, as the women chanted, "Do it." All the while she was looking at Shawn with a look that could only be described as provocative, alluring, and defiant, as her gown was now above the knee.

Shawn was more than surprised that she had gone that far as he bent down and whispered in her, "Baby, if you go there, you leave me no other choice. I'm going to have to call your bluff. I have some things up my sleeve as well. Don't do this . . ."

He nervously chuckled, while Sandra, having no idea what Shawn was saying, was on the other side of Serenity whispering in her ear and telling her, "Girl, don't listen to the hype. You take it to the limit. He's going to back down, watch . . ."

Serenity turned to Sandra and whispered in her ear, twirling her locks and biting her bottom lip, "San, I can't do this. I can't. He's bolder than I am. Let's just go one more inch, and if he doesn't give in, then let's throw in the towel, OK?"

Sandra was animated about what Serenity had just told her. Shawn couldn't hear, but from the body language he could see Sandra wasn't too enthused with what Serenity had just conveyed to her. But that wasn't what he was going by. He was going by Serenity's body language. He knew she was about to surrender. He could not hear a single word she was saying, but her gestures were screaming. He knew that whenever she twirled her locks and bit her bottom lip, she was nervous.

He could smell victory as he raised his arms and shouted to no one in particular, "I got this. I see it loud and clear."

Sandra put her head down in playful defeat, and then she looked at Serenity and saw the same thing Shawn was looking at and quickly went down to her ear, "Girl, he's toying with you. He's going by the signals you are giving him." Serenity wrinkled her nose, not understanding what her friend was talking about. Sandra said, "Stop biting your lip and twirling your locks. He knows you do that only when you are nervous. Girl, he just played you like a bootleg flick. Show him, call his bluff." Serenity looked up at Shawn who looked back at her with a cocky smile. Serenity held his look, closed her eyes for a brief second, slowly opened them up, and looked at him, and with all the seduction she could muster up, she licked her lips slowly and spread her legs a little wider. The guys in the place went wild, making animal noises, howling and hooting, and cocking their heads to the side for a better view. Some cocked their heads so much to the side they playfully fell over. Sandra pretended she fainted, and the women wanted to cheer but were speechless. So they applauded with their mouths wide open. Shawn knew he was in trouble as he froze in place, unable to move or speak.

Serenity, never seeing Shawn that way, applied the pressure even more, like a wrestler applying a submission hold. The gown went up higher, just a little bit above the knee. The guys were now coming in closer as they saw legs that they only wished could wrap them up. Shawn looked at Serenity and knew he had to do something. As the music started playing, Shawn took off his jacket and flung it. The gesture didn't faze Serenity as she continued with that seductive look, and she pulled the gown up midthigh along with the garter belt that started at the ankle. The women were still cheering. The guys were seeing a leg that was strong, firm, and long. Some of the guys were playfully biting their hand just to prevent themselves from screaming. Shawn thought he saw some of them salivating. Sandra, who had pretended she had fainted, sat up and looked around. She looked at Serenity and where the gown was and pretended she had fainted again; people erupted in laughter.

Serenity looked at Shawn, who did not show any signs of surrender, and lifted up her dress as far it could go, inching the garter item with it. Shawn's eyes opened wide as he grabbed a towel from a nearby table and waved it in surrender. The women went berserk, as they cheered for Serenity, while the guys prompted Shawn for going that far and gave him sympathy high fives. Sandra was helped up by some of the other women, and she acted as if she was dazed as she gave two thumbs up to Serenity, who beamed with a smile. Shawn playfully and reluctantly walked up to Serenity and stood as a lowly servant. The guests, both women and men, loved it as they laughed and clapped.

Serenity, playing it for all it was worth, signaled for a microphone. As she was handed the microphone, she gave her victory speech, "Today, my fellow-ladies, we stand victorious." The women cheered, and the men, who did not want to but had to give them what was their due, clapped as well. As she looked at Shawn with those sexy eyes and with the excitement still burning in her cheeks, she winked and said, "You may bow down to the queen." The women once again erupted in applause as they laughed at the fun moment while Serenity continued, "You may kneel and remove the ribbon corsage from my sexy, shapely legs, my defeated comrade and companion." Shawn playfully nodded, kneeled, and removed the garter belt.

The women cheered and chanted "victory" over and over again. Serenity raised her arms to silence her female comrades; she asked Shawn, "Do you have anything you want to say, my servant?"

Shawn, still playing the lowly servant role, took the microphone with humility, slowly lifted the microphone to his mouth, and said very slowly, "Thank you, Queen Serenity." The men chuckled and the women laughed, enjoying the fun. The more he talked, the bolder and confident he became. "You are the queen. Long live the queen. Reign in your victory, my queen, for tonight my queen . . . I shall rule as king." The men as well as the women, not expecting such words, applauded with cheers and laughter. Serenity blushed and just smiled. She got up and hugged her man, and he held her twice as tight as he lifted her up and over his shoulder while she yelped in surprise, not because of falling, but because of the sudden burst of energy from Shawn. As the music started, he carried her over his shoulder to the door while Serenity faked and pretended that she was going to throw the garter. The women were jumping and running, all excited to catch the lucky charm.

Serenity found Sandra and quickly gave her a look that said that she hoped Sandra would catch it, but she as well as Sandra knew that she could not show any partiality. She continued to fake as if she was going to throw it. Each time the women would scream, laugh, and talk out loud in fun to each other. Shawn finally made it to the door. The women knew the moment was coming as they eagerly waited for the garter to be tossed. According to tradition, one who catches it would be the next one to get married. For women, it was an exciting moment; for some guys, it was a moment where they hoped and prayed that their woman wouldn't be the lucky recipient. Perhaps as they went for the corsage they would trip or slip or something crazy.

Serenity continued to taunt the women by pretending she was going to throw the garter. Then the moment came when she started counting, "One for the money." Her arms swung hung high in the air as she continued, "Two for the show . . ." As her arms went high again. "Three, you better get ready." The arm went high again. "And four, I'm getting ready to let it go . . ." Serenity, still lifted on Shawn's shoulder, swung her arms as best as she could. She let go of the garter belt as it soared high in the air. The women scampered, scrambled, and laughed like children as they went for the garter belt. Sandra desperately pushed and knocked her hips around in the crowd, knocking women over like bowling pins. She was a desperate heifer. She reached up to grab the prize and slipped and landed on her backside. Serenity was laughing quite hard. Taking advantage of the moment, Karen, Shawn's secretary, caught the garter belt; the women clapped and applauded. Shawn was pleased and thought that if anyone deserved a break it was Karen. Shawn gave her two thumbs up as he let out a male howl; the other men followed suit. The place was roaring with laughter. As they left, the music started up again and the people went back to the dance floor.

Shawn and Serenity got into his car and was going back to his place, but Shawn decided that that was the best time to come clean.

As they sat there, Serenity wondered why he wasn't moving the car. She looked over at him and saw a look of concern and apprehension on his face, something as far as she could recall never having seen before. She became very concerned and placed her hand on his leg and asked him, "Shawn, what's wrong? What's the matter? Are you OK, baby?"

Shawn closed his eyes for a brief second to gather his thoughts. He knew sooner or later, which he wished was later, that that subject would have come up, but he felt this was the best time. *Get it out of the way, move on.*

Shawn responded in a sober and serious tone, one that she wasn't used to. She became very uncomfortable as she waited for his response and braced herself. "Serenity, you know how much I love and adore you. You are the best thing that I ever experienced in a woman, and I've loved you since that first day that I met you. And since we've been together, I have never enjoyed myself as much as I have, baby. You are my life and the air that I breathe. I love you so much that it hurts inside to think what I would do if I didn't have you. I would cease to exist." He took her hand, kissed it, and placed it back in her lap. When Shawn picked up her hand, he could feel it shaking. She wasn't sure if it was him or her, but she got that answer when he let go of it and placed it back in her lap. She could feel it shaking against her leg. In her mind, Serenity cut him off. She just felt that Shawn wanted to say something but didn't know how to word it.

Oh my god she thought. She hoped he wasn't sick or anything crazy. She wouldn't know how to handle that news. It would crush her; it would shatter her into bits and pieces. She took a deep breath, gathered up whatever resilience she had in her reserve tank, held his hand, and said, "Shawn, please tell me. I could handle it. Don't look at the tears. I hurt because you are hurting. Please don't keep me in the dark. Are you sick? I mean, is it medical? What is it, baby? Has something happened to someone in your family? What, baby?"

Shawn looked at her and saw the fear and anxiety in her eyes, and he looked down and saw her hands shaking before she could hide them by folding them together. He took her folding hands and placed each one in his own. As his hands engulfed hers, he smiled at her that million-dollar smile to calm her nerves, and he chuckled and said, "No, baby, it's nothing like that. Come on now. Don't try to get rid of me already." He winked at her to reassure her it wasn't what she thought as he continued, "Baby, I'm as healthy as a horse. You are going to have to deal with me for a long time, and everyone in the family is fine."

Serenity felt a weight drop off her shoulders, but then a little bit of that anxiety crept back as she looked at him with all seriousness and said with concern, "Then what in heaven's name is going on? You're not a cross-dresser, right? Because you cannot be wearing my thongs. You would have to buy your own."

They both laughed at that; easing the rest of the tension, she looked at him and said, "Shawn, what is going on, baby? I am not a mind reader." Shawn was still thinking about how she would look like wearing a thong. The thought made his jimmy get hard.

Shawn pushed the thought aside for the time being. While still holding her hands, he said with a bit of reservation, "Well, quite some time ago, about ten months ago to be exact, give or take, you said . . ." Shawn wanted to back out. It wasn't the right time, not on his honeymoon night, but he knew he had started and now he had to finish. Serenity looked at him and while twirling her locks and biting on her bottom lip responded, "What? Tell me. What did I say? Something that hurt you. If I did, I'm sorry, baby. You know, back then—"

Shawn cut her off and smiled at that ever-familiar look of her twirling her locks and biting her lips. *What a turn-on centerfold look!* He pushed that thought on the back burner and continued, "No, baby, you didn't do or say anything to hurt me, please relax."

Serenity nodded her head up and down quickly, took a deep breath, and said, "OK." She was fine. Shawn continued, "You mentioned that you wanted to meet the other woman."

Serenity's breath caught in her throat and whatever shaking her hands were doing stopped. Shawn could feel her hands wanting to curl up into fists as she snatched them from Shawn's grip and her whole attitude went from sadness to madness. She blinked several times, looking at Shawn in astonishment, and said with a tone that was on the verge of controlled mania, which is a smile on the outside with thoughts to do harm to someone on the inside, "Shawn, what are you saying or implying? Are you telling me . . . just so I can understand and make sure all the pieces fit together, OK . . ." She still had that maniacal smile on her face. She looked . . . crazy as she continued, "Here I am thinking, oh my god something was terribly happening with you . . . Well, you know, the way I feel about right now. That something still may be happening to you and is still a possibility, but by these hands of mine . . . I can't believe you would sit there and drag this thing out as if something crazy happened, and secondly, I can't believe you would wait on our honeymoon to tell me this, Shawn. What made you think that I would want to meet some woman on my honeymoon or meet her, period, for that matter?" Shawn sat there speechless with a half-smile on his face. He loved to see her get worked up, but Serenity would have loved to take that half-smile and smack it off his face as she waited for him to respond. She continued, "Well, finish putting the noose around your neck, Shawn. I can't believe this." Shawn tried to hold her hands, but Serenity avoided his reach and said, "Ooh, don't touch me."

Shawn said in a calm, mellow tone, "Serenity, calm down so I could finish. You are jumping to—"

Serenity's eyes cut right into him like a laser beam as she cut him off, "Don't you dare tell me to calm down, don't you dare treat me like a school age child, and don't you dare act as if this is a small matter? It is our wedding night, you pompous whore. On our wedding night, of all nights, you bring this up. What? You want to do a threesome. Well, three is a crowd. You could have a threesome. Look, you could play with her, she could play with you, and you could play with yourself. There goes your threesome, you jerk." Serenity looked at him and made an angry grunting sound. The dashboard of the car lit up like a Christmas tree. Serenity stopped in the middle of her grunting and looked at the dashboard. She shook her head, ignored it, and said in frustration, "OK, are you finished?" Then she said out loud to no one in particular, "Dead man walking." Shawn tried his best to hold it, but couldn't help burst out laughing. Serenity, looking stern, cut his laughter down to a chuckle and from there to a dry cough and then to clearing his throat. The dashboard lit up bright again. Serenity looked at it and said with frustration, "And what is the deal with this car? Is it possessed or something?"

Shawn was holding back another laugh. She cut her eye at him like a parent would do to a child. He quickly said, "OK, OK, it's not what you think. If you just listen to what I . . ."

Serenity was fuming. If she was fire, she would be a four alarm, out of control. She responded with a sneer, "Oh really, then what should I think? What conclusion should I arrive at . . ." As she poked him in his chest with each statement, she continued, "when your man," Poke. "your husband," Poke. "your friend," Poke. "And was soon to be your lover." Double poke. And she continued, "Tell me, Mr. Intelligent, what should I think when your husband says, 'Oh, I want to talk to you about the other woman'? I'm not supposed to be pissed off, right? What are you a jackass. Lord, forgive me." She looked at him, still astonished. "You realize these are grounds for an annulment in a court of law. A court would not even spend five minutes to come to that decision, and wipe that stupid smile off your face. I don't have time for this."

Shawn took his hand and dragged it down his face. Under any other circumstance, she would have been laughing, but right now, at that moment, she was steamed. "OK, lover boy, where does she live . . . this other woman? Start up this car. We are going over there. You will make a decision tonight. As a matter of fact, I want to meet the slut, and then I will make the decision whether or not to kill you and then leave your whorish ass, Lord, forgive me, or leave you and come back and then kill you." Shawn wanted to laugh. He was doing his best to hold it in. Serenity, who was looking down, shaking her head, looked up at him and said, "You better not laugh either. You better try to control yourself. I mean it, Shawn, or I am out of here." Serenity noticed Shawn controlling his laughter and knew it was killing him as she continued, "Now, where does this floozy live?"

The dashboard turned bright red. Serenity jumped a little at the sight and turned her attention back to Shawn, who once again stifled a laugh and said, "She is pretty close, closer than you think."

Serenity, shaking her head and looking at him, said, "What does that supposed to mean . . . ?" Shawn was getting ready to answer but was cut off as she continued, "Man, I should have seen this coming. I should have known. You in your slick Rick rap, that smile and white teeth. I should have seen it coming. How long have this been going on, tramp?"

Shawn stated in a matter-of-a-fact tone, "I've known her for years, way before we met."

Serenity, who was fed up, said through clenched teeth, "Well, that is obvious, you jerk You know, for an intelligent person, you can really sound like a complete jackass, and if you've known her that well and you two were supposed to be that tight, why didn't you marry her?"

Shawn put his head down, chuckled, and looked up at Serenity. "Because like I said a million and one times, I love you."

Serenity felt as if she wanted to pull her hair out as she put her head down in her hands, made a frustrating sound, and looked up at Shawn with daggers that wanted to go right through him; she said, "You really like playing with women's feelings, don't you player? Thank God I found this out. Boy, did you have me fooled. You are good, damn good. Forgive me, Lord. How close are you two?"

Shawn wanted to laugh so bad, he rubbed his hand down his face like he had done earlier. He behaved as if he was in anguish and said, "OK, we are close. She has been there for me. I can't count how many times."

Serenity felt as if her insides were going to explode. She was in tremendous emotional distress. She loved this man like she never loved any other man. Tears streamed down her face. She may sound tough and say tough things, but she wanted this man and no one else. She thought, *Please, God, let this be a dream. I know or I thought this was the man I prayed for and you sent to me. I didn't see it at first, but eventually I did and I do, but . . .* Shawn interrupted her thoughts by calling her name, and she responded, "Shawn, I want to say congratulations. You are the first of many firsts. You are the first man I ever loved, and you are the first man who has ever hurt me the way you have hurt me tonight. You have done such a perfect job. You have ripped something out of me that no one will be able to replace because I will not trust another man for a long time. Here, take back your ring." She went to take it off, but Shawn prevented her by holding her hand and pleading with her to listen to him. She pulled back with all the anger she could muster up against all the love, compassion, and memories of this man. Her anger was weak. She pulled back as if she had no more fight in her, and she said in a sneer, "Don't touch me. You are worse than a deadly disease. I can't believe all the things we've been through and the things we've said to and about each other on your part. I guess it was all a lie . . ." Shawn, while shaking his head, was trying to tell her what it was all about, but she cut him off again, "Hush, I am not finished yet. Once I'm done, you can spit out more lies. So while you and I were having a good time, I guess the Mr. Hyde was seeing someone else. Have you told her the same things you've told me? Have you taken her to our favorite spots? When? How often? How did you pull it off? You are such a busy man. How could you, Shawn? I want to hate you right now, but I . . . I . . . love you too damn much . . ." Through tears she was able to finish her sentence, "That's why this hurts so freaking much." She wanted to claw his skin off him.

He put his head down and thought enough was enough, but one thing he knew from day one and now he knew even more and it was that he loved this woman so much. She had become truly bone of his bone and flesh of his flesh. Without her, he would crumble and slowly fade out and would no longer exist. He looked at her as she dealt with something she did not quite understood, and he once again made a plea to express his feelings, "Serenity, I love you like I never loved anyone before you, and I would never find anyone after you."

She put her head down and cried as her shoulders shook from the crying as well. She quickly looked up and smacked Shawn on the arm. The blow didn't hurt; just the idea that she did it surprised him. She said through her tears, "How dare you mock me, you male chauvinist bastard? Forgive me, Lord."

She hit him in the arm again. Once again there was nothing behind the hit, but it was enough for Shawn to speak up, "I had about enough of this crap, Serenity. You are the one who wanted to know about the other woman. You want to know a few facts. Like how often do I see her?" Serenity leaned back a little due to Shawn's anger. She knew she had pushed too far. She should have never put her hands on him, but she did not show fear as she raised her chin in defiance, while Shawn continued,

"I see her every day. When? Time is no factor, Serenity. Sometimes I saw her, and she dropped me off to see you." Serenity cursed at him under her breath. Shawn rolled his eyes and continued, "She is my means to get from point A to point B. I like to get all that I could."

Serenity looked at him and, in disgust, said, "You are one sick brother."

Shawn mumbled, "Whatever."

Serenity continued, "I'm out of here, Shawn. I do love you, but I guess the saying is true. True love is ignorant, but it is not stupid." She went to unclick the seat belt, but it was jammed. She said in frustration, "The damn thing is jammed again!" She struggled to click it, but it was jammed. It was of no use, and she was becoming more frustrated by the minute. "Shawn, get me out of this car, *now!*"

Shawn looked at her and started the car; he ignored her request and responded, "As soon as you meet the other woman, then you make the choice. You will be free to go if you choose . . . I will not stop you."

Serenity looked at him in astonishment, then looked up, and said, "Lord, I'm not going to wait to Sunday to ask for forgiveness for what I'm about to say and do to this man. I know, I hardly ever speak this way, but send your angels to cover your ears and close your eyes for a brief second. That's all I need." That was it. Shawn could not hold back his laughter any longer as he laughed so hard tears started to flow out of his eyes. Serenity, frustrated, hit him in his arms with several slaps that had no power behind them; they were more or less like love taps. Shawn, ducking as if the blows were hard, laughed even harder, especially when she hit him and hurt her own hand in the process. He looked at her as she made a painful sound rubbing her hands. Once he knew she was OK, he laughed even harder.

Serenity said, still rubbing her hand, "What's so funny? Let me out of this car right this minute, Shawn, male chauvinistic, jackass, low-life Cook."

Shawn finally calmed down, looked at her, and with all seriousness and in a firm tone said, "No, sit back and shut your mouth. You can leave when I'm ready to let you leave, so sit back and shut your pie hole. Do we understand each other, Serenity?" Serenity's eyes opened up and her mouth dropped. She was about to open up a can of verbal slaps again, but Shawn beat her to it. When she was about to speak, he raised his hand and said, "Don't say a word, Serenity Cook."

She sneered, "You wish."

He sneered and spoke hard in that baritone voice of his, which caught her off guard, "Don't you think about saying another word. You just sit back. You wanted to meet the other woman. Well, this so-called jackass, male chauvinistic low life, who loves you like crazy, will introduce you two to each other." Serenity started to protest, but Shawn raised his hand and said, "I said to hush. Don't say anything." Shawn drove three feet along the curb and stopped.

Serenity looked at him, baffled, thinking that perhaps he had changed his mind. She thought about it and said to herself, "That is a good idea."

Shawn looked at her, and said, "This is what I've been trying to tell you. Serenity, meet Complex. Complex, meet Serenity." Nothing happened. Shawn sat there with his arms spread out as in the case when one introduces someone.

Serenity looked at Shawn as if he had lost his mind. She said under her breath, "Oh my god, I've married an escapee from the nuthouse."

Shawn, with confidence, called out, "Complex." Nothing.

Serenity said, "Ooo . . . kay, perhaps this is one morning you missed your medication. I think this would be a good time for me to get out."

Shawn gave her an annoying look and said, "Complex." The dashboard came to life. It lit up like a bright Christmas tree. The lights were going crazy. Her seat belt clicked off, releasing her. She quickly turned in that direction, and her seat belt slid back in its original place. The passenger door became unlocked. She yelped at how things were happening so fast around her. She looked at Shawn for an explanation. He did not give one but stared straight ahead. The next thing she heard shocked and surprised her.

That was it. That was the voice she had heard. When she had spent that wonderful night at what she now called as Shawn's shack, under the stars, she recalled them playing Uno and Monopoly and listening to music. She also remembered hearing that voice, so sexy and strong, and then she looked back up and down, thinking that six months ago she had heard that voice while zooming through the streets to the hospital. And she remembered it sounding strong, confident, and sure.

Serenity looked at Shawn and said in a tired tone. Her voice was weak, zapped from exhaustion, and she said to him, "Shawn, what's going on?"

Shawn looked at her with such deep compassion in his eyes and said, "Baby, you'll see. Please be patient . . . please."

Serenity looked at Shawn and made a face, when Complex said, "Good evening, Serenity, this is the so-called slut you refer to me as . . . And how are you?"

Serenity looked at Shawn as if she was going to pop out of her skin. She looked everywhere in the car, and she whispered to Shawn, "That's the voice. Who is she?"

Shawn chuckled and started to speak, but Complex cut him off, "You can talk to me. I'm Complex, not the cleanup woman, but I am the other so-called woman. But it's all good, girl. It is what it is." Serenity looked at Shawn, who was smiling from ear to ear.

Serenity's seat quickly went all the way back in a flat position, and she grabbed onto Shawn. Complex told her that it was OK, and for the next two and a half hours, Serenity and Complex talked right there in that same spot alongside the curb. Shawn on several occasions tried to get a word in, but it was useless. When they were finished, Serenity's seat was brought back up in the sitting position, She was shaking her head, still digesting everything that was said. Shawn could not count how many times she apologized to both Complex and Shawn for doubting his love. She knew that they were like peanut butter and jelly and that man had treated her better than any other man besides her father.

Shawn went into the whole history of how Complex came about and everything along those lines. Serenity was astonished by such technology. Complex was advanced in years, so advanced she did not like to be referred to as a piece of technology, but she was almost as human as a human could get. Her system was so sensitive. Shawn had only tapped the surface of what Complex could do. Shawn completed the history and was exhausted with all the evening's events. He said, "OK, my two favorite ladies, I don't know about you, but I am exhausted. Can we go home?"

Both Serenity and Complex said at the same time, "Sure thing, baby." Serenity laughed and Complex's dashboard lights fluttered in different patterns.

Shawn got out of the driver's side, walked around to the passenger side, and opened the door for Serenity. She looked at him, and he said, "Come sit with me in the backseat."

Serenity looked at him with an unsure smile and said with hesitation, "I thought you wanted to go home." Shawn, still holding his hand out to help her out, did not say a word as Serenity took his hand. He helped her out and led her to the backseat, which was very roomy and comfortable. Serenity looked uneasy, and Shawn asked her what was wrong.

She said, "I want to go home. We are not sixteen years old any longer."

Shawn smiled and said to Complex, "Complex."

Complex responded, "Yeah, baby."

Shawn responded, "Set your itinerary for Shawn's place."

Complex responded, "Yes, sir. Would you like the designated driver decoy to be deployed?" Shawn gave the affirmative. Serenity looked on in awe. She was speechless as the front-seat driver side opened up and a lifelike person emerged from the seat. Serenity was spellbound. The lifelike person moved its head, arms, and other parts of his body like a real person.

Serenity shook her head in amazement; Shawn smiled and said, "Complex, can we have some privacy?"

Complex responded, "Sure thing, baby." Serenity was so caught up with everything that she started feeling giddy. She started giggling like a teenager talking about her first date. Shawn enjoyed this side of her. He enjoyed everything about her. He had such a deep love for her that he felt it deep in his soul. He knew that that love was special. It had endured the test of time. He sat there with his arms around the woman he loved. He was in deep thought, trying to define the relationship between him and Serenity. He started to smile and thought, *This is unbreakable love.*

Serenity looked at him, placed her hand on his chest, and began to massage it. She said, "What are you thinking about?" Shawn instructed Complex to play the love song CD. Serenity was a little startled by the surround sound and smiled once again as she was amazed by Complex's capability.

Shawn smiled and looked at her, and he responded to her question, "Well, Mrs. Cook, I look forward to spending the rest of my life with the one I love and adore with every inch of me." Serenity reached up and Shawn bent down slightly, and the two kissed passionately.

Epilogue

Warning: The Following Contains Serious Adult Content.

Shawn and Serenity got back to his place, which was now their place. Complex took her time going back, which gave the two lovebirds passionate time with each other. Both Shawn and Serenity were still on a high, a high of caressing and kissing. Even though they were tired, they both looked forward to lying down, holding each other, and falling asleep in each other's arms. Shawn got out, quickly went around the back of the car, opened up Serenity's side, and led her out. He then swept her up in his arms. Serenity smiled and hugged his neck real tight, not due to the fear of falling, but due to the fact that she loved her man so much she could not get enough of him. She giggled all the way into the house. Shawn didn't know how he held her and switched off the alarm at the same time.

He walked with her upstairs and gently put her on the bed. He stood over her as they both looked at each other with such passion of deep love mixed with desire. Whatever fatigue was there was slowly fading away, and energy was slowly surging in; they both felt it. Shawn lay down next to her, and the two kissed passionately while their tongues did a tango. Both were feeling such a raw need to go further.

Shawn began to undress Serenity. Her gown was long and awkward, but his passion and need was so strong, he had no time for patience as he helped her take the wedding dress off. He unbuttoned the string of buttons in the back. She, in turn, began to undress him. Her fingers could not move fast enough for undoing the buttons. She reached his shirt and decided to take the express route as she started from the top and pulled the shirt apart. Buttons were flying everywhere. The act gave Shawn such a hard-on that he thought he would come on himself.

They both stood there; they were down to practically nothing, Shawn had his briefs on, and Serenity had stripped down to her bra and the thong she was wearing. Shawn came closer to her and undid her bra. Serenity stood there allowing him to have his way with her. She knew that he was more experienced than she was, so she thought she would follow his lead as he stood there and pulled the bra off her breasts, which he only had a chance to see till then with her clothes on. From that perspective, he knew she was the perfect size, the way he liked it. He slid the bra off completely, and her breasts stood there firm with her nipples erect and hard.

Shawn was more than pleased. He was looking at perfect nice-size breasts. He wanted to put as much of his mouth on her erect nipples and whatever else his mouth could take in. He swallowed hard as the weight of his erection hung hard in his briefs. Serenity looked at the package, and her breath caught in her throat. She thought that it would take two hands to wrap around that monster. She still had her thong on, and Shawn could tell from the way her cat was shaped that she could probably handle all of him. She noticed that the front of his briefs, where the head of his pump was, it was wet. She wondered what he tasted like as she reached down and grabbed a handful of his hardness. She heard his breath catch in his throat as she moved along the length of it seductively and smiled with satisfaction; she said, "I need to take a quick shower, if you don't mind? I am really sticky and sweaty." And she gave his Johnson one more feel along its length.

Shawn said through shallow breath, "Whatever you want." Serenity turned her back at him and turned her head slightly to look back at him with the most seductive smile he had ever seen. She slowly pulled down her thong to the ankles and bent down as if she was touching her toes while pressing her butt into Shawn's Johnson. Shawn almost lost it after seeing the visual of her shapely backside, and having that backside rubbed up against him almost sent him out of his mind. She looked back at him, smiling, and then down at the wet spot on his brief. The spot was a little larger. She knew if she kept this up, Shawn's manhood was going to blast off.

Serenity knew her way around his home and went into the linen closet to get a towel. She then went into the bathroom to take her quick shower. When she closed the door behind her, she leaned against the door, holding her heart. She was so nervous. She could not believe that she did what she had done. She could not explain where she had got such boldness from, but she smiled and thought that since the ball was in her court she had to continue to find the courage to finish what she had started. She thought as she turned on the shower, *Tonight she was going to send her man to a place where no man has gone before.*

Shawn was in the bedroom, setting the mood. He had put on a music CD that had love songs. He knew he had to adjust the lighting. On the wall, he had four control levers. He pulled the lever for the regular lighting to be down to the point that the room was completely dark, and a few seconds later, he pushed up the lever that controlled the red light, which gave the room a dim red look. There was enough lighting where they both could see every inch of each other, and Shawn didn't want to miss anything, but it still wasn't to his satisfaction. To him, lighting was a key aspect in the beginning stages of foreplay. Poor lighting such as the time when it is too bright where you can see a person's stretch marks or blemishes is a turn off, or if a person has to shield her eyes when she walks into a room, then that should give a clue that it's too bright, or if a person is bumping into things and hitting her toes against stuff or when you have to ask the person to keep talking so you can find her, all these points should give an indication that it's too dark. But when a person walks into a room where the lighting helps that person to put down her defenses or when the person doesn't have to worry about certain marks such as stretch marks or conversational pieces such as old operation scars, knife scars, or scars that may have occurred when they were younger, that type of lighting makes the person comfortable.

Shawn worked with the lighting until he found the right combination. Then he went around to two of the four outlets in the room, and each one had an air freshener plug that sprayed a mist just by pressing the button. The two that he used were called Jasmine, which he knew was Serenity's favorite scent. The scent went with the lighting. Shawn had created the perfect aphrodisiac atmosphere that would stimulate her emotions,

He then took out some enhancing massage oils and a few other surprises. He thought, *Maybe she may not be into this stuff, but if she was willing to try he was more than willing to do it.* Lastly, Shawn put out a few of her favorite pieces of chocolate. He figured he was killing two birds with one stone in the sense that she loved this kind of chocolate and also, whether she knew it or not, chocolate was a wonderful aphrodisiac.

Shawn placed three lit unscented candles in different areas of the room to enhance the romance; he wanted to stimulate her emotionally, mentally, physically, and spiritually.

Shawn tapped his forehead as he just then remembered the most important thing. He went to his drawer and took out a box of non-latex polyurethane condoms, which he liked the best because they gave a nice sensitive feel. Yet they were twice as strong as other condoms, which meant if things got wild and crazy he knew the condom would be strong enough to deal with it; also he liked the idea that if he had to add a lubricant to get into those tight areas then that was the right condom. Shawn stood back and made sure he had everything; he was pleased. He looked down, and he still had a semi-erection. He could not believe that in the heat of the moment that woman wanted to take a shower. In a way, Shawn was happy for the pause, but he wanted to also get busy. However, he realized the way he had hooked up things, he would rather have it that way than rush through it. He wanted the night to be special. It was the first time he was making love to his woman, his wife, his best friend, and he knew deep down that she deserved the best.

Shawn was beyond horny. He wanted Serenity with such a raw passion, he could not wait. *She was about to get a big surprise,* he thought as he smiled to himself.

Shawn took the lubricant mood oil, which when rubbed on the body would slowly make that area become warm to very warm. Shawn wanted to give Serenity a back rub with that stuff and let whatever had to happen, happen. In the meantime, Shawn removed his underwear, and he took some of the oil in his hands and began to massage his penis. Immediately his penis responded and was pipe-hard again. He was ready; he headed toward the bathroom. He was going to join Serenity in the shower.

Serenity was enjoying the warm semi-hot shower. It felt so good. She didn't want to come out as she told herself, "Just a few more minutes." She was relaxed. The nervousness had dissipated. She wanted Shawn. Just the thought of him inside of her made her nipples hard and erect as she circled them with her finger, tantalizing her imagination. Her vagina was becoming moist. She was physically ready for him, but she just wanted a few more minutes. She stopped as she thought she had heard the door open, and she stiffened a little. She realized it was Shawn. *Perhaps he has to go to the bathroom.* She listened carefully to see if he was going to lift the seat up on the toilet, a plus for him if he did so.

However, instead she heard the shower door sliding back, and she saw Shawn, all six foot three and 225 pounds of him, come into the shower. His presence was huge: broad shoulders, wide chest, and strong arms as he stood behind her, his erection, his penis, lightly touching her. No words were said. Just the sound of the shower and their breathing could be heard. It was as if they were in a heavy rain. Then Shawn took a washcloth and soaped it up, and he began to wash her up as he kneeled down, as if he was kneeling to royalty. He began to wash her feet as he slowly lifted one leg to complete the task. Serenity balanced herself by holding on to the wall with one hand and the shower door with the other. No words were spoken. Serenity was a little nervous. She stood there with her back to him. She could feel his manhood lightly up against her. She liked the way it felt. It wasn't an intruder. It was more of an unexpected but welcome guest.

Serenity put down her leg to lift the other one up so that Shawn could do the other foot. No words were spoken again but Serenity enjoyed what she was feeling. She thought, *A simple washing was turning her on.* She wondered what would happen if he got to those other areas. She would probably fade into oblivion. Shawn worked his way to her calves. He felt her firm, shapely calves. The feeling alone was turning him on. He washed both calves; no words were said. He washed her thighs; no words were said. Then the moment came. Shawn spread her legs slightly apart and washed the outside of her mound, and then he worked his way to the inside as he gently washed it. The sensation made Serenity close her eyes and enjoy the feeling, and then he inserted one large finger into her vagina.

Serenity gasped with her eyes opened wide. She had a look of rapture on her face as Shawn continued to finger her vagina with his long thick finger. She began to moan and groan, and yet no words were spoken. Shawn was turned on by the pleasure/pain expressions on her face. He then inserted another finger and went in and out of her joy spot. The sensation brought tears to her eyes as she felt the sensational wave of an orgasm hitting her. Shawn felt the wave as well too. Her body prior to orgasm tensed and then released, and that was what he felt. He knew she was coming as the sweet sensation surged throughout her body. She wanted to yell, shout, cry, and scream all at once, but she could not express any of those things. The only thing she could do was make sounds. Shawn added another finger and filled Serenity up to the max. Her eyes opened up wide in surprise. She was moving up and down to the rhythm of Shawn's fingers going in and out of her yoni. Serenity got lost in the rapture of another orgasm.

Shawn slowly removed his fingers from her love zone, and he continued to wash her up. He was now moving to her breasts. Shawn looked at her swollen, erect nipples and washed underneath her perfectly sized breasts, and when he was done, he kissed them and nibbled on them while Serenity held her head back and the water slid down her face onto her breasts into his mouth. The sensation for Shawn was amazing as his manhood continued to feel the strain of wanting to release. He could feel his penis pulsating. He didn't know how long he would be able to endure such ecstasy and exhilaration. He wanted her and he needed her. He wanted to explore every inch of her, and he wanted to go where no man had gone before.

As he continued to lightly rub the tips of her nipples, the simple act brought on another wave of orgasm. Shawn was pleased with the way Serenity was responding. She wasn't timid or intimidated. She just wanted him the way he wanted her. He turned her so that her back was facing him. He admired her back; it was beautifully shaped and strong in its firmness. Shawn began to drop love kisses all over her back, starting with the shoulder blades, and he kissed and licked her back all over. The act sent a tinkling sensation up and down her spine.

He washed her back slowly, working his way down to her legs, and then he bent her over and began to wash her ass, slowly wiping with the cloth, going in and out a few times. Then when she thought he was done, Shawn reached back toward the space saver, opened up a jar of Vaseline, applied a little to his middle finger, and slowly stuck his middle finger up Serenity's ass. At first, she flinched. The experience was new. She thought she would have to go to the bathroom and that could have been embarrassing, but then she relaxed and found the feeling exhilarating. She found the act such a turn on as she bent over for Shawn to go deeper, which he did one time, and her breath was caught in her throat. She felt as if he was going to go through her as his strong fingers penetrated hard and deep. He then slowly pulled his finger out of her ass and washed his hands. He turned her around to him, and they both looked into each other's eyes as the shower rained on them. They both felt the raw need to go even further. Serenity thought, *How much further can this man go? What more can he do to her?* He had already turned her into a freak, allowing him to do things to her that she would have had reservations about with any other man, but with Shawn it was a different story. She trusted and entrusted her heart and body to him as they looked at each other with raw desire. Still no words were said between them and as if reading each other's minds, their lips came together, and they kissed hard and long with passion. Their breathing was ragged and rough as he pulled on her locks and she carved into his back with her fingernails, causing an expression of either pain or pleasure, she did not know which, to be released from his mouth as they continued to explore each other's mouths with their tongues.

Serenity reached for a clean washcloth. She soaped it up and began to wash up Shawn. She started with his back and worked her way down to his legs. She bypassed his butt. She had something else in mind for that. She turned him around so he was facing her. She saw the size of his manhood and she was impressed. *He hung well enough,* she thought. *This was the thing her best friend, Sandra, was fixated on, the size of a man's Johnson.* She would talk about that that one hung well, that other one joystick should have been in the world book of records because he was huge and how he ripped her open, while that other one that she had dated and she had first seen his "Little Richard" she had thought that was the right name for it, but she said that when homeboy used that thing, that thing was packed with so much TNT she screamed just like "Little Richard." Serenity wasn't experienced enough to know, but she was smart enough not to listen to her best friend, which if she did she would make that old adage "the blind leading the blind" come true. Serenity relied on the experts and the little experience she had, which wasn't much, but she had read somewhere that it was not about how large one was, it was about how one used it to give that person an experience that they would never forget, but always remember. She was brought back to the present moment, which was looking at the size of Shawn's manhood; she hoped that the lion was as big as its roar.

Serenity wrapped her arms around his neck, slid her hands down his chest, and continued to go further down to his stiff cannon XL. She started from the base and worked the full length of it as she formed her hands like a loose fist and went up and down on the joystick. Shawn put his head back and moaned out loud as she continued to bring him to the edge of coming. She could feel his strong Goliath pulsating in her hands as she continued to work it up and down like a pump. His breathing became faster and uneven. She could feel the beat of his heart. His eyes rolled back in his head. He was at arousal speedway. She grabbed his twins, ball one and ball two, and could feel that they were very heavy. She grabbed them and pulled on them with enough pressure while at the same time she kept on doing the hitchhiker's move on his hard pole. She could tell the twins were begging for release. She could see he was trying to gain some control but was failing. He was full and at the point of coming, but she thought, *This may be the right place, but not the right time.* Serenity eased up on the stroking, turned her back to his outstretched pole, and purposely dropped the soap so she could bend down and pick it up. She bent with her hump in the air and her joy spot clearly visible as she stood up, smiled at him, and cut off the shower.

They both got out of the shower. She was drying herself off when he snatched her up and carried her to the bedroom. When they entered the bedroom, she was impressed with the way he had transformed their paradise. She liked the way he gave the room enough light to the point that she started to feel a sense of calmness as well as eroticism. For some reason, the dim light made her more relaxed, sexier, and even a bit hornier.

It removed all distractions and gave her feeling as if she was still in the shower. Serenity looked around and could tell that Shawn had totally transformed the room. Nice, soft love ballads came through the surround sound speakers. It was as if the artist was right in the room with them. She heard every note and every musical instrument. It was amazing.

Once again, Serenity was caught up with the lighting. It was perfect; the three candles made their images look sexier and younger. It seemed to give her a burst of sexual energy, and when the candlelight coincided with the black lighting, it set her arousal to another level. She thought, *This man knows what he's doing.* Serenity looked at the nightstand and the items on the stand, and she was impressed. She saw some toys put out as well and then the thing that sealed the deal. When she saw the condoms, it proved that that man was thinking with his top head and not his bottom head. If he was that thoughtful to put them out, that meant that man was thinking about both of them, and that drew her even closer to him.

The first words were spoken by them after the foreplay in the shower had taken place. She was trying to tell him she wasn't fully dried off, but it was useless as Shawn covered her mouth with his and dipped his tongue all around. Serenity followed suit, and the two stood on common ground as they kissed each other with such passion. Their tongues did that familiar dance as he worked his kisses down to her neck, which was one of her erogenous zones and which Shawn picked up on immediately while in the shower. Serenity was becoming aroused again as her joy spot began to become moist again and her nipples began to stand out and hard. As she moaned to the love assault on her neck, Shawn took the assault further ahead by nibbling on her neck with love bites, leaving sure signs of ownership.

Serenity did not want to stop him. It felt so good, but she knew if he kept it up rolls and rolls of orgasms were going to start coming. Shawn must have read her thoughts. He wanted her to last a little longer. He wasn't finished with the assault as he moved down to her midsection, kissing that area and at the same time tweaking her nipples. He was applying enough pressure to the extent she felt the yin and yang, the pressure and pain, as he tweaked one nipple and assaulted the other one with his mouth.

Serenity felt the first roll of an orgasm coming on. Her body began to shake. Her breathing became heavier and faster as the assault continued, and then it was there. She came as Shawn got down to her love zone and kissed all around it, and finally he went into her love zone with his tongue. The sensation made her gasp and moan as her hands gripped the soft sheets and pulled and yanked them. As he inserted his tongue into the very essence of her womanhood, he tasted her juices. For him, it was an aphrodisiac. It made his pole even more taut. He felt as if his manhood was going to break out of its skin like the Incredible Hulk bursting out of Banner clothes.

Shawn, for the time being, left that area and went north to her clitoris. He teased it with his tongue by flicking at it. Then he sucked on it, and then he applied his whole tongue to it. The sensation sent Serenity into a different hemisphere. Her head was spinning. She felt intoxicated as she moved and wiggled and twisted and writhed to the sensation. She began to moan louder to the extent that she began to tremble and quiver from the sensation. She could not take the sensation. She felt as if she was about to explode. It was too much as Shawn continued to apply pressure to her clitoris.

Serenity's eyes opened wide, and she told Shawn to give her more. Shawn went the extra mile. While he had his mouth on her clitoris, his tongue had it locked in place, he took his thumb and inserted it into her yoni and began to go in and out at a slow pace at first and then he picked up the pace as he went deep enough to touch areas she did not know about. On the alphabet he was tapping and hitting that G-note. She was now at the point of screaming his name, "Oh my god, Shawn, I can't take anymore. Oh my god, don't stop. Oh . . . oh . . . oh . . . I can't, baby, I can't take . . . Don't stop." Shawn continued to suck on her clitoris and used his thumb to go in and out of her love spot, causing waves and waves of orgasms after orgasms to come. As he used his other hand to tweak one of her nipples, the medley assault of sexual pleasure overtook her, all of it at one time. He was overwhelming her. She thought it was too much as her eyes opened wide. "Oh my god, Shawn, what are you doing? What are you trying to do to me? Oh my ggg . . . yo . . . u are . . . I can't take it, too much, too much, *oh my god . . . Shawn, I'm coming . . . I'm coming . . . I'm coming . . .* I can't stop, *oh my god.*" Wave after wave, she came hard into his mouth. He did not stop. He swallowed her juices and kept the assault going. She screamed his name, "I can't stop coming, baby, enough. You are going to kill me. *Oh sh . . . I am coming again . . .*" Serenity felt any minute she was going to collapse. Finally, the sexual storm was over as Shawn embraced her and told her he loved her. Serenity began to shake and cry. The experience was too much. She was overwhelmed with pleasure she had never felt before. Shawn held on to her for a few more minutes and then he collapsed next to her. She was trying to catch her breath, trying to get herself back into some kind of balance, as she mumbled over and over again, "Oh my god, oh my god." She made all kinds of sounds, describing her rapturous experience; she was in her own sexual soliloquy.

Serenity regained some sense of control and equilibrium as she rolled on top of him and looked him in the eye; her face was still flushed. Shawn thought she had never looked as sexy as she did right then as she kissed him hard with passion. Shawn was still rock hard. She reached behind her to take hold of his rock. She then mounted him slowly, guiding his iron pole into her love hole. He was big, but she was more than wet and adjusted very quickly as she came down on him slowly. He let her set the pace. At first, it was hard for him just to lie there, but once she found the rhythm it was her ensemble, her beat, and her sound. She was in charge, and she enjoyed the way his manhood went deep into her joy spot as she tilted her head back and rode him. Shawn was at the brink of coming, but he had to gain some control as her tightness made him feel every inch of her. He moaned and groaned, allowing her to set the pace, but the tide of control turned.

Shawn grabbed hold of her waist and began to add to her beat as he met her when she came down on his pole. He came up as he shoved her waist down his long John Silver. The sensation made Serenity writhe and squirm. He knew how to use his equipment very well. She felt that when he came up into her and pulled her down by her waist into him, he was going very deep, but that made her even more determined to ride him harder.

She could feel his hardness going in and out as the feeling brought on another wave and she was coming again. And as she was coming, the muscles in her love zone grabbed him, pulled him, and pushed him. He could feel her strong grip. At first, he stopped as he felt he was about to release, but he gathered his composure and, when the sensation dissipated, he continued to match her pace. He could feel her juices drip down his penis. She looked at him intently and could see the expression of pleasure and pain—the pleasure of the feeling of being in her love zone, but the pain of trying to hold his own release. The look turned her on. As she rode him even harder, he moaned and his breathing became harder and faster. She rode him like a bronco. He could not take it. He could not keep up with her pace as she came again, releasing her juices over his manhood. He was about to release when he quickly rolled her off him and placed her on her knees, and he got behind her and entered her from the backside. He entered her slowly. Her breath got caught in her throat as she felt every inch of him. He felt long and hard.

Once he was in her love zone, he increased the pace. He could feel her tightness, and he was in her very deeply. He was at the point where he could not take it much longer. He began to go deeper. With each thrust, she yelped, squealed, shrieked, and screamed, whatever sounds that could come out of her mouth she made them. He was taking her to another level. Just when she thought that he had gone deep, that doggie position made it feel he was going deeper. She gave him a side-glance as he thrust harder. "Oh my goodness . . ." She gave a yelp. "Oh my god, Shawn . . ." And she gave a shriek. She continued to glance at him wild-eyed.

He continued to be turned on with the look as he pounded away in her love zone. She felt the pleasure and pain and glanced back at him as he continued to go deeper and deeper, and she squealed, "Oh my god, you are going to break me. I'm going to come again." Still looking at him as he worked his magic with his Johnson, she screamed his name and said, "I'm coming all over you. Do you want that, huh, huh . . . ? *Oh my goodness!*" She came again. Shawn was about ready as Serenity began to match his pace and slammed into his manhood. The sensation made him dizzy. It was her turn to rock his world as she continued to pound into him. He couldn't take it any longer as he quickly switched positions and laid her on her back. They were both at the point of joyous exhaustion as the only thing one could hear were moans and sounds coming from both of them. Shawn pulled her to the edge of the bed and positioned himself standing up between her legs. Serenity was sore, but she wanted more. They brought new meaning to the missionary position. As he placed her legs on each shoulder, he now had wide access as he entered her. This time he did not go easy, but he thrust his hard pole into her. She yelped with eyes wide open.

She could feel how big he was. She told him through clenched teeth to take it and also told him to go deeper. Her words were like added fuel to the fire. As he began to take her hard, she was about to come again. She was now full. All of him was in her. He could not go any deeper. As his pace began to quicken, she felt it, but she wanted more. It hurt her so bad, but it also felt so good as she screamed and shrieked, grabbing and pulling the sheets. The bed was a mess, Shawn didn't want to come like this; he wanted her on her knees.

She got on her knees. She was so sore, but Shawn knew that a few more thrusts and he would come. He entered her with such force that he began to pound her love spot with such energy. She could hear the sound of his breathing changing, flesh slapping up against flesh. She knew he was about to come, but in the meantime his pounding brought on wave after wave of orgasms. She would have never thought she could have so many.

She had heard about it, but now she was experiencing it for herself. Shawn continued to go as deep as he could.

Serenity was feeling the fullness of his manhood as she grabbed whatever she could and screamed sounds of pleasure as he was about to let loose. He asked her if she wanted him to come in her mouth. She didn't know how to answer. She had never done that before, plus she was so caught up she didn't know up from down or her right from her left. She was twisted with pleasure. She just nodded her head. He on the other hand was spinning out of control. She kept up with him and turned him inside out, but he was there. His thrust became harder and deeper to the extent that with each thrust it was lifting her up as she screamed, yelped, and called his name, but she took all of him with pleasure. He told her that he was about to come. She glanced back at him to see his expression. She had been always told that a man's expression when he's about to come and when he is coming was such a powerful experience to behold, the pain and pleasure, that yin and yang. So he was ready as he thrust a few more times, and then with agonized pleasure, he screamed, "*Oh my god, Serenity!*"

He pulled out, and she turned toward his fire hose and put all of him in her mouth. The sensation made him see stars as he made inaudible sounds and grunts and shot his love seed into her mouth. He came hard, grunting and shaking. She was sucking him like a vacuum. The sensitivity of his Johnson made him squirm and writhe as he held on to her locks. She tried to suck every bit of come out of him. His breathing came faster and faster as he screamed and grunted, "Oh no, I'm com . . ." He was coming hard. She decided to make good of the promise that she had made in the shower about his ass. She wanted him to come even harder. She stuck her middle finger up his ass. He opened his eyes wide and screamed her name with passion and pain as he came even harder. She kept her finger in his butt until he was completely finished coming, moving it in and out. When it was over, she snatched her finger out of his butt, and he collapsed first. And she was more than exhausted and collapsed next to him.

They were both breathing hard, jagged breaths and sweating profusely, lying next to each other and not saying a word, but trying to gain some sense of balance or something. Finally, they embraced one another in such a way one could not tell where one ended and the other began. They both had expressed their love for each other. They truly had hearts that were unbreakable.

Shawn and Serenity fell asleep in each other's arms. He got up around 3:00 a.m. and just looked at her, noticing her beauty. Her lips were a little swollen from the previous night. His mind quickly went back to the previous night, and he began to get a hard-on. He began to kiss her, showering with her with kisses. She squirmed and moved, but he continued. Then he decided he wanted her. His passion was raw and he was sore, but he wanted her. One would think that the previous night would have been enough, and to him it was more than enough. He was full to the max, but it wasn't out of the need to have, it was out of the desire to make love to the woman whom he loved like no other woman. He had to be inside of her.

He took her; she was still sore. When his manhood went inside of her, she gasped. He was amazingly hard. *Where did he get such energy?* she thought. But he took her. She felt every thrust, and she pleaded with him, "Shawn, take me. I'm all yours, baby. I can't take it. I can't hold it, Shawn, mmm, Shawn, so good, oh my g . . . g . . . g . . . I'm coming, *I'm coming, baby.*" He felt her juices all over him, squirting out. Shawn at the same time was about to come as the pressure was too much. He pulled out, and she took his hard pole and let him come all over her as he groaned and grunted. She pumped his manhood hard and fast of its juices. He came all over her breasts and wherever else he shot it. She looked at him seductively, and he said, "Let me get you a wet washcloth." She asked him to wait as she licked the come off the nipples of her breasts. The act turned him on as he kissed her passionately. They both lay down still exhausted and fell into a deep, comfortable sleep.

    Later that morning, around eight, they woke up, and that time Serenity made the first move as she played with his joystick. She was surprised that it was limp. She kept playing with it, trying to bring it to life. He stirred until he finally opened his eyes and brought her to him and kissed her with such passion. Serenity pushed off gently and went down to his Johnson to perform some magic as she took him in her mouth. His joystick became hard quickly as she continued to take his large manhood as deep as possible in her mouth. She deep throat him to the point she was gagging. The sensation for Shawn was exhilarating. The room felt as if it was spinning out of control, it was a mind boggling experience for him.

    Shawn was moaning and grabbing her hair. It was too much for him as she slowly pulled him out of her mouth. Shawn was overtaken with such passion that he had to have her as he got on top of her and brought her legs up to his shoulders. He wanted her to feel every bit of him his manhood was hard and large. She was sore and made whimpering sounds to express her soreness, but at that point, his raw passion had one thing in mind and that was to make love to her as he took her. They made love to each other, this time slowly and deeply. She moaned and called his name with such emotion it turned him on more, as he was reaching his climax. She could feel it, and she begged for him to give her all of him. He told her he was coming, and she opened her legs even wider and lifting up her hips to give him more access. He came hard once again inside of her this time. She felt and welcomed the hot lava juices that came from him. After it was over, he embraced her and she was crying. He asked her what was wrong, and she said, "Nothing, baby."

He retorted, "Then what's up with the tears? Did I hurt you?"

She smiled and responded, "These are tears of joy and thanksgiving, and no, you did not hurt me. You are such a passionate lover."

Shawn kissed her tears and then her lips. "You are also."

Shawn paused and looked at her in such a way that she became concerned. "What are you thinking about?"

He smiled, nodded his head, and said, "Us, you and I. Do you realize that I—"

She cut him off and responded, "That you came in me, yes, and I felt something when you did. It was . . ."

Shawn excitedly spoke, "Yes, I thought it was just me, but I felt it when I came in you. There was a connection, Serenity. I felt it. I know it sounds crazy, but . . ."

She kissed his lips and said, "No, it doesn't. I think this morning I conceived. Maybe that's why I am happy, I don't know." Shawn got up out of bed and pulled back the curtains. It was such a beautiful day. The sun was just coming up, the grass was wet from the dew, the birds were chirping, and the squirrels were chasing each other. Shawn didn't know whether he felt like lovers or like young teenagers, but he knew he was married to the most beautiful woman in the world.

Serenity looked at him, "What are you doing?"

Shawn looked at her with moist eyes and said, "We are going out for breakfast to celebrate the new addition to the family." Serenity smiled and protested out of reasonable logic, but Shawn stopped her and said, "Whether it's real or not, one day it will happen, but I have reason to celebrate anyway."

Serenity looked at him, still smiling and crinkling her nose, a look that Shawn had come to love, as he responded, "The love I have for you will last forever, Serenity. It's meant to be, and most of all . . . it is unbreakable."

Serenity smiled, nodded her head, kissed her man passionately, and said, "That's right. You are so right, baby."

The End